JORDAN'S SHADOW

ALSO BY ROBIN JOHNS GRANT

Summer's Winter

PRAISE FOR *SUMMER'S WINTER*

Part murder mystery, part Hollywood dream-world and part thought-provoking Southern lit, *Summer's Winter* takes the reader on a romantic ride, filled with movie-star moments that plummet into hair-raising hairpin twists and turns. Jeanine and Jamie's relationship crackles with sparring, spirituality and suspense, leading to an ending worthy of your favorite Hollywood finale.
    ~Elizabeth Musser, author of *The Swan House* and *The Sweetest Thing*

The twists and turns in *Summer's Winter* kept me reading into the night...I couldn't wait to reach the end! Robin Johns Grant's *Summer's Winter* is a heartwarming read in which good and evil collide. I loved it!
    ~Nancy Grace, HLN host and author of *The Eleventh Victim*

In Grant's debut novel, a young woman's fascination with a Hollywood star affects her life in ways she never could have imagined. This complex story is told in lush, heated prose...A passionate, well-wrought mystery by a Christian novelist to watch.
    ~*Kirkus Reviews*

Robin Johns Grant's *Summer's Winter* is the most inventive take on fan fiction I can imagine -- because it's a romance-thriller about fandoms, especially if not explicitly the Harry Potter fandom, and explores the important intersection of literature, spirituality, and imagination. Delightful!
    ~John Granger, the HogwartsProfessor, author of *The Deathly Hallows Lectures*

JORDAN'S SHADOW

ROBIN JOHNS GRANT

Mount Carmel Books

Published by Mount Carmel Books

Macon, Georgia, USA

Mount Carmel Books

http://robinjohnsgrant.com

http://www.facebook.com/robinjohnsgrantauthor

Cover design: Laura K. Wilson

Cover photo: Anna Gregg

PUBLISHER'S CATALOGING-IN-PUBLICATION DATA

Grant, Robin Johns.
Jordan's shadow / Robin Johns Grant.
pages cm.
ISBN-13: 978-0692364796 (pbk.)
ISBN-10: 069236479X (pbk.)
1. Mother-daughter relationship—Fiction. 2. Georgia—Fiction. 3. Time travel—Fiction. 4. Mystery fiction.   I. Title.
PS3625.G73 J67 2015
813`.6—dc23

In memory of A. O.
The best daddy any girl could have had.

PART I

Rose, 1984

CHAPTER ONE

The night they found Jordan was the first time Rose had gone back to the old quarry pond in quite a while. She had been trying very hard to avoid the place, but no matter how hard she tried to stay away, the pond seemed to work just as hard to pull her back to it—as though it could brood and feel and scheme. So when Hunter turned the Camaro off the paved road onto the logging trail that ended at the pond's edge, for a second she blamed the water instead of him. But only for a second.

Turning to glare at Hunter, she braced herself with her hand against the dash. The Camaro's wheels bumped over the uneven ground, and darkness pressed against the windows as the thick pines shut out the moonlight. Rose tried to keep her voice from sounding hysterical. "You're going to the pond!"

He turned to glance at her. Even in the dim light, she could see his mouth set in a determined line. "*We* are going to the pond."

Rose snapped around and faced forward. She wanted to argue, but then again she didn't. She hated it when Hunter was mad at her.

When he spoke again, she could hear the edge in his voice. "That's okay, isn't it?"

"You know the answer to that." She tried to keep her voice level and calm, the way he liked it.

"True. What I don't know is why it's not okay."

The woods started to thin as they reached the clearing, and the end of the road. As always back here, the radio lost reception and went to static, cutting "Thriller" off in mid chorus. Hunter sighed as he switched off the engine, leaving Rose's ears ringing in the sudden quiet. Or maybe the buzzing came from rain frogs. She could see the water glittering and tossing in the moonlight, restless in the stiff breeze. They were in for a storm.

In spite of herself, Rose's words came out loud and sharp. "Of course you know why it's not okay."

He laughed. "I don't think the water can hurt you if you're just sitting in the car looking at it." He reached for Rose's hand—no, it was her wrist he grabbed, pulling her toward him. But his lips and his voice were soft as he brushed her mouth with his. "Maybe it's not your water phobia bothering you. Maybe you're just scared to be alone with me back here in the woods."

Rose giggled, happy that he didn't sound angry. "Are you kidding? I want to spend my whole life alone with you." Running her thumb across the humble diamond engagement ring on her finger, she reassured herself of its presence for about the hundredth time that day. It was a magic ring, her passage to freedom. There would be one more year of bondage before then, including nine long months while Hunter went back to the University of Georgia and she stayed here under Mamma's critical eye. But come next May, everything would be different. The minute she crossed that stage and had her high school diploma in hand, she was going to climb into this very Camaro and head for Athens with him.

She closed her eyes and breathed deeply, trying not to think of the dark sky outside the car, strobing with heat lightning. Instead, she willed herself to picture a neat little apartment for married students at the University of Georgia. The sunshine of an autumn morning streaming through the windows. The bustle of football crowds rushing across the campus outside, while she sketched or painted for one of her art classes. Noise and sunshine and purpose and love. Think about that, she told herself, rubbing her thumb over the ring so hard she almost cut her skin.

Hunter was saying something. "Yeah, I like that whole life alone together thing. Let's start right now."

"Wh-what?"

"A little moonlight swim. Just the two of us."

"No!" Rose pictured herself diving into the mouth of that dark water, its wind-rippled teeth glittering as she slid down its throat. "I-- no. I just couldn't."

He pulled his hand away from her. "Fear of water, fear of other women, of what your mamma thinks…I can't have a wife that's scared of everything, you understand?"

"Yes." She felt the diamond ring slipping around on her sweaty finger. "I understand." And she did. Hunter Isaacs had big plans. Law school, politics—how could she be a governor's wife, or even a candidate's, if she was afraid of everything? Lifting her head, she tried to smile. "So maybe we should try that swim."

His mouth stretched into a grin. "That's my girl." He tugged playfully at a stray lock of her hair. "We'll whip you into shape yet."

Hunter got out of the car and came around to Rose's side, opening her door and taking her hand to help her out. Now she felt safe and protected and silly for being terrified of her own family's pond, which wasn't even particularly big or scary. Not as though it had sharks or anything. Although it was deep. People said the quarry had been like a bottomless pit before it was abandoned and left to slowly fill itself like a giant bathtub. But she could swim just fine, so what did that matter? Hunter was right to be mad at her for being so silly.

He dragged her to her feet and into an embrace, and for a long moment she forgot where she was, forgot about the pond and the woods and the darkness. There was nothing in the world but the two of them.

When he finally pulled away, he sighed dramatically. "Darn. Too bad you don't like coming to the pond."

She laughed and slapped at him—playfully, of course—and as she did, she marveled for the thousandth time that someone like him could possibly be interested in a little mouse like her, with her messy blondish hair and her tiny—okay, short—frame. He was as perfect as a Greek god, tall and muscular, his black, silky hair shining in the moonlight.

He was moving in for another kiss when she saw movement, a blur of white near the edge of the black water. She twisted her face away from his so she could see better.

Hunter threw up his hands in frustration. "What's the matter now?"

"Look." Rose raised a shaky finger to point. "You see it, don't you?" For a panicky minute she was afraid he wouldn't see it. With her family history, she didn't want him to think she'd started imagining things, too.

He sighed but followed the line of her hand, and Rose was relieved to feel his shoulders jerk with surprise. Apparently he did see.

His eyes were wide as he turned to Rose. "Who is that! Do you know her?"

Her? To Rose, the thing standing near the edge of the pond appeared ghostly, a human form with feminine curves, but glowing white and swaying from side to side like a young tree in a breeze. She forced herself to look again. A girl? Well...maybe. But why would any girl be standing in the woods in the dead of night? And was she naked?

Never taking his eyes off the whatever-it-was, Hunter backed around the car until he got to the driver's side, then reached in and switched on the headlights. The figure spasmed as though in pain, then went still. In those seconds, Rose decided that it was indeed a girl, with dark hair that looked wet and stringy. And she wasn't naked, but she wasn't fully clothed either. Just a camisole and a filmy skirt, both of which clung to her as though wet, and had some kind of dark, irregular stains that looked terribly like...

"Blood!" Hunter gasped, just as Rose came to that same conclusion. "She's got blood on her." He broke into a run, racing toward the girl.

Rose crept along a few paces behind him. Something was dreadfully wrong. The girl just stood there, turned in their direction but apparently not seeing them. If it was just a girl, why didn't she move? Why didn't she speak?

"Hunter, wait!" she called.

He didn't listen to her. He didn't slow down even when the girl raised her hand, as though gesturing him to stop. He rushed on, like a sailor to a siren, heeding nothing.

Two paces from the girl, Hunter slowed, then stopped. Rose caught up in time to hear him clear his throat and say, "Uh, miss? Are you okay?"

She didn't say anything. She didn't look at them. She just stood and stared into the light from the Camaro's headlamps.

Hunter looked at Rose, as though unsure what to do, and she opened her mouth to tell him to go call the police or an ambulance or something. Then she closed her mouth and considered. They were on her family's land. What would Mamma say? They weren't ever supposed to go back in these woods. Mamma was as scared of the pond as Rose was—although Rose suspected that Mamma was scared of lawsuits and hospital bills, not anything as silly as phantoms and dark water. She would throw a fit if she found out Rose had disobeyed her and come back here, even if it was Hunter's idea, but that fit would probably be nothing compared to how she would react if they called the authorities without consulting her first.

Hunter was still focused on the girl. "Miss? Who are you? What happened?"

Slowly, she brought her hand up in front of her face. Her mouth moved, as though she was trying to speak. In spite of her fear, Rose leaned closer and managed to hear the girl say, "That light. It hurts my head."

That's when Rose saw she had blood on her face, too. "Hunter, I think she has a head injury." Rose felt a warm rush of compassion, melting her fear away in an instant. Without a second thought, she touched her fingertips to the girl's arm and felt clammy, wet skin. "What happened to you? Did you fall in the pond?"

The girl just looked at her, but now Rose knew why. Her eyes were glassy and dazed. The skin of her arm felt cold against Rose's fingers, even in the muggy night air. Feeling Hunter moving closer to her, Rose said, "I think she's in shock."

Rose remembered vague instructions from TV shows about keeping shock victims warm. In movies, someone always had a blanket handy. Unfortunately, it was May. Rose was wearing as little clothing as Mamma would let her get away with and certainly wasn't hauling blankets around. But it was all right. Hunter was stripping off the shirt that hung loosely over his Aerosmith tee and approaching the girl with it, like someone sneaking up on a bird with a net. She stared at him and didn't move, so he draped it around her shoulders.

The girl pulled the covering tighter and actually spoke. "Thank you."

He cleared his throat two or three times before he said hoarsely, "You're welcome."

The girl, who was taller than Rose, tilted her head and looked at Hunter. Noting the girl's long, lean figure, Rose felt a pang of something ugly as she thought how stunning they were, standing there together, two black-haired beauties lost in each other's gaze.

Of course, the girl had a head injury, which probably explained the dreamy trance she seemed to be in. But what was the matter with Hunter? The longer the moment stretched on, the tinier Rose felt, until she finally blurted out, "Come on. Let's take her to the house."

Hunter blinked, as though waking. "The house? We need to get her to the hospital."

Rose hesitated. "I don't know."

"You don't know?" He spat out the words, making her jump. "Oh for Pete's sake, if you're worried about your mother, I'll take the heat for it."

Hunter slid his arm around the girl's waist to support her. She swayed in his embrace, so he bent and lifted her from the ground while barking orders at Rose. "Go open the car door." She ran to obey, and he gently deposited the girl on the back seat. "You ride back there with her and look after her."

Again, Rose did as she was told, sliding in beside the girl, even taking her hand to comfort her. The girl's fingers lay in Rose's, limp and icy. Then she raised the hand to her damp hair, pulled a strand forward and started wrapping it tightly around her index finger. So tightly Rose figured it must hurt, although the girl continued to do it, over and over, releasing the hair and then twisting it tight again, cutting into her finger with it.

"What's your name?" Rose asked her. Still no answer.

Rose waited, giving the girl time to collect herself and think. But her gaze grew distant, and she started to hum some tune that seemed vaguely familiar. Jiggling her hand, Rose tried to bring her attention back. "What's your name?"

Again that tilt of her head as she seemed to consider the question. "I don't...I'm not sure."

Rose never was certain that the girl was telling the truth about that. But she was sure of one thing, at that moment and in the years to come. She should never have let Hunter take her back to the pond. They certainly shouldn't have thrown open the car doors and meddled with the night. The minute they did, the darkness that had pressed against the car windows won. It streamed inside with them, into their safe little world, and blotted out all her sunny dreams. There would be no wedding with Hunter, no cozy apartment at the University of Georgia, no blissful escape. The darkness swallowed it all.

And the darkness was in the shape of a pale-faced, raven-haired girl.

Part II

Ginny, 2009

CHAPTER TWO

Ginny lay in bed, waiting for the sickness to come and trying not to call Mom—at least not yet. She knew what was wrong, but that didn't mean she wasn't scared, especially after that trip to the hospital last time. She started shaking and pulled the covers up tighter, watching the glowing numbers on the clock change from 12:59 to 1:00. A little longer, she told herself. Don't make a fuss until you're sure.

A wave of dizziness crashed over her, and she wanted to throw up.

"Mom?" The weak, pathetic sound of her voice made her feel panicky. Maybe she had waited too late. What if she passed out before anyone heard her? She pulled herself into a sitting position with great effort and took a deep breath. "Mom! I'm sick!"

She heard movement. A dull thud as someone's feet hit the old shag carpet. Then Daddy's voice calling, "Rose, do you hear? Ginny's sick again."

It was Daddy who appeared, breathing hard and practically running until he was just inside her doorway, then pulling up short as though not quite sure what to do now that he was here. He had flipped on the hall light and she could see his face, wide-eyed as he took in her appearance. His reddish-brown hair was disheveled, and as he ran his hand through it—a sure sign of nerves—it only got messier.

Ginny shivered again. "I wanted Mom."

He mumbled under his breath but she could still hear him. "Yeah, well, don't we all." He slapped his hands together and, putting on his usual "I'm-in-charge-here" Daddy face, moved briskly to her bedside. "So what do we need to do? Is it the blood sugar thing again?"

She wasn't letting him off the hook that easily. "Maybe Mom just didn't hear. Her room is further away than yours."

Daddy turned on a lamp and started picking through the junk on her nightstand. "So where's the monitor thingy?"

Anger surged through her, giving her strength. She threw the covers aside, feeling the cold air hit her clammy skin. "Just forget it. I can do it myself." She sat up, then bent down to reach for the monitor on a shelf of the nightstand near the floor. Adrenaline, low blood sugar, and quick movements made a terrible mix. She felt herself falling over, her head nearly colliding with the floor before Daddy caught her and eased her back down on the bed.

"Be still. I've got it." He pulled the monitor's black nylon case off the shelf and unzipped it. A moment later, he threw it back down on the nightstand, scattering a pile of pens and paperback novels. "There's no test strips." He sounded disgusted. He looked vaguely around the room, as though expecting a package of strips to materialize out of thin air.

"Mom knows where they are," Ginny said.

He looked at her. "So there are more?"

"I...I think so."

"Well, I'm amazed. I wouldn't have figured she would have bothered with that, either." He started toward the doorway. "I'll find them."

Ginny hugged her arms to her chest, listening to him stomping and grumbling his way to the kitchen. She heard a bump, a sharp curse. Daddy stumbling over a box. Then came a sharper rattle and thud. That would be Daddy kicking said box. Through it all he fussed at Mom, as though she were listening, as though she had actually come out of the bedroom. As though she cared. "Blast it!" he yelled. "How long does it take to unpack! We've been in this stupid house for weeks now and it's complete chaos. Chaos!"

Briefly, Ginny remembered Mom's story of how she got together with Ben Crosby. "I very seldom dated," she had told Ginny. "I had...well, I'd been hurt really badly before. But when your dad came into the office where I worked to replace a cracked window, it was like he brought the sunshine into that place with him. His smile...the way he made me feel. He brought laughter back into my life."

Ha! Ginny thought. There hadn't been much laughter in this house of late.

By the sound of things, Daddy was now rummaging around on the kitchen counter, tossing items around in his search. She heard the soft slide of the open bag of sugar, the plastic clacking of the calculator, the jangle of Mom's keys, and the clanking that was either unwashed silverware or the candlesticks that couldn't seem to find an appropriate place in this house. Then came an "aha!" from Daddy. Apparently he'd found the strips.

Again he rushed into her doorway, then stopped, but this time the look on his face was puzzled, distant.

"Daddy? What's the matter?"

He shook his head, as though clearing it. "Oh, nothing. Sorry." He started toward her, but his voice still sounded distracted. "I thought I saw something on the counter that didn't belong there. Something odd."

Ginny laughed, the sound coming out more hysterical than she had intended. "You're kidding, right?"

Daddy's eyes came back into focus, and he laughed, too, although he didn't sound terribly amused. "Yeah, how silly of me."

He got the strip ready in the meter and loaded the needle into the lancet. But after pulling her hand toward him, he went a little green. She pulled her hand back and took the lancet from him. "I told you I could do it." She viciously rotated the dial and turned the pressure from a two to a three, jammed it down against her fingertip, and pressed the button hard. A little shock of pain went through her as the needle shot in with a satisfying click.

The reading was sixty-nine, low but not unmanageable. Daddy gave her orange juice and sat by her for a while, fidgeting in her rocking chair while she squirmed around in the bed. Eventually he supervised another glucose check and, after confirming an okay reading, went back to bed in the guest room.

Ginny lay staring at the black ceiling, thinking about Mom holed up in the master bedroom, listening to her own daughter call for help and not making a move. She figured she would never be able to get back to sleep thinking such angry thoughts, but she must have drifted off, because the next thing she knew was the sound of her parents' arguing voices coming from the direction of the kitchen.

"I can't believe you're not staying home with her today, Rose."

That would be Daddy.

"Why don't you stay with her?" Mom chimed in. "Isn't that why you were so determined to be self-employed? So you wouldn't have a boss to explain to?"

Daddy snorted. "Those lazy bums at the construction site won't lift a finger if I don't show up to make them."

"Look, Ben, Ginny's not that sick. Her sugar never did go that low this time. I think she milks this hypoglycemia thing."

Gee, thanks, Mom.

The woman ranted on. "She's well enough to go to school. If she doesn't want to do that, she'll be fine at home by herself."

"I don't know. It's all been hard for her lately, and anyway...you know Ginny. She looks way older than fifteen, but sometimes she acts like she's twelve."

Ginny felt a pain go through her. She'd never heard Daddy say anything like that.

She heard him sigh and add, "It's a terrifying combination for a dad."

"Ben, please—even if she were twelve, that would be old enough to spend a day at home alone," Mom said.

Then the back door slammed. Ginny got out of the bed and pulled the soft pink afghan off the rocking chair, wrapping it tightly around her shoulders as she went to the window. A sagging car shelter, big enough for two cars plus the tractor, stood on the far side of the back yard. But Mom always parked out in the open, closer to the house. Ginny could see her picking her way down the porch steps, trying to keep from stepping on the hem of her long skirt while clutching a sweater, purse, and tote bag in her arms.

Why hadn't she come when Ginny called her last night? Why hadn't she at least come in to check on her this morning? Mom might avoid her every other moment of the day, might not even want to look her in the eye when she couldn't escape talking to her, but she was always there when Ginny was sick. It was the one thing Ginny could still count on. Or so she had thought.

At the Escort, Mom set her coffee mug on the top as she held the sweater and bags in one arm and wrestled the car door open with the other. As always, she looked too small and fragile for whatever job she was tackling. Ginny remembered her thirteenth birthday, when Mom had hugged her before her party and then laughed.

"Good grief. What's with you? You become a teen-ager and automatically you're taller than me?"

It was true when she was thirteen, and over the next couple of years, Ginny had shot up much taller than Mom, who was only five-one and small-boned. With her long blonde waves of hair and the flowy clothes she liked to wear, Mom had always seemed a little other-worldly to Ginny, like a fairy. Ginny had wanted to look just like her, but instead of Mom's blonde hair and blue eyes, everything about Ginny was some shade of brown, including her hair and eyes. In kinder days, Mom said her eyes were like Aunt Livvy's. Ginny at least wanted to be petite and graceful like Mom, but instead, she just kept growing taller, and her shoulders got broader until she felt like she was built more like Daddy than Mom. Which was fine for Daddy, but Ginny felt like a giant towering over her dainty fairy mother.

Maybe that's why Mom is scared of you lately.

Well, that was a stupid thought. Not that Mom was scared of her, because obviously she was. But it was ridiculous to think that Mom's fear had anything to do with Ginny's size. Mom wasn't scared of Daddy, and he was six feet two—all of it solid muscle from working construction the last year or so.

Anger bubbled up through Ginny's veins, into her head as Mom leaned across the driver's seat of the Escort, arranging her stuff before getting in. Ginny saw herself in her mind's eye standing behind that car door, grabbing it and shoving it, crushing it against her mother's back and legs. The will to strike out and hurt grew so strong that, for a moment, Ginny believed the door really would slam against her mother.

It didn't, of course. Mom simply got in and drove away. The anger drained out of Ginny as quickly as it came. She sat back down on the bed before her knees gave way. What would happen if one day she wasn't watching from the window when one of these moods struck her? What if she stood behind Mom, within easy reach of a car door—or something even more lethal?

Maybe Mom had a reason to be scared of her, after all.

Ginny's feet were cold, but she made no move to get back in the bed. She sat staring at nothing, growing colder and colder and wondering for about the thousandth time what was wrong with her.

On their last visit to the doctor, Mom had pulled the man aside and tried to ask him something without Ginny hearing. Ginny pretended to be out of earshot, but she heard Mom trying in her own blundering way to ask that same question—what was wrong with Ginny? The girl had changed drastically. Why did her moods change on a dime? The doctor answered that the hypoglycemia could cause some irritability and aggression. Then he laughed and said, "Of course, she's also a teenage girl. So what do you expect?"

Very funny. Ginny had wanted to smack him, too.

"Hey, sport, how you feeling?"

She jumped at the sound of Daddy's voice, as though he had caught her in some vile act. She hugged the afghan around her. "Better."

"Well that's good to hear."

"Not good enough for school, though."

He sighed. "Uh-huh." He sat down in the white wicker rocker at the foot of her bed. It looked so tiny under him, she expected it to break any minute.

Ginny stared down at her bare toes, hoping he wouldn't start nagging about school again. She needed a pedicure. Of course she'd only had one pedicure. Her friend Amy treated her to it, along with a manicure, as a going-away present the day before they moved from the city. But her nails were ragged and ugly again now.

"It'll get better," Daddy said.

Yep. He was nagging again.

"School, I mean. It's only been a few weeks. It'll get better."

"Yes sir."

No way would it get better. It had started out all wrong, when Heather Tanner got kicked off the basketball team right when Ginny transferred in to the school, wanting to try out. Apparently Heather had been temporarily suspended for various infractions before, but Ginny replaced her so well that Coach didn't take her back this time. Kelsey Shaw, captain of the team and Heather's best friend, knew a lot of tricks for making a new girl's life miserable on and off the court. At practice, she had "accidentally" knocked Ginny down more than once. But much worse than that had been the day that Lanie Jefferson came to Ginny with a huge smile on her face, holding out a big plastic bag to her.

"What's this?" Ginny had said, hearing a few titters of laughter nearby as she accepted the bag.

Lanie had leaned in and said in a stage whisper, "A gift for you.

From the clothing drive."

"Clothing drive? But I—"

"Now, now," Lanie shushed her, patting the hand holding the bag. "Your name was given to us. We know your dad's out of work and you're having a hard time."

"He's not out of work. He's starting his own company—"

But Lanie had held up a hand to quiet her again, given her an "understanding" smile that infuriated her, and hurried away. And Ginny had seen Kelsey disappearing around a corner right before the loud laughter broke out. It was pretty easy to guess who had given Ginny's name to the clothing drive. Dropping the bag of second-hand apparel into the nearest trash can—and wanting to crawl in with it and close the lid over her head—Ginny had fumed at the double insult. Ginny tended toward rather artsy, flowing clothes that had been perfectly acceptable at her Atlanta school, but not here in the suburbs. Kelsey had found a way to get in a jab at Ginny's fashion sense and ridicule her family's financial struggles at the same time.

Daddy knew none of this, of course. All he knew was that she was on the basketball team. Hooray!

As though hearing that last thought, Daddy said, "I'm really proud of you for making the team. That'll help you make new friends. You'll see."

How could the man be so totally clueless? Feeling grumpy, she grabbed one of her pillows and shook it a little more violently than was necessary to fluff it up. "I don't understand why Mom could keep her job in Atlanta but I had to change schools."

"Because there are rules about school. You have to live in the district. You can work anywhere you want to, if you're crazy enough to make the commute."

She dropped her voice and muttered, "I knew Mom was crazy."

She didn't really mean for Daddy to hear her, but of course he did. His voice rose a couple of decibels. "Don't say things like that about your mother."

Even if we both think it. "Yes, sir."

"Anyway, you better be glad your mother's willing to make that commute. Her income's all we've had lately."

"But you're working now."

"Yeah, sort of. But new businesses take some time to pay off." He smiled. "Just like new schools."

"I didn't know you were so grateful to Mom. I didn't think you had a very high opinion of her anymore."

"Why would you say that?"

"You haven't slept in the same room for weeks. Did you think I wouldn't notice?"

He picked at a broken piece of wicker on the chair arm, pulling at it. She knew she had upset him because he normally went around fixing everything, straightening pictures, making everything just right. Now he sat picking apart her chair. But his tone remained light as he answered. "I've driven your mother crazy for years with my snoring. Now we've got a big enough place she can finally get some sleep."

"So it was her idea?"

"Uh-huh."

Yeah, right. Not the way the doors had slammed that night, with Daddy doing most of the slamming as he huffed out of his and Mom's room and up the hall, into the guest room. Mom had huddled behind the closed door of the master bedroom and cried, so quietly that Ginny couldn't hear her until she crept right up to the door and knocked. She wanted to go inside and comfort her mother. Actually, she wanted to be comforted. But Mom had told her to go away.

Daddy suddenly switched gears. "You feel up to breakfast?"

As if on cue, her stomach growled. They both laughed.

He stood up. "I'll go see what I can find."

She started to stand up, but he motioned for her to be still. "Stay put. I'll bring you a tray."

Wow. Breakfast in bed. She lounged back against her pillows and stretched out her legs on the bed again. Maybe she should be sick every night.

After settling the breakfast tray across her legs, Daddy plopped down into the rocker and absently looked around. She didn't think he was really seeing her or her room, but was thinking of the big hole in the ground that marked the foundation of his latest construction project. So he surprised her when he nodded his head toward the wall opposite her and said, "What are those?"

She glanced where he was pointing and for some reason felt a stab of guilt. "Oh…those. I, uh…I found them in a drawer when we moved in."

Daddy stood up and went to study the row of charcoal sketches that Ginny had thumb-tacked in what she thought was an artistic arrangement. He glanced in her direction, then back to the drawings as he said, "Huh. Wonder why these appealed to you."

Embarrassment warmed her face, and she saw the sides of Daddy's mouth twitching.

"I just thought they were really well-done," she said, indignant.

"I'll bet."

She gave up the battle. All the drawings featured one or both of two lanky, well-built boys, so Daddy would never believe anything other than teenage hormones had made her like them. And true, hormones were probably part of it, because both the boys were cute. Actually, one was downright gorgeous, with close-cropped dark hair and eyes that appeared brooding, but kind—as though he was fully aware of some pain or suffering but determined to fix it. She had nicknamed him "Soulful."

The other boy who was in some of the pictures looked like the gorgeous one—and yet he didn't. His dark, silky hair was long and messy, and he was a little bit shorter and slighter of build. In all the drawings, his mouth was tilted in a grin, and his eyes were smaller and beadier. Well, maybe that was unfair. The eyes were still nice enough, they just hadn't been drawn to be so soulful and luminous, and they looked more devilish. Like the boy who would have sat behind you in third grade and pulled your hair when the teacher wasn't looking. She mentally called him "Trouble."

Some of the drawings were just angles and lines, cheekbones and eyes and chins. Others were detailed, showing the guys lounging beside a lake or river, practically hidden in the lush grass of the bank or by low-hanging, leafy branches. In fact, it almost appeared as though the artist were spying on them from behind a tree, furtively stealing their image. In some of the drawings, there was a girl with the guys, and she looked a bit familiar but Ginny couldn't quite place her. Maybe that was because she wasn't drawn as sharply as the boys. That made Ginny think that another girl had drawn the pictures, because of where her obvious interest lay.

Daddy was shaking his head, gesturing toward Trouble. "Look at the hair on that one! I'd forgotten how we used to look back then."

Ginny's head jerked up. "Back then? When?"

"Late seventies or early eighties, by the look of it. The guy looks like he'd just discovered mousse."

Ginny thought for a moment. "What do you mean…how 'we' used to look?"

He laughed. "Oh, I had a mop like that, too." Winking at her, he said, "Hard to picture, huh?"

Ginny said nothing. His words had given her an odd little pang, and not because she was picturing super conservative Ben Crosby with long hair and holes in the knees of his jeans. She didn't even bother trying something that impossible. No, the odd feeling came when she considered these boys still existing somewhere, but middle-aged, with business suits and wrinkles and probably pot bellies from sitting at desks all day. She wasn't sure why that idea was so jarring. Because she hadn't thought them any more real than characters in some racy teen novel? Or because the drawings seemed to have frozen them in time, forever brooding or plotting mischief, forever young?

"I'll bet Rose drew these," Daddy said.

"What!" Again her stomach dropped. "No, she didn't."

Daddy raised his eyebrows at her. "Who else would it have been? You think your Grandma Carla would have spent her time sketching teenage boys?" He shook his head. "Your mom was the only one in this house with any artistic leanings."

Ginny opened her mouth to protest, then closed it without speaking as she remembered standing next to Mom in her bedroom in their old apartment, so young that Mom was actually taller than her. Mom was painting a mural of night sky and a castle turret, with a snowy owl circling it because Ginny was obsessed with Harry Potter. Ginny had been so fascinated to see Mom producing Hogwarts and Hedwig out of thin air, with flicks and swishes of her brush, as magic and powerful to Ginny as if she had conjured the image with Harry's wand. And then Mom had given her a paintbrush and let her add the full moon, showing her how to shade it and stroke it so that it truly seemed to glow with light.

That was the first time she had ever seen Mom draw or paint, and for a while after that she had driven the woman crazy, begging her to draw owls and wizards and dragons. She had pleaded for Mom to show her how to do it herself, and Mom had tried. Only the art really was like something magical, because no matter how hard Ginny tried, she couldn't produce anything as wonderful as Mom had done with those casual flicks of her brush.

Even at the ripe old age of fifteen, Ginny had cried over leaving the castle mural behind when they moved here, into Grandma Carla's house. But she hadn't thought about Mom painting for ages. She had practically forgotten that Mom ever did anything artistic. Never once had it occurred to her that Mom, as a kid growing up in this house, might have produced these drawings. Or known boys like this. Heck, it had barely occurred to her that Mom might have ever been young.

She was about to ask Daddy if he knew who the kids in the picture were when he said briskly, "So. You gonna finish your breakfast?"

"Oh, right." She had completely forgotten the eggs on her plate, which were now cold and congealing. She wrinkled her nose at the sight. "I'm finished."

He picked up her tray, then just stood there, fidgeting. "Look, it appears you're doing okay. You don't mind if I run out to the work site, do you? Just to make sure the guys showed up and know what they're doing?" Her expression must have made clear she did mind, because he started making excuses. "It'll only be for a couple of hours. I just need to check on things."

Her stomach lurched. The taste in her mouth turned sour, and she swallowed hard. "Maybe I could go with you."

He frowned. "Maybe you could go to school."

School or this creepy old house. What a choice.

"No, I…sure, go ahead. Do what you need to. I'll be fine."

"You sure?" He said it the way people do when they want you to reassure them—even though they intend to do as they like no matter what you think.

She said what he wanted to hear. "I'm sure."

Relief lit his face. He shot to his feet, setting the chair to rocking feverishly, and leaned over to give her a peck on the cheek. "Thanks, honey. I'll be back in a flash. You'll barely notice I'm gone, you'll see."

The front door slammed a nanosecond later. Ginny slid back down in the bed and watched the rocker going back and forth, back and forth. The house settled down on her, like a weight on her chest.

When they moved in, she had picked this room to be her bedroom instead of the guest room down the hall. Years ago, before Grandma Carla did the renovations, it was the house's living room. It retained a working fireplace from those days, and she thought it would be cool to have a fireplace in her bedroom, like in all those romantic books and movies. Plus the room gave her a huge picture window overlooking the back yard and outbuildings and the pecan grove beyond. She even had her own door opening onto the back porch. Daddy had raised an eyebrow when she claimed this room as her own. "Not planning to sneak out at night, are we?" Yeah, right. Considering her nonexistent social life, what would be the point?

Instead of being cool, though, this room—like the rest of the house—had started to creep her out. Things fluttered and squeaked inside the chimney. Daddy said it was just starlings, but the idea of things nesting inside her walls didn't comfort her a lot. On windy nights, stuff bumped around on the back porch, and shadows shifted on the other side of the filmy curtains. Sometimes she lay awake watching the door, her eyes convinced that the handle was turning and her thudding heart waiting for the door to burst open.

Just now, something on the roof made a little scratchy-scratch noise. Over and over. Scritch-scratch. Just like that. Squirrel, maybe? Probably, but who knew? She pulled the sheet up to her face, peeking out over the eyelet edge. She'd never heard sounds like that back in their apartment in the city. But then, they'd been on the middle floor, with another family above them arguing, and playing hip-hop music, and watching TV shows that featured lots of gunfire and bombs, and running the shower at two o'clock in the morning. Whole armies of squirrels could have been marching across that roof, clawing tunnels into the attic, and no one would have heard a thing.

She suddenly noticed her rocking chair was still rocking, even though she must have been daydreaming for a couple of minutes. Swoosh, swoosh, swoosh…it made a soft but rhythmic noise as it swayed back and forth on the ugly green carpet. And it didn't seem to be slowing down. Swoosh, swoosh…How long had Daddy been gone now?

Ginny threw back the covers and got up. She reached out a tentative hand to stop the rocker's motion, then drew it back. What if it wouldn't stop? What if something pushed back against her hand, cold and unyielding?

She made a beeline out of the room.

CHAPTER THREE

For a while, Ginny tried watching television. Usually, TV made everything normal. It was hard to get scared with sitcoms blasting canned laughter throughout the house.

Hard, but not impossible. Their one functioning TV was located in the "New Room," which in Ginny's mind was a pretty bizarre place all on its own. It had started life as a garage, but years ago Mom's family decided to expand the house and turned it into a living room. The old den became a third bedroom—now Ginny's room—with a bathroom and closet carved out of the floor space. All that happened before Ginny was born, and yet her weird family still called the renovated garage "The New Room." It had a separate entrance to the porch, and also had French doors from the kitchen that would shut the room off from the rest of the house. Add walls of windows looking out onto woods and pecan trees, and you had a fair beginning toward creepy. But none of that was the worst of it.

When the garage was enclosed, the narrow staircase down into the unfinished basement had been enclosed along with it. So now, their living room featured a dark hole down into that pit of a cellar. Even with *The Fresh Prince* blaring, Ginny couldn't help but glance in the direction of the stairwell from time to time, halfway expecting to see scaly creatures climbing out of the hole.

And then there was the fireplace area. On the mantel was an urn with her Aunt Livvy's ashes. How gross could you get! But that's where they had rested all these years, and Mom refused to shift them when they moved in. Above the mantel was her grandmother's portrait. She didn't even want to think about Grandma Carla, if she could help it, but it was hard not to with the woman staring down at her.

The whole subject of Grandma had always been a little strange. Even though Grandma Carla was Ginny's only living grandparent—and had only lived about an hour away from their city apartment—they hardly ever visited her. And Grandma never came to their place. On the rare occasions they did see her, Mom turned into a whole different person, her face strained and quiet. How weird it was now to be living in Grandma's house. But Daddy had insisted they move in here after Grandma went into the nursing home. Money was so tight with him starting up Crosby Construction—and being unemployed for a long stretch before that—that living rent-free in this vacant house was the only logical thing to do. So Daddy said.

Oh, great. Now all Ginny could think about was Grandma, and that one awful visit she had made with Mom to see her in the nursing home.

Come to think of it, was that when Mom had started behaving so weirdly toward Ginny—after Grandma freaked out on seeing her? The frail old woman had become so agitated they had to leave. Ginny got all shivery remembering Grandma struggling to lift her hand to point at her, working her mouth and trying to speak, although she hadn't been able to say a word since the stroke.

Violently shaking her head to clear away the memory, Ginny picked up the remote and started flicking through the channels. She was *not* going to think about Grandma and the nursing home visit today, when she was already a nervous wreck. Because everything about Grandma was connected in her mind, and she would soon be remembering other things.

Racing through the channels, she heard blips of noise from game show hosts, jewelry salesmen, and sitcom laugh tracks. The abrupt sounds were jarring, but that was okay. They smashed to pieces the memory that was starting to form in her head, about that time when she was seven or eight and came to stay with Grandma. This was not the time to start thinking about that. Not hardly.

Suddenly, even over the TV chatter, Ginny heard something.

She sat up straight on the sofa and concentrated, but the sound did not repeat. What had it been exactly? A distant, muffled sound, something like the cry of a child. And it definitely came from down there, down in that dark pit of a basement.

She picked up her cell phone and tapped in a message to Amy. "I hate this weird house. I think it's haunted."

Then she started flipping channels again, waiting for Amy to respond.

She heard the scratchy-scratch noise again. Was it coming from the roof this time, or from the basement?

She got up and crept toward the dark hole, leaned over the railing and tried to see down the stairwell. But she couldn't make out anything beyond the first step or two. She leaned further over the railing, straining her neck...

A high-pitched squeal came from down there, somewhere. She jerked away from the railing, dropping the TV remote in the process. It clattered down the steps, down, down, one step after another. Ginny didn't hear it land. She skedaddled out into the hallway.

Well, this was just peachy. At this rate, she'd be out in the yard soon, afraid to come into her own house. Only it wasn't really her house, was it? It was Grandma's.

She glanced down at her pajama bottoms and bare feet. Maybe she'd better get dressed before the next hair-raising adventure, so at least she wouldn't be quite as humiliated if she had to flee into the road. Not bothering to take a bath, she hurriedly pulled on black jeans and a black cotton shirt, and finished off by slipping into her tennis shoes. All set for running, ha ha! After jerking a brush through her hair, she wandered back in the direction of the New Room, not quite sure of her next move. She patted the pocket of her jeans, making sure her phone was there.

Maybe it was because she was thinking about her phone, but an idea came to her. She wanted to call Mom. She wanted to tell her mother about all the strange noises, about that thing in the basement. Maybe Mom would be able to explain it. Maybe she had heard that very noise every day when she was a kid in this house, and it was really no big deal.

Yeah, Mom won't mind you calling for this, she told herself as she punched in the numbers. She'll be able to tell you exactly what it is.

As she listened to the ringing on the other end of the line, waiting for Mom to answer, a little voice in her head nagged at her. *You don't want her to explain anything. You just want her to feel sorry for you and worry about you and maybe even come running home. Idiot. Daddy was right about you acting like you're twelve.*

"Connor-Fielding. Mr. Fielding's office. May I help you?"

The woman's voice broke into her thinking so abruptly that Ginny almost said, "Mom?" But after a split second's thought she knew this wasn't her mother's voice. "Umm…may I please speak to Rose Crosby?"

"I'm sorry. Ms. Crosby no longer works here," the woman answered, in a voice so flat and efficient she almost sounded mechanical.

"Wh-what?" Ginny shook her head, trying to pull herself together. "No. That isn't possible." Maybe this woman, whoever she was, hadn't heard her correctly. "I'm looking for Rose Crosby. She's Mr. Fielding's assistant."

"Ms. Crosby hasn't worked here for at least two weeks. I'm Mr. Fielding's new assistant. May I help you?"

"No, uh…thanks." Ginny shoved the phone back into her pocket.

After a moment's thought, she dialed again, this time trying Mom's cell. It went straight to voice mail. Probably a dead battery, Ginny thought. Mom was always forgetting to charge it.

Feeling dazed, she drifted out of the house and stood on the front porch, staring across the road at the thin strip of trees that screened the new subdivision that was under construction. Her mind dimly registered the hum of heavy equipment, the occasional sound of workmen shouting orders to one another. It would have been a comforting sound, reminding her of trips to Daddy's work sites, if she hadn't made that phone call to Mom's office.

Mom's former office.

Mom hadn't worked at Connor-Fielding for two whole weeks? Two weeks! But this morning, she had argued with Daddy about how important it was for her to go to work, had sworn there was no way she could stay home with Ginny. So what the heck was going on?

The question filled her with a desire to scream, to do something. The feeling expanded inside her and pushed against her head and chest, propelling her down the steps and across the yard. Her Nikes pounded the dirt, the crunchy pre-spring remnants of grass, carrying her forward and away, away from the creepy house and her weird family and the sounds of civilization across the street. Just away. She didn't give a thought to where or even think about it, until she was brought up short by a huge limb—half a tree more like it—and she looked around and realized she had taken a path into the woods. Not only that, it was *the* path, the one leading back to the pond.

Don't go back to the pond. It's dangerous.

That's what Grandma Carla had told her when she stayed here that one summer. That's what Mom had said when they moved in a few weeks ago. As a matter of fact, it was one of the few times that Mom had looked at her, really focused on her and talked to her, in months. She had looked directly into Ginny's eyes and almost pleaded with her. "You understand me, don't you? That pond could be a hundred feet deep. And it's in the middle of nowhere—cell phones and radios and stuff won't even work back there—so there wouldn't be anyone around to help you if you got into trouble. You don't need to ever—ever—go back there."

Part of Ginny had wanted to laugh. Mom was so notoriously afraid of water that it was silly. She really didn't even like bathtubs, and now she was making it sound as though the pond were a lion or a bear. Some kind of beast that could chase her and grab her and pull her in. But Ginny hadn't laughed, because another part of her had been filled with a warm fuzzy feeling, enjoying the concern and the fear in Mom's eyes. Fear for Ginny.

She stood still on the path, considering the downed tree for only a few seconds. Then she climbed over it. She managed to snag a hole in her thin cotton t-shirt in the process, but that was okay. Except for the draft. It was one of those typical Georgia February days that couldn't decide whether it was winter or spring. When the breeze was still, the sun felt warm like spring, but then a chill wind would kick up and break the illusion.

The pond came into view suddenly, as she rounded a sharp curve between two sycamore trees. Several things struck her, one right after the other, as she caught sight of it. First, it didn't look dark and frightening at all, but sparkled like a jewel in the bright sunlight of the clearing. Second, it didn't seem as isolated as Mom had said. Maybe Mom was remembering how it used to be, before the road had been widened and lots of the trees cut down, but Ginny could actually glimpse the highway through the pine trees. Curious, she pulled out her cell phone, prepared to decide her mom had been fibbing about everything just to scare her. But by golly, she had no service on the phone. Weird.

She looked up to see what might be blocking the signal, then froze. A boy was standing on the shore on the other side of the pond, dead still and looking exactly like one of the drawings on her wall.

It was "Soulful," living and breathing and staring down into the water from the edge of the quarry cliff.

CHAPTER FOUR

Ginny's dream of "Soulful" abruptly shattered.

The boy dove into the pond, immediately surfaced, and let out an undignified howl as the icy cold water hit him. She knew that was what was wrong with him, because he let out an impressive stream of curse words interspersed with adjectives like "freezing" and "freakin' cold" as he shot out of the water.

Okay, so he wasn't a ghost. Still, she drew back into the cover of the trees at the edge of the clearing, not sure whether the boy had seen her. She could see the muscles in his shoulders and back working as he pulled a shirt over his head. And while she was relieved that he was a live boy—or disappointed, she wasn't entirely sure which—she realized her mother had been right about how isolated the pond was. Even though she could see a tiny section of the highway several hundred yards away, there would be no one around to help her if anything happened.

Don't be a wimp like Mom, she told herself. It's just some guy that wanted a swim.

He lifted his head, and for a moment his profile stood out sharply against the bright daylight. And then she recognized him from school. Alec Matthews, one of the jocks. Girls, including the infamous Kelsey from the basketball team, swooned over him. Ginny had never thought him that attractive before, although he looked pretty good right now. Not as good as the guys in the drawings, though. Not at all romantic, as he stood honking and clearing water out of his sinuses.

She had fallen into a daze, hunkered behind a sycamore and watching him dry off, so that she nearly fell over backward when he suddenly looked straight at her. "I see I'm not the only one playing hooky today," he called.

She shrank back further into the shadow of the tree, but it was no use. He was still looking directly at her and smirking, and she felt ridiculous. So she stepped out into the sunlight, folded her arms across her chest and said, "I'm not playing hooky. I'm sick."

He snorted—kind of like when he was clearing his sinuses. "And came down to the pond for a little therapeutic swim, I guess."

"No, I just..." She trailed off, not wanting to admit she was scared to be alone in her own house. In the middle of the day. "I needed some fresh air. That house is sort of...stuffy."

"Okay." He grinned as he said it, obviously wanting "okay" to convey "you're lying but I'll be nice and go along."

She resisted the urge to smack him. "What are you doing here?"

"I told you. I don't mind admitting it. I'm playing hooky."

"No, I mean here. On our property. It is ours, you know."

"Oh, yeah? I heard Ole Lady Remington sold it, but I thought it was to a corporation or something. I heard they were gonna build an apartment complex."

"Well, you heard wrong." Ginny felt herself bristling, but wasn't sure why. How could Alec Matthews know what a sore subject this was in her household? A brief replay of that last fight flashed through her mind. It was the same argument as usual, with Dad insisting that selling just a few acres of the land would end their financial troubles, and Mom insisting that it would be a betrayal of her mother's trust. Daddy pointed out that Mom didn't even like the pond, acted as though she was terrified of it, so why wouldn't she agree to sell it, for the good of the family?

The last time they quarreled about this was the night of the big fight, when they ended up sleeping in separate rooms. Sounding really frustrated, Daddy had reminded Mom that he was the one Grandma had trusted with her power of attorney. "Maybe she realized how crazy you were going to act about all of this," Daddy had said.

Things hadn't been the same since those words came out of his mouth.

Needing to vent, Ginny said, "Don't call her Ole Lady Remington. She's my grandmother, and she's in a nursing home."

"Yeah? I didn't know the old lady had family. Never heard of any."

"You know Grandma?"

He didn't answer the question. He cocked his head and studied her. "Wait a minute…maybe I do remember something." He thought for another minute, chewing on his bottom lip with the effort.

Ginny squirmed, feeling herself starting to flush. Surely he didn't remember her from that time she stayed with Grandma, from that thing at the church. Surely not.

He snapped his fingers. "I know you! You came to visit when you were, I don't know, eight or nine, didn't you? That was you in that ruckus at the church, wasn't it?"

Now Ginny didn't just feel a little flush of embarrassment, she was burning up with it. She might just burst into flames.

She tried to deflect him. "You want to hear something really weird? Before I came outside, I heard these noises—"

He cut her off with a crow of triumph. "It was you! I remember you now." The grin faded, swallowed up by a hungry look of curiosity. He leaned toward her. "So what actually happened that night? How'd you pull that little stunt?"

"I have no idea what you mean."

"Oh, come on." He laughed. "That was the only time I remember being in that church and not being bored out of my mind. I always wanted to thank you."

She pulled forward a strand of her hair and fidgeted with it, wrapping it around her finger so tightly she felt pain. Desperately, she blurted, "Look, that's old news. This noise in my basement, it's like a kind of squealing noise. Like a baby, or like something crying."

"Oh, yeah?" He didn't sound terribly interested. "That thing at the church really freaked some people out. But my mom said you faked the whole thing."

"What!" She was being drawn back into this conversation, like it or not. "And why would I do that?"

He put up his hands. "Hey, Mom said it wasn't your fault. She said your granny was such a fanatic that she had made you hysterical."

Ginny let out her breath in frustration. "There was nothing to fake, okay? It was all a stupid misunderstanding. It was hot and I got sleepy and I was a little girl. I crawled under the bench—"

"Pew."

"Pew. Whatever. And I went to sleep. Next thing I know, I wake up and people are in an uproar. Talk about hysterical. One deluded woman thought she saw something and started the whole thing."

Alec shook his head. "Not just one old lady. I saw it, too."

"You—you what?"

"I was looking straight at you when it happened. I saw it, too."

For a moment, Ginny was speechless. Since she was eight years old, she had gone back and forth between two ways of thinking about The Incident at the Church, as she had come to refer to it in her mind. First, she would be convinced that something amazing had happened to her, something worthy of the uproar it had caused. Second—and this was most of the time—she was sure that while she had tried to take a peaceful nap under a bench—uh, pew—her crazy grandma had hallucinated something, then humiliated Ginny so badly she never wanted to set foot in this town again.

And yet, here she was. Not only here, but with a boy who apparently had a front row seat to the action that night? Suddenly, Ginny was hungry to talk about it, to tell him what she had felt and experienced. To know what he had seen.

She opened her mouth to speak, still not entirely certain what she was going to say, when a sudden movement up at the highway made her close it again. She saw a flash of red through the trees and heard the sound of a car engine slowing down, then cutting off. The car had angled off the highway and come to a stop on the side of the road, conveniently parked so she could see it pretty clearly through a gap in the pines. It was Mom's Escort. The door opened and slammed shut, and Mom came around the front of the car. She moved slowly, in stops and starts, as though unsure of her purpose. Finally she stopped altogether on the shoulder of the road and gazed down through the trees toward the pond, right in Ginny's direction.

Ginny drew back into the sycamores, grabbing Alec's arm and pulling him with her.

"Hey, what—"

"Shhhh!" For a fraction of a second, she realized she had just manhandled and shushed one of the most popular guys at school. Then she saw flashes of white paint as another vehicle pulled along the road and stopped just beyond the Escort, and forgot everything else as she watched Mom turning toward the vehicle, shading her eyes with her hand and appearing to talk to someone. Frustrated, Ginny moved around Alec and craned her neck, trying to see as Mom walked toward the other vehicle, but a thick stand of pines screened it from view. All Ginny could see were a few flashes of white paint, and she could tell the vehicle was big, much taller and wider than the little Escort.

"Hey." Alec's theatrical whisper right next to her ear made Ginny jump. "What are we doing?"

Ginny whispered back, even though Mom couldn't possibly hear them from this distance. "That's my mother up there."

"Oh." A brief silence. "I thought you weren't playing hooky."

"I'm not. She is."

"O-kay…"

Alec drug the word out as though he thought Ginny was crazy, but she ignored him, focusing all her attention on trying to hear or see something that would tell her what Mom was up to. Preferably without letting Mom see or hear her, which made the first goal more difficult. She just couldn't seem to get in a position to see much of anything. The murmur of voices drifted down on the breeze, but no clear words. Then there was the sound of car doors opening and closing, and the white vehicle pulled away. Mom did not reappear, and the Escort stayed put. Silence fell.

Ginny turned to face Alec, staring at him as she tried to think.

"What'd I miss?" he said. "I couldn't see a thing back here where you pushed me, but it must have been pretty exciting the way you were carrying on."

The words came out of her mouth before she had fully considered the idea—or the wisdom of sharing it with Alec. "I think I just saw my mom cheating on my dad."

His eyes widened. "Right there by the side of the road? Man, I did miss a lot."

"No, you idiot." She shoved him out of the way and started to march down the trail, back in the direction of her house. "Forget I said anything, okay?"

She nudged the puzzle pieces around in her mind as she walked, trying to make them fit. Mom was lying to Dad about her job, pretending to go to work same as usual. Instead she was meeting some unknown person by the road and going off with him. What she had blurted out to Alec seemed obvious, but even if Mom was cheating, what did that have to do with her losing her job? And lying to Daddy about it?

Mom cheating!

How could those words have formed in her mind so easily? A few months or a year ago, they would have been unthinkable. Ginny would probably have rushed up to the roadside, thinking that Mom was being kidnapped. But she had known that Mom was changing, had changed, even before today's lies were shoved in her face.

Startled by a noise at her shoulder, she whipped around and found Alec trudging along behind her. "What…where are you going?"

"I thought you might not want to be alone right now."

Her palms felt hot and sweaty. Wiping them against her jeans, she said, "That's crazy. Just because I heard some weird noises, that doesn't mean I'm scared to be alone in my own house."

"Really? What kind of noises?"

"Were you listening to me at all a while ago?"

"When?"

She threw up her hands. "When I told you about the noises!"

He tilted his head and considered her. "I have no idea what you're talking about, but you just told me you saw your mother cheating on your dad. I thought you might be a little upset and want some company."

"Oh."

Now she didn't know what to think. Or what to do. All the stories she'd heard about this guy made her think he was the stereotypical jock. A complete, stuck-on-himself jerk. But he was actually showing some signs of a decent side. And it was true. She didn't want to be alone right now.

Of course, if Daddy or Mom came home right now and found her alone in the house with a boy—especially when they were both supposed to be in school—they would freak. At that thought, something inside her went cold and hard. "Yeah, maybe you're right. Some company would be nice. Thanks."

As Alec followed her into the house, her stomach fluttered, reminding her of last night's sickness.

He stood gazing around the kitchen. "Got anything to drink? I'm melting."

"Oh, sure." Ginny didn't see how he could be melting, when she was on the verge of shivering. Come to think of it, she didn't know why he had wanted to swim on a day like this. But whatever.

He stood at the counter and gulped a Coke in a few swallows, then plopped the empty can down on the countertop and wiped his mouth with the back of his hand. "So. You gonna give me a tour?"

"A tour?"

"Of your house."

"Oh." She started clumsily toward the New Room. She tried to think of witty things to say but found that her tongue could barely form words. Her brain was tied up with other thoughts: *If Daddy comes in and finds me with a boy in the house, he will kill me. What is Alec up to? Do boys usually ask for house tours? Or does that mean something else? Am I supposed to know that he's actually asking to see my bedroom? Did I just agree to something? I'm such an idiot.*

She pointed out the various bedrooms from the hallway. Alec sauntered to the door of her room and studied it. He grinned as he turned back to look at her. "You've got your own door in and out of the house?"

Ginny shrugged. "It used to be the living room."

"Man, you don't even have to bother sneaking out a window or anything. How cool is that!"

She resisted an urge to snort. Oh, yeah, that was her. Sneaking out to parties every night.

Alec pulled out a pack of cigarettes. "Okay if I smoke in here?"

Another flash of memory—Mom going ballistic when Daddy had some of his friends over to watch football and one of them smoked in the house. "Sure." She smiled. "It's fine."

As they settled back into the New Room, Alec froze with the smoke halfway to his lips and cocked his head as though listening. "Did you hear that?"

Ginny was about to say no, but then she heard the same noise that had driven her from the house earlier, the thin, high cry of …something. And it was coming from down the stairs.

"See? I told you!" she said.

"Told me what?" Alec stuffed the cigarette into his Coke can— gross!—and bounded toward the stairs. Ginny slowly followed him. By the time she reached the bottom, Alec was pacing around the basement, head still tilted in that listening attitude. For a moment, they heard nothing but silence. Then Ginny jumped back toward the steps when a high-pitched squeal ripped through the dank basement.

Alec turned toward her and laughed.

"What's so funny?"

"You." He shook his head. "Surely you're not terrified of a kitten?"

"A kitten! Where?"

He swung around, eyes searching. "Not sure yet. But we've had enough strays for me to know a kitten when I hear one." He pulled at a stack of boxes, peering behind them. "You got any? Strays, I mean."

"No. Well..." She thought for a moment. "I've seen a cat around here a few times. It's so wild, it runs when you open the door. It certainly hasn't come in the house."

Another squeal. They both looked up, in the direction it had come from, and found themselves looking at a patchwork of water-stained ceiling tiles. Alec grabbed a rickety wooden chair, one belonging to Grandma's old dinette set, and dragged it to the middle of the floor, then climbed up to stand on the seat. He pushed up a tile and peered upward.

Ginny watched him for a moment. "You need a flashlight?"

"Not yet. There's some light coming in from a crack in the wall on the back side of the house. I imagine it's right at ground level. Probably just big enough for mamma cat to squeeze through."

"Do you see her?"

"No, but I don't imagine she's in here, or this little guy wouldn't be carrying on like that."

Alec reached in and felt around. Ginny shuddered. Kitten or no, she wouldn't stick her hand up in there for any amount of money. Finally, Alec started to pull out his arm. As he moved, he dislodged a wad of paper. It bounced off of Ginny's head and hit the floor.

"Hey, watch it." Without thinking, she picked up the paper while keeping an eye on Alec's acrobatics. Part of her registered that the paper wasn't really a wad of trash, but carefully folded. It also felt damp and disgusting. She glanced back down and saw brown water stains on the yellowy paper. The ink had run in spots but some letters were distinguishable. She saw a partial date: Ju __, __84. And then a couple of words that appeared to say "ax Mom." *Ax Mom?* Yikes! A couple more partial words: "I'm JO." And then just an "ny" at the bottom, written in cursive when the rest was printed.

Ginny sighed. More creepiness. Would this house ever exhaust its supply? Who had stuck a piece of paper up into the ceiling, anyway, as though hiding it there? Was it a note, or what? She looked more closely at the letters at the end. She could make out i-n-n-y, written in cursive.

Kitten shrieks, close by her head this time, grabbed her attention. She looked up and saw Alec dangling a squirming little gray ball over her head. She shoved the paper into the pocket of her jeans and reached up to take the tiny animal from him. She cuddled it against her body and almost immediately, the crying stopped. She felt herself smiling all over as she cooed to it, stroked its soft fur and gazed into the grayish-blue eyes. The kitten was gray all over, except for a funny patch of white on its forehead that looked almost exactly like a star.

She stopped as a thought hit her. "Wait a minute. Should we have taken him out? Won't his mother be looking for him?"

Alec shrugged. "I don't know. Have you seen her lately?"

Ginny tried to think. "I don't think I've seen her for a couple of days."

"She could just be out hunting for food, or who knows? Lots of bad things happen to stray cats."

Ginny felt her stomach knotting. She didn't know much about animals, but she knew this baby probably needed its mother to live. His tummy felt round and fat, but he was obviously hungry. He rooted his little face eagerly in her hand, as though looking for a milk spout to latch onto.

She looked up at Alec. "What do you think I should do?"

"I don't know. Your folks probably don't want animals nesting in the house, though."

Ginny thought wryly of the starlings in the chimney. Daddy hadn't been too swift to jump on that problem.

"Your dad will probably want to fix that hole. Maybe you should just leave the little varmint outside and see if its mother comes back for it."

Ginny frowned at him. "I don't like the sound of that."

Again he shrugged. The gesture was starting to annoy her. "Suit yourself," he said, glancing down at his watch. "Whoa, I gotta get going. I didn't realize I'd been here this long."

Ginny trailed up the stairs behind him, watching him light up another cigarette and wondering what in the world she was going to do with the little life cradled in her hands. As they reached the top of the stairs, the door from the kitchen swung open, and they found themselves face to face with Mom.

Everyone froze. Ginny could hardly breathe, as she thought how this must look. Alone in the house with a strange boy. *And* they were coming up from the basement together. Smoke from his cigarette fogged the room. Ginny was clutching a contraband animal.

She tried to force out an explanation. "Hey, Mom. This is…this is Alec Matthews, a boy from my school. He just…" She trailed off, not able to think of any explanation that wouldn't cause her a world of hurt.

Oddly enough—and what wasn't odd about Mom's behavior lately?—Mom was totally ignoring the boy, the cigarette smoke, and Ginny. Her eyes were wide and wild, staring only at the kitten in Ginny's arms. "What is that!"

"Umm…a kitten?"

"Where did it come from?"

Ginny opened her mouth and stammered, trying to get out an answer.

"I said, where did it come from? Where!" Mom demanded.

"I—we—found it. Downstairs in the basement."

"The basement!" Mom went white. "What do you mean? How is that possible unless someone put it there? How?"

"I don't…uh, Alec?"

Even Alec Matthews looked a little cowed by Mom's hysteria. But he cleared his throat and rallied. "Up in the ceiling tiles, Miz Crosby. The mamma probably got through a crack from outside."

Mom turned from him to Ginny, actually looking into her eyes for the first time in ages. Ginny felt a little thrill go through her. "Get rid of it," Mom said roughly.

"But Mom, it may starve."

"I said get rid of it. Now!"

As Mom almost ran in the direction of her bedroom, Alec turned to Ginny with wide eyes. "Wow."

"Yeah. Tell me about it."

CHAPTER FIVE

Ginny would rather do almost anything than go to this stupid dinner that Mom had planned at Kelsey Shaw's house. Of all people in the world, why did Mom have to be friends with Kelsey's mother? And then there was Kelsey's weird stepbrother, Max Ferguson. What a fun evening this would be.

"Oh, c'mon, Rose, let her stay home and watch TV," Daddy said as he slipped on his jacket. "That's what I'd like to be doing."

Ginny thought of being in this house alone at night, sitting in the living room with the TV and that stairway to the pit. "Umm…maybe you could drop me off at the mall."

It was bizarre, but Mom actually seemed to want her company tonight. "Ginny needs to go," Mom said, not looking at her, of course. Talking about her like she wasn't in the same room. "Anna has kids her age, and she needs to get to know people."

"That's the trouble." Ginny crossed her arms tightly across her chest. "I do know her kids. Kelsey's mean as a snake and Max is just strange."

"Oh, great." Daddy sighed. "Sounds lovely."

"You don't have to play with the kids, Ben."

Ginny threw up her hands. "But I have to?"

Rose picked up her purse and turned her back on Ginny. "Yes, you do."

Ginny looked at her dad in silent appeal, but he threw his arm around her and propelled her toward the door. "Sorry, sport, but I may need you to protect me from the mean kids."

Ever since taking in the kitten, Ginny had been on shaky ground with both parents, so she couldn't really push the matter. She'd been forced to show the little cat to Daddy the night she and Alec found it. She had watched for its mother all evening, and even left the baby out in the grass, just outside the crack in the foundation, for an hour or two while she watched from the window. But Mamma Cat didn't seem to be coming back. By then the poor kitten was practically hysterical with hunger.

Daddy had looked so weary and worn-down as she showed it to him that she felt a pang of guilt for adding to his burdens. She had half-heartedly planned to tell him everything she had found out about Mom, too. But she couldn't pile it all on him at once, and the kitten was urgent.

"What am I supposed to do?" she asked Daddy. "I can't just let it starve."

He had sighed. "No, you can't." He reached out and touched the white star on the little gray forehead. "Does your mother know about this yet?"

"Yes."

"How'd she take it?"

Ginny told him, leaving Alec Matthews out of the story entirely. The creases in his forehead seemed to deepen as he heard about Mom's latest explosion.

"I'm sorry she's so upset," she finished. "But I have to take care of it. It doesn't seem to have a mother anymore. And trust me, I know what that feels like."

"Ginny." There was a quiet warning in his voice. Then he nodded and picked up his car keys. "Okay. First things first."

Daddy had driven her to the pet superstore, where a clerk showed them some high-priced formula for orphaned kittens. Daddy shook his head and looked even sadder as they went through the checkout.

Ginny gave the eager baby his bottle as they drove home. He clutched Ginny's fingers and latched on with his needle-sharp claws as he sucked and gulped at the formula. Her skin stung where he held onto her, but her heart ached even worse as she watched him.

"Ginny?" Daddy's voice broke her focus on the baby. "If your mother is still upset about the cat when it gets old enough to feed itself, we'll have to try to find it a home. For now, just take care of it like that lady at the pet store told you to. And for Pete's sake, don't let your mother see it."

"I'm sorry to cause so much trouble, Daddy."

"Oh, honey, if it weren't this, it would be something else," he had answered.

Ginny had been careful since then to keep the kitten out of Mom's sight, and Mom didn't even seem to remember it. Probably too much on her mind, what with having an extra man in her life and running her own con game, Ginny thought. But that was another fight for another time, when Ginny could figure out what she should do about it. For now, she just wanted to keep the peace as much as possible.

So, even though she hated the idea of this dinner at the home of two of her least favorite people at Westside, she resigned herself to her fate.

When they arrived, Kelsey let them in. "I'm sorry I won't get to eat with y'all. I have a date." She smirked at Ginny. "But you enjoy your big evening."

Ginny felt herself growing hot all over as Kelsey continued to grin at her, silently implying that only a loser on the grandest scale would be at a dinner party with her parents. Then the doorbell rang, and things got even better. Kelsey's date was standing on the other side of the door—and it was Alec Matthews.

He smiled at Ginny, completely unabashed, and waved a careless hand in her direction as Kelsey hooked her arm through his and dragged him out into the night. She flashed a gloating smile over her shoulder at Ginny, as though she'd just beaten her in a wrestling match.

And Ginny tried to think why. What had she ever done to the girl—to any of these whispering, cliquish girls in this county who seemed determined to cut her out like a sick calf from the herd? She caught a glimpse of her reflection in a long panel of glass next to the door. Jeans, white polo shirt. Ugh. She had even changed the way she dressed, as though that was going to do any good. She was so boring-looking she was surprised she still had a reflection, hadn't disappeared altogether.

Ginny suddenly realized she was standing alone with Max, who stared at her. Max always stared at her—not just tonight. She constantly caught him at it, when she turned her head his way in Biology class, as she stood at her locker in the hallway, when she glanced up at the bleachers during basketball practice. There he would sit (or stand), with his wild Albert Einstein hair, studying her exactly the same way he studied the frogs they dissected in Biology lab. Concentration, fascination—a sort of detached, scientific curiosity. Only the frog never caught him at it, never got offended. She often did, and she would attempt to glare at him and put him in his place, but she never really got a chance. He looked away too fast, blushing a fiery red and turning quickly to some other activity.

And then there were his t-shirts. Without fail, he wore a shirt emblazoned with some religious slogan. Tonight's shirt read, "Jesus>The World." The kid was a walking billboard for God. Not that Ginny had anything against Jesus, or religion, but Mom did. She said a little bit of religion was a good thing, but when people overdid it, it made them crazy. Looking at Max, Ginny tended to agree with Mom.

Tonight, as they ate an assortment of meat that his dad had charred on the grill, Max sat at one end of the dining table while Ginny sat on the side, next to his mother, or stepmother, or whatever the term was when the parental units were only living together. She could see him out of the corner of her eye. He was staring at her. She sighed and took a bite of her potato.

Mom wasn't acting much better than Max. Only instead of staring straight at Ginny, she bobbed her head back and forth from Ginny to Ms. Shaw and back again, as though watching for something. Sometimes she said something embarrassing, like "Ginny, tell Anna about your science project." How lame could you get—and totally unlike Mom. It was almost as though she were inventing excuses to make Ms. Shaw look at Ginny. Or maybe she just wanted the woman to look away from Daddy.

Ms. Shaw was beautiful, with the most amazing white teeth and smooth skin. Her blonde hair was cut in an elegant bob, and she had a way of sitting and moving that screamed sophistication. Worst of all, she and Daddy definitely seemed to be hitting it off, cracking jokes that no one else seemed to understand and smiling at each other. There would definitely be parental fireworks over this little display later. Occasionally Mom broke her rhythm of looking back and forth from Ginny to Ms. Shaw by glaring at Daddy.

Daddy didn't seem to notice, at least not yet. He smiled at Ms. Shaw and said, "So. How is it you and Rose know each other exactly?"

"We knew each other when we were kids," Mom muttered, making it sound as dull as dirt.

Ms. Shaw, on the other hand, flashed a wicked smile with those gorgeous teeth. "We practically grew up together. And when we were teenagers, we were engaged to two brothers."

Ginny dropped her fork. As she picked it up, she saw that Daddy looked surprised, too, while Mom looked totally uncomfortable.

Ms. Shaw, however, continued to babble happily. "Oh, yeah. Hunter and Jake. We were crazy about them, weren't we, Rose?" She laughed. "Or maybe we were just crazy, period." She lifted her glass in a toast. "And I should know. I'm a therapist."

"We were really young," Mom said, fidgeting in her seat.

"Well, this is interesting." Daddy looked from one woman to the other. "Engaged to two brothers. But neither of you married the guy." He laughed, and the sound was harsh and scratchy. "Or maybe you did. What do I know? I didn't even know Rose was engaged before me."

Ms. Shaw's eyes grew wide. "Really? Oh, my."

Mr. Shaw—oops! Mr. Ferguson, that is—piped up for the first time. "No, Ben, you were right. I'm pretty sure I know the names of all of Anna's ex-husbands, and there's not a Jake or a Hunter among them."

"Very funny," Ms. Shaw said, but she didn't sound particularly upset by the comment. She just gazed mildly at Max's dad, who continued to eat with his face turned down toward his plate.

Daddy finally tore his eyes away from Ms. Shaw and said to him, "So, Henry, Rose tells me you're a professor at Tech. Are you an engineer?"

Mr. Ferguson shook his head without looking up. "No. I'm in the physics department."

"Oh." Poor Daddy, who dropped out in his first year at the University of Georgia, seemed to have nothing to say to that.

Ms. Shaw grimaced in Mr. Ferguson's direction. "Henry's official title is associate professor, but he doesn't teach much."

He glanced up briefly, flashing a smile through his beard.

"That's what TA's are for."

The woman continued, "Henry is totally absorbed in his research."

Daddy nodded politely. "Anything we would understand?"

Mr. Ferguson put his fork down on the side of his plate. He leaned forward on his elbows and folded his fingers into a little tent. "I'm working with a team attempting to measure the entropy budget of the universe."

"A-ha," Daddy said, as Ginny tried not to laugh. "And that would be…what, exactly?"

"Well…how to put it simply…you're probably familiar with the basics, right? Like the Second Law of Thermodynamics?"

"Uh…not really, no."

Mr. Ferguson smiled—not in a snotty, know-it-all way, but almost looking excited to have a chance to talk about this stuff. "You're familiar with it, even if you don't realize. Basically, that law of physics states that things naturally move from a state of order to one of chaos." He tapped the glass of iced tea in front of him. "The ice in this glass melting is an example."

Daddy laughed. "Or Ginny's room."

Mr. Ferguson grinned. "I won't go there. But yes…think how things naturally decay over time."

Max jumped in, obviously reciting, "'The whole creation groans…subject to its bondage to decay.'" He looked around, blinking. "The apostle Paul said that, in the Bible, a couple of thousand years ago. Amazing, huh?"

There was a moment of silence.

Daddy cleared his throat and turned back to Mr. Ferguson. "So how does your research tie into this…this law of decay, or whatever?"

"Well…accurately measuring the entropy level of the universe can tell us so much—about how the universe began, about the origin of life."

And then Mr. Ferguson got really excited, and he started to talk. And talk. And talk. Occasionally a word here and there jumped out, like "black holes," and "measurements" and "entropy" and "arrow of time." To Ginny, the words were totally disconnected and devoid of meaning. Looking around at the glazed eyes and open mouths around her, she didn't think she was the only one.

Max was the only one who appeared even vaguely interested, but then Ginny saw him glance at her and redden. Clearing his throat, he said, "Dad, you left us somewhere in the supermassive black holes."

Mr. Ferguson stopped short. He blinked and looked around, as though trying to orient himself. Finally he turned to Max. "Even you?"

Max laughed. "Even me."

"Oh." Mr. Ferguson let out a long breath. "I guess it's a good thing I have teaching assistants."

Max looked over at Ginny, smiled and shook his head. He actually appeared human, for once. She couldn't help but smile back.

Ms. Shaw produced a gorgeous turtle cheesecake for dessert, gushing about the new bakery she had discovered, complete with a former pastry chef from the Ritz Carlton. Mr. Ferguson murmured that he shouldn't have any, since he was diabetic.

"But you know you're going to." Ms. Shaw glanced at him, looking a little annoyed. "Either leave it alone or just enjoy it now and kick up the insulin later." She turned her gaze back to Daddy. "I believe in enjoying the moment."

Daddy grinned at her in a way that was sure to make Mom seethe with jealousy, which under normal circumstances would have made Ginny feel sorry for Mom.

Sure enough, Mom broke into the conversation, sounding sour. "Interesting attitude for a therapist."

Before tonight, Ginny hadn't known Ms. Shaw was a shrink. She was surprised Mom wasn't afraid to be around her. Although insane people might not realize they were nuts.

Ms. Shaw was raising her glass to Daddy. "A therapist exists to help people enjoy their lives, doesn't she?"

"Sounds good to me." Daddy was still grinning at Ms. Shaw like an idiot.

Mom was still glaring at Daddy. Ginny wondered what Mr. Ferguson thought of this little exchange, but he was bent over his cheesecake, scooping it up with a fork and apparently enjoying the moment.

Mom shoved her chair back, scraping it loudly across the hardwood. She picked up her dessert plate and reached across to grab Daddy's, even though it still had half a slice of cheesecake on it. "I'll help you clear, Anna."

"Hey." Daddy waved his fork in protest. "I wasn't finished with that."

"I also believe in equality. You don't mind clearing the dishes, do you, sweetie?" Ms. Shaw said to Mr. Ferguson. The corners of her mouth tilted as she looked at Daddy. "So I can stay out here and talk to our guests?"

"No problem." Mr. Ferguson scraped his plate, then stood up and started gathering dishes.

One elbow on the now-cleared table, Ms. Shaw leaned her head to rest on her hand and looked at Daddy as though about to speak. Mom, however, plopped herself down in her chair and shoved the dessert plates across the table at Daddy. "Sounds like the men are going to clear, honey." She said the word "honey" as though it was a synonym for "jerk." "So why don't you help Henry?"

Daddy gave her a look, but didn't say anything. Lips pressed tightly together, he grabbed the plates and followed Mr. Ferguson into the kitchen.

The sound of another chair scraping made Ginny remember Max.

As he got to his feet, Ms. Shaw raised her eyebrows. "Where do you think you're going?"

"*Lost* is on."

"So record it. Or ask your guest if she would like to go watch it with you."

Max turned toward Ginny, with such a look of panic on his face that she had to struggle not to laugh. She wasn't sure whether he was sort of intrigued but terrified at the thought of being alone with her, or simply horrified at the idea of her messing up his program.

Either way, she quickly set him at ease. "It's okay. I've never watched it, and I've heard it's pretty complicated to catch up on."

Max guffawed. "That's an understatement."

She pushed back her chair. "I'll just go help with the clearing up."

Max scampered away, obviously happy for the reprieve.

Pushing the swinging doors with her shoulder while balancing a stack of plates, Ginny saw Daddy loading the dishwasher and Mr. Ferguson sitting at the breakfast table, pulling out a black bag like the one that held her glucometer.

He shook his head as he pulled out something that looked like a pen. "Cheesecake is going to be the death of me."

Daddy straightened up from the dishwasher and froze, staring at the little gadget that Mr. Ferguson was holding. "What's that?"

Mr. Ferguson glanced over at him. "Oh, sorry." He got to his feet and held up the pen thing. "My insulin. Anna gets onto me constantly about using this stuff in the kitchen. I'll just duck down the hall and—"

"No, no, no need for that," Daddy assured him. "It doesn't bother me. I was just trying to think..." His voice grew thoughtful. "I've seen one of those things—recently. But where would it have been...hmmm."

Mr. Ferguson, apparently reassured by Daddy, was pulling up his shirt. Grasping a fold of skin on his stomach, he aimed the little gadget at his middle.

Ginny dropped the dishes on the counter. "I feel a little queasy. I think I'll go back to the women."

"Oh, I'm sorry, honey," Daddy said. "I didn't think." He gestured toward Mr. Ferguson. "Ginny's been having a lot of experience in this department, lately, herself. She's been really sick a couple of times."

"You're diabetic?" Mr. Ferguson said to her. "Maybe that's why this injector pen looks familiar, Ben."

"No, I don't think so. You don't use one of those, do you, Ginny?"

"You know I don't. Insulin is the last thing I need."

"Ginny is hypoglycemic," Daddy explained to Mr. Ferguson. "Her blood sugar has started dropping really low and—"

"Excuse me. Where is your bathroom?" Ginny broke in.

Mr. Ferguson pointed her down a hallway. As she started in that direction, Daddy frowned at her in concern. "You're not getting sick again are you, honey?"

"No, I'm fine."

And she was, after splashing water on her face and sitting on the toilet with the lid closed for a few minutes. If only this miserable evening would end. She just wanted to put her pajamas on and crawl into her bed and stay there for about twelve hours. No, correction. She wanted to crawl into her bed in their old apartment in Atlanta.

Forcing herself to her feet, she washed her hands and face one more time and stared at herself in the mirror. What were Kelsey and

Alec Matthews doing right now? she wondered. Whatever it was, it was sure to be better than this.

She meandered down the hallway in the direction of the dining room. There were no swinging doors to maneuver from this direction. In fact, the dining room was open to the hallway, and something about the hushed sound of her mother's and Ms. Shaw's voices made her slow down as she approached. Their voices sounded like hers and Amy's when they were exchanging juicy secrets. Thinking about seeing her mother up by the highway this afternoon, getting into a car with someone and driving away, she stopped before she came into their line of vision and stayed perfectly still, hoping they'd speak loudly enough for her to get some answers.

She felt a little shock of surprise when the first thing she heard was about her.

It was Ms. Shaw speaking. "I'm just not sure what you mean, something strange about Ginny. Are you asking me as a mom, or as a therapist?"

"Actually, I'm asking you as someone who—who's known me for a long time. Who knew me in 1984."

"I'm not sure I understand."

It sounded as though Mom started whispering. Ginny strained, trying to hear over her own thudding heartbeat. She couldn't hear everything, but made out the words, "Ginny remind you of anyone?"

Ms. Shaw's laugh sounded harsh and shrill after Mom's whisper. "Everybody reminds me of someone. Must be age. And all these teenage girls look alike. They all have the long straight hair, and good grief! Lately they're all tall and curvy. We didn't look like that, did we?"

"One of us did."

"Excuse me?"

"Doesn't Ginny remind you of someone from back then, back when we were young?"

"I'm not sure."

"Think about it."

A brief silence followed. Then there was a long sigh, apparently from Ms. Shaw. "I'm sorry, Rose. I'm not sure what you're getting at. If you'd just tell me—"

"No, no. Don't worry about it." Mom's voice grew louder. "You either see it or you don't. It's not important."

Ginny heard the sound of the swinging doors and the men coming in from the kitchen, and knew she had heard all she was going to hear.

The car ride home was only about five minutes long, but it seemed much longer. Mom stared out the window, and Daddy talked about that stupid injector pen.

"I finally remembered where I saw one like it," he said, as they turned onto the dark road to Grandma's house. "There was one lying on the kitchen counter the last time Ginny was sick during the night. You know, when it took me so long to find the test strips."

Mom finally spoke. "Right. Because I'm such a disorganized mess that you couldn't find anything."

Daddy sighed, a long deep sigh. "Rose, please don't start. That's not what I meant, or—I don't know. Maybe it is."

"What?"

"I'm trying to figure out why there was—or is—an insulin injector pen in our house. Did your mother use one?"

"I don't know. Maybe. Yeah, I think she did."

"And we still have random stuff like that lying around?"

"Ben, I don't know what you're talking about. I haven't seen a pen like that."

"So where did it go? It was on the counter that night—"

"Maybe it's still there."

"I don't think so." He pulled behind the house and shut down the engine. He was out of the car in a flash, crossing the yard with long, determined strides. By the time Ginny and Mom straggled in, he had the kitchen lights blazing and was gesturing them in. "You see? It's not here now. So what did you do with it?"

Mom blew a wisp of hair out of her face. "Ben, what is this about?"

"I'll tell you what it's about. I asked you to make sure this house was cleaned out before we moved in. That all your mother's poison was out of here. What about our daughter?"

Mom laughed sharply. "It's not as though we have to baby-proof the house anymore, Ben. That Ginny is long gone." Mom whirled and faced her, looking her directly in the eye for the first time in so long that it took Ginny's breath away. "Isn't she?"

"Wh-what?" Ginny took a step back, startled.

But Mom was in her face. "My Ginny is gone, isn't she?"

Ginny struggled to speak, fought to make sense out of what she was hearing. Before she was anywhere close to forming a response, or even a question, Mom had turned on Daddy again.

"You know what I think this is all about? You're trying to take the attention off the total fool you made of yourself this evening."

And they were off now, in the direction Ginny had expected ever since Ms. Shaw had sent that first flirty smile in Daddy's direction. Now Mom was yelling at him about "coming on" to other women, and betraying her right under her nose, with her own friend, and Ginny felt sick again. She wanted to crawl off to a cool, quiet bathroom the way she had at Mr. Ferguson's tonight, but something wouldn't let her. She felt fascinated, watching Mom rant at Daddy about his behavior when she knew it was Mom that was being deceitful, who was maybe even cheating. Several times she opened her mouth, ready to tell Daddy about Mom and the big white car. But she couldn't. The accusation was just too horrible, and she didn't know for sure, and the blood was pounding in her ears so hard that she was about to pass out.

And just when she had decided to let it go, let it pass, let them work this stuff out for themselves, the words slid out of her mouth. They felt like hot bile rolling across her tongue, catching her by surprise like a sudden fit of vomiting. "Mom's been lying to you for weeks. She doesn't have a job anymore. She's going...somewhere else."

Silence fell. Deep, intense silence.

Daddy's eyes were wide with surprise. He turned to Mom. "Rose?"

But Mom was staring at Ginny. For the second time in one evening, she was actually looking Ginny in the face. And her eyes were full of hatred.

Ginny was sick again that night. But again, when Ginny called out, it was Daddy who came. Daddy who checked her blood sugar, and Daddy who gave her juice and got her sugar level back into the normal range pretty quickly. All very anticlimactic, really.

So Ginny made a promise to herself. She would not be sick and call out for her mother ever again.

CHAPTER SIX

Ginny sat in the back of the Escort on the way to her game, watching the stiff, erect backs of her parents in the front. They stared straight ahead. No one spoke. Although Ginny had been wishing for days that they would stop fighting and just be quiet, she hated the cold silence.

Of course, she had started it all with that bombshell about Mom's job. Here they were, over two weeks later, and just this afternoon they were still fighting because of what Ginny had said—at least indirectly. She should have kept her mouth shut and let Daddy find out some other way. But how could she have known how things were going to escalate? How could she know that Daddy would use all this as an excuse to go out and sell five acres of Grandma's land, including the pond?

Mom had practically fainted this morning, when Daddy told her. Gasping for enough breath to speak, she hissed at him, "You had no right! I've told you over and over we were not going to sell that land."

"I had every right to do it." Daddy had started to wash his hands at the kitchen sink, completely calm.

"Maybe legally," Mom said. "But not morally."

"Your mother obviously trusted my judgment more than yours, or she would have given you power of attorney."

"My mother…" Her voice trailed off. Ginny peeked up from the textbook she had open in front of her and saw Mom seem to deflate. Her voice grew smaller. "You should at least have talked to me first."

Daddy snorted, turning from the sink to face her. "Like you talked to me about your job? When did you intend to tell me, Rose? How long did you think you could lie to me and trick me?"

"I wasn't lying." Mom's quivering shoulders made her voice shake. "I just...I was afraid to tell you."

"I guess you were. I talked to Tom yesterday. He told me why he let you go. How spacy you'd gotten. How he just couldn't trust you with deadlines or important documents anymore."

Mom's shoulders sagged, and she looked down at the floor.

Daddy was breathing hard. "You should have told me, Rose— the minute you got fired. I had a right to know."

Mom's head snapped up, and her eyes were blazing. "Don't you dare talk to me about what you had a right to know. Not when you sold my land out from under me without a word to me."

"We need the money—now that you have no income."

And off they had gone again...

Even though she wanted the fighting to stop, Ginny really couldn't blame Daddy for anything. Mom had changed, was doing all kinds of secretive, bad stuff lately. Ginny squirmed in the car seat, trying not to think about her missing kitten. But she just couldn't stop herself. The kitten had gotten tired of being shut up in Ginny's bedroom, had taken to hollering and scratching at the door. Fearing Mom's wrath, she had started letting little Star out to play in the yard while she was at school during the day, hoping he would stay out of Mom's sight. But a couple of days ago, she couldn't find him when she came home, and she hadn't seen him since. And she couldn't help but wonder just what this new Mom might be capable of...

Ginny jumped as Mom's harsh voice broke the silence in the car. "By the way, Ben. I imagine Anna will be at the game, too. Do you suppose you could keep your eyes in your head and try not to humiliate us all?"

Daddy slammed his hand against the steering wheel. "You have got to do something about this jealousy, Rose. It's a sickness."

"Not if it's true."

"Let's see. First there was my secretary, Jessica. You got so paranoid about her, so determined we were having an affair that you almost got me fired from that job."

Ginny sighed. Even she knew this old argument well enough to know that Ms. Mulholland was next.

Sure enough, Daddy said, "Then there was Pauline Mulholland. You were horrible to that poor woman."

Ginny remembered Ms. Mulholland. They went to a pool party at her house once, and her torso was as long as poor Mom's whole body. Daddy had talked about her constantly. He told Mom how Ms. Mulholland dressed, and offered to find out where she shopped so Mom could dress like that. Yeah, Mom probably had a right to be snippy about that one.

Back then, Ginny and Mom had spent so much time together, redecorating their little apartment with practically no budget but with plenty of imagination. Mom taught her to sew and they made slipcovers, even a ruffly white one for the footstool, which Mom called "shabby chic." And then there was that beautiful castle mural that she painted on Ginny's wall. Every afternoon, Ginny had practically run home from school so they could work on the transformation, because Mom wouldn't dare work on any of it without her. And they had hours together, bringing beauty out of nothing, because Daddy was always working late.

Working late…with Ms. Mulholland?

No. Ginny shook her head, shaking away the nasty thought like a dog shaking off mud. Daddy wasn't the one who'd lied about going to work and then met up with someone by the roadside. He didn't deserve the way Mom was treating him lately. And neither did Ginny. He'd had to force Mom to come to her game today, even though it was a tournament.

As they all climbed out of the car in front of the gym, Mom slammed the door way too hard and marched toward the entrance without waiting for them. Even though Ginny had wasted the thrill of several wins wishing Mom had been there, she now wished that Daddy had just left the woman alone. Let her stay home by herself if that's what she wanted. Or sneak off to meet somebody. Whatever.

Taking a deep breath and squaring her shoulders, she headed toward the entrance with Daddy. She almost wished she were playing football instead of basketball, something a little rougher. As she marched inside, she targeted several people she would love to tackle—hard. Weird Max loitered in the doorway, staring at her as she went in. His stepmom stood a few feet away, and Ms. Shaw smiled so brightly at Daddy that Ginny wanted to go wipe the grin off her face for her. And when she finally made it to the locker room, Kelsey was the first person she saw. After making brief eye contact with Ginny, Kelsey turned her back, closing ranks with her little circle.

The game itself started out fine. Flying down the court and pounding the ball against the floor were therapeutic as usual. Ginny breathed deep breaths of the stale gymnasium air and yet felt refreshed. Her head started to clear. Then suddenly, everything took a turn.

On her way to the free-throw line, she made the mistake of glancing up into the stands and saw Daddy seated between Mom and Ms. Shaw. Mom's head was turned slightly away from them. She stared off into the distance, clearly focused on something other than the game. Daddy's and Ms. Shaw's faces bounced back and forth, toward the game and then back toward each other. They gestured toward the action on the court and talked with great animation, obviously enjoying the game together. Daddy sat a respectable distance from both Mom and Ms. Shaw. And yet, in some odd way, Daddy appeared to be miles away from Mom, while he seemed to be melting into the other woman.

Ginny missed the free throw. Kelsey cursed at her. Ginny whirled to face the other girl. In a low tone, she growled, "You'll shut your face if you know what's good for you."

Apparently no one else heard, but Kelsey did. Her eyes widened in surprise, but she didn't appear intimidated. Instead, her mouth tilted up at the sides as though she exulted in drawing emotional blood.

You had to hand it to her, though. Kelsey wanted to win the tourney. So when she saw Ginny was clear, she threw to her. Ginny pulled off a couple of difficult shots, and all was well again. Until Ginny stood with her back to Kelsey, waving her arms and guarding the Demons' star Brittany Jessup, and felt an elbow drive into her ribs.

A pain shot through her, then ebbed just as quickly. She knew right away there was no serious physical damage, but the surge of anger didn't weaken when she turned to look at Kelsey.

The girl quickly put up her hands. "Sorry." The ref blew the whistle. Apparently, one of the Demons girls had fouled Kelsey and driven her into Ginny. The situation was being handled. But Kelsey looked at Ginny for the briefest moment and twitched her mouth again, twisting it into that same irritating—no, that same evil—smirk that she seemed to wear whenever she looked Ginny's way.

Something in Ginny snapped.

Time seemed to skip. She found herself falling down to the floor, almost surprised to see Kelsey falling under her. The smirk was gone, at least. Kelsey wore a highly satisfying expression of shock as they both hit the ground and Ginny attempted to slap her. But hands were already pulling Ginny up, off of Kelsey and away from her. Kelsey jumped to her feet, and went for Ginny—but hands pulled her back, too.

Ginny heard madhouse sounds. Whistles blowing, girls screaming, parents cursing. Feet thudded down the bleachers as spectators swarmed the court. Ginny searched the stands, focusing in on the place her parents had been sitting. She found Daddy a few rows down, heading for the court. Mom was standing still, her hand clapped over her mouth and her eyes huge as she stared down at the brawl. No, be honest. She was staring at Ginny, and Ginny alone. Their eyes made contact across the distance, and Ginny felt herself melting at the sheer horror in her mother's expression.

Mom's terrified of me.

The thought had nudged around Ginny's mind many times before, searching for an opening, but Ginny had refused to let it in. Now, as she watched Mom push her way through the mob, the door into her mind crashed open and the realization streamed in.

She looks at me and sees some kind of monster. But why? Why!

Mom fought her way against the crowd, struggling toward the exit door and away from the court as everyone else ran toward the action—but then, no one else was terrified of the girl who had started the fight.

As tempers settled, Ginny felt the fingers that restrained her loosen their grip, and she took immediate advantage. She twisted and jerked, freeing herself, and sprinted for the door to the outside. Voices screamed her name, or screamed other things at her. She heard the ref demanding she come back. She even heard Daddy. But she kept running, in her own way just as scared of the monster as Mom obviously was.

Running blindly, she ran full-force into someone and bounced back. Arms again gripped her, and a familiar voice said, "Whoa, whoa. Where you think you're going in the middle of the game?"

She jerked her head up. Relief flooded her as she recognized Alec's face. Obviously he must not have been inside yet, hadn't seen the craziness in there.

"Get me out of here, Alec."

"Yeah, okay, but what…I mean, what's going—"

"I mean it, Alec. Get me out of here. Now!"

He looked bewildered, but finally he nodded, turned on his heel, and headed toward the parking lot.

CHAPTER SEVEN

Not long after they peeled away from the gym in Alec's truck, big fat drops of rain started to fall on the windshield with heavy, plopping sounds. Soon after, their staccato beat gave way to a constant roar as rain fell in sheets. Alec turned on the lights and leaned forward slightly in the seat, frowning as he struggled to see where he was driving.

After a few minutes, Alec pulled into a big parking lot of some kind, but Ginny couldn't really tell where they were. He killed the engine, and for a few minutes they sat in silence, just watching the rain. It blurred Ginny's vision of anything beyond the hood of the truck. The roaring of the downpour was the only sound. Through the wall of water, she could vaguely make out the line of flat, boxy buildings of a strip shopping center with a tattoo parlor, but she saw no signs of life. Finally she spotted one other vehicle, a pick-up truck set up high on oversize tires, crawling past them in the parking lot. Then there was no more movement.

Alec reached in his pocket and pulled out his cigarettes. "So. You gonna tell me what happened?"

Ginny wasn't even sure he could hear her over the rain, but she told him anyway. About the fiasco at the gym, the fight with Kelsey, even the way her own mother looked at her and ran from her, as though she had morphed into something hideous right there on the court. She told how it had been coming on for months.

As she talked, Alec sat looking straight ahead, blowing smoke toward the windshield. The cab was filling up with noxious fumes, but she didn't want to complain. It had just occurred to her that the last time she saw Alec, he was picking up Kelsey for a date, so he probably wasn't feeling all that happy with Ginny right now.

"I'm sorry," she blurted.

He turned toward her as he blew out more smoke, causing her to cough a little.

"Sorry? About what?"

"You know. What I did to Kelsey in the game."

He guffawed. "Are you kidding me? That girl's a piece of work. I'm sure she deserved it."

Ginny's mouth fell open. "But aren't you…aren't you dating her?"

"Nah. We went out a couple of times. She's a looker and all, but she complains constantly. Nothing's good enough for her."

Ginny felt her spirits rise the tiniest bit, until she remembered her mother's scared face. Mom running terrified from the gym. She heaved a deep sigh. And then she felt Alec touch her lightly on the arm.

She turned and found him studying her.

"Everything's gonna be okay," he said.

"I don't know," she whispered.

"I do. Come here."

Alec pulled on her arm, and Ginny could feel him staring at her, but she stared straight ahead, through the windshield. "All I want is for my mother to look me in the eye—really look at me for once—and tell me what's going on."

Alec dropped her arm. "Maybe you need to stop worrying so much what they think…what she thinks. You just need to do what makes you happy."

"Yeah." She drew a deep breath, feeling that tired deflated feeling that always came after one of her bursts of anger.

"Time to grow up, start thinking of yourself for a change."

"Is that what growing up is?"

"Yeah, it is. Come here."

Alec put his hand under her chin and pulled her toward him. He brushed her lips tentatively with his, as though testing the waters—or her mood. Ginny was amazed to find herself kissing him back. She had only kissed a guy once—Josh Smith, a few months ago. They'd sat together at a couple of football games, and once, when they had found themselves alone in the school hallway together, he had given her a quick peck on the lips. But she had never been in a situation quite like this—alone with someone like Alec, in a cozy, warm bubble far away from everything, hearing a soft voice stroking her, calming her, telling her how special she was, how wonderful.

She leaned against him, forcefully returning his kiss. Alec pulled away slightly to look at her, a surprised expression on his face. He grinned and moved back in, and for a moment it was all quite lovely.

Then Alec's hands started to wander, and a little alarm went off in Ginny's head. This was turning serious. Pulling out of his grasp with some effort, she turned and faced front again.

"What's the matter?" he asked.

"I, uh…I know you'll think this is stupid, but I'm really not supposed to date or be out with boys until I'm sixteen."

Alec laughed. "You're not supposed to beat up your own teammates on the basketball court, either, but apparently you did."

She smiled weakly. "Yeah, well, maybe I should limit my crimes to one per day."

Alec chuckled, but she couldn't find it in her to laugh. A cold wave of fear washed over her as she considered the enormity of what she'd done.

"Oh, Alec," she moaned. "I can't believe what I did."

"It was only a kiss."

"No, not that. The game." She shook her head, trying to clear it. She felt as though she had just woken up. "What possessed me? I've been working for years, working for a scholarship." Panic rose in her voice. "You know they'll throw me off the team. I'll probably get expelled." Reality hit her full force. "And Daddy—Daddy's going to freak!"

"Calm down, okay," Alec said sharply. Ginny had a feeling his patience was wearing thin. "So what do you want me to do? Take you home?"

Ginny tried to think. "No…I'm not ready to go home and face the music yet. Anyway, I need to do some thinking—before the yelling starts. Could you just drop me off at the mall?"

He took a deep breath and cranked the car. "Sure, why not?"

For an hour or so, Ginny wandered through the mall, for once barely noticing the gleaming white Nikes or the sparkly miniskirts in the store windows. In fact, the whole time was a blur, except for one moment when Ginny walked blindly into some poor man who appeared to be distracted, himself, by a display in a Victoria's Secret window. As they bounced off one another, the man's cell phone dropped to the floor.

She gushed, "Oh, I'm so sorry. I didn't see you!"

They bent down at the same time to pick up the phone. Ginny reached it first.

"No, no, my fault. I didn't look where I was…" The man's voice trailed off in mid sentence as he stood up straight and looked at her. His mouth hung open, giving him a sort of stupefied look.

Probably struck dumb by my outrageous beauty, Ginny thought. *Yeah, right.* Anyway, the guy was pretty old, probably her father's age, at least.

"Mister?"

He cleared his throat. "I'm sorry?"

"Want your phone back?"

"Oh yes, yes, of course! I just…" Again, the words faded away. He made no move to take the phone she held out to him. She waved it in front of his face, trying to break his trance, and finally he blinked and reached for it. "Oh, sorry. Thank you. Thanks very much."

He was starting to creep her out, but then he stuck the phone in his pocket and walked briskly toward the Dillard's entrance. She shrugged and moved off in the other direction.

The more she walked, the more frightened she got about facing Daddy. He was all she could think of. Even though this whole mess had started because she was mad at Mom, she didn't even care what that woman thought right now. Ginny had let Daddy down, when he had done nothing to deserve it. He would be hurt. He would be furious.

As her fear increased, so did her desire to just get this whole mess behind her. It was definitely time to go home. Did she dare just call Daddy to come get her? She felt naked and vulnerable as she realized she had nothing with her. No purse, no money, and horrors! No phone. How did a person even go about making a call without a cell? Did they have pay phones anywhere anymore?

Maybe she'd just walk home. No sense begging for help now. She'd made this mess, she should deal with it herself.

She wrapped her arms tightly around her and stepped out into the late afternoon. The rain was gone, but it had left an ugly scene behind—gray clouds and a damp, chill wind. She decided to cut through the parking deck. Not only was it a shorter route to the road, but the structure might give her a little protection from the cold.

"You're not walking, are you?"

Ginny jumped. She hadn't realized anyone was behind her.

It was the same man—the one she'd bumped into. Which was okay at first. He had managed to close his mouth and didn't look so weird. And he was clean-cut and well-dressed. Better dressed than her contractor father ever was, in fact. Daddy never wore an actual suit like this man's, not even to nice restaurants.

"Yeah, I'm walking. It's not far," Ginny answered.

"You don't need to be out walking all by yourself. A young girl like you—it's not safe."

Why did his supposed concern for her safety suddenly made her feel unsafe? The parking deck seemed to stretch out in every direction around her for miles. And naturally, no one else was around. Had he followed her out here? Ginny wondered.

He moved away from her, held out his remote like a magic wand and brought forth a flashing of lights and sound from a silver Lexus a row over. She breathed a sigh of relief. It was a coincidence. Besides, serial killers and perverts didn't drive such nice cars, did they?

He opened the door and threw a bag into the back seat. "Why don't you let me give you a lift?"

Ginny's hackles were back up. "Oh, uh...no thanks." She tried to smile. "You know, don't talk to strangers, all that."

"It's okay. I'm not a stranger. I know your mother." He smiled, but suddenly he looked frightening, his teeth sharp like a wolf's. He was breathing faster. "I haven't seen her in a long time, but you—you look just like her." He took a couple of steps toward her. "Why don't you let me drive you home? I'd love to see her again."

Ginny backed away, keeping the distance between them. "You know what? I just realized, I—I forgot something. Something I was supposed to get for my mother, as a matter of fact." She turned and walked back toward the store, walking as fast as she could without breaking into a sprint, which she desperately wanted to do. But she had a feeling it would be like running from a mad dog or a lion or something, that it would just make him come charging after her.

She was halfway back to the Penney's door now, the inside glowing like a lighthouse in the fog. She allowed herself a glance back over her shoulder. He was standing by the Lexus, his hand resting on the open door. He was staring at her.

This time, she did allow herself to run.

Of all people, Kelsey's mom ended up rescuing her. Ms. Shaw found her wandering through the mall and offered to give her a ride home. Since her only other choice seemed to be walking home and risking the stalker guy catching her without people around or a store to duck into, Ginny accepted.

As they walked out to Ms. Shaw's SUV, Ginny expected the woman to start lecturing her about her behavior at the game. Instead, Ms. Shaw peeled back the plastic that covered two silk dresses she had just purchased and held them up for Ginny to see.

"Pretty," Ginny mumbled, thinking it was a little odd that the woman was out shopping so soon after her daughter had taken a public pounding on the basketball court. She slid into the passenger seat as Ms. Shaw carefully hung the dresses in the back and smoothed them down so they would hang straight.

"Um…how's Kelsey?" Ginny made herself say.

As she cranked the car, Ms. Shaw turned to look at Ginny. She appeared surprised, and Ginny would have sworn it took her a second or two to remember the fight. When she did, she waved her hand dismissively. "Oh, Kelsey's fine. No big deal." She snorted. "As long as you didn't damage her looks, Kelsey's all right. That girl can be terribly vain."

Glancing back at the plastic-covered dresses, Ginny figured it was a safe bet where Kelsey had gotten that trait. Again, Ms. Shaw's unconcerned attitude was a little odd, but it was also heartening. If she wasn't all that upset, maybe Mom and Daddy weren't, either.

"Do you have any tattoos?"

The question jerked Ginny's thoughts away from her impending doom. "What?"

Ms. Shaw laughed. "Tattoos. I'm sure you probably do. That's what girls do to look cool these days, isn't it? Kelsey's got about five of them—plus a belly button ring and who knows what else."

"No," Ginny said. "I don't have a tattoo. My folks would freak."

Ms. Shaw chuckled. "You mean Ben?"

The cozy way the woman said "Ben" made Ginny's flesh crawl. "Both of them."

"Oh, really?" Ms. Shaw leaned toward Ginny, causing the car to swerve to the right a little as she inadvertently moved the wheel. "Let me tell you a secret. Your mother and I went together to get tattoos when we were teenagers."

"What!"

"That's right."

"You're kidding!"

"Nope. I can prove it. Here, look." She grabbed at the neckline of her shirt, trying to pull it and expose her shoulder. The car swerved again. "Oh, blast it."

"It's okay." Ginny put a hand out to stop her. "You can show me when we get to my house. But seriously…my mom has a tattoo?"

"Oh, no. She chickened out after we got to the place. She couldn't even stand to sit with me while I was getting mine. She ended up sitting in the car."

That figured. Still…

"I just can't picture Mom even considering a tattoo."

"She probably wouldn't have if Hunter hadn't said something about it being sexy."

"Hunter?"

"Her fiancé. You remember at the dinner party, I mentioned that Rose and I were engaged to two brothers, Hunter and Jake."

"Oh, yeah." Ginny thought of the drawings of Soulful and Trouble that she had tacked on her bedroom wall, and wondered briefly if they were the brothers. But no, there was another girl in most of the pictures, and the girl wasn't Mom or Ms. Shaw. Unless Ms. Shaw looked really different back then.

"Anyway, the four of us were somewhere one day, and a cute girl walked by with a low-cut top and a little flower tattooed right about here." Ms. Shaw gestured toward her chest. Ginny seriously wished she would keep her hands on the wheel and the car in the right lane. "Which of course just drew the guys' attention to that location even more. Rose and I started talking about how trashy it looked, because back then, girls just didn't get tattoos unless they were trailer trash or something. But the guys both kept insisting it was sexy, so Rose and I said fine, we'll go get one if you like it so much.

"I think Rose thought Hunter would be appalled, because he was a pretty conservative guy. But he got a kind of gleam in his eye and said he would love it, as long as she got it somewhere that no one could see it except him. So a couple of days later, she and I went. We had our designs all picked out. But then, like I said, once we got in the tattoo parlor it only took Rose about two minutes to get scared and change her mind."

A little silence fell. Ms. Shaw kept glancing at Ginny, as though she wanted to say more. Maybe she was still just dying to show Ginny the tattoo and prove she didn't back out, or how cool she was.

But Ginny had to ask, "What kind of tattoo was Mom gonna get?" She smirked. "Her fiancé's name?"

Ms. Shaw shook her head. "No, actually. She decided to get a design in honor of her sister. A dove with an olive branch."

"Uh…I don't get it."

"Livvy's real name was Olive, you know. Olive Anne."

Ginny didn't know that. She knew hardly anything about Mom's family, but she didn't say that.

"Livvy always hated the name and wouldn't let anyone call her that, but she loved the concept. The olive branch stands for peace, you know. And I think there's something in the Bible about a dove and an olive branch…I can't remember. But it means peace with God. Livvy hadn't been dead all that long. Two or three years. So that's what Rose decided on."

"Doesn't sound sexy, if that's what she was going for," Ginny said.

Ms. Shaw wiggled her eyebrows. "Depends on where you get it."

Oh, gross. Ginny felt herself growing hot, and was extremely relieved to see that they were approaching her driveway. At least until she remembered what she was facing inside.

As they pulled into Ginny's yard, Ms. Shaw's attitude abruptly changed. All of a sudden, she seemed like a professional therapist— or at least a concerned mother figure—and she insisted on walking Ginny inside to make sure that everything was okay. Before Ginny could get her front door open, she knew she was wrong to hope her parents would take the basketball fiasco as lightly as Ms. Shaw apparently had. They could hear the shouting from inside, and

Ginny's hands started to shake so hard that Ms. Shaw had to take the key from her and open the door herself.

The sound of Daddy's raised voice hit them first.

"I don't know what we're gonna do, Rose, I swear I don't. Except...we gotta get you some help. I know that."

"Me! Get some help for me?" Mom's voice was shaking. "So I was right. You do think I'm crazy. You've been thinking that all these years!"

"No, I didn't think anything of the sort, until..."

"Until now?"

"Yes, frankly, until now!"

"Oh, thank you very much for—"

"No, you listen, Rose. I've always tried to be patient with you, just like your mamma told me to. But this—well, I don't know what to do, honey. This is just nuts!" A brief moment of silence, then, "You said things turned ugly between you and this Jordan person. How ugly?"

Jordan?

"What do you mean, 'how ugly'?" Mom asked.

"I mean, why are you so afraid of her? Or let's just say hypothetically that this crazy idea of yours is true. Why would she want to come back and haunt you? You said you hated her because she stole your boyfriend, but did you do something to her? Sounds like maybe you've got some unresolved guilt—"

"Stop it, Ben! Stop!"

Come back and haunt you? Mamma was worried about being *haunted?*

For some reason, Ginny turned toward Ms. Shaw—maybe hoping she would understand what the heck her parents were talking about. Maybe hoping this professional woman would know what to do. But Ms. Shaw stood frozen, her fingertips to her lips and a rapt expression on her face as she listened for all she was worth.

Daddy was saying, "I'm just trying to understand—"

"No you aren't. You're making fun of me."

"I don't know what to say to you." There came the sound of a chair scraping the floor. Keys jangling. "I gotta get some air. I gotta think," Daddy said. Ginny heard the kitchen door open, but not close, and after a moment, he said, "I can't leave, can I?"

"What do you mean?"

"Lord, Rose, what am I supposed to do? Leave you here alone with Ginny? Is it safe? I mean, you might…" Daddy's voice faded away.

"Might what?" Mom said. "Are you actually saying I might hurt Ginny?"

Daddy started talking again, but his voice was so low that Ginny couldn't make out the words.

That did it. Ginny started toward the swinging door into the kitchen, planning to slam through it, slam into this mess of a conversation and make them tell her just what the devil they were talking about.

But a hand on her shoulder pulled her back. Ginny snapped around and found Ms. Shaw at her shoulder, her eyes gleaming with intensity. In a hushed voice, the woman told Ginny to go to her room.

"But—"

"Go. Now!" Ms. Shaw's grip on her shoulder relaxed a little, and she whispered. "I deal with situations like this all the time. It usually sounds worse than it is. Now go."

Dragging her feet, Ginny did as she was told and went to her room. But Ms. Shaw hadn't said anything about closing the door, so she stood just inside, leaning against the door jamb, and listened as hard as she could, trying to breathe as little as possible. She made out almost no words, except a couple of curses and exclamations from both her parents right after Ms. Shaw went in.

Then the back door slammed. The voices grew very hushed, but she could tell from the low vibration that one of them was Daddy, and the other sounded too calm to be Mom. So Mom had probably slammed out and left. Ginny ran to the window of her room and, sure enough, saw Mom's Escort whipping around the side of the house and out of sight.

For a long moment, Ginny stood at the window, dazed. The sound of voices in the hallway finally snapped her out of her trance. She crept to her doorway and watched as Daddy walked Ms. Shaw to the front door. His face was turned, but she could tell his skin was dead white, and he kept running his hand through his hair the way he did when he was nervous. Or at least, he kept it up until Ms. Shaw took the hand and squeezed it. Ginny had no idea what the woman was saying, but she kept up a soothing-sounding monotone while

Daddy occasionally just nodded. Their heads were very close together.

Finally, they pulled apart. Ms. Shaw left.

Daddy turned and was facing Ginny, but he didn't seem to see her. He stood there for a long moment, looking past her, as though she were invisible. As though she were a ghost. Then he went into his bedroom and closed the door.

CHAPTER EIGHT

Mom picked up the plate of cold waffles that sat in front of Ginny. "You didn't eat much. I thought waffles were your favorite." She smiled brightly.

Sheesh. It was like having a Stepford Wife for a mother.

"I'm not very hungry."

Now Mom frowned, oozing concern. "You're not sick, are you?"

"No, I'm fine." Ginny got up and grabbed her jacket and backpack. "I better head out. I'm gonna be late."

"Want me to drive you?" Rose beamed at her again, although, after a second, her eyes skittered away from such direct contact with Ginny's.

So Mom hadn't turned completely into a Stepford Mother. She was acting all sweet and concerned, but that was just on the outside.

"It's okay. Dad said he has time to drop me off." Ginny's heart sank at the look of relief that passed across Mom's face.

As they drove away from the house, Daddy barely spoke, which was fine. Ginny didn't feel like talking either as she replayed the breakfast scene in her head. She didn't know whether to be glad that her mom was at least trying to be nice to her again—or upset that the woman was being forced to pretend to care.

That's what Ginny figured it was, anyway. Force or coercion or blackmail, something like that. Ginny hadn't been able to make out what Daddy and Ms. Shaw were saying with their heads pressed together the day of the fight, but a couple of days later, Mom started seeing Ms. Shaw professionally, like a shrink. And Mom started plastering these big fake smiles on her face and being all nice. So either Daddy had threatened to leave her if she didn't shape up, or Ms. Shaw had told her she was headed for the funny farm. Something like that.

It was really strange, but for some reason, Daddy seemed more upset with Mom after the fight at the game than he did with Ginny. He had, of course, punished Ginny, but his heart didn't seem to be in it. (Grounded for two weeks. Yeah, that'd teach her. As though she ever went anywhere, anyway.) Mom never even mentioned what had happened at the gym. Ginny would give anything to have heard that whole fight in the kitchen, to know what had happened between her parents that had shocked Daddy out of punishing her within an inch of her life.

Twisting the rear view mirror toward her, Ginny checked her hair.

"Hey!" Daddy said. "I need that to drive, you know."

She grinned at him. "I'll give it right back." She smoothed her hair down with her hands and flipped one side of it back over her shoulder. She started to put the mirror back right, but stopped as she noticed the car behind them—a silver Lexus. She twisted a strand of her hair around her index finger, twisting and tightening.

"Ginny, you okay?" Daddy said.

"Yes sir."

He cleared his throat, a sure sign he was about to say something fatherly. "Are things starting to get back to normal at school?"

Needles of ice shot through her stomach. "Yes sir."

True enough. Abnormal had been the first few days after she completed her suspension. Everyone stared at her. A few bold ones were downright mean. Someone taped a copy of the school newspaper to her locker, with its front page article about the brawl at the game. An editorial blamed her not only for losing the tournament but practically for treason. "People lose their tempers in the heat of battle, sure. Fights happen. But you don't attack your own team. If you don't understand that, you've got no business playing sports at all."

That's what the first few days were like. But yeah, things were back to normal now. Boys ignored her. Girls snubbed her and whispered behind her back. Perfectly normal.

She kept her eyes on the rear view mirror as Daddy started one of his speeches about tough times not lasting but tough people do, something like that. She couldn't concentrate. The silver Lexus crawled along behind them, maintaining a steady distance.

She broke into his speech. "Hey, Dad? You notice that car back there?"

He glanced at the rear view. "Yeah. Sweet, huh?"

"No, I mean…it's been behind us the whole way. All the way from our street."

"So?"

"So I've never seen a Lexus in our neighborhood before. And besides—" Ginny licked her lips and wondered why she was hesitating. Why shouldn't she tell her father that a creepy guy at the mall had a car like that? Because he might freak out, and she couldn't deal with any hysterics right now, maybe? Then again, if it was the weird guy, maybe a little hysteria was perfectly acceptable.

In the rear view, Ginny saw the Lexus signal a right turn and disappear onto Oak Street. She caught a brief glimpse of the driver's head. All she could make out was that he was talking on a cell phone and wearing a red baseball cap.

"Ginny? What were you saying about the car?"

Creepy guy probably wasn't the type to wear a ball cap. Too suave. And whoever was in that car was occupied with his phone, not with her. She shook her head. "Nothing. It was silly."

She thought it was silly until about thirty seconds after Daddy dropped her in front of the school. Daddy's truck had just pulled out of sight when the silver Lexus cruised slowly past the school, and the driver in the red baseball cap turned his head and looked straight in her direction.

She flew up the steps into the school, tripping on the top one and banging her knee. She didn't stop to inspect the damage. For once, she wanted to be inside with the pushy teachers and snotty students and the hundreds of warm solid bodies that could stand between her and…what?

She opened her locker and stood staring inside it, seeing absolutely nothing. The picture in her mind was too strong. That silver Lexus driving past, the scary guy behind the wheel staring at her.

What did he want? What should she do? If she went right now and told the principal, would he believe her? Would he call the police? Would everyone stare and point at her as she walked to class, whispering that that was the girl the police came to talk to? She could hear them now. *What's she done this time? More fighting? That girl's nuts.*

The bell rang, shattering her trance. She grabbed her Geometry book and closed the locker door, still having no idea what to do. She turned and, for the five thousandth time at least, caught Max Ferguson gawking at her. She thought she had gotten used to it. But not today. Enough was enough.

Obviously, he knew he was busted. He whirled and tried to move away from her, but she jumped in front of him and blocked his path—then surprised both of them by starting to yell at him. "What is it with you—and everybody else in the world, apparently! Why does everybody stare at me all the time? Am I that much of a freak?"

Max's jaw dropped. His eyes were huge and gaping, but not like usual. The boy was terrified.

"I mean it. Tell me! Why do you stare at me?"

He gulped and stammered. "Because—because you're so pretty. And nice." His mouth tilted upward in a smile, and for once he looked almost human. "Not at this particular moment, maybe. But usually."

Ginny felt her anger deflating. She didn't want it to, because if she wasn't angry, she'd be scared again. "So what, you're stalking me or something?"

Max snorted. "Oh, please. I said pretty, not beautiful. I'm not obsessed with you or anything."

"Yeah, well, you coulda fooled me."

Max put up one hand, the one that wasn't balancing a stack of books. "Hey, don't worry. Won't happen again. Trust me, the glow is fading."

Ginny watched him walk down the hall and sighed. Great. Now she felt guilty, on top of scared and angry. She watched him walk down the hall. His movements seemed such a pathetic imitation of Alec's carefree swagger that she couldn't stand it. "Max, wait!"

He stopped and turned toward her. She walked quickly in his direction but refused to run.

"I'm sorry," she said when she reached him. "I didn't mean to yell at you like that. Things have just been kinda weird lately."

His expression softened. "Yeah, I know. I understand."

His deep blue eyes were so full of compassion, Ginny's anger came surging back. Considering that his stepmother was her mom's shrink, he probably did understand, but that just made her even madder. She hated that he knew.

"Yeah, well, I better get to class." As she moved away from him, her muscles felt so stiff she was afraid she would shatter if anyone touched her.

ᑢ

Alec dropped by that evening. Ginny felt absurdly happy to see him. He'd been civil when he saw her around the school, but that was all. She didn't know whether he was still mad that she'd pushed him away the day of the tourney fight or was just embarrassed to be seen talking to the school pariah. Either way, she was glad all that nastiness seemed to be blowing over.

The two of them and her dad shot some hoops in the driveway while Mom did something or other in the house. Daddy tired out first and went inside. She and Alec settled on the porch steps in the twilight. It was nice and cozy, but as usual, she could feel eyes boring a hole into her back. At least this time she understood the reason. Daddy was keeping an eye on them through the picture window.

She told Alec about creepy Max and their conversation, ending with her anger that Max knew her mother was seeing a therapist.

Alec picked up the ball that was lying at his feet and studied it as if it were crystal. "I bet he knows a lot more than that."

"What do you mean?"

"You know his stepmother's office is in their house, right?"

"Yeah."

"Well, a year or two ago I heard him bragging to some other kids that every word she and her patients said to each other shot right through the air ducts into his room. He started telling some of the weird stories he'd heard."

"You gotta be kidding."

"Nope. I don't know, maybe he was just trying to get attention. But that's what he said." Alec stood up. "So, you feel like shooting a few more?"

Ginny stayed seated. "I don't think so. I don't feel too great."

He frowned down at her. "Oh come on. You're not gonna let a little geek like Max Ferguson get to you, are you?"

Yes. "No." Alec didn't look convinced. Maybe that's why she told him the rest. "Something else happened today." She told him about the Lexus, and her belief it was the same guy from the mall.

To her utter amazement, he laughed. Laughed!

"What is your problem?" she said, pulling a strand of her hair forward and wrapping it around her finger, very very tightly.

"I don't have one. What's yours?"

"What do you mean?"

"Oh please, what is it with girls? Y'all see stalkers everywhere these days. A guy looks at you twice and you think he's after you."

"That's not exactly the case here."

"You don't even know for sure it's the same guy, do you?"

"Well, not a hundred percent sure, but—"

"Exactly. Look, Ginny, don't be paranoid, okay? You don't want to end up like your mother, do you?"

She stood up. "I'm going inside, Alec. I really don't feel too well."

He shrugged. "Okay. Whatever."

As she climbed the porch steps, she wondered why every encounter with Alec ended on a sour note. And why she always wanted another one.

Sleep didn't come easily that night. At one point Ginny realized she was clenching her teeth so hard that her forehead and neck hurt. She took a deep breath and tried to calm herself, but the minute she relaxed she saw that silver Lexus, cruising slowly past the school. Then creepy Max's eyes watching her. She heard Alec's voice, first calling her paranoid, then telling her about Max's eavesdropping. Little weasel.

But wait a minute.

Ginny sat up in bed. If Max made a habit of eavesdropping, maybe he could tell her just what the heck was going on with Mom. Maybe he had listened in on Mom's sessions. That thought didn't exactly fill her with joy. In fact, she squirmed and felt her face burning at the thought of it. Calm down, she told herself. You can kill him later. Or at least tell him what you think of him. But for now, maybe he could be of use in this whole mess.

She dropped back against the pillows, flat on her back, and stared at the ceiling.

Maybe she shouldn't have called him a stalker.

CB

Ginny fidgeted on the passenger seat of the truck, sliding forward to look in the rear view mirror, squirming around sideways so she could look out the back and sides.

Daddy glanced over at her. "What is the matter with you this morning?"

She froze, midway between the rear view and craning to look past his face at the intersection. She made herself slide back into a normal position and try to appear relaxed. "Uh, I don't know." She grinned. "Too much coffee, I guess."

He snorted. They both knew she detested coffee.

Why didn't she just tell him about the Lexus, about the scary man? Why did she almost feel guilty, as though by attracting some kind of weirdness she had done something wrong herself?

Partly because of what Alec said? Because Mom seemed to be infected by weirdness lately—and Ginny didn't want to appear to have caught the bug? For whatever reason, she just didn't want to tell Daddy.

Once again, though, she felt grumpy and nervous by the time she reached school. Once again, Max was right there handy for her to vent her frustrations on—and she almost did. He was rummaging around in his locker, but he glanced and nodded at her politely, then looked away like a good boy. No staring, just as he'd promised. Somehow that made her mad, too. He was being sarcastic, wasn't he? Trying to make her feel bad?

She took a deep breath. Calm, calm. *He has something you want, remember?* Namely, an air duct right over his stepmom's psycho-babble room.

"Hey, Max! Wait up!"

He turned and looked at her, frowning suspiciously. He hugged his books to his chest, like a shield, as she approached. "Yeah, what do you want?"

She put up both hands. "Truce, okay?"

He shrugged.

She stopped a couple of feet in front of him. "Okay, first I want to…" She twisted her hair around her finger, feeling it cut into the skin. Boy, this was hard. "I want to…apologize…for the way I acted yesterday."

He frowned even more deeply, as though waiting for the punchline. "Yeah?"

"Yeah. I was kind of freaked out when I got to school yesterday, so I guess I took it out on you and—"

"Freaked out?" He was still frowning, but it was different. She realized with shock that he appeared genuinely concerned. Quite different from Alec's reaction.

His distress threw her. She tried to wave it off, but found herself stammering and saying more than she had intended. "Oh, yeah, I'm sure it was nothing, but there was this car…I've seen it before, and I thought maybe the guy had followed me." She laughed nervously. "I guess I had stalkers on the brain when I came in here, and that's why I lit into you."

Max didn't seem concerned about the apology. "What did your parents say? About the car, I mean."

"Oh, I didn't tell them. I'm sure it's no big deal."

"But what if it is a big deal? You gotta tell your folks, Ginny."

"I'm not even sure it's the same guy. Anyway, my parents have enough on their minds right now."

Max nodded. "Yeah, I know."

Her blood surged, heating her face. "Yeah, I guess you do."

"What? Did I say something wrong?"

She hadn't intended the conversation to go this way, but she blurted it out. "I heard about how much fun you have, eavesdropping on your mother's clients."

Now it was Max's turn to flush red. He probably felt as hot and sticky right now as she did. When he finally responded, his voice was so quiet she had to step forward to hear him.

"I haven't done that in a long time," he said.

"Oh really?"

"Yeah, really." He looked down at the front of his shirt, which made her look at it, too. Today's tee read, "Fearless!" A bunch of small print was under that. Probably a Bible verse.

"That was before I got saved," he said.

Oh, brother. Her shoulders sagged. "Oh, I see."

"You don't seem very happy about it."

She considered him for a moment, then decided to confess. "Actually—even though I think that eavesdropping on people you don't know is absolutely atrocious—I was kind of hoping you might, uh…"

"What?"

"Well, maybe let me hang out in your room next time my mom was over there."

Max crowed with triumph. "Oh, so it's atrocious when you listen in on strangers, but it's perfectly acceptable if you do it to your own mom."

She let out her breath in frustration. "You don't understand, Max."

"No, I guess I don't."

She felt her throat starting to ache, threatening tears, but she fought them back. Still, she couldn't stop her voice from shaking. "I've got to find out what's going on with her. It's—it's about *me*."

The bell rang, and Max's gaze flickered toward the door of his class.

"I'm sorry," she said, turning toward her own class. "I don't know what's wrong with me."

He touched her arm, holding her back. "No, I'm glad you told me. Let's talk at lunch, okay?"

Maybe they both had too much time to think things over before lunchtime—to regret making this appointment. For whatever reason, they ate the bland cafeteria food mostly in silence, giving the chicken fingers and corn far more attention than they deserved. Max finished eating ahead of Ginny and started staring at her. Naturally. She continued to eat tiny bites of chicken and wish the bell would ring.

Max spoke so suddenly it made her jump. "I think your mom made a poor choice—choosing Anna to be her counselor."

In spite of herself, Ginny was curious. "What do you mean?"

"I mean that woman has serious issues herself. How can she tell other people what to do if she can't fix herself?"

"She seemed pretty amazing that night we came to dinner. So confident and self-assured. Nothing like Mom."

"Yeah, well, you don't live with her. Anyway, I think your mom could teach Anna a few things."

"About what?"

"Parenting." He leaned across the table and said in a stage whisper, "Have you seen how her daughter turned out?"

Ginny burst out laughing. "Uh, yeah…we've definitely met, as you may recall."

Max blushed a deep red. Had he forgotten her altercation with Kelsey on the basketball court? Apparently so, because he mumbled, "Sorry. Didn't mean to bring that up."

"It's okay." She tried to lighten up the moment. "Anyone who has to live with Kelsey Shaw is bound to be a little muddled."

"Yeah, true…But you know, as mean as she can be, sometimes I feel kind of sorry for Kelsey. Anna never pays her any attention, and who knows where her father is? Anna Shaw has had so many men, she probably can barely remember that particular one."

"Hmm…" Ginny looked down at her food after making the noncommittal noise. She just couldn't bring herself to feel too sorry for Kelsey. "Well, maybe she'll get bored with your dad pretty soon."

"That's what I'm counting on."

They fell silent again. Ginny pushed her corn around with a fork.

Max watched her. For the second time, he broke the long silence. "So what did you mean? That your mother's seeing Anna because of you?" He smiled, teasing. "What did you do?"

"I don't know." She hated the way that came out, all tiny and scared-sounding. But she told him what she did know.

As she talked to him, he gawked at her, of course. But for the first time, she really noticed the sapphire blue color of his eyes, his long lashes, the way his mouth was set in concern. He really could be a fairly decent-looking guy if he didn't go out of his way to appear so geeky. Those t-shirts. And the long, untamed hair. Why would he let himself look so scruffy?

As she stopped talking, Max looked down at his plate. He had no food left to push around, so he tapped his fork against the plastic tray until she wanted to scream. Why did she keep telling boys these things? They couldn't understand.

Max surprised her. He looked up and said, "Everybody assumes we're the ones changing. Kids, I mean. But parents can change, too."

Ginny nodded. "You can say that again."

"My dad changed when he met Anna."

"How?"

Max crinkled his forehead in thought. "My mom died when I was little, and Dad really stepped up to the plate. He's always been into his work, but he made time for me, too. And he'd tell me about his research. He'd draw diagrams and make models out of salt shakers and oranges, until I had at least a vague idea of what he was doing. He bought me a chemistry set and we played with it." Max took a deep breath. "Then he met Anna. He became completely obsessed with her. I'd barely see him for days at a time. And when I did, she was there, too." He made a face. "Anna and Kelsey. I couldn't believe it when Dad said we were moving out here to the boonies to live with the two of them. I didn't think I'd survive."

Ginny sighed. "Yeah. Tell me about it."

Max squared his shoulders. "Still, that would have been fine if Dad was happy. But he wasn't. His work has always been the most important thing in his life, and even it started to slip."

"How do you know?" She thought of her own father. "Did he lose his job?"

"No, worse. He lost a research grant. A couple of them, actually." Max shook his head. "He published some of his research not long after we moved out here, and it got slammed. Other researchers accused him of shoddy work. Poor controls. A couple repeated his experiments and got totally different results. It was awful."

Ginny puzzled over this. "So…how is that Anna's fault?"

"It's not her fault, exactly. Except for being so demanding of his time. Man, even when I was a kid I understood how important his work was. She always has him guessing, wondering what she's doing when he's not there. Whether she'll just move on to someone else if he lets her get bored. They're not married, you know." Max shook his head, as though clearing away that thought. "Anyway, I only brought all this up to say…parents go through phases, too. They do dumb things and get into trouble." He leaned across the table, toward Ginny. "Sometimes we have to be the strong ones. Sometimes we have to look after them."

Now Ginny leaned toward him, so close she caught a whiff of milk breath, but it didn't bother her. "That's what I want to do, Max. Look after my mother. And to do that, I have to understand what's going on. Will you help me?"

He fell back in his chair, away from her, almost as though she'd pushed him. "You mean sneak you into my house, and let you listen in on your mom's session?"

She nodded.

He took a deep breath. "Oh, man." Then he shrugged. "I guess it's for a good reason. Yeah, I'll help you."

CHAPTER NINE

Ginny didn't mention to Max that she was supposed to be grounded. She was straining his conscience enough, as it was. Herself, she didn't care. This was too important.

When they got to Max's house, they walked through the front door as though it were perfectly natural for Ginny to be there—as if they weren't up to no good. Ginny could see Ms. Shaw in the kitchen, but she was standing with her back to them, talking on a cordless phone. Still, Ginny felt like ducking, or sliding along the walls, or doing something to camouflage her presence.

Max snickered at her as they reached the stairs. "Will you relax?"

"Won't your mom—or stepmom, or whatever—won't she get upset if she sees us going up to your room together?"

"Are you kidding? She'd probably be thrilled."

Ginny decided she'd chew that one over later. "I don't want my mom to know I'm here when she comes."

"She won't."

The neatness of Max's room disturbed her. Where were the clothes on the floor, the crumpled potato chip bags, the unmade bed—all the elements she'd pictured making up the average boy's room? Not that you could call Max average. The shelf of trophies (science fairs and chess matches) proved that. A desk jutted up against a wall, right under a window overlooking the shady back yard. A laptop and small printer were its only occupants. A table next to the desk held a chess board with little figures carved out of some kind of stone. On the various squares, wizards pointed wands and warriors flexed swords above their heads. Each stone gleamed as though recently polished. Not a speck of dust showed itself anywhere, although Ginny had an urge to get down on her knees and check under the bed for dust bunnies.

She stood in the immaculate room and turned a slow circle, trying to get an angle on Max Ferguson. Her gaze came to rest on a terrifying-looking sword hanging over his chest of drawers. "What the heck is that!"

Max put his hands on his hips. "Please. Show some respect. That is an exact replica of Aragorn's sword." When Ginny looked at him blankly, he said, "From the *Lord of the Rings* movies?"

"Okay. If you say so." She wandered over to his bookshelf. Along with *The Lord of the Rings* trilogy and a lot of fantasy titles she didn't recognize, she found the complete Harry Potter series in hardback. She felt a lump in her throat as she touched the spine of *Harry Potter and the Deathly Hallows*. "You know, I still haven't read this one," she said.

"You're kidding! It's amazing."

"Mom and I read all the other ones together and somehow…well, we never got around to this one." She didn't add that, by the time the seventh book came out, Mom had already started acting weird. Had stopped looking her in the eye. Had stopped wanting to be alone in a room with her. She did, however, tell him about the mural that Mom had painted.

"That's so funny," he said, when she finished.

"Funny?"

"I mean…a coincidence." He opened his closet and started to pull a quilt down from the top shelf. When he unrolled it across his bed, Ginny saw squares depicting Hedwig, the castle, the Hogwarts Express…on and on, square after square, each one pieced together out of teeny tiny snippets of fabric.

As Ginny exclaimed over it, Max said, "Yeah, my mom made this for me before she died."

With an uncomfortable feeling that they might both start bawling any minute, Ginny searched for something light to say.

But then Max glanced down at his watch. "Your mom's gonna be here any time. Here. Let me show you." He dropped into his desk chair and wheeled it to the left a few inches. Then he pointed down at a vent. "That's where the sound comes through." He looked up at her. "I didn't go looking for it. I was just sitting here at my desk and started hearing voices from downstairs." He smiled sheepishly. "I did maybe bend down and concentrate pretty hard a couple of times, but sometimes I really can't help overhearing stuff."

Ginny nodded. "Can they hear you, too?"

"I don't know. Probably. Doesn't really matter. I never make any noise. I use headphones when I listen to music." He blushed again. "And I normally don't have visitors in here."

Ginny grinned at him. She couldn't resist. "Not even girls?"

He turned so red she was afraid he would keel over. But he didn't answer the question. He stood up, almost turning the chair over in the process. "You can sit here if you want to. Although you might want to sit on the floor right next to the vent so you can hear better." He slapped his hands against his legs a couple of times. "Well, I guess I'll leave you alone now."

Ginny felt a flutter of panic. "Where are you going?"

Max paused with his hand on the doorknob. "You don't want me to hear whatever your mom has to say, do you?"

"Oh, no...I guess not." She didn't, really. On the other hand, she hated to be alone. "Why don't you stay until they start?"

"Okay."

They sat cross-legged on the floor, Ginny next to the vent and Max facing her. They could occasionally hear movement downstairs, or the phone ringing. Max cautioned her to be quiet, so there they sat, perfectly silent and staring at one another. Ginny wondered if her face looked as intense as Max's, and then of course that thought struck her as deliriously funny. She tried to hold in the bubbling laughter, but her shoulders shook and she occasionally let out a little snort. Max glared at her and made a slashing movement across his throat, but that only made her want to laugh more.

Then she heard the door of Ms. Shaw's office open and shut, followed by the woman's voice. "Hello, Rose. Ben."

Ben? What was Daddy doing here?

Ms. Shaw asked him basically the same thing.

Daddy's answer boomed through the vent. "I think there are a few things you need to know. Things Rose hasn't been telling you."

Ginny didn't feel like laughing anymore. She was only vaguely aware of Max getting up and slipping from the room. She hunkered down over the vent, almost touching her ear to it, as Mom started to talk in her soft, hesitant voice. Ginny could only make out a few of her words, but Daddy was clear enough.

"I'm not paying a hundred fifty bucks an hour for nothing. I started asking Rose some questions about these sessions, and I found out she hasn't even told you the real problem."

Mom and Ms. Shaw started talking at once, and then Daddy jumped in again, so Ginny missed a little of what came next. She caught Ms. Shaw saying something about therapy progressing differently for each individual, and not rushing things, and then Daddy blew up again.

Finally everyone stopped talking but Mom, and this time her voice wasn't so soft. It was shrill, at least in the beginning. "You told me to come here and talk to Anna, so that's what I've been doing. Every week, just like we agreed."

"But you haven't told her anything."

"Ben, Rose and I have talked a great deal. I think we're making good progress—"

"Oh, please! She's conning you."

Ms. Shaw's voice was firm. "Ben, we don't talk that way in here. Now this is Rose's session, and I think it's time for me to ask you to—"

"He wants to make sure you believe I'm crazy."

"Rose, please don't start this again."

"No, it's fine. Fine." Mom's voice grew softer again. Ginny closed her eyes and concentrated, shutting out everything but Mom. "What Ben wants me to tell you is that…" There was a long pause. "That I've been noticing something about Ginny for some time now."

"And what's that, Rose?"

"That she's turning into someone else."

Ginny's pulse started to thud in her ears, threatening to drown out her mother's words. She held her breath, trying to hear, but that only made her heart pound harder.

"Somebody else?" Ms. Shaw's voice was flat, professional. "You mean she's changing? That's not really surprising, is it? When kids go through adolescence, they often seem to change into totally different people."

"No, no, no," Daddy said. "That's not what she means. Is it,

Rose?"

A soft murmur. Ginny thought Mom had said "no," but it was hard to be sure.

Mom's voice grew louder. "Let me ask you a question, Anna. Do you remember Jordan?"

"Jordan who?"

"Good question. We called her Jordan Banks but that was just because nobody knew her name. Surely you remember that, that girl—"

"Oh! That girl you and Hunter found wandering by the road? The one with amnesia?"

"That's right."

"Good heavens, I haven't thought of that girl in twenty years! Whatever happened to her, anyway?"

Daddy laughed harshly. "According to Rose, she's sleeping in Ginny's bedroom."

"Uh...excuse me?"

"Ben, please..."

"Well, that's a good summation, isn't it? There was this strange girl in your past—who knows, maybe she wasn't even a real girl. Maybe a spirit or something who showed up in your life back then. And now she's possessing your daughter."

Ginny leaned back against Max's desk for support.

"I don't...I never said it like that," Mom was saying.

Ms. Shaw cooed, "Ben, why don't we just let Rose talk right now? Rose, can you tell me what exactly you do think is happening?"

A long, long silence. When Mom started to speak, she sounded out of breath, gasping for air every few words. "I started noticing it a couple of years ago—or I don't know, maybe even sooner. You know how girls change when they hit puberty. Overnight, she started looking so different. Not like the little girl I'd had. But that's not what disturbed me. At first, I just had this nagging feeling that not only did she not look like Ginny anymore, but she *did* look like someone else."

"Jordan?"

"Yes. The bone structure in her face, her height...she was so tall. The way her hair lifted away from her forehead—in fact, Ginny complained to me one day that she wished she could get it to lie down sleek and straight and I looked at her and saw that the fullness, the way it fanned back was just like Jordan's. I mean…so many physical things. Her golden eyes—"

"Okay, but there's probably a good explanation for her gold eyes, right?" said Ms. Shaw.

"What do you mean?"

"Well, I know you all said that Jordan's eyes were very much like Livvy's. Your sister would be Ginny's aunt, so it would be natural for her eyes to be that color."

"But Ginny's weren't always so gold like that."

"Of course they were," Daddy scoffed. "Or anyway…they were a kind of gold-brown, and I think she's just using some make-up or something that makes them look a little different now."

"Anyway, there were other things. The way her voice got so husky and deep, exactly like Jordan's. The way she walks. The way she twists her hair around her fingers when she gets nervous."

"Rose, that's all complete garbage! Little stuff, that you could notice about anybody if you started looking," Daddy said.

"I tried to tell myself that for a long time, Ben. And then one day I took Ginny with me to visit Mamma in the nursing home. When I had been visiting Mamma, she hardly even reacted. Never moved or spoke. But when I took Ginny, she knew her, too."

Ms. Shaw's voice sounded sharp for the first time. "How can you possibly know that? Your mother can't talk."

"She did when she saw Ginny. She called her Jordan. She hummed the song that Jordan used to hum. Mamma saw it, too."

"That's when all this started, I guarantee you," Daddy declared. "Carla Remington's brain was completely fried by that stroke. She's said maybe five words since she had it, and they never make sense when she does. But all because she spit out the name 'Jordan' when Ginny came in the room—"

"It wasn't only because of that. That was just confirmation."

"Look, Rose…why doesn't anyone else see what you see? Why doesn't Anna recognize her? You don't, right, Anna?"

"I…I can see a small resemblance…maybe. To tell you the truth, I can hardly remember what the girl looked like. But I don't think my memories are all that relevant. I just want to know what Rose thinks. What do you believe is going on with Ginny? Are you saying you think Ginny is possessed?"

Ginny felt dizzy. She pressed her hand against her forehead and fought the urge to get up and flee the room.

"I don't just want to know what Rose believes," Daddy said. "I want to know what she plans to do about it."

"What?"

"I'm scared to death about all this, and not just because it sounds so bizarre. I'm almost sure she's been trying to poison Ginny."

"What!"

"Ben." Ms. Shaw was the only one still sounding calm and reasonable. "That's a very strong accusation."

"Let me just ask Rose something. Where's your mother's insulin?"

"Her insulin! What are you talking about? We don't have any of her meds left."

"Oh really?"

"Ben, what are you getting at?" Ms. Shaw said.

"That last time that Ginny was so sick, I was looking for test strips and noticed a gadget on the kitchen counter. It struck me as funny at the time, but I was in a tizzy and didn't take time to look at it. I realized later it was an insulin injector, like the one Henry uses. Why would there have been insulin in our house? Especially the night that Ginny got sick? I looked it up. If you give insulin to someone who doesn't need it, that can cause hypoglycemia. It can kill them."

Mom's voice sounded strangled. "Ben, you're not...surely you don't think I made Ginny sick? That I would ever make her sick on purpose?"

"Not the Rose that I've known all these years, no. But this one, the one that's filled with all these delusions...yes, I do."

Ginny started to shake her head. She wanted to shout at him to be quiet, he didn't know what he was talking about. She pulled herself to her feet and jerked open the door of Max's room. She tried to run down the stairs but was so unsteady she almost fell down. Max was in front of the TV, swinging his arms wildly, causing his avatar on the screen to swing a sword and cut the head off some grotesque something. Ginny shuddered looking at it and grabbed at the railing.

Max dropped the game control when he saw her. "Are you okay?"

She tried to answer him, to tell him no, she most certainly was not okay. But nothing would come out. She just shook her head and ran for the door. Max tried to come after her, but she pushed him aside and slammed the door behind her.

She started to run down the middle of the road, in the direction of home, but after a block or two she slowed down, slowed, slowed, until eventually she stopped. She stood vacantly in the middle of the road until a woman driving a Blazer blew her horn at her. Ginny moved to the grass but still stood looking around aimlessly.

Where exactly should she go?

"Ginny!"

She turned, back in the direction of Max's house, to see who had called her name. The voice sounded so distant, she wasn't sure. Part of her hoped it would be Daddy, running to scoop her up in a bear hug and promise her everything was going to be okay, that he had everything worked out. Instead, she saw Max, standing on the pedals of his bike as he coaxed it up the hill. She felt like crying again as she saw his face, red with effort but determined to reach her as quickly as possible.

Then she heard her name called again. It wasn't coming from Max.

Alec's truck blew past Max, flying up the hill in her direction. When he reached her, he didn't bother to pull out of the roadway, just stopped next to her.

"Hey, where ya' been? I've been trying to call you." Unlike Max, he didn't look or sound concerned. But he didn't know what just happened, Ginny reminded herself. "Wanna go for a ride?"

Yes, she did, very much. As far as she was concerned, they could drive until they hit the bottom most tip of South America. She glanced back at Max, who had halted right where he was when Alec drove past. He was still looking at her, but his expression had changed. She walked around the truck to the passenger side and opened the door. She waved at Max, hoping he would interpret the gesture as, "Thanks, but I'm okay. Don't worry."

He didn't wave back, just turned his bike and started walking it back toward his house.

CHAPTER TEN

L oud voices. Arguing. Horrible words.

Ginny turned up her music and tried to concentrate on her problems, but the symbols and numbers swam under her eyes.

She heard Mom shouting. "Anna, Anna, Anna! I am so tired of hearing that woman's name. I told you I'd never be able to talk to her."

"So, fine. Just choose somebody else." Daddy's loud voice. The one that made her run to her room when she was a kid. "But you've got to get help."

"Oh, really? And is that why you're running over there to Anna's so much? Because you need help?"

"You bet it is. And I'm not ashamed to admit it. It helps me to talk to her, to try to sort this all out, even if you don't want to do it."

"Oh, I'll just bet she helps you. She's giving you just what you need, isn't she?"

"Rose, please…"

"The two of you probably engineered this whole thing just so you could be together. You're probably trying to convince me I'm crazy just to get rid of me."

"Rose, don't be paranoid."

Paranoid. Ginny sat up straight. That's what Alec had called her. Was it just a mean thing that guys said to make girls feel silly? Or was there something seriously wrong with her mother? Something that was maybe being passed down to her?

The phone rang. Ginny waited through a couple of rings, but apparently the grown-ups were having too hard a time pulling away from their fascinating fight to answer it. She glanced at the caller i.d.

and saw it was coming from Max's house. She hesitated with her hand above the receiver. She wouldn't mind talking to Max, but what if it was Ms. Shaw? Well, probably better for her to answer, if it was. If Mom heard that woman's voice right now, she'd explode.

Oops, too late. Mom had spotted the name on the caller i.d., too, and was hurling a few accusations at Daddy about it. She still wasn't answering the phone, though, so Ginny jerked up the receiver. "Hello?"

"Hey. I was about to hang up. I didn't think anybody was home."

Max! Thank goodness. She cupped her hand over the mouthpiece and yelled toward the front of the house. "It's for me. It's just Max."

"Gee, thanks," said his voice in her ear.

She laughed—and boy, did that feel good. "You know what I meant." He probably didn't, but she didn't want to go into all that now. "What's up?"

"I wondered if you'd like to go to church with me tonight."

Ginny froze. She couldn't speak.

"Uh, Ginny? You still there?"

"Yeah, I, uh…uh…"

"Oh, for Pete's sake. It's not that outlandish an idea, is it?"

"Well, no…or kinda. It's not even Sunday."

"Lots of places have Wednesday services."

"Oh."

"I'm mainly asking because it's kind of a special night."

Uh-oh. All kinds of things ran through Ginny's mind. What could be special? Visiting speaker? Scenes from TV shows ran through her mind. Fire-and-brimstone preachers with greasy hair holding revivals under tents.

"Special how?"

"I got a car today."

"A car? You have your license?"

"Yeah, as of this month. The car's just an old Civic, but—"

"No, no, that's amazing. I'd love to have my license. And a car." The fiery preacher in her brain gave way to vistas of scenic country highways, herself in the driver's seat, all alone. Complete freedom.

"So anyway. Want to go?"

"Max, only you would celebrate getting a car by driving to

church!" As Max chuckled, she stretched out her legs and said, "Why choose me for this special occasion?"

"I couldn't think of anybody else. Wait…That didn't come out right."

Ginny burst out laughing. "It's okay. I know what it feels like to be desperate."

"I can't imagine that. Especially not when you're hanging out with Alec Matthews." A slight beat. "He won't mind, will he?"

"Alec Matthews does not own me, Max."

"All right, all right. Just checking."

They both fell silent again. In that moment, Ginny heard the voices from the front of the house again. Not loud anymore, just intense, like a low growl from an angry dog. "You know what? I'd love to go with you to church."

Max drove quite differently from Alec. He came to a full stop at stop signs and observed the speed limit. Ginny hated to admit it even to herself, but she felt relieved. They drove away from town, east of the Interstate and into an older, run-down area. As he pulled carefully into a parking place, she observed all sorts of folks streaming into the little brick building. Old and young, black and white and Hispanic, ladies in knit pantsuits and kids with holes in their jeans.

Ginny unbuckled her seatbelt. "Not exactly what I expected so far."

Max threw open his door and stuck one foot out on the pavement, but stayed seated. "What did you expect?"

"I don't know. Something more like your house. Something that shouts successful professional people. New and elegant and vanilla. That sort of thing."

Max's mouth twisted in a mischievous grin. "That's exactly why I chose this church. Originally, anyway. Because it's not all those things."

"What do you mean?"

"I originally started going to church as a childish act of rebellion. I figured it would drive Dad and Anna crazy, which is exactly what I wanted to do. They're both so scientific. They tend to look down their noses at spiritual things. And oh my word, fundamentalists or evangelical Christians—especially if they have a thick Southern accent—are like fingernails on a blackboard to both of them."

"And that's exactly what you wanted to be. Another set of screeching nails."

"Well, yeah. Especially when I could come home from church services and throw in little digs about them living in sin." Max's grin faded. "Then something happened."

"What?"

"To begin with, I met lots of nice people here. Good, sincere people. I started feeling bad, because of the way I was using them. I was sort of making fun of them, if you got down to it. But the big thing that happened…" Max looked down and picked at a thread in the cloth seats. "Jesus."

"Oh." She squirmed in the seat, suddenly unable to sit still and meet his eyes. "That's cool."

"I know that look. It's the same one my dad gives me when I talk about this stuff." He shrugged. "I know it sounds lame, but it's true. One night it was almost like I heard his voice in my head. Like he put out his hand to me, and I took it and pulled him right inside me. He filled me up." He shook his head a little.

Ginny shivered. "You make it sound like being possessed."

"I guess it is sort of like that. Possessed by the Holy Spirit. But it's a good thing. You're never alone. And you're never the same."

"Don't say 'you.'" She hugged her arms to her chest. "I don't want to be possessed at all, not by anything." Tinkling piano music came to her ears. She noticed they were alone in the parking lot. The service must have started. A chorus of voices joined in with the piano. Diverse voices. Bass and tenor, tuneful and flat, but all loud and joyful. Her chills increased, especially as the tune progressed and she realized she had heard it before. Recently.

Max didn't seem to be concerned that they were late. In fact, he leaned back against the seat and looked through the windshield and started to tell her a story. "We all have to be filled by something. There's a story in the Bible, where Jesus cast a demon out of a man. But he warned that the demon might come back, and if he found his former 'house' empty, he would occupy it again—and bring his friends."

Ginny couldn't make any sense out of Max's babbling. She didn't particularly care right now. "Max, what's that song?"

Max's mind changed course with some effort. "What song?"

She pointed toward the church windows. Light and music

streamed through the stained glass panes, and she could vaguely see shadowy figures moving on the other side in time to the tune.

"Oh, let me think…it's something about the river Jordan. Let's see." He started to sing, so off-key she had a hard time picking the tune out of the noise. When she did, her shivering increased. He sang, "On Jordan's stormy banks I stand and cast a wishful eye, to Canaan's fair and happy land—"

"Okay, okay, that's enough."

He frowned. "What's the matter?"

"Max, I'm sorry, but I changed my mind. Could you please take me home?"

"Sure, but—I didn't mean to scare you with all that possession talk." He tried to sound light. "It's a church, not a haunted house. Sorry if I made it sound that way."

"No, not, it's not that, I just—I want to go home."

"Okay. No problem."

Max almost missed the turn into Ginny's drive. As a result, one tire went off the pavement, bouncing Ginny in her seat, and leaving a deep tread mark in the soft grass. Daddy would probably have a fit, but she didn't care right now.

Max pulled up in front of the porch steps and put the car in park. Ginny turned to him. "I'm sorry I screwed everything up. Especially on the first day you have your car."

"It's okay. I'm sorry I screwed up your lawn."

She grabbed the door handle and looked toward her house, but didn't get out. After a moment, she let go of the handle and dropped her hands in her lap. "I want to tell you why I freaked out back there, if I can figure it out myself."

"Okay."

As usual, Max watched her, waiting. Funny, it didn't bother her now. His staring didn't feel like weirdness or stalking anymore. It felt like concern.

"I've been thinking so much about my mother, and wondering if she's mentally ill. If it's something that runs in the family. I've been thinking about that a lot, and I started getting nervous at the church back there. And then I heard that song."

"The one about the Jordan River." It wasn't a question from Max, but a statement, urging her on.

"That's right. A few months ago, I went with Mamma to visit Grandma in the nursing home. She's partially paralyzed from two strokes, and she can't talk anymore. She can make sounds, and she tries to talk, but she can't make words very often."

"That's awful."

"Yeah. It was the first time I'd seen her since she got sick like that—the first time I'd seen her in years, actually. Anyway, her eyes got real wide when she saw me, and she stared and stared. She kept making these horrible strained sounds, like she was trying to talk."

"That's normal, isn't it? I mean, you are her granddaughter, and she hadn't seen you in a long time. I'm sure she was excited to see you."

"Yeah, but you haven't heard the whole thing. I told you she can make sounds. She used to have a beautiful singing voice, and she can still hum tunes now. So she starts looking at me, all wild-eyed, and wiggling around in the bed, and she starts to hum a tune. Over and over, the same tune. At first it's sort of pretty and soulful. But the more agitated she gets, the faster she hums, and it starts to get off key. It sounds crazy, and I'm about to freak out."

"Was your mother there with you?"

"Yeah, but she was no help. I looked at her, and she was white as a sheet. She had her hands on Grandma's shoulders, trying to calm her down, and she kept saying, 'What is it, Mamma? What are you trying to tell us?'

"All of a sudden, Grandma gets quiet, but she's still staring at me. She takes a deep breath, as if she's trying to muster up her strength, and then she says one word as plain as day. 'Jordan,' she says. 'Jordan.'"

"Wow. Did your mom seem to know what that meant?"

"I asked her, after we got out of there. Which we did in a hurry, trust me. She said she didn't know, but that I should forget about it. She said that Grandma could occasionally speak a word that sounded clear, but that it wasn't necessarily the word she was really trying for, so I shouldn't take it too seriously. She just wanted to talk to me, and it was just a random word. I asked Mom, if that was true, why she seemed so upset, and why we practically ran out of the room. She said it was just so upsetting to see her mother like that."

"That all sounds pretty reasonable," Max said.

"Yeah, I thought so, too. I tried to forget about it. Until this week."

"What's different now?"

She exhaled, a long slow breath. "I didn't tell you what I overheard in your mother's office. What I heard my mom saying."

"No, but I knew it upset you. You don't have to tell me."

"I want to tell you." And she did, holding nothing back. She didn't know whether to be pleased or scared that her story made his mouth fall open.

"Man, that's weird. I mean, along with all this other Jordan stuff."

"I know."

They fell silent. Max appeared to be thinking. For once, Ginny stared at him. Finally she prodded, "So what do you think?"

"I don't know."

"Back at the church, you were talking about people being possessed by…things. So do you think I am? Possessed by this girl, Jordan?"

"No, I don't."

"You sound so sure."

"I am sure. Ginny, I wasn't talking about some ghost-story gobbledy-gook like you see in horror movies. I was talking about something spiritual."

"You also talked about Jesus casting out demons."

Max made a noise, sounding frustrated. "Boy, am I ever sorry I brought that up. Ginny, you're not possessed by a demon, trust me. And anyway, that's not what your mother was talking about, right? She was talking about some girl she used to know. A flesh-and-blood girl, not a ghost or goblin."

"I guess."

Max ran his hand around the steering wheel. He didn't look at Ginny when he spoke next. "I can think of one explanation that's pretty simple, but that you probably won't like."

"What's that?"

"Okay." He took a deep breath. "As far as the thing with your grandmother, I think your mom was probably right. She was excited to see you and she got all worked up, and she just couldn't make the right words come out. But then maybe your mother's been fretting over it. She's been under a lot of stress lately, and she knew this girl Jordan in the past that she didn't like, or that hurt her somehow. And somehow she starts to mix it all up—what your grandmother said, and what she remembers from the past, and—"

"So I was right. My mother's crazy and probably my grandmother, too. That's what you're saying."

"Ginny." The word sounded like a plea—a plea for understanding, or calm. She grabbed the door handle, and this time she did throw open the door.

Max lunged across the seat and grabbed her hand. "Ginny, wait."

For some reason, she did. His eyes were all concerned and earnest again. "I'm sorry," he said. "I don't know what I'm talking about. I don't know anything about your mom, or about what's going on. But I understand why you're upset. I mean…man, what a thing to be going through!"

She nodded. "Thanks, Max. I appreciate that."

He let out his breath. "I'll keep thinking about it, though. There's got to be an explanation."

As Ginny walked into the house, she wondered if she would ever find that explanation. And if she did, would she like it?

CHAPTER ELEVEN

The next day, Max bounced up to her at her locker and, without greeting or small talk, said, "You know how you were worried about being weird?"

"Umm…" She tried to shift her mind away from her pending Geometry test and figure out what he was talking about. "I sort of remember saying crazy, not weird."

"Well, whatever. I decided you just need some perspective."

"How's that?"

"You need to see that, compared to other people, you are blissfully normal. I've decided to help you with that."

"Oh, really? How do you plan to do that?"

A grin spread over his face and his eyes twinkled. "By showing you how truly strange I am, for example."

She burst into laughter. "Oh, Max. I knew that already, trust me."

"You didn't know this." He leaned in closer. "Guess what I like to do on certain weekends in the spring?"

"Turn into a werewolf?"

He creased his forehead in thought. "I believe that involves a full moon every month—not just weekends in spring."

"I can't imagine, then."

"This is just between us, right? I don't want Kelsey and Anna to know this."

"Max!" She really was starting to get curious.

"Okay. Here goes." He took a deep breath, then said in a rush, "I've been taking sword fighting classes for a couple of years now—"

"Sword fighting!" she squealed.

"Shhhhh!" He glanced around, and so did Ginny, but she didn't see anyone looking at them. He lowered his voice and said, "Can you keep it down, or is this just too exciting for you?"

She nodded her head, trying to look solemn. "I can handle it."

"All right, then. Not only am I pretty decent at sword fighting, but every year at the Renaissance Festival, I dress up in a costume and play a character and fight some of the other characters."

For some reason, this idea filled Ginny with a warm glow. "That sounds amazing!"

"Really?" Happiness flooded Max's face, too. "I mean, it is weird, but…I was hoping you might think it was strange in a good way."

"Absolutely. When does all this happen?"

"Starting this Saturday. So…" Max cleared his throat. "Want to come?"

"Just try keeping me away."

"All right, then. It's a date." Max's face went white. "I mean, I didn't mean…I mean, it's all set, then."

"Okay, Max." Ginny chuckled. "All set."

Daddy dropped Ginny off at the gate of the Renaissance Festival. From the moment she started down the shady, wooded path leading from the ticket booth and parking lot to the festivities, she was enchanted. Costumed singers and musicians lined the way, and she could feel herself slipping away from Metro Atlanta and her world with all of its troubles.

Aside from tourists in shorts and t-shirts, the time travel illusion continued. Yes, you could buy a Coke—but the machinery was hidden in the back of wood huts that looked for all the world like an ancient village. Smells of smoking meat and soft notes played on stringed instruments added to the feel. She closed her eyes and soaked it in, almost forgetting about Max until a loud voice shouting, "Make way, make way!" broke her from her spell—and also made her leap out of the way as two characters in loose shirts and hose gleefully pulled a two-wheeled cart at breakneck speed right through the crowd.

According to Max, his swordplay with other characters was supposed to look spontaneous, but actually followed a set schedule.

So she consulted the map and headed over to the jousting area, where he was supposed to be performing next. She heard before she saw an altercation. A tall, thin knight was shouting at a broad-shouldered youth in knee boots, something about splattering mud on him. As the youth retorted, the knight drew his sword and lunged, and the fight was on—and only then did Ginny realize that the lanky youth crossing swords with the knight was Max!

The "fight" lasted five minutes or so. Ginny's mouth hung open the entire time. She just couldn't get over that this was dorky little Max—his shaggy hair hanging out of a piratey head scarf, his mouth set in an intense but confident line as he thrust and parried with the equally realistic knight.

Max had warned her he could only break character when he took breaks and got out of sight every now and then, so when the defeated knight fell to his knees, Max simply winked at her as he bowed deeply to the crowd and stalked away. Ginny shook her head in wonder, amazed at the cocky spring in his step. Who was this person! Where had this Max been all these weeks?

After she meandered around in the shops for a while, she met him at the Tea Room, which was really sort of an open air café, with a roof but no walls, shaded and draped in greenery and with ample views of all the silliness going on outside. Max swept over to her table, still transformed and drawing quite a few admiring eyes in his leather tunic and tall boots.

As they ate meat pies and Cornish pasties and sipped tea, Max continued to sprinkle his speech with "your ladyships" and "thees" and "thous." Then, dropping his voice almost to a whisper, he leaned his head in toward her and broke character. "Hey, your birthday's coming up, isn't it?"

"Yeah, it is."

"I was just wondering…" Max's voice faded away.

"Yes?"

He chewed on his lower lip for a moment, as though trying to build up his nerve. Then he sat up straight, squared his shoulders, and spoke in the swordsman's voice. "Wouldst my lady care to accompany me to sup that evening, in honor of the noble day of her birth?"

"Wow, I think that's the nicest invitation I ever got." She beamed at him and almost said yes, and then it hit her. "Actually,

Alec and I already have a date for that night."

"Oh." Max seemed to deflate again.

"But maybe you and I could do something the next day? It's Saturday. We can spend the day together if you like."

His eyes brightened a little. "If you want to, and you think it's okay, then…yeah, sure."

"Of course it's okay. And I'd love it."

She meant that. She did love the idea. As she walked to the front gate of the Festival a few minutes before Daddy was supposed to pick her up, she realized she was looking more forward to spending the Saturday with Max than seeing what Alec had planned for her birthday.

Before she turned off the lamp on her nightstand that evening, her gaze went, as usual, to the drawings on the wall. Both boys in the picture still stirred some sort of yearning in her she couldn't quite identify. But she realized with a jolt that the one with the soulful, kind eyes no longer reminded her in the least of Alec Matthews. Now, she was reminded of the concerned puppy eyes of Max Ferguson.

She sighed at the thought of having two such guys in her life. Maybe Daddy was right. Maybe things would work out in this school, in this house, after all. With that happy thought, she drifted easily into sleep.

The sound of loud voices crashed into her nice dreams. She sat up so quickly she felt dizzy and heard Mom and Daddy going at it again. But wait…why would they be fighting in the middle of the night? They didn't even sleep in the same room. She glanced at the clock and saw that it was three a.m.

Then she heard Daddy's voice. "Blast it, Rose, did you do this to me!"

Her brain cleared, the drowsy fog burned away by his words. Running down the hallway, she found Mom standing at the door of the bathroom.

Ginny put her hand against her chest, where her heart was thudding, and tried to breathe. "What's wrong?"

Mom turned toward her. "Your dad's sick."

"Ginny!" It was Daddy's voice, calling her weakly.

She edged into the doorway. Mom made room for her, but her face clouded over and she glared first at Ben, then at Ginny.

Daddy was a mess. He knelt by the toilet, and he lifted his head with apparent effort to look at her. He was shaking violently, and beads of sweat stood out on his face. "I think I need to go to the emergency room, baby." He rubbed his chest, and he sounded breathless when he spoke. "My heart, it's going a mile a minute."

"I'll get my purse," Mom said, turning to leave.

"No! I'm not going anywhere with you."

"Daddy, what's going on?"

Mom crossed her arms. Tears spilled from her eyes. "Your father thinks I did this do him. Poisoned him or something."

"Daddy, that's crazy!" Ginny cried. "Anyway, you've got to let her drive you. I can't."

"No, no...call Anna," he said.

Ginny stood still, not knowing what to do. Then Mom choked out, "You heard him, Ginny. He wants Anna." So she started to shuffle out of the bathroom. But then Daddy also called out, "And bring your...glucometer." Gasping for breath, he finished up, "I want to see...if she did the same thing to me... that she did to you."

Ginny couldn't bring herself to call Anna. She called Max to come drive Daddy to the E.R. Then she checked his blood sugar, which was indeed scary low—almost coma level. She ran for a glass of juice and tried to get it in him, but by that time, he was groggy and limp and she only managed to get a few drops into him. And even then, she almost strangled him.

Max had shown up by this time, his hair standing out in all directions and sleep in his eyes. She had never seen a more beautiful sight—especially when he went confidently into the bathroom, took one look at Daddy, and said, "I think we should call an ambulance."

And in fact, Max was the one who did the calling. By this time, Mom was laid out on the bed with her face in a pillow, and Ginny absolutely had to go check something in her bedroom.

She picked up a big floppy teddy bear from the floor, where he landed every night when she threw back the covers. She laid him across her lap and shoved his head way forward, exposing a torn seam where his head and torso were sewn together. She reached inside, her fingers touching the injector pen she had stuck in there weeks ago. The pen was empty and couldn't harm anyone. It couldn't have hurt Daddy tonight.

So what did make him sick? What—or who?

CHAPTER TWELVE

Ginny couldn't believe it, but in spite of the butterflies in her stomach, she felt hungry.

She padded to the kitchen. According to the wall clock, it was two in the afternoon, but there was no sign of cooking. When they got home from the hospital this morning, Mom had gone straight to her room and shut the door, and Ginny hadn't heard a sound from there since.

With a deep sigh, she opened the refrigerator and peered inside. Didn't normal families have left-overs from meals, or lunch meat and stuff for sandwiches? Yeah, normal families. So she should have expected these empty shelves. Opening the drawer at the bottom, she found a bag of pre-packaged salad that had expired a couple of days ago but didn't look too brown or slimy. No dressing, though. Scrounging through the cabinets, she found a bit of olive oil and cider vinegar, which she mixed with some oregano from an old spice jar. Tasting it, she decided it wasn't too bad. She also turned up a wedge of cheese that was hard but didn't look moldy and a few slices of bread, so she made some cheese toast. When the toast was ready, she studied her scanty meal for a minute, thinking about Mom, who must be empty and hungry, too, even though her butterflies must be monsters compared to Ginny's.

According to Daddy, Mom had poisoned him. If that was true, why should Ginny worry about whether the woman ate or not? But how could it possibly be true?

They had kept Daddy in the hospital overnight. They had gotten his blood sugar back to a normal level fairly quickly, but after all his ranting about being poisoned with insulin, they were keeping him to run tests. Even though she didn't think they really believed him. She'd been standing nearby when one snotty-sounding doctor said, "Well, Mr. Crosby, don't you think you would have noticed if your wife—or anyone else—stuck you with a needle without your permission?" And after Daddy insisted that Mom had been dosing Ginny with Grandma Carla's insulin pen for weeks, too, the doctor sneered at Ginny. "What about you? Your mom been jabbing you with needles? Ever wake up and find mysterious puncture wounds?"

So, she doubted they were going to try very hard to find anything. Still, no matter how the tests went, Ginny couldn't imagine any way this could turn out well. Happy couples did not accuse each other of attempted murder.

Trying to shake those thoughts away, Ginny busied herself dividing the food into two plates. Then she went and knocked on Mom's door. After a moment, when there was no answer, she cracked the door and stuck her head in. The blinds were closed, and the room was gloomy but not dark. Mom was curled up on the bed.

"Mom?"

Her mother woke at the sound. She lifted her head and looked toward Ginny. "Oh, uh…Yes?"

"You want something to eat?"

Mom looked at the clock on her nightstand, appearing confused. "Is it time to eat?"

"Well, it's the middle of the afternoon, but I haven't eaten—"

"Oh, I'm sorry." Mom started to pull herself up, her movements clumsy and stiff. "I lost track of time."

"No, no, that's not what I meant. I made a salad. You should come eat."

"Oh. Thank you, Ginny."

Like a robot, Mom got to her feet and followed Ginny to the table in the kitchen.

They sat across from each other, stabbing hunks of lettuce and staring down at their plates. Occasionally Ginny glanced up, and a couple of times Mom bobbed her head up at the same time, and their eyes met. Then they would both look back down at their food.

Finally, Mom put down her fork and pushed her plate away. "Ginny…" That's all she seemed able to say. Just the name.

Ginny stopped pushing lettuce around on her plate and looked up.

Mom tried again. "I uh, I just want you to know…I didn't poison your dad."

Ginny dropped her gaze back down to her plate.

"You know that, don't you?"

Finally Ginny looked up, leveling a hostile gaze at her mother. "There's a lot of stuff I know. And a lot of stuff I don't."

"That doesn't really answer my question."

"I'm not sure how to answer it. It really depends on, well…the stuff I don't know."

Mom nodded slowly. "Okay. So what do you need to ask?"

"You'll actually tell me the truth?"

Mom's face clouded over, and she hesitated. But then she nodded. "Whatever I know myself, I'll tell you."

"You promise?"

"I promise."

Ginny's heart started to race. "Okay." She almost couldn't find the breath to speak, and tried to calm herself as she wondered where to start. "This is one you should be able to answer. A few weeks ago, when I stayed home because of my blood sugar, you left because you supposedly had to go to work." Even Ginny could hear the sarcastic tone creeping into her voice, and she saw Mom's expression growing colder. *Don't waste this*, she warned herself, again trying to calm down. "Anyway, I needed to get out of the house so I…" *Don't mention the pond.* "Uh…I went for a little walk, and at one point I could see the highway through the trees. I saw you meet someone. Saw you get into their vehicle and drive away." She was surprised to hear the steadiness of her voice as she finished up, "You were lying to Daddy about your job for some reason. Were you meeting a man? Are you having an affair?"

To her amazement, Mom laughed.

"This is funny?"

"Well, kind of. I thought you said you could see the vehicle. You didn't recognize it?"

"I couldn't see it very well. Just a flash of white, and I could tell it was big…"

"Exactly. It was Anna's big white SUV."

"Anna! I mean…Ms. Shaw?"

"That's right. Obviously I had things on my mind." Mom took a deep breath. "As you just pointed out, I was covering up the fact that

I'd lost my job, and things weren't going at all well between your dad and me…" Her voice drifted off, and she gazed into the distance for a moment, then seemed to pull herself back to Ginny. "Anyway, I'd pulled over just to have a private moment to think. Anna saw me and stopped to talk, and she ended up taking me to lunch."

"Oh." For some reason, Ginny felt deflated, even though she knew she should be glad. "Okay." She searched her mind, trying to remember her next question, and when she did felt a surge of anger return. "Okay. What about my cat?"

Mom frowned, looking confused. "What cat?"

"You know what cat. The little gray kitten you freaked out about."

Mom jumped as though startled, and her eyes darted around the kitchen. "I'd forgotten about that cat. Where is it?" Mom looked as though she were about to jump onto the table or stand in her chair, like a woman in a cartoon trying to get away from a mouse. If she was acting, she was doing an amazing job.

Ginny continued, but with a lot less confidence, "I don't know where it is. That's why I'm asking you."

"What do you mean?"

"It just disappeared one day. Vanished."

"Vanished? That's strange. Just so…strange."

Mom's eyes were starting to look a little wild. Ginny was beginning to wish she hadn't brought this one up. But she had to finish it. "I know you didn't want it here. You sure you didn't…I don't know what. Get rid of it somehow?"

Mom shook her head violently. "No. I never touched that kitten. I swear." Mom's voice dropped to a whisper. "You believe me, don't you?"

For a moment, Ginny didn't say anything.

"Ginny…" The word came out sounding like a groan of pain. "How can you believe I would do these things? Do something to your kitten? Hurt your father!"

Ginny slammed her water glass down on the table. "How can you believe what you do about me?"

"Wh-what?"

"I know what you think of me. That I'm some sort of demon or…or possessed by one or…I don't know what. You think I'm some horrible girl named Jordan that did bad things to you and you hate." Ginny felt tears coming to her eyes. "You gave birth to me! How can you not know who I am?"

Mom's mouth dropped open. "Where in the world did you hear something like that?"

"Doesn't matter. I know what you think. And I know it's not true."

Mom appeared to be struggling for breath...struggling, period. Her face contorted, and she chewed on her lip as she stared at Ginny, as though battling something inside herself.

And then her features seemed to relax. She sat up straight and nodded. "I know you're not a ghost, baby. I know."

"You do?"

"Yes. Well...most of the time."

"I don't understand."

"Ginny, your dad's right about one thing. Not all the time, but sometimes...I get sick."

"Sick like, mentally?"

Mom nodded.

"What's wrong with you?"

"Well, when I was young like you, I had to go into the hospital. First my father had killed himself and then my sister had died. Maybe it was too much. Anyway, I had what they called a psychotic episode."

"What's that?"

"It's when you...maybe just for a little while...can't tell what's real."

For a long moment, Ginny sat listening for more, but Mom didn't speak. Ginny heard the clock ticking, as loud as a bomb, and a mockingbird fussing outside the window.

"Was that the only time that happened?"

"No. It's happened a couple of times since."

"And was it ever about..." Ginny licked her lips nervously. "Was it about that girl? Jordan?"

Mom drew a deep breath. "How about we go get comfortable in the living room? It's a long story, but I think it's time I told you everything. From the beginning."

A few minutes later, Ginny was seated on the couch, clutching a throw pillow to her chest as though it were a life preserver. Mom sat to her right in an arm chair, staring out the window as if she could see not the pecan orchard, but straight back into her past. And then she started to speak.

"The old quarry pond always pulled at me like a magnet, so strong it was like magic. No matter how I struggled to avoid the place, it worked just as hard to drag me back there. So when my fiancé Hunter turned the Camaro off the paved road onto the trail to the water, I almost felt madder at the pond than at him. Almost…"

Part III

Rose, 1984

CHAPTER THIRTEEN

Even if the girl hadn't appeared in their lives in such a dramatic way, Rose would have known there was something strange about her because of the effect she seemed to have on everyone, starting with Hunter. He sat in the waiting area of the emergency room, slumped forward in his chair and twisting his hands with worry as they waited for news of the girl's condition. When Rose tried to talk to him he merely grunted, and when she put her hand on his shoulder, he shrugged it off. Finally, Rose hugged her arms around herself and fell silent, wondering if he would have been this anxious if she were the injured one. Still, the girl was pretty, and Hunter was the protective type. So his reaction was understandable.

Then Mamma showed up.

For the first little bit, the scene proceeded exactly the way Rose had imagined it. As Mamma strode toward them, her loosely-tied raincoat slapping against her bare legs, her face was purple with suppressed anger. Bobby Carter, the deputy sheriff, was striding along beside her.

Mamma didn't ask how the girl was doing. She didn't ask them what happened, or anything else for that matter. Without greeting or preamble, she got in Rose's face, so close that Rose could smell the cheap white wine on her breath as she growled, "Bobby here told me you two found an injured girl back at our pond. I told him he must have gotten his wires crossed. No way you were back at that pond, were you?"

"No, Mamma, of course not." The words were out of Rose's mouth automatically, just a sort of reflex, long before she had time to think about it. She saw Hunter's eyes widen with surprise, and she felt herself flush, but she didn't take the words back.

Bobby frowned and looked at Hunter. "I thought that was what you said when you called in."

Rose looked down at the floor, unable to meet Hunter's eyes. The silence seemed to stretch on forever, but finally Hunter spoke. "I guess y'all misunderstood me. I said we found her by the road, near the turn-off to the pond."

She jerked her head up, dizzy with gratitude, but found Hunter studying her with such profound disappointment that she dropped her gaze again.

"She wasn't on our property, was she?" Mamma demanded.

"Oh, no, Mamma." Inwardly, Rose kicked herself. What was the matter with her? Why did her fear of Mamma automatically take control of her, when she could feel Hunter withdrawing from her with every word?

"Well, it's a good thing. I've had enough trouble from you already tonight, young lady," Mamma said.

"What do you mean?"

"You know what I mean. You were in such a hurry to take off on your date with Hunter that you left the house in a mess. Water sloshed out of the bathtub, puddles out in the hall—"

Rose was genuinely puzzled. "No, I didn't, Mamma. Anyway, I bathed this morning and I swear I didn't—"

"Don't lie to me! When I come home from work, worn out from trying to keep food in your ungrateful mouth, I don't appreciate having to spend a half hour cleaning up your messes and—"

Deputy Carter cleared his throat. "I'll take it from here, Carla."

But before he could ask any questions, Hunter's mother, dressed in her white nurse's uniform, appeared through the swinging doors that led off into some mysterious part of the emergency ward. Hunter had said she was on duty tonight, so Rose wasn't surprised to see her—only surprised it had taken her this long to appear.

She gave both Hunter and Rose a peck on the cheek and a quick hug as she cooed over them, as though they were the ones who had been injured. Then she nodded and greeted Mamma stiffly. "Hello, Carla."

Mamma grunted. "Lacey."

"How's the girl?" Hunter asked anxiously. "Have you seen her?"

Mrs. Isaacs nodded. "I think she's going to be okay. She doesn't seem to be injured other than that bump on her head. She probably has a concussion."

"Is she still humming that tune?" Rose said. Even to herself, her tone had come out too rough.

"You mean 'On Jordan's Stormy Banks'?" Mrs. Isaacs asked. Seeing her and Mamma's blank looks, she explained, "It's a hymn." In a sweet, clear voice, she started to sing, "On Jordan's stormy banks I stand and cast a wishful eye, on Canaan's fair and happy land where my possessions lie—"

"We wouldn't know about religious nonsense like that," Mamma interrupted, bringing the song to a crashing halt. "The girls' father had an unhealthy interest in all that foolishness, but I didn't let him ruin my daughters with it."

Hunter was glaring at Rose. "Mamma just said the girl has a concussion, so that would explain the humming, okay?"

"I didn't mean anything," Rose said, her voice now feeling too small and meek. She just couldn't get it right.

Mrs. Isaacs rubbed her arm. "It's okay. I know you both must be pretty upset after a thing like this. But no, she's not humming anymore, mostly because she's asleep. They're going to keep her here tonight for observation, but hopefully she'll be good as new then." For the first time, Mrs. Isaacs spoke to Deputy Carter. "Any idea who she is?"

He shook his head. "Not yet. But we'll probably hear from some panicked parent soon. She still doesn't remember anything about what happened?"

Mrs. Isaacs sighed. "She doesn't remember who she is right now, let alone what happened."

The deputy shifted position and tapped his hand against the side of his leg. "Doesn't take a rocket scientist to figure it out, though, does it?"

"What do you mean?"

"The girl's half-dressed, next to the road. Sounds like her and her boyfriend had a disagreement about how far she was willing to go. Things got a little rough and he dumped her out."

Mrs. Isaacs's eyes widened. "That's horrible!"

"But not that unusual. Don't worry. Soon as her memory comes back we'll pull the little jerk in."

"And what if her memory doesn't come back?" Hunter said quietly.

The deputy frowned. "What do you mean?"

"Where will she go—if it's time to leave the hospital and she still has no memory?"

"I'm sure DFACs will find a foster home or—"

"She says she's eighteen," Mrs. Isaacs said.

"What?" Deputy Carter sounded annoyed. "I thought you said she didn't remember anything. Maybe I need to be questioning her right now."

"Memory is a funny thing," Mrs. Isaacs said. "There's all different kinds. If you sat her behind the wheel of a car, she would know whether she could drive, for instance. She says she knows she's eighteen."

I'd probably be sure I was eighteen, too, if I thought they were about to stick me in a foster home, Rose thought. But she didn't say it out loud. Why should she cause the poor girl any more misery?

Mrs. Isaacs was waving one hand in dismissal. "Well, anyway, she can come stay with us if she's eighteen."

"I want to see her," Mamma suddenly said.

They all looked at her, surprised into a moment of silence.

"Ummm…" Mrs. Isaacs cleared her throat, looking as though she were trying hard to think of a good way to say no. "I'm not sure that's such a good idea, Carla. She needs to rest."

"Nonsense. When my Livvy was in here with a concussion after that bike accident, you people woke her up all the time. Said it wasn't good for her to fall into a deep sleep."

Rose felt herself flushing with embarrassment as she heard a slight slur in her mother's speech. She hoped no one else could tell how much Mamma had been drinking.

"Well…why exactly do you want to see her?" Mrs. Isaacs was asking her.

Carla shrugged. "I don't know. I feel bad for her, lying here by herself."

Clearly, Mrs. Isaacs didn't think it was a good idea, but as usual, Mamma got what she wanted. Rose knew from experience that it was so much easier to give in than to deal with the scene Mamma would cause as the situation dragged out. So Mrs. Isaacs cautioned them not to wake the girl, but led them all into the room—because Hunter insisted that if Mamma got to see her, he and Rose should, too.

They all stood around the bed, hushed and still, staring down at the waxy figure lying there. Rose shifted on her feet, uncomfortably reminded of staring down at Daddy in his casket. Mamma shot her a look for her fidgeting, but Rose thought it was more an automatic reaction than true anger. Truth be told, Mamma seemed to be relaxing as she stared down at the long, lanky figure in the bed, as though she had expected to find something gruesome or gory and was reassured by the sight of a normal, sleeping girl.

In spite of the look she had given Rose, Mamma broke the rules herself by sniffing and saying, "Doesn't look like anyone from around here. Very strange-looking."

"I think she's beautiful," Hunter said. "You can't see her eyes now, Carla, but it's amazing. They're that same sort of gold color that Livvy's were."

Mamma flinched. Frowning, Mrs. Isaacs motioned them all from the room.

As they filed out, Mamma grabbed hold of Rose's arm—her eyes on Hunter. When he was a safe distance from them, Mamma hissed, "You make sure that girl doesn't go stay at the Isaacs' house."

Rose made a half-hearted effort to pull away. "How am I supposed to manage that?"

Mamma hesitated, then said firmly, "Bring her to stay with us if you have to. But keep her away from Hunter."

"Stay with us?" Rose's chest went tight, and she struggled to breathe. "You're kidding, right?"

"No, I'm not. What's the matter with you?"

"What's the matter? Mamma, this girl came out of nowhere, in the middle of the—" Just in time, she stopped herself from saying *in the middle of the woods.* "—night. In the middle of the night, wandering around and half crazy. We don't know anything about her."

Mamma huffed. "Tell me you're not afraid of a weak, injured girl." She peered shrewdly at Rose. "Or are you thinking she's something else? A ghost? An angel?"

Rose felt her face burning, as though Mamma's sneering words had scraped her raw. But she said nothing.

"That Hunter is going places," Mamma ranted on. Releasing Rose's arm, she stood staring deep into her eyes. "It's amazing you landed him in the first place—you wouldn't have if you weren't

Livvy's sister."

"Mamma!" Rose gasped. Mamma had never said this out loud, even though Rose had always known she thought it. Even though, not too far below the surface of her mind, Rose believed it, too.

Mamma shrugged. "If you're going to live with him, you better face the truth now. He loved your sister. That didn't stop because she died. He's always thought you're as close as he can get to Livvy, but…well, you need to do whatever it takes to hold onto him."

Rose stared at her mother, unable to speak.

"Do you hear me?" Mamma prodded.

Rose managed to nod, and Mamma started walking again. Rose watched her swoop down the hallway and thought that for once, she and her mother were in total agreement. One way or another, Rose had to get out. Whatever it took, she had to hold on to Hunter.

○З

The fact that Carla Remington took in a stray girl with no name and no memory was a wonder to the whole county. Everyone knew that Carla Remington was not exactly the charitable type.

Both sides of Rose's family had been in Georgia for generations, but until Carla Brown and Dan Remington got together, they didn't mix much. The Remingtons were dreamers, with soft unfocused eyes and overgrown lawns. The Browns had eyes as sharp as eagles' and hard, lean bodies that could take anything life dished out. Livvy had always told Rose that Mamma and Daddy were happy until his business went under and money was so tight, but Rose didn't remember any of that. Her memories were sort of like a movie trailer—short scenes and pictures and scraps of dialogue glued together, telegraphing the story of two people that never should have been together.

The clearest scene Rose could remember from start to finish was of Mamma jerking a Bible out of Daddy's hands and telling him to get up off his lazy behind and do something to save his family, instead of expecting some kind of magic fairies to come and save them. Rose remembered his wounded eyes, genuinely bewildered, focusing on Mamma as though he'd never seen her before and whispering, "Not fairies. God." Rose wasn't sure how long it was after that, but in her mental movie trailer, the next scene was Daddy's funeral, with Mamma standing straight and dry-eyed by the casket receiving their neighbors, who walked away whispering words like "suicide" and "no surprise with a wife like that," as soon as they thought they were out of range of any Remington's hearing.

Livvy and Rose were half-breeds, pragmatists who studied hard so they could go to college, but only because they wanted to be art teachers or open up a free vet clinic. They washed cars and babysat because they lusted after cold, hard cash—but then spent their money on paints and books and other "nonsense" that Mamma refused to buy them. Or at least, that's how Rose and her sister were until the year that Livvy slowly, subtly began to change.

After Daddy's death, Livvy went a little odd. She developed an intense interest in the afterlife. She sensed the presence of angels—or demons—everywhere. Mamma prohibited the two girls from going to church, thinking it was feeding Livvy's unhealthy obsession. Rose tried to be more like Mamma, tried her best to be practical, to please her and—later—to please Hunter and to plan for a nice, normal life.

And then came this strange girl with no memory and no past.

From her first night in their home, the girl slept in Livvy's room, or at least, Rose assumed that she slept. Rose locked her door every night, not liking the idea of this creature loose in her house while she was sleeping and vulnerable. But Rose often heard the shuffle of her feet as she wandered through the halls, and the girl told them she was having trouble sleeping.

Gradually, Rose's tense muscles started to relax around the girl. Yes, Jordan was a little peculiar. (Jordan was what they called her, after the tune she had hummed so relentlessly the first day or two.) Yes, her gaze would be dreamy and faraway one moment, and frighteningly intense the next. But that was probably because of her injury, the terrible struggle she must be going through, trying to remember.

Almost against her will, Rose became attached to the girl, partly because Jordan seemed determined to be Rose's friend. She wanted to be near Rose, but not like a puppy, or a younger girl who wanted to look up to her. Even though Jordan was the one injured and lost and alone, Rose often got the feeling the girl was trying to protect her—even from Mamma.

One evening, as Rose was loading the dishwasher and putting away the dinner leftovers, the sunset caught her eye through the kitchen window, startling her with a dusky shade of mauve she had never seen before. Feeling her heart squeeze with a longing to capture it, to hold it forever, she grabbed her sketchpad and colored pencils and bounded onto the porch. Over the next fifteen minutes, she worked like a madwoman, shading and laying on color in the swiftly-changing light. Alternately soaring with joy and wanting to scream at the limitations of her tools, she completely forgot about the leftover pot roast and vegetables that needed to be transferred to Tupperware dishes. As usual, Mamma had spent her Sunday cooking, producing one amazing Sunday evening feast and enough leftovers so she wouldn't have to cook after work for the next two or three days. And Rose left every bit of that food out on the counter to spoil, seeing nothing but that other-worldly glow of pink light.

Reality came back to her in a flood the next morning, when she pushed open the door to the kitchen in search of cereal and saw Mamma standing in the middle of the room, her hand over her mouth as she surveyed the mess that Rose had left everywhere. Horror washed over Rose in a dizzying wave. Mamma would kill her. A whole Sunday—half of her weekend away from the job she hated—literally down the drain.

Slowly, Mamma turned to face Rose, her face ashen with fury. She moved her hand away from her mouth, and Rose braced herself for the blast.

But before Mamma could speak, the door swung open and Jordan appeared. Rose saw the girl taking in the scene and, no doubt, drawing an accurate conclusion about what was going on. Rose felt a flicker of irritation. It was bad enough for Mamma to constantly remind Rose how stupid and forgetful she was. Having witnesses always made the scenes worse.

But then Jordan gasped. "Oh no, I'm so sorry! I can't believe I did that."

Mamma frowned. "Did what?"

The girl made a sweeping motion with her hand, taking in the whole kitchen. "That. Ruined all your beautiful food."

Mamma's stern expression eased the tiniest bit, weakened by uncertainty. "You did all this?"

Jordan nodded. "You know I haven't been very hungry lately, but I woke up in the middle of last night and was starving. I don't..." She licked her lips nervously. "I mean, I remember coming down here and getting the food out, but I don't know…I don't really remember much after that."

Stunned into silence, Rose watched the struggle in her mother's eyes, watched her clenching and unclenching her fists. Amazingly, compassion seemed to win. The woman nodded and said, "You're probably still not quite right after that head injury. Well…" She turned and surveyed the mess again. "Couldn't be helped."

Jordan spoke in a rush. "You don't have to worry one bit about cooking when you get home from work tonight. I'll do it."

Mamma raised her eyebrows. "You know how to cook?"

The girl laughed. "I guess we'll find out." Her eyes grew serious again. "I know I need to pay for the food, too. I'll be more help around here, I promise. I want to make everything up to you."

Before Rose's amazed eyes, her mother turned to mush. "Don't you worry about any of that. We're happy to do it."

As Mamma blew past Rose, leaving the kitchen without a word of apology (not that she really owed Rose an apology, since she had been right about her scatterbrained mistake in the first place), Rose couldn't understand what she was feeling. For the first time she could remember, someone had taken the rap for her. Someone had put her head in the lion's mouth and had actually tamed the beast.

As she murmured her thanks, the oddest memory came into Rose's mind, seemingly out of nowhere, of a time when she and Livvy and Mamma blew out a tire in a really bad section of Atlanta. Mamma immediately started fretting and fussing, even more so when Livvy said they should pray, and started to do it. Out loud.

Almost immediately, a nicely-groomed man in a mechanic's uniform showed up at the car and asked if he could help. Within minutes, he had the tire changed and, waving off Mamma's offer of payment, he walked away.

"God sent him." Livvy had breathed. "He was an angel."

"Oh, nonsense," Mamma scoffed. "According to his shirt, he works at Danson Tires."

"He just appeared out of nowhere."

"He walked up from behind the liquor store."

"You actually saw that?" Livvy demanded.

"Yes." Mamma made the pronouncement immediately, and yet her voice didn't sound sure.

Why that memory came back to Rose as she watched Jordan

start to clean up the kitchen for her wasn't at first clear. It became clearer after the calamity at Rose's eighteenth birthday party.

For the occasion, Mamma invited about twenty people over to grill hamburgers—some of them more her friends than Rose's, but still, it was nice. Hunter came, along with his mom and dad and Jake, and Jake's girlfriend, Anna. Mrs. Isaacs brought a six-layer chocolate birthday cake while the rest carried a pile of presents. Mr. Isaacs and Mamma fiddled with the grill and fussed over the correct height of the flame, and the rest of them sipped Cokes and chattered and munched chips. Jordan was quiet, as usual, but they had all met her before and so the afternoon felt relaxed and comfortable. At least it did, until Rose was almost finished opening her presents. She had beamed on opening a delicate silver bracelet from Hunter, and grown warm with happy embarrassment when she received a hand-made quilt from Mrs. Isaacs for her future home. For her and Hunter's bed, she thought, but did not say.

The odd thing happened when she picked up a pretty box from Anna and, without warning, Jordan lunged across the picnic table and knocked it from her hand.

Everyone gasped and stared at the girl, who was breathing hard and looking wild.

"What do you think you're doing?" Mamma demanded.

"I—I had to. That—" She pointed at the pretty box, which had landed on an ant bed. "That would kill her."

"What!" Anna laughed harshly. "What the devil do you mean by that?"

Even Mrs. Isaacs' brow was creased with concern as she studied the girl. Rose was glad she was there, in case the girl was having some kind of left-over brain trauma from that head injury and was about to need medical help.

Anna snatched up the box and slapped her hand across it, knocking off the ants. Then she held it out to Rose, who tentatively put her hand out to take it.

"No!" the girl cried. "I'm not kidding."

"What is your problem?" Anna demanded. She jerked the top off the box and held it out for everyone to see. "It's soap, not a bomb."

As they all looked at Jordan, she nodded. "Yes, soap. Almond soap, isn't it?"

"No…well, yes. Almond-scented…It's just some kind of natural, hand-made soap I bought at a craft fair in Savannah last week." She shrugged. "I thought Rose loved that kind of artisan stuff."

"I do," Rose murmured. "It's lovely, but it probably has almond oil and…"

"She's deathly allergic to almonds," Mamma muttered, sounding dazed.

Anna's eyes widened. "Seriously?"

Rose nodded. "I can't even touch them…the oil…almonds could kill me."

Silence fell, as they all stared at Jordan, who looked just as ashen-faced and shocked as everyone else. She stood in the center of them, tugging nervously at a strand of her hair and wrapping it tightly around her finger.

Finally Mrs. Isaacs spoke. "But Jordan…how did you know?"

She shook her head. "I don't remember, but I guess someone must have mentioned it. That um…" She nodded in Rose's direction, as though she had suddenly forgotten her name as well… "that she has these allergies."

"Yes, but…how did you know what was in the box?" Mrs. Isaacs asked.

The girl didn't answer right away. After a long moment, she said, "I don't know. I just had a feeling."

"Well, thank God you did," Hunter declared.

Jake chuckled, his mischievous eyes sparkling. "Maybe it's like a Stephen King book or something. You got knocked on the head and now you're psychic."

Hunter gave him a little shove. "Shut up, Jake."

As Rose stacked her gifts into one pile and gathered up the torn paper and ribbons, she realized why Jordan constantly reminded her of that scene with Livvy and the Good Samaritan who had changed their tire. If Livvy had been present when Jordan saved her life this afternoon, she would have declared on the spot that the mysterious Jordan was an angel, sent to watch over her little sister.

Her sister…

A shiver went through Rose at the thought of her sister, her ashes in an urn on the mantel, her soul…where? Mamma had always said there was no such thing as a soul, that the whole idea of Heaven was made up so that mortal people could comfort themselves. Sort of like plugging a night light into a dark room. Of course, Mamma hadn't said that so much since Livvy died in that car wreck.

As for Rose, she chose to believe in what Livvy believed, because that way, she could still believe in Livvy's existence somewhere. Could maybe even believe that Livvy had sent this golden-eyed girl to watch over her...

Even as that shivery-warm thought was coursing through Rose, she looked around and noticed that the girl had gone missing. And so had Hunter.

She pushed her way through the people still clucking over her in concern—even Mamma! Nodding and murmuring something comforting to Anna, who was still wringing her hands and babbling over her near-fatal mistake, Rose headed for the house, carrying a stack of presents for cover. "Just stashing my goodies," she called over her shoulder. "Be right back."

After dropping the packages on the kitchen table, she made a quick check of Jordan's bedroom—the old converted den—hating herself for what she was thinking. Finding the room empty, she made a stop in the bathroom to splash water on her face and try to think. Why would Hunter and Jordan both be missing at the same time? Where could they be? For some reason, she immediately thought of the pond.

For once, she wanted to go down to the pond, just to put her mind at ease. As she drifted out of the bathroom, she came to a halt in the hallway, wondering if she could really get up the courage to walk into those woods, to end up alone at the pond.

Then she heard a sound from the basement. A sort of scraping noise, and a soft thud. As quietly as possible, she edged to the top of the stairs in the New Room and peered down, but she couldn't see anything. Heart pounding with dread—not of ghosts or anything so vague, but of something common and solid and ugly—she placed one silent foot after another down the steps. On about the fourth step, she was able to see the whole room. And there, just as she had expected, was Jordan.

Instead of finding Jordan and Hunter stealing kisses, however, she found the girl alone. But that didn't ease Rose's mind, because Jordan looked so guilty. She was standing next to an old chair, her hand posed a little too casually on the back, and she was breathing heavily and flushed. She looked exactly the way she would have if Rose *had* caught her kissing Hunter.

Rose glanced around, certain he must have nipped into hiding somewhere. But there was no way he could fit into any of the piled-up boxes, and there was really nowhere else for him to be.

Trying to keep any accusation out of her tone—after all, Jordan had just saved her life—Rose asked, "What are you doing down here?"

"I just...I thought I heard something." She couldn't seem to meet Rose's eyes. "Guess I was wrong." She darted toward the stairs before Rose could ask any more questions.

As the sound of Jordan's footsteps were dying away, and Rose was turning to leave, she noticed the window.

There was a little window at the top of the far wall—the one wall that rose above ground level. When you were outside, you had to kneel down to peer through it. Or to climb through it, into the house, and down onto the old dining room table positioned strategically below it—a technique that Hunter and Jake and Livvy had perfected when they were kids. They hadn't used that window much lately, since the New Room was built and the old den became Livvy's room, with its own door to the outside. Still, if someone had been down in the basement, doing something they weren't supposed to, and needed to make a hasty exit when they were about to be caught...

Right now, the little window above the table was wide open, with its filmy white curtain fluttering in the breeze...as if someone had just made a hasty escape.

CHAPTER FOURTEEN

In Rose's mind, she couldn't remember much about the days in between the Birthday Incident and the Picnic Incident, as she came to call them in her mind. All she knew was that, as one blurred into another, her muscles remained clenched to the point of pain and her feelings about the girl swung wildly back and forth between affection and repulsion. The day of the picnic, she and Hunter, Jake and Anna, plus Jordan spread blankets on the grass next to Peachtree Lake and flopped down on them, leaving just a little space in the middle for the food. Two couples plus the girl—but Rose was the one feeling like a fifth wheel.

Jake lolled back against a tree, his wavy brown hair brushing his shoulders. He grinned at Anna as she unpacked sandwiches from a basket. "You're not gonna poison anybody this time, right?"

Anna slapped at him playfully. "I didn't poison her. How did I know she was allergic to almonds?" To Rose, she said, "But just in case you're worried, I was really careful with the food. Tuna, mayonnaise, and a little salt and pepper. That's pretty much it. Unless you're allergic to the bread."

Rose laughed. "No problem."

Hunter sat next to Rose and ate silently, while Jake chattered and joked, as usual. Jordan was quiet, too, but her eyes were hungry, taking everything in. To Rose, she had seemed different ever since the day of the birthday party, when Rose had found her skulking down in the basement. Lately, the girl's silence seemed less dazed and more brooding. Calculating. She seemed to watch everyone with an intensity that was almost frightening, as though she were no longer confused, but was now busy hatching a plan. Probably a plan involving Hunter, Rose thought cynically.

Anna didn't seem threatened by the girl, but looked perfectly relaxed as she picked at a plate of fruit and smiled at one of Jake's jokes. Watching her, Rose leaned back and tried to relax her shoulder muscles. She needed to be more confident, like Anna.

After a couple of kids threw a Frisbee right into the middle of their food for the second time, though, Anna didn't seem quite as relaxed. She hurled the Frisbee back, coming suspiciously close to hitting one of the boys' head, and said, "Honestly, Rose. I just don't understand why your mother thinks it's okay for us to hang out at this overcrowded lake, but she won't let anyone go near that nice, private pond right in your back yard. This is ridiculous."

Rose shrugged. "I guess she figures if one of us drowns here, she won't get sued."

Jake ran one hand through his long, disheveled hair and laughed. "That sounds like what your mom would be worried about. Her money, not us." He looked at Jordan and wiggled his eyebrows. "We have been known to sneak back to the pond, anyway."

Jordan smiled. "Yeah, I know. That's where I came into the story."

Jake's grin wobbled. "Oh, right. Sorry." He cleared his throat. "We really haven't done much of that lately, though. Defying the old lady and having little private parties back there, I mean. Not since Livvy, I guess…oops." Now he looked mortified.

Anna shook her head. "Why don't you just go ahead and plant your foot in your mouth and leave it there, Jake?"

Hunter stuffed the last of a sandwich in his mouth, then unfolded his long brown legs from underneath him and stood. "Come on. Let's go swim."

Jake immediately jumped up, but Rose said, "You can't swim right after you eat."

Hunter scoffed. "Yeah. I'm sure that's why you don't want to go."

Rose felt her face burning with shame, but Hunter wasn't finished. "Like mother like daughter, I guess."

"What do you mean?" Jordan asked.

"Rose is terrified, too."

"Of getting sued?" Jake laughed. "We won't sue you, darlin'."

"Of water," Jordan said quietly.

Rose stared at her. "How did you know that?"

Jordan flushed and started to twist her hair around her finger, so tight it appeared it would cut off the circulation. "I'm sorry. I don't know anything."

Rose got to her feet and faced Hunter, although she still had to look up to meet his eyes. "Have you been having little chats with Jordan about my shortcomings?"

"Rose, c'mon. You're humiliating yourself."

Anna cheerfully changed the subject. "So, Jordan, do you swim?"

"I don't know."

"You would know if you tried though, right?"

"I guess."

"So try."

"No. Y'all go ahead. I'll stay here." She glanced over at Rose. "Unless you—or Anna, of course—unless one of you goes in, too."

Rose felt Anna's hand patting her shoulder. "No. Rose plainly told you she's terrified, bless her heart—"

"I didn't say terrified—"

"So I'll stay here and keep her company," Anna continued. "Y'all go ahead."

"I'll stay, too," Jordan said.

"Okay," said Jake.

But Rose saw the mischievous look he shot at Hunter, and saw the answering twinkle in Hunter's eye, and braced herself.

Sure enough, as though responding to an unspoken countdown, the guys suddenly made a dash at Jordan. One grabbed her under the arms and one grabbed her legs. Laughing wildly, they ran to the end of the dock and tossed her in, then jumped in behind her. The girl thrashed for a second, then disappeared under the water.

Before Rose could even realize what she was doing, she found herself at the edge of the dock, sailing off of it. The water shocked her to her senses, amazingly cold to her sun-warm skin, rushing up past her nose, pushing into her sinuses, closing over her head. She knew how to swim—in fact, had once been rather good at it—but panic made her start to thrash and choke. She opened her eyes but it made no difference. There was no light, just darkness, wet and burning in her head and her chest.

And then, strong hands took hold of her, pulled her up, up to air and life. She gasped in sweet lungfuls of hot Georgia air until she came to herself again. She turned her head, expecting to see Hunter's face. Instead, she found Jake's eyes peering into hers as water dripped from his shaggy bangs onto her nose.

Anna was right behind him, looking over his shoulder at her. "Are you okay?"

"Yeah." With a great effort, she grabbed onto Jake's arm and pulled herself up.

He chuckled. "So now we know. Neither of you can swim."

Anna smacked him on the arm. "That wasn't funny. They could have drowned."

"We were looking out for Jordan. We had everything under control if Rose hadn't jumped in, too. Why'd you do that, Rose, if you can't swim?"

"I can," Rose said.

"Sure didn't look that way."

"I got dizzy. I almost blacked out." She gave Jake a little shove to the side, trying to see past him. "Where's Hunter?"

"Uh…"

There was no need for them to tell her. He sat a few yards away, wrapping a towel around Jordan, rubbing her shoulders with it and cooing words that Rose couldn't make out, as solicitous and attentive as he had been that night they found her. The girl's face was as ashen as it had been that night, too, but her eyes were clear and focused as she met Rose's gaze. Then Hunter turned, apparently wanting to see what had grabbed Jordan's attention. As he saw Rose, he gave a little shake of his head, as though disappointed.

Rose wondered vaguely why she had jumped in, when she hadn't been able to go near water without trembling for years. Why the instinct to save this girl had been so strong, when Rose hated her more than she had ever hated anyone.

ഇ

As Anna squeezed her hand and talked in a low, serious voice, Rose went icy all over, almost as though she were going numb.

"I'm only telling you this because I'm your friend," Anna said.

Funny. Rose had spent a great deal of her free time in Anna's company over the past couple of years because they were dating the brothers, but it had never occurred to her that Anna might be her friend. When Anna had first appeared in their lives, she had made it obvious that she thought of Rose as a bratty little pest, and Rose had assumed she still felt the same way.

Through the numbness, she vaguely felt Anna squeeze again. "You okay?"

"Yeah…it's not as though I wasn't expecting something like this."

"Really?"

Rose nodded. Of course she had expected it, ever since she saw the way Hunter looked at the girl shining in his car's headlamps that first night by the pond. Even before that, somewhere down inside her, she had always known that Hunter would leave her, that it was too good to be true, that it wasn't really Rose that he loved. So when Anna had dropped by this evening just to "chat," as she put it, and had looked at Rose as pityingly as a doctor about to deliver news of a terminal illness, Rose had known what was coming. Anna had been over at the Isaacs' house visiting Jake and had overheard Hunter on the phone, making plans with Jordan to meet…

"…at the pond?" Rose murmured.

"What's that?"

"I was just thinking…I knew Hunter was interested in her. I just don't understand them meeting at the pond. I mean, you'd think Jordan wouldn't want to go anywhere near that place, after her bad experience there."

Anna's eyes narrowed, giving her a shrewd look. "Oh, I know exactly why they're going there." She held Rose's puzzled gaze for a moment. "Because they know you won't go there."

The ice in Rose thawed, as suddenly as though a burning torch had been touched to her skin. Heat rose through her, pumping her blood faster through her veins, making it thud in her head. It propelled her to her feet, toward the door, without any thought for Anna or the niceties or explanations. She only remembered Anna as she felt a hand grab her arm and pull her back from the doorway.

"Where are you going?" Anna demanded.

"To show them that they're wrong," Rose said.

Still feeling that unaccustomed throbbing of heat and power, she threw off Anna's arm and headed outside, into the night.

Part IV

Ginny, 2009

CHAPTER FIFTEEN

G inny sat waiting for more of the story, but no more came. Mom sat staring out at the pecan orchard, her arms crossed tightly.

"So what happened then?" Ginny prompted.

Mom turned to her, looking sort of surprised to see Ginny sitting there. "Oh." She cleared her throat and laughed a little. "I've been going on for ages, haven't I? I'm getting hoarse."

"I'll get you some water." Ginny jumped to her feet, not wanting Mom to have an excuse not to finish the story.

"Would you get me some aspirin, too?" Mom called after her. "I can feel a bad headache coming on."

Ginny fumbled in the cabinet for the aspirin bottle and sloshed the water in the glass as she hurried.

As soon as Mom had swallowed the pills and set the water glass down on the end table, Ginny leaned toward her. "Okay, so what happened then? What's the rest of the story?"

Mom rubbed her forehead. "There really isn't any more. Nothing worth hearing, anyway."

"But what about...you were going down to the pond, to confront them." Almost whispering, Ginny asked her, "Did she do anything to you? This Jordan person?"

Mom lifted her shoulders in a shrug. "Not unless you count turning Hunter against me."

"So they ended up together, like you were afraid of?"

"Not in the long run, but…she managed to break us up before she…went away. Just as I'd expected." Getting to her feet, Mom picked up the empty water glass. "Pretty dull ending to the story, isn't it?"

"That's it?" Ginny felt bewildered. "That can't be the whole thing or we wouldn't be having all these problems, would we?"

Mom whirled around to face her, eyes flashing. "Oh, so my story isn't bad enough for you? Okay. So what if I tell you that watching Hunter gradually fall for Jordan and leave me for her was enough to put me back in the hospital? And that while I was in that place—half the time so out of my mind that I thought monsters were pulling me down into a deep black pit and I was struggling to breathe—Hunter not only broke off our engagement, but asked my mother to get the ring back for him."

Ginny held up shaky hands. "Okay, okay."

But now she couldn't seem to get Mom to stop. "Or how about that I've had to watch you grow more and more like that girl every day for years, not knowing whether I was losing my mind or whether you're her, whether it's all some sort of divine judgment or…no." Shaking her head from side to side, Mom repeated the word. "No."

Feeling tears running down her face, Ginny said. "No? What do you mean?"

"I mean, no. I will not do this anymore."

Mom took two long, deep breaths, then smiled shakily and took a step toward Ginny, who shrank back into the couch. Mom stopped in her tracks, wiping tears away but moving no closer to Ginny.

"Am I really just like that strange girl? Exactly like her?" Ginny whispered.

"No, there are differences, of course." Mom went silent for a moment, her eyes glazing over. Throughout her story she had done that, going quiet, seeming to lose herself in the memory so that Ginny had to prompt her to start talking again. She had a feeling Mom still hadn't told her everything, and it nagged at her, as though the sound on a movie had cut out and she had missed an important part of the plot.

Finally Mom said softly, "Baby, I can admit I'm probably not seeing you clearly right now. I know I've had problems, and that they run in my family. But don't worry, because I'll get help. I'll get treatment or medication or whatever I need to do to keep us together, to keep you from being hurt anymore. Do you believe me?"

After a long moment, Ginny said, "I believe you'll try."

Mom laughed sharply. "That doesn't sound too optimistic."

Ginny shrugged. She could feel Mom studying her.

"What is it, Ginny? We might as well get it all out now."

Ginny lifted her head and met her mother's intense gaze. "It's just…I think I do understand how you feel. I think there's something weird, something wrong about our whole family. Including me."

"What do you mean?"

"You know when I was little, and you went into the hospital…" Ginny stopped as a sudden thought hit her. "The hospital…I never knew exactly what was wrong with you, did I? Was it…was it like when you were younger, and you didn't know what was real?"

"Pretty much. Mainly I was depressed, but the doctors used the word 'paranoia.'"

A shudder went through Ginny. She'd heard that word applied to herself lately.

"You know…well, you know what a flirt your father can be, but I started getting really freaked out about it and I caused a scene at his job and…"

"It's okay. I get it." Ginny breathed in deep, then blew it out slowly. "So anyway, when that happened, I came to stay with Grandma, remember?"

"Of course."

"And she took me to her church. And something bizarre happened."

"I remember that, too. She told me a little about it when she brought you home. She had to, because you were still so upset, and it made me furious. She would never even let us go to church when we were young, and then she later changed into such a religious fanatic that she took you to some holy-roller place and let them traumatize you."

Ginny was shaking her head. "No, it wasn't like that, really. It wasn't the church being weird. It was me."

"What?"

"I don't know what Grandma told you, but the way I remember it…well, the preacher was preaching, and my mind started wandering, and I behaved really badly. Grandma got onto me a couple of times for squirming and fidgeting, and then I actually slid down onto the floor and played for a bit. And then I got sleepy, down there, and Grandma left me alone—maybe because I was at least being still and quiet. I remember looking up through people's legs to the front of the church, and thinking how funny it was to watch the preacher's legs pacing back and forth as he talked, and that his shoes were really dirty and scuffed. And then things blurred and went black, and I heard voices—I don't remember what they were saying—and just when I started to get really terrified of the dark, things got light again.

"I was still in the church, still looking up to the front of the church through people's legs, only it was different. I couldn't see the preacher stomping back and forth. Where he had been there was a...well...a casket."

"A casket!" Mom's eyes grew wide.

Ginny nodded.

Mom swallowed hard. "Who...who was in the casket?"

"I don't know. It was closed. But it gets even stranger. There were people standing around the casket, but I couldn't tell who they were. From under the bench...uh, pew...I could only see then from the waist or so down. But there was an old, white-haired lady in a wheelchair, and she was crying. And then she turned sideways in the wheelchair and touched the coffin, and I could see her better, and even though she was really old and wrinkled, and one side of her face was drooping, I knew...I knew..."

Mom sat down on the couch next to Ginny, and took her hand. "What did you know, baby?"

"That it was Grandma. A really old, sick Grandma." Ginny raised her face and looked at her mother. "The way she looks now."

Mom's eyes were getting crazy big, too, as she listened to Ginny. But her voice was soothing as she said, "It sounds like a really scary dream, honey, but I'm sure that's all it was."

"No, no, you haven't heard the whole thing. Grandma was crying and praying, and I wanted to help her. I started to crawl under the benches toward her, but then I felt sort of a jerk, or a tug, like I was falling backwards, and things went dark again.

"When I opened my eyes, I was under the pew and the church was in an uproar, because apparently they thought I was missing." Ginny licked her lips nervously. "Grandma had apparently looked around and I wasn't next to her anymore."

"So all the hubbub was because you had crawled under the seat to sleep, and she didn't even bother to look before she got everyone hysterical?" Mom shook her head. "Amazing. Your grandma never was one to go at things quietly or calmly."

"No, that's the thing. She did look, or at least she said she did. She tried to look around quietly for a minute, but it was a small church, you know. So first a couple of people around her got in on the act, and then finally the whole service came to a halt while everyone looked. They swore that for a few minutes, I just wasn't there." Ginny paused, shoving back her hair, which was suddenly damp with sweat. "And then suddenly I popped out from under the pew and asked them what was going on." Laughing shakily, she said, "One lady actually screamed when I did. Well, they never did finish the service the way they had planned it that night. Half the people laughed and shook their heads and said—just like you did—how silly the whole thing was. How I had been way up under the seat asleep the whole time. Fooled 'em good.

"But there were a few others, especially the ones sitting around Grandma, that didn't laugh it off." She went quiet for a second, remembering even now how the white, scared faces of Grandma's friends peering down at her had scared her so, especially after just coming back from the spooky old woman in the wheelchair. "They swore they had looked under that pew and every other pew, had looked everywhere, and that I absolutely was not in that little church."

A moment of silence passed. Then Mom ventured, "But…you were, right?"

Ginny lifted her shoulders, let them fall. "You tell me."

"But Ginny. How could that possibly be?"

"I don't know. How could I be turning into this girl you used to know?"

"I told you, baby. I don't…it's not real. It's just…it's what I see. I mean, Anna knew Jordan, too, and she's not freaking out. Apparently it's just me."

"So maybe I'm just crazy, too," Ginny said. "But if we're all just crazy, then—if we're all just full of delusions and we're just remembering things wrong, then how come Alec Matthews says people are still talking about what went on at that church that night? How come I knew exactly what Grandma was going to look like almost ten years later, after she had a stroke?"

"I don't know, baby." Mom shook her head slowly. "I just don't know."

CHAPTER SIXTEEN

When the doorbell rang, Ginny ran for it, not even stopping for a last-minute check of her hair or make-up. She dearly wanted to get to the door before Daddy or Mom.

Too late. As she skidded into the hallway, she saw Mom pulling the door open. Amazingly, right after that, she saw Mom smile and usher Alec in. Then Daddy shuffled in from the direction of the New Room and stood glowering. The world had turned upside down.

One way or another, the pain was short-lived. She and Mom had already had a little girl talk about Alec and her birthday date, so even though Mom made Alec stay for a few minutes so they could chat and "get to know one another," she made the whole business seem non-threatening and downright normal. Daddy might be in a foul mood but he had already met and approved Alec on an earlier occasion, so there wasn't much he could say right now, even though he had made it clear he didn't like Ginny going off with Alec on her birthday.

Too bad, Ginny thought, as she sailed through the door toward Alec's truck, finally free of the parental approval ritual and ready to have some fun for a change. If Daddy had really wanted to celebrate her birthday, he could have made an effort to behave better and make her happy.

Daddy had offered to take her out on a father-daughter date to Atlanta, to some fabulous restaurant or the zoo, or both—whichever she wanted. When she told him that would be great if the whole family could participate, he'd frozen on her.

"That's just not possible right now. You know that," he'd said stiffly.

"No, I don't know any such thing. Mom's made a huge effort to put all this ugliness behind us. She and I are doing okay now. So why can't you?"

Daddy had sighed deeply. "We can't just pretend none of this ever happened."

"None of what? I mean…surely you're not still saying Mom tried to kill you, are you?"

He wouldn't answer her, not right then. But Ginny knew that's exactly what he was still thinking, even though the hospital had found nothing to back up his claims.

A few hours later, the big date had wound down to a hamburger at one of those retro drive-ins with wait staff on roller skates.

As she reached across to grab her Coke from the carhop, she said, "This is amazing. We can celebrate my birthday without even getting out of the truck."

He huffed in protest. "We got out when we got your tattoo."

She touched her shoulder, where the brand new drawing of a dove with an olive branch had become a part of her. "Very true. Thanks again, by the way."

He shook his head. "Weirdest present I ever got for anybody, but if that's what you wanted."

"It's what I wanted. And I couldn't have done it without you, being underage and all."

Alec grinned. "Yeah, I do know some useful people."

"Useful and unusual," Ginny agreed, remembering the artist that Alec had taken her to. The woman's entire upper body had been covered with various breeds of intertwining dragons.

Alec took a huge bite of his burger. While chewing, he asked her, "So did you do it to tick your mother off?"

"Of course not. Anyway, I think she'll love it."

"Yeah, right. Moms always love tattoos. And your mother in particular is just so darn reasonable."

Her fist tightened. She forced herself to relax it, to draw a deep breath. "Actually, she was going to get one just like this when she was a kid, in honor of her sister. It's a long story."

"She was going to? But she didn't."

"No, but that was just because she was afraid of the needles. Doesn't mean she won't like mine."

"Okay. I want to go in and see you show it to her."

Ginny felt a twinge of pain from her shoulder and of irritation toward Alec all at the same time. Suddenly the tattoo felt wrong, like something that would turn into a festering sore that she would have to show Mom and that would just set them off arguing again. What had she been thinking? She'd been thinking of doing something that would actually impress Mom, of course. But if she was wrong, a tattoo was a pretty permanent mistake. Oh well, at least she didn't have to show it to anyone, if she didn't want to. It would take a pretty skimpy outfit for the tattoo to show.

Alec swallowed the last of his burger and pointed at her fries. "You're not gonna finish those?"

"No."

He grabbed and tossed a couple of them down. It reminded her of a pelican she had seen recently on a nature show, gobbling down a fish. She wondered briefly why in the world she kept going out with this guy. Then he finished eating, wiped his mouth and hands with a napkin, and gathered up all the trash. He turned and grinned at her, and caressed her knee with his hand. Oh yeah, now she remembered why.

"So, your birthday's almost over. Want to go for a drive?"

"I'm supposed to be home soon."

"A quick drive, then."

Ginny shrugged. "Okay. Whatever."

The drive was actually pretty nice for a while. They cranked up the radio and let the windows down. The May evening was cool enough for the breeze to be pleasant.

"Hey, Alec."

"Hey," Alec said, tightening his hand on her knee.

"Ha ha. I just remembered something—something I've been meaning to ask you for a long time." Ignoring the butterflies in her stomach, Ginny continued, "The first time we met, you mentioned that you had seen something—you know, when I was little and came to visit, and there was that crazy scene at Grandma's church."

"Oh, yeah." Alec glanced at her, then back at the road, and she could see his eyes had widened. "I can't believe I'd forgotten that."

"So what did you see?"

"Well, I was down on the floor, helping look under the pews for you—and having the time of my life, I might add. Most interesting church service I ever went to. And I swear to you, I was looking straight at this one spot. One second you weren't there, and the next you were. Poof! Like watching a magician onstage. How did you do it?"

Ginny wasn't sure what she would have said, if she had been able to speak. As it was, she felt the greasy fries burning in her chest and throat, and she clamped her hand to her mouth to keep from puking all over Alec's truck seats. And Alec.

He jiggled her knee. "Come on. Tell me."

Her mind was numb, except for one repeating sentence. *Alec saw it. I really did disappear from the church, go somewhere else…*

Then Ginny felt her stomach muscles tighten even more as she noticed they were approaching her road. "You taking me home already?"

"Umm…no. Not exactly. Whoa! Almost missed it," he said, twisting the wheel to the left so sharply that she bounced against his arm. For a moment she was relieved that, at least, she didn't have to try to change the subject. Then she noticed he appeared to be turning into the woods. As he slowed in front of a gate with a familiar "No Trespassing" sign, she realized it was the overgrown road back to the pond.

"What do you think you're doing?" she asked, knowing full well what he was doing.

Alec had halted in front of the closed gate, but was throwing open his door and preparing to get out, as though he had a plan. He reached across and caressed her knee. "I thought it would be nice to spend a little time together. Nice view of the pond in the moonlight. Just the two of us."

Briefly, Ginny wondered how a normal fifteen-year-old—wait, sixteen-year-old—girl would react to a statement like that. Was she supposed to giggle and flutter her eyelashes? Be flattered that this was how the guy was choosing to celebrate her birthday? Be thrilled at the idea of some kind of rite of passage into womanhood?

But of course, she wasn't normal, was she? Alec's story had just confirmed that.

A normal girl would be feeling nervous right now if she had heard Mom's story about her own trip down this path with her own boyfriend. Shouldn't Ginny be feeling foreboding, or fear at the idea of the dark woods and the strange girl that had come from nowhere?

Apparently Ginny just couldn't manage normal. Because all she felt was extremely annoyed.

"That thing is padlocked, you know," she said. "To keep people like you from breaking their necks or drowning in the pond."

He paused to grin back at her. "Doesn't seem to have been deterring me so far, does it? Remember the day we first met?"

"Vividly."

"Seriously, when's the last time your folks checked the lock?"

"I don't know. It's not ours anymore, anyway."

Ginny watched him in the spotlight of the truck's headlamps, fiddling with the padlock, dropping the chain, and then shoving the heavy gate inward. Pity he was wasting all that effort.

As he slid back into the driver's seat and reached for the gearshift, she gripped his arm. "Wait."

He turned to her with an innocent expression. "What?"

"Did you ever think of asking me whether I want to do this?"

He blinked, looking blank. "Well...we've been hanging out for a while, so I thought...I mean, why wouldn't you want to?"

Ginny let out her breath slowly. "For so many reasons I don't even want to have to list them all."

"Oh, really?" His voice was developing an edge to it.

"Yes, really."

"I see." He sat silent for a moment, facing forward and drumming his fingers on the steering wheel. Apparently he'd been regrouping, because when he twisted around to face her, he was smiling again. Rubbing her arm, he said in a low voice, "I know you don't have much experience, but there's nothing to be scared of, really." With his mouth next to her ear, he whispered, "I'll take good care of you."

"Oh, puh-leeze!" Ginny gave him a shove. "Alec, I really just want to go home, okay?"

He folded his arms. "What is it with you? You're always running after me, but then the minute I show any interest, you get scared and want to run home. Maybe you need to grow up a little before you go out with me anymore."

"Okay. I believe I'll go home and get started on that right now." Throwing open the passenger door, Ginny's feet hit the gravel of the drive and she skidded about a foot and almost fell before she managed to grab the truck's door and steady herself.

Alec was laughing at her from inside. "Calm down, little girl. You don't have to run away from the big bad monster. I'll drive you home."

"No, thank you." She slammed the door shut and walked to the shoulder of the road, turning toward her driveway. She could see a vague outline of her mailbox a couple hundred yards away.

Alec pulled up beside her, rolling down his window and calling out, "Ginny, this is ridiculous. You don't have to go walking down the road in the dark. Get in the truck."

"Contrary to what you think, I'm not the least bit afraid. I'm just seriously ticked off. You, on the other hand, should be terrified, since you're driving on the wrong side of the road."

"All right, then. Fine." The engine screamed as the truck leapt away from her, its headlights quickly disappearing around the curve. Thankfully, he appeared to at least have pulled it into the right lane.

Ginny sighed and started to trudge toward her driveway. Oddly enough, she had told Alec the truth. She didn't feel frightened. The moon was bright, and though trees lined both sides of the road, she could see streetlights peeping through from the new subdivision on her right. And not far away, on the left-hand side, was home.

Home. For once, she felt as though she were going home. Even though Daddy was acting the way that he was, she had to believe it would all get better. With Mom seeming to come to her senses more every day, anything was possible.

By the time she finished her trudge up the driveway, the adrenaline surge that had fueled her tirade against Alec and her optimism had faded, leaving her feeling more shaky and doubtful as she climbed the porch steps. She paused for a moment in front of the door, going over the evening in her mind and trying to prepare for the worst.

One, she had confirmed from Alec that something really bizarre had happened that night in Grandma's church. At least maybe that couldn't get her in trouble tonight. But two, she had gotten a tattoo. And although she had done it in a warm rush of sentiment toward Mom, it now seemed like a really stupid idea. Just another idiot way to pick a fight with Mom. She fingered the sore spot on her shoulder. Maybe she'd better give that one some time and let that remain her secret for now.

Three, she had just offended the only popular person at school who didn't already hate her. A gorgeous jock. The only good thing to come out of her experience at that stupid school. The only boy who had ever shown interest in her. Well…that wasn't entirely true. There was Max.

Part of her wanted to burst out laughing at that thought. But not because it was ridiculous. Because it was…

"Mom!"

The door had popped open suddenly, and Mom was standing there. Ginny sucked in her breath, then relaxed. Mom was smiling.

"Hey," she said. "Where's Alec?"

"Don't know, don't care."

"Uh-oh." Mom stood aside to let Ginny in. "Doesn't sound like you had a very good birthday."

Ginny just shrugged. "I guess not, but I certainly can't say it's the worst day I've had lately."

She headed toward her bedroom, and saw to her surprise that Mom was following her.

As Ginny dropped her purse on the bed and turned, she found Mom standing just the other side of the threshold. For a fleeting moment, there was a kind of struggle in her face, but then she stepped across and into the room.

Ginny felt her face breaking into a smile. "Good for you! You did it!"

Mom laughed, a little sheepishly. "It shouldn't be that hard to come into your daughter's bedroom, should it?"

"But it was, so I…I do appreciate it."

"I just wanted to make sure you're okay. What happened?"

Ginny started to say, "Nothing," and be done with it. Instead, she found herself spilling the whole story. Well, the part about the fight with Alec, anyway. She decided not to bring up the church weirdness…or the tattoo. Somewhere during her sordid tale, she sat down on the edge of her bed, and Mom settled in to the wicker rocker to listen. Ginny was pleased to see nothing but concern in Mom's face as she talked—and even admiration and approval when she reached the part about storming out of Alec's car.

Ginny felt herself glowing with warmth as Mom shook her head and said, "Wow. That's amazing! It's so similar to what I told you the other day, about Hunter pressuring me, only…well, you stood up for yourself. I never seemed to have the confidence to do that."

"I never usually have confidence, either," Ginny mused. "I don't know...Alec's been getting on my nerves for quite a while now. Maybe if I'd been with someone I liked more, I would have let him pressure me into doing whatever he wanted."

"No. I don't believe that. You're a strong girl, Ginny."

Out of the blue, she felt her eyes filling with tears. A picture of herself, lying in bed and waiting for the sickness to hit her, calling out for her mother like a six-year-old, filled her head. "No, I've been terrible lately. I've been so weak and I've done such stupid things."

Slowly, Mom reached out and touched her hand—tentatively at first, looking the same as when she had forced herself to enter Ginny's room. Then she grasped Ginny's hand in both of hers and squeezed. "We all do stupid things. Me more than most. But we're going to be fine. I'm very proud of you tonight."

Ginny sniffed hard and, reaching for a tissue with her free hand, nodded.

Mom cleared her throat and looked around the room, as though searching for a change of subject. When her gaze swept the wall of drawings, Ginny heard her gasp. "Where did you get those!"

Ginny's muscles clenched in an automatic response to the surprise in Mom's voice. Normally, she'd be needing to prepare herself for battle, but she hoped they were past that kind of normal. Trying to sound calm, she said, "They were in a drawer when we moved in. Daddy said you might have sketched them. Did you?"

Mom didn't answer right away. She got to her feet and walked over to study the charcoals, crossing her arms and appearing to look them over the same way she had studied the Monet paintings at the High Museum when she took Ginny to an exhibit a few years back.

Finally she said, "Yes, I did them."

Since Mom didn't sound angry, Ginny slid off the bed and went to stand next to her. "They're amazing. I'd forgotten how good an artist you are."

A trace of a smile touched Mom's lips. "Thanks. I was just a kid when I drew these."

"Who are they? The kids in the pictures, I mean." A quick flash of her disastrous evening with Alec flashed through her mind. She sighed. "I wish guys like this were real."

"What do you mean?"

"You know. These guys look so..." Ginny groped for words,

but couldn't find the right ones to express the way she felt whenever she allowed herself to fall into the world of the drawings. A place not quite real, where anything bold and beautiful might be possible. A place where boys were soulful, or heroic, or larger than life. She blurted out, "You know. Not real-life jerks like Alec Matthews."

To her surprise, Mom burst out laughing. "Oh, honey."

"What?"

Mom jerked her head toward the one with the deep, kind eyes. "That's Hunter Isaacs right there. The one who bossed me around and thought mainly of himself—same as Alec Matthews." She sighed and pushed her heavy blond curls away from her face. "There's nothing new under the sun, I'm afraid."

Ginny felt a stab of disappointment and rather wished she and Mom weren't having this talk. Just in this brief second, the boy's face seemed to be changing, its charcoal lines growing harsher.

Her face softening, Mom touched the face of the girl in one of the drawings, and said to Ginny, "Don't you recognize your Aunt Livvy?"

"Oh, is that who the girl is! I knew she looked sort of familiar, but to be honest, I haven't seen all that many pictures of Aunt Livvy." Observing the soft look on Mom's face as she drank in the picture of her sister, Ginny again thought of the tattoo. She went so far as to tug at the collar of her shirt, wanting to show it to Mom and please her with her tribute to Aunt Livvy—which had been Mom's idea in the first place, according to Ms. Shaw. Again, she stopped herself. And Mom said she was brave. Ha!

Mom turned away from the wall, but she stood with her arms folded, looking out into space, as though not really seeing Ginny. "We used to be a foursome, once upon a time. Livvy and me, Hunter and his brother, Jake. From the time we were little kids."

"Tell me." The words had come out so low, she wasn't sure Mom had heard her. She cleared her throat and tried again. "Tell me."

Mom settled back into the wicker rocker. "Well...we didn't always live in this house, you know."

Ginny shook her head. "I didn't know that."

"I guess we moved here when I was about eight and Livvy ten. Mamma wasn't altogether thrilled about buying this property with the quarry pond on it. And it's true, people do sneak onto land with ponds like ours and do idiotic things, like diving off of cliffs and hitting their heads on rocks, or freezing in water they didn't expect to be so cold, or just plain drowning because there's no one around to save them. So the minute we moved here, she started fussing about us not going back to the pond."

Ginny smiled and dropped down onto her bed again. "So naturally you were dying to check it out."

"Of course." Mom stopped and gave her a stern look. "Just because I'm telling you this doesn't mean that pond isn't dangerous."

Ginny was indignant. "Hey, I had a perfectly nice opportunity to go back to that pond tonight—with a gorgeous guy, at that—and I got out and walked home, didn't I?"

Mom laughed. "Yes, you did. Sorry. Where was I? Oh, yeah…so Livvy and I went exploring, and we got down to the pond, and we did find something really odd."

"Oh yeah. Not as weird as a lost girl with amnesia?"

"No, not that odd, but still…it was pretty strange. There was a tiny gray kitten out in the very middle of that pond, floating on a log. It was squealing its head off."

"A kitten! How did it get there?"

"I have no idea. I was sort of obsessing over that very question, because it frankly freaked me out a little, but Livvy snapped at me that that really wasn't the point. The point was, how were we going to get it out?"

"Neither of you could swim?"

"Yeah, we could, but it was early spring and the water was really cold. Anyway, we were talking over various ideas when we heard a noise in the bushes—giggling, to be exact. I was ready to run back to the house and never disobey Mamma again, but Livvy marched over to the bushes and more or less pulled these two boys out."

Ginny sat up. "They had put that poor kitten out there? And they were laughing about it!"

"No, no—or at least they said they didn't, and we ended up believing them. Supposedly they'd been trying to figure out how to rescue the thing, too, when they heard us coming and hid because they were trespassing. They were laughing because they thought our 'girlie' ideas were idiotic, so they said." Mom snorted. "But guess who ended up rescuing the kitten? Livvy got tired of the talk, and just jumped in and did it. She was nearly frozen, not to mention scratched, when she made it back to shore with the little cat, but she did it. Even the boys were impressed.

"That was the start of the four of us being inseparable, having all kinds of adventures. The three of them were all older than me, but that didn't matter for a while. Not until puberty hit, anyway."

"Did they start leaving you out or acting like they were too old for you, then?"

"Not intentionally. Things change. That's life. The first thing that changed was the way Hunter and Livvy felt about each other."

"Oh, yeah." Ginny could just imagine, the friends growing older, growing up, starting to notice each other in a new way. She sighed as she looked at the pictures, thinking how romantic it all was, until it hit her, and she gasped. "Wait! Hunter and Aunt Livvy? But I thought…you said he was your fiancé."

Mom fidgeted with her hands, picking at the loose wicker on the rocker the way Daddy had done. "Yeah, he was. Eventually. But when they first started to develop feelings for each other, they were fifteen or sixteen. I honestly think I developed a crush on Hunter long before Livvy did, but he didn't think of me that way. I was still just a bratty kid that he put up with, you know?"

"That must have made you feel terrible, when they started dating."

"Well, a little, but it seemed pretty natural to me for Hunter and Livvy to get together. I thought Livvy was the most beautiful, most wonderful girl in the world, so I didn't mind as long as I was still part of the group."

"But they just wanted to be alone together all the time?" Ginny had had that happen to her before, when one of her friends suddenly got a boyfriend and dropped Ginny like a hot potato. Eventually, when the couple broke up, the girlfriend would come running back, but it always hurt. Always seemed so unfair.

"They didn't necessarily want to be alone all the time." Mom laughed, and the sound had a sharp edge to it. "I told you Anna Shaw and I go way back. She moved into town at the worst time possible for me, when the guys were starting to notice girls, but I wasn't old enough yet to be noticed. Anna was something new and fresh, and she was pretty and fun."

"I'm sure you were, too," Ginny said indignantly.

Mom lifted her shoulders, let them drop. "No, not like Anna. So anyway, there was still a foursome, only it didn't include me anymore."

Ginny almost blurted out, "So how did you end up with Hunter?" But she realized just in time and adjusted her question, speaking softly as she said, "So were they still dating when Aunt Livvy died?"

Mom frowned and appeared to be thinking hard. "It's hard to say, really. They dated for a long time—or at least it seemed long back then. But for the last year or so, Livvy was changing. I don't think her focus was on Hunter all that much and, well...it's hard to say whether they broke up or were drifting apart."

"I just realized...I don't know how Aunt Livvy died."

"She had gotten a scholarship to a college in Florida, and she drove down to check it out one weekend, and..." Mom cleared her throat. "There was a car accident, a few miles before she got there."

Mom was getting to her feet. "It's getting late, and I'm pretty tired," she said. Before she went, though, Mom patted her hand and said, "I know I said it before, but I'm proud of you, Ginny. If only I had been as smart as you about boys, well...some bad things might not have happened. You keep it up, okay?"

Mom vanished through the doorway.

CHAPTER SEVENTEEN

As long as they were eating pizza or exploring the used bookstore, Max made an all right companion. After that he was pretty useless. When Ginny slowed down at the second shop window, Max sighed.

Ginny scowled at him. "You make a lousy girlfriend."

"My father will be relieved to hear that."

"Kindly remember this is my birthday outing, so you have to do what I want." Ginny inched down the sidewalk, stopping again outside a hairdresser's window as she sipped her Coke. With all the little noises of frustration Max was making, he sounded like he was about to explode. "Ginny, puh-leeze!"

She vaguely heard him. "Just a minute." Her gaze flickered across the photos of the glamorous models with their wild hair and flaming make-up. An idea started to take shape in her mind. She tilted her head up, then down, studying the different looks. Finally she turned to look at Max. He stood with his arms folded tightly across his chest, glaring at her.

"Go on home, okay?" she said to him. "I decided how I'm gonna spend my birthday money from Mom and Dad."

Now he looked at the pictures of the models. They didn't appear to please him. "You're going to get your hair done?"

"Yep."

"Why?"

"I don't know," she lied. "Because it's fun, I guess."

Max shook his head. "Seems like a waste to me." He walked over to stand beside her. "Which one?"

She pointed. Max studied it for a minute, then turned to her with wide eyes. "You're kidding."

"Nope."

He looked at it again. This time he turned back to her with an expression of hope. "You just mean the cut, right? The bangs? You don't mean the color."

"All of it. Color and all."

"Oh, man."

They were both silent for a minute, drinking in the model's face and hair as though Leonardo Da Vinci had painted her. Finally Max said, "You know you're going to look like a total Goth, right? Is that what you're going for?"

"Oh, don't be silly."

"Then what—"

"Max, it's a girl thing. You wouldn't understand. Just go on home, okay?"

"Are you kidding? I wouldn't miss this for the world."

"It may take a while."

He held up his sack from the bookstore. "I'm good."

Ginny put her hands on her hips. "You are not going to sit in there and watch me have goop put in my hair."

He put up his hands. "Fine, fine. I'll be right here on this bench if you need me."

He plopped himself down on the bench, stretched out his legs, and started to pull his paperback treasures out of the plastic bookstore sack. Ginny opened the hairdresser's door, but paused when Max called her.

"What is it now?" she asked.

"You know your mother's gonna have a fit, don't you? She's gonna hate this?"

Ginny just rolled her eyes and went inside. How could she tell Max that he couldn't be more mistaken? How could he understand that this new look was not a gift for herself, but that she was actually doing it for her mother? Anything to make her look different—less like that Jordan girl that her mother saw in her and feared—had to be a good thing.

Ginny gasped when the hairdresser spun her around to face the mirror and she saw a total stranger staring back at her. A black-and-white, moon-faced stranger. The hairdresser, Nikki, gushed over the outcome. But then, her own spiky strands were an unnatural shade of fuchsia.

Ginny's bangs had been cut so they brushed straight across her eyebrows. The rest of her hair had been tormented into submission with blow dryer and brush until it hung docile and straight. Its black surface shone like a dark jewel, like a table made of slick onyx. By itself, it did have a kind of beauty.

"But I look so pale," Ginny protested.

"That's because you're not wearing any make-up." Nikki stood behind her, placed her hands on either side of Ginny's face, and tilted her head. "You have a perfect blank canvas. You won't believe how the colors will just pop now." She reached for something on the cluttered countertop—a lipstick tube. She rolled it so the bright crimson color showed. "Do you mind?"

When Ginny walked outside, she found Max lying on his back on the bench, holding up his graphic novel an arm's length above his face. He glanced toward her, then back to his book.

"Max. It's me."

He turned his head toward her. He dropped his book, which smacked him on the nose and then fell to the sidewalk. He sat up and rubbed his nose, but mostly he stared at her.

"Oh, sh—" He caught himself. She knew he was trying not to cuss. "Oh wow. I mean, wow."

Ginny's stomach fluttered as she pictured Daddy going through this same shock. No, worse. Max had been expecting it. "Okay, so it's a shock. But how does it look?"

"Oh, wow."

"Yeah, you said that already. Could you be more specific?"

"You look so…old."

Ginny threw up her hands. "Old? Old people have gray hair and wrinkles." She grabbed up a handful of her hair. "They do not have hair like this."

"I didn't mean gray hair old." Max's face reddened. "I meant like college or something. You know, like…a sophisticated woman."

"Oh. I guess that's not so bad." She shifted her shoulder bag, settling it higher up on her arm. "Come on. I better be getting home."

When they pulled up outside her house, Max turned to her and grinned. "Can I stay and watch the fun?"

Ginny jerked on the door handle. "Go home, Max."

Ginny's steps slowed as she approached the front steps. She could see the truck under the shelter, so Daddy was definitely home. She wasn't so worried about Mom for once, but Daddy had been known to freak out just because he thought she was wearing too much make-up. And Nikki had piled it on her pretty good. The hair and make-up together might just put him back in the hospital. She pulled out a Kleenex and wiped at her cheeks and lips. She didn't have a mirror. She just had to hope that helped.

She pushed open the door a crack. The old hinges creaked as she tried to peek inside, trying to gauge who was where. Creeping into the hallway, she heard dishes clanging in the kitchen. Probably Daddy. He'd taken to doing most of the cooking lately. Mom's bedroom door was closed. That's how she spent much of her time lately, behind her closed bedroom door. Ginny stood for a moment in indecision. She could slink into her room and put off the inevitable, but she hated dreading things. She squared her shoulders. No, better to face the shock right now and move on past it. She looked from Mom's doorway toward the kitchen, then back again. Probably smarter to at least have Mom on her side before facing Daddy.

She tapped on Mom's doorway and heard a groggy "Come in." She pushed open the door. The blinds were completely shut, blocking out most of the afternoon sun. She searched for her mother in the gloom and assumed that the lumpy form on the bed was her.

"Mom?"

The woman lifted her head. Ginny stood silhouetted in the light from the hallway, so Mom could no doubt see that something was different. She raised up to a sitting position and fumbled for the lamp switch, knocking over a water glass in the process. Ginny looked at the rivulets of water streaming down the nightstand as the room burst into light, but Mom ignored the mess. Her eyes were fixed on Ginny. She blinked as though trying to clear the sleep away. "Am I dreaming?" she whispered.

Ginny shook her head. "No. I got my hair colored, that's all.

Mom, are you okay?" She took a step toward the bed. Mom scrambled backwards across it, her bare feet and legs shoving the covers to the floor in her haste.

Ginny had the urge to flee, herself, but she made herself go to her mother, who had drawn her knees up to her chest and buried her face against them, blocking out the view that was obviously so upsetting. Ginny shook her head. What now?

"Mom?" She gingerly touched her hand to the woman's arm, then jumped as she snapped her head up and grabbed at Ginny.

On the second try, she got her fingers around Ginny's wrist, and she hung on. "What have you done with my daughter?"

Suddenly everything turned around. Ginny was backing toward the door, wild-eyed, with Mom coming after her. In fact, Ginny sort of pulled her along as she tried to get away, because the woman wasn't letting go. Her nails were digging into Ginny's flesh.

Ginny started to whimper. "Mom, it's me."

"I know who you are. I know why you're here, but it's because of me. Me! Ginny has nothing to do with it. You give me my daughter back."

Ginny jerked her wrist, and it came free of the crazed woman's grip. Immediately, Mom started flailing at her with the flat of her hands. Ginny threw her arms up, trying to shield her face, and she felt the slaps, the sting of Mom's fingernails scratching the backs of her hands. She jerked and twisted and backed toward the door, crying out as she managed to hit her head against the edge of the open door in the process. And then other hands pulled at her, gripping her waist and dragging her into the hallway. Now she screamed in earnest.

Daddy's voice boomed in her ear as the hands let her go. "Ginny, get into the New Room and close the door!"

She lurched and swayed as everything seemed to halt. No pulling, no slapping hands. She dropped her fingers from her eyes and saw Daddy roughly pushing Mom backward into her bedroom.

"Daddy, stop it!"

He briefly glanced at her, looking so angry she shrank back. "Ginny, I'll handle this. Get in the other room."

She saw Mom drop to the floor, her back against the bed and her face once again buried against her knees, shutting out the light. Then Daddy slammed the bedroom door.

Ginny ran for the phone in the kitchen and stabbed at the digits.

Ringing. Ringing. "Oh, please answer, please, please—"

"Hello?"

At the sound of Max's voice, she burst into tears. "Max!"

"Ginny?"

"Go get your mom, okay? Now."

CHAPTER EIGHTEEN

"You come up with anything?" Max asked her.

Ginny glanced up from her laptop to look at him. They were sitting at either end of her dining table, and she could barely see him over the tower of books in front of him. Just a couple of eyes peering over the top. In spite of her mood, she smiled and said, "I don't think even Google can compete with that pile."

"I hope that's not true." He sighed and pushed the books aside. "These things are so out of date. One book still calls Iran Persia. I swear, if they want to assign us these stupid papers, you'd think they'd have some appropriate books in the library." He looked at her and repeated his question. "So you haven't found anything, either?"

"No, not really." She dropped her gaze back to the keyboard and felt herself flush, even though she had technically told the truth. Her searching hadn't turned up any answers—but then she hadn't been looking for information on the current state of politics in Iran. She'd been looking for information on Jordan.

She didn't have much hope when she started. She had so little to go on. Just that one name, really. "Jordan." Try typing that into Google and see how many hits you have to wade through. She tried everything else she could think of. The name of her town and the phrase "unidentified girl." "Lost girl." "Missing girl." She tried her mother's maiden name but came up with nothing. Finally she went to the local newspaper's online archives in hopes of browsing the year or two in question, and found that the stories only went back to the mid nineties.

She jerked her head up as a shadow fell over the computer. Max was standing over her, looking down at the screen.

He snorted. "No wonder you're not finding anything useful. We're doing Iran, not Jordan."

"Oh, I—no, I'm sorry." She folded the screen down and closed the laptop with a click. "I couldn't concentrate on the project."

"I know."

She looked up again and found Max studying her with nothing but concern in his big blue puppy eyes. He really did have very nice eyes.

The doorbell rang. They both fell quiet, listening as Ginny's dad opened the front door and greeted someone. A second later, Ms. Shaw swept into the kitchen with Daddy trailing behind, an idiotic grin on his face. Ms. Shaw's hands were wrapped in oven mitts and she carried a large casserole dish.

Max frowned at her. "What are you doing here?"

"Me?" Banging the dish down on the counter, she smiled archly. "I swear, Max, you're over here so much folks are gonna think Ginny's your girlfriend."

Max's mouth tightened into a straight line. "Oh, really? Then I guess folks will think Mr. Crosby is your boyfriend, huh?"

Max flushed as silence fell and the two adults glared at him. Judging by the look Ms. Shaw was giving him, Max was in for a beating when they got home. At least a verbal one. The woman put her hands on her hips. "That was a terrible thing to say. Ben and Ginny need our help while Rose is in the hospital."

Max flipped open the top book. "And here I am. Helping."

Ginny could feel Daddy staring at her. *While Rose is in the hospital.* Also known as loony bin. The thought made her head feel heavy on her neck, as though she'd never be able to lift it again.

Daddy cleared his throat. "Ginny and I appreciate you both very much. I don't know what we would have done without you. Isn't that right, Ginny?"

With effort, she nodded her heavy head.

A couple of hours later, Ginny held up the now-empty casserole dish and watched the soapy water drip off of it. Burnt-on cheese stuck to the glass sides like cement. Ginny grabbed a scouring pad and attacked it, scrubbing it as though this very dish was responsible for everything that was wrong in her life right now.

"Whoa, whoa!" Daddy set down the dirty glasses he was carrying and pulled the casserole pan away from her. "That's glass. You don't use that pad on glass."

Ginny didn't answer him. She folded her arms and watched him as he took a washrag and efficiently cleaned up the dish the right way. Everything he did was so blasted efficient. She had a sudden memory of her and Mom in the kitchen of the apartment, making Christmas cookies. Mom's cookies were fabulous, melt-in-your mouth wonders, and the decorations she invented turned them into works of art. They had laughed and played in colored frosting and sprinkles and wrecked the kitchen, then collapsed on the floor under the tree with warm sugar cookies and milk. They would have cleaned up, the two of them together, but in their own way and own time—okay, Mom's time. Instead, Daddy jumped in immediately and fixed it. He didn't say anything, but the noise of him slamming around in the kitchen somehow ruined the taste of the cookies.

Ginny unfolded her arms and nervously watched Daddy putting up dishes. "So. Is it true?"

Daddy paused with his hand on a cabinet door and looked at her. "What?"

"Are you Ms. Shaw's boyfriend?"

"Ginny!" He slammed the door shut. "What's gotten into you?"

She felt herself starting to shake. "I know how you feel about Mom."

He slapped the dishrag onto the counter. "Ginny, she might have killed you."

"She's not evil."

"I know that, but she's very disturbed."

Ginny picked up the dishrag and rubbed at the countertop, watching her fingers move instead of looking at her dad's face. "So where is she, exactly?" Daddy didn't answer. Ginny glanced up at him. "Well?"

He drew a deep breath. "You don't really need to know that."

"Why not?"

Daddy laughed harshly. "Do you remember the effect you had on her last time she saw you?"

"I know that. I don't have to go see her right away. But I'd still like to know where she is."

"Why?"

Ginny felt hot tears started to spill out of her eyes. "Why? Because she's my mother, that's why, and I want to know she's all right."

"She's being well taken care of. It's a nice hospital. She'll get the rest and the help she needs."

"How far away is it?"

"Ginny, please."

Ginny tore off a paper towel and wiped roughly at her eyes. "So when she gets out of this lovely hospital and she's not disturbed anymore, will everything be like it used to? Will you love her again?"

"Ginny." He rubbed his forehead, as though her questions hurt. "It's not that simple, okay?"

"Why not?"

"Because I don't know what's going to happen. I don't know how long it'll take your mother to get well—or whether she even wants to get well." He took his hand away from his forehead and met Ginny's gaze. "But I can tell you one thing. I will not allow you to be hurt. I'll have to have some pretty strong guarantees that your mother is over these delusions before I'll ever allow her near you again."

CHAPTER NINETEEN

Ginny leaned against Max's car and waited for him to get out of his last class. Mr. Pace always droned on past the bell. She shifted her heavy backpack and wiped her sweaty bangs—her sweaty Goth-black bangs—out of her face. A couple of cheerleaders walked past on the way to their own cars. They glanced at her, then quickly looked away as she met their gaze. They walked by with their heads close together, whispering. Whether they wanted her to hear was anybody's guess, but she heard enough. "So this is what happens when you get kicked off the basketball team," one of them hissed.

It was the whispers she couldn't quite make out that really got to her. When only a word here and there made its way to her, and her imagination filled in the rest. But then, she had certainly given them plenty of fodder, hadn't she? New girl at school. She makes the basketball team. She has a meltdown and gets kicked off the basketball team. Takes up with the local Geek/weirdo/Jesus freak. Dyes her hair black. Has a crazy mother. Yeah, she'd talk too if she were in their shoes. She looked down at her flip-flops. Trouble was, she wasn't in their shoes.

Max came jogging up, huffing a little under the strain. She smiled at him. "You didn't have to hurry. I know how old Pace is."

He waved off her words. "Yeah, he's a pompous old coot. But that's not why I was hurrying. I just had a thought."

"Yeah?"

"I know you bombed out trying to find newspaper articles about that girl online, but just because they're not on the Web doesn't mean they're not out there, you know?"

"What do you mean?"

"I called the public library. They've got the paper on microfilm all the way back to the fifties."

"Micro...what?"

He rolled his eyes. "I'll explain later. Let's go."

Actually, a friendly librarian explained the microfilm and showed them how to thread the big, scary-looking readers. Each spool of film held three months' worth of papers, so Ginny and Max split up a few reels from the early eighties. Ginny found the lighted pages on the screen to be fascinating—so much more interesting than most of the stuff she found online. Something about the grainy black and white pages, the low hum of the machine and the quiet of the library, the glow of the screen around the ads for hair salon perms and old movies back when they were new, and stories about the Reagan-Mondale presidential election when it was real and serious, not just history.

Max tapped her on the shoulder. "Don't stop to read everything. We'll never get through this."

"Okay, okay."

She had only been forcing herself to focus and turn quickly through the pages for a couple of minutes when, this time, Max broke her concentration.

"Oh my G—oh, wow."

"What is it?" Ginny asked, wondering what had almost made Max take the Lord's name in vain, as he put it.

"You're not gonna believe this."

She jumped to her feet and leaned over his shoulder to get a view of his screen. She had to shift positions a couple of times, trying to see the image through the layers of glass and dust and glare from the bright modern lights. Then she found it, just the right position so the picture popped into view, like a swimmer's face rising to the surface of the water and suddenly breaking through. She gasped and dug her fingers into Max's shoulder. The swimmer's face was her own.

The oval lines of the face in the photo were hers, as were the slightly pointy chin and the too-skimpy eyelashes. This girl tilted her head the same way Ginny did when she was confused. In fact, the girl's eyes appeared groggy and dazed—probably exactly like Ginny's right about now. The only difference Ginny noticed right off was a bandage on the girl's forehead. Most amazing of all, the girl's hair appeared to be dead black, and it hung straight to her shoulders with the bangs brushing across her eyebrows. The exact haircut, the exact color that Ginny had gotten a few days ago.

"Ginny."

She felt Max's fingers on hers, trying to unlatch her from his shoulder. She unclenched her fingers. "Sorry."

"It's okay." He studied her face, then stood up and motioned to the chair. "Here. You sit down."

She did it. She probably would have done anything anyone told her to right about now. She felt incapable of logical thought, herself. She tried to focus on the words, but the words seemed to drift randomly around the page, as though they were swimming around underwater the way the girl's face had earlier.

"Max, what does it say? Is it her?" She swallowed hard. "Is it Jordan?"

Max pulled the chair from the other microfilm reader and sat down next to her. His eyes rapidly skimmed the words. Apparently they were holding still for him. "They didn't know her name. It says some kids found her wandering next to the road—"

"Mom and her boyfriend," Ginny whispered. She rubbed her forehead, feeling her new bangs. Did Mom ever tell her Jordan had black hair? Of course not, she couldn't have, because Ginny had been trying very hard to look different from Jordan, hadn't she?

"The girl had a head injury and was dazed. They're asking anyone who might be able to identify her to contact the police and—oh. This is interesting." Max looked up at her. "It says she had a tattoo. You don't have a tattoo, do you?"

Ginny didn't move. Her fingers were clenched as tightly to the sides of the chair as they had been dug into Max's shoulder earlier.

"I mean, because this is really funny. This would pretty much clinch the thing, because it says here that the tattoo is—"

"A dove with an olive branch."

Max's forehead crinkled as he stared at her, waiting for her to explain. Instead of saying anything, she lifted her hair, shifted the elastic of her peasant blouse and exposed the tattoo she had gotten on her birthday.

Max blushed, but he couldn't seem to take his eyes away. He leaned in closer. Now it was his turn to whisper. "Oh, man."

Ginny sat on the low wall outside the library and watched the shopkeepers on the town square locking up for the day. They traded greetings and, apparently, jokes. Their laughter floated clearly down the street and to Ginny's ears, but their words sounded fuzzy and far away. Then a loud pop sounded right next to her, and she jumped and whirled around to find Max opening a Coke can.

"Sorry," he said. "Didn't mean to sneak up on you." He gave the opened can to her, then popped open a Dr. Pepper for himself.

"You didn't sneak up on me." She automatically took a sip of the drink but could barely taste it. The cold felt good in her mouth, though, so she held the icy can against her throbbing forehead. "I'm just kind of in a daze."

"I can't imagine why." He sat down next to her on the wall. "So why did you get a tattoo?"

Ginny started to laugh—weakly at first, but then it just got funnier and funnier. "Oh, Max," she gasped. "You are amazing. Out of everything that's going on, that's what you want to know?"

He shrugged. "I guess I was trying to start with something simple." He gulped down what must have been half of the Dr. Pepper, then smacked his lips together and looked at her, waiting.

Ginny breathed in deeply, trying to calm herself after the hysterical laughter. "Okay...believe it or not, I originally thought I was doing it for my mom."

"Where in the world did you get an idea like that?"

"From your mom, actually—I mean, from Ms. Shaw," she amended quickly, seeing the dark look Max gave her at the word "mom." "Anyway, she told me that back when she and my mother were young, they made a plan on a dare to go get tattoos. And my mother was going to get an olive branch in honor of her sister Livvy who passed away—her full name was Olive Anne. Anyway, Mom and I had actually started getting along again, and I wanted to do something nice, and I don't know...I guess I wanted to do something the popular girls do, too. Who knows? Anyway, I did it on the spur of the moment on my birthday, but then for some reason, I was scared to show it to Mom after I got it."

Max snorted. "And a good thing, too. If she freaked out over your hair color, can you imagine what she would have done if she had seen that tattoo?"

Ginny shuddered. "Mom told me about finding Jordan, but not all that much about what she looked like. With all the fuss she was making, I assumed she looked just like me—like I used to." Looking into Max's thoughtful blue eyes, she felt a little steadier, and before she could think about it, she blurted, "I'm so glad you're here."

"Are you kidding? I wouldn't have missed this for the world."

She laughed. "That's what you said about my hair cut."

"That was pretty good. But this is much better."

Her smile flattened. She felt her stomach flutter and felt queasy. Max, bless him, grew serious, too. She asked him, "So what does this mean?"

"I don't know exactly, but I do know one thing." He looked down at the top of his Dr. Pepper can and traced his finger around its circular top, almost as though he were reading tea leaves. He looked up at her again. "Your mother's not crazy."

CHAPTER TWENTY

Ginny was supposed to be doing homework as she sat at one end of the kitchen table. Daddy was supposed to be sitting at the other end, writing out checks and paying bills. Neither was working out. Daddy paced around with the cordless phone, arguing with one of his suppliers. Ginny kept lifting her notebook, sneaking peeks at the printout of Jordan's face.

Twice she had started to pull it out and show it to Daddy, hoping an adult could figure this thing out and explain it to her. Twice she had pushed it back under the notebook. Her mother was an intelligent adult, and she'd landed in a mental hospital trying to figure this out. Anyway, the printout from the microfilm wasn't as clear as she would have liked. She wished she had an original of the newspaper to show him.

Daddy hung up the phone and sat down across from her. He picked up the top envelope on the pile in front of him and ripped it open. He scanned the pages for a few seconds, shaking his head the whole time. "I swear, Rose barely landed at that place before they started sending the bills. If she's there very long, they'll bleed us dry."

She watched as he tore into a couple more envelopes, muttering the whole time. Nervously tapping her pen against her notebook, she said, "How long do you think she'll be there?"

"What? Oh...I don't know, Ginny. Let's not start all that again, okay?" The phone rang again. He jerked it up and punched the button. "Hello? You gotta be kidding me! How could they not have our order?" He sat in silence for a minute, frowning, then shoved the chair back, got up and started to pace again. He stopped at the kitchen window, peering out as he talked.

Ginny stared at the papers he had dropped when he answered the phone. He still wouldn't tell her where Mom was, and she desperately needed her mother right now. She glanced at Daddy's back, then slid her hand across the table and took hold of the top paper, turning it so she could hopefully read it.

The columns of tiny numbers and letters swam under her hurried gaze. She tried to calm down and focus, but this thing was like a maze made of ink. She looked for a logo and for a moment thought she had been rewarded, then realized that it was the insurance company's info, not the hospital's. This must be some kind of statement about what they would pay. But surely they would have to spell out *who* they were paying somewhere, right? The name of a doctor or hospital had to be here somewhere—

She jumped and gasped as the paper was jerked from her hand. Daddy was towering over her, holding the paper in his hand and frowning. "Ginny, I asked you to let this go."

"How can I just let it go, like it doesn't matter? She's my mother, and it's my fault." She swallowed hard, forcing back the tears that were threatening. "Anyway, what if Mom is right?"

"Don't be silly."

"I'm serious, actually."

"So you honestly believe you're being possessed or taken over by some girl your mother knew twenty-five years ago?"

"I don't know," she mumbled. "I don't know what's happening."

"Ginny, I can tell you what's happening, because it's happened before. Your mother has had…problems…off and on throughout her life."

"Not like this."

"What do you know about it?"

"She told me. About the times she's been in the hospital. But it wasn't through her whole life, and anyway, she was mostly depressed."

"This kind of thing runs in her family, Ginny. Her father was a pretty strange old bird from what I hear. Her sister, too."

"That would be my grandfather you're talking about. And my aunt."

"Yeah…"

She looked at him sharply. "So that's the point you're trying to make? That my whole family on Mom's side has been insane, and so if I say something you don't like, I'm probably crazy, too?"

"I didn't say anything like that." He sighed and, pulling out the chair next to her, sort of fell into it. "I'm pretty sure it was your mother making you sick for the past few months." He added quickly, "I don't think she can help it, mind you. In her own way, she's sick, too."

"And all this is because of seeing that insulin injector on the kitchen counter that night?"

"Not just that, but everything together. The way your mother obviously feels about you."

"You're wrong."

"Wrong?"

"Mom didn't hurt me, not with that insulin injector or anything else. Which means she didn't hurt you, either."

"Ginny, listen—"

"No, you listen." The chair screeched across the linoleum as she jumped up. "This one, at least, I can prove."

Running to her room, she grabbed her old teddy bear and headed back to the kitchen. Daddy looked bewildered as she started to rip stuffing out of it. "Ginny, are you okay?"

"I am now, but..." She ripped the injector pen from the bear's innards and threw it on the table. "I wasn't when I was giving myself shots with this."

Daddy cursed. He hardly ever cursed, especially when he knew she was listening, so she knew he was beyond shock. He stared at her, wide-eyed, then looked down at the injector pen as though it were a snake. Reaching out a finger, he touched it gingerly, still looking as though he expected it to bite him.

"Don't worry. It can't hurt you. It's empty."

"But...but...you were making yourself sick?"

She nodded. "Not just with that thing. Even before we moved, I...well, I did several disgusting things that I won't go into. Finding that injector pen when we moved in was just a bonus."

"Ginny, you could have killed yourself! Are you..." His voice trailed off.

"Am I insane? Is that what you were going to say?"

"No, no, of course not."

"Well, according to you, insanity runs in the family and I'm the next in line for it."

"I did not say that. Ginny, I…frankly, I don't know what to say, but I'm scared to death." He tilted his head to one side, studying her. "Why? I just don't understand…why would you make yourself sick on purpose?"

For a moment, Ginny sat silent, thinking back. "I guess it started a few months ago, when I fell on the stairs, remember?"

Daddy nodded.

"Mom had already been acting funny toward me for a while—"

"Yeah, I know."

"So you know how it was. She wouldn't talk to me, or do anything with me. She would barely look at me. It was as though I didn't exist. But then when I fell, she came running. She fussed over me and took me to the doctor. I know this is awful, and it makes me sound like I am crazy…or at least like I'm about five years old. But I liked it. I liked her fussing over me. But a couple of days later, I was well and she was over it. So…" Ginny shrugged. "I decided to fake it."

"Oh, Ginny," Daddy moaned, leaning his face in his hands. "Why didn't you just come to me?"

"I did depend on you for a long time. To tell you the truth, that's why I was so desperate to get on the basketball team the minute we moved here. Basketball was something we could share. But…I don't know. I still wanted Mom. And it wasn't just about me. Most of the time, it brought the two of you together, too. You'd both rally around me and…it was the only way I knew to bring the family together again."

Fear darkened Daddy's eyes. "So…did you make me sick that night, too? What was the point of that?"

Ginny rolled her eyes. "No, Daddy. I didn't poison you and neither did Mom. Give it up, will you? Sometimes we really do just get sick."

Daddy got to his feet, somehow looking older and tireder than when he sat down. He went to the sink and turned on the faucet, first splashing a little on his face, then filling a glass and taking a big gulp. Finally he turned back to her. "This has got to stop, Ginny."

"It already has stopped," she said. "The pen is empty and, anyway, it didn't work anymore. Mom started ignoring me when I was sick, too, and that just made y'all fight more. It was pointless."

He shook his head. "No, that's not good enough. I can't just let this go. We've got to get you some help."

Her laughter sounded harsh in her ears. "Like you're helping Mom, you mean? Fine, stick me in the loony bin with her. Maybe at least I'll get to see her, then."

Slamming the door behind her, she ran out into the cool evening air, breathing in deep gulps of it and trying to calm herself. She looked around vaguely, wishing she could drive. Wishing she had a car and she could jump in and just leave, just hit the interstate and head to Florida and the beaches. Or at least that she lived in the city and could go somewhere. She could walk back to the pond, she supposed, but that didn't sound all that appealing right now.

Ginny was taking her frustrations out on her basketball, slamming it rhythmically into the concrete of the driveway and calling it dribbling, when Max appeared. She captured the ball and hugged it to her chest, moving out of his way as he parked under the hoop at the top of the drive. He threw up his hand in greeting as he climbed out of the car.

She nodded toward him, still hugging the ball. "I didn't know you were coming over."

"I know, I should have called."

"No, it's okay. I'm glad you're here."

He beamed, his whole face lighting up at her words. Uh-oh. She hoped she hadn't given him the wrong impression. She cleared her throat. "So what's up?"

"Well, partly I just wanted to make sure you're okay."

She smiled wanly. "Oh yeah. Fabulous."

He sat down on one of the porch steps. "I also wanted to tell you I bombed out on finding an original of that picture, at least as of now. I went to the newspaper office, but their records are on microfilm, too. They said we could maybe try the historical society."

"Oh."

He peered up into her eyes. "You don't sound very interested."

"Oh, I'm interested, it's just…" She sat down on the step just below him, laying the ball down next to her feet. "To tell you the truth, I'm more interested in finding my mother."

"She's not really lost, is she?"

"She is to me. Daddy refuses to tell me where she is. He thinks

I'll go barging in to see her somehow—and of course that's exactly what I want to do. He's sure she'd have a meltdown at the very sight of me, but—" Now it was Ginny looking up at Max. "I think if I could just talk to her, could tell her that she was right and she isn't insane, everything would be all right, don't you?"

Max leaned over his knees and fidgeted with his shoe laces. "I don't know, Ginny. I don't know if it would be that easy."

"You said yourself she's not crazy."

"Not in thinking you're Jordan, no. But—"

Ginny stiffened. "But what?"

"Well, just because we saw that picture doesn't mean we've figured out what's going on, does it?"

"No, but…obviously there's nothing for her to be afraid of anymore."

"So you're not afraid?"

Defiantly, she held his gaze for a moment, but then she broke and looked down. "I'm terrified."

"Of course you are."

Her gaze fell on the basketball lying at her feet. She grabbed for it, but had trouble making her trembling fingers grab hold of it. Good thing she didn't have a team to let down anymore.

"So you think I should be scared?" she asked him, realizing she sounded harsh, but somehow unable to stop herself. "You think like Mom did, that some girl from the past is taking me over?"

Max shook his head. "No, of course not. That doesn't make any sense."

Ginny laughed. "Of course this doesn't make sense. Did that just now occur to you?"

"No," Max said, not seeming to notice her sarcasm. "But I've been thinking, and I've decided your mother has it all backwards."

"What do you mean?"

"Jordan isn't coming from the past to haunt her. I think you're going to go back there."

"Huh?"

Max paused, apparently for dramatic emphasis, then announced, "Time travel."

"What?"

"I think you're going back there, to 1984."

Ginny started to laugh. Ignoring Max's indignant protests, she laughed until she could hardly gasp for breath. She tried to stand up, but collapsed back onto the steps, doubled over with giggles.

When she finally calmed down, he was still sitting on the steps, chin propped in his hands and watching her. "So, you finished?" he said.

"I guess."

"So now that you're finished mocking me, think about it logically and tell me where I'm wrong."

"Because it's impossible, that's why."

Max took his copy of the microfilmed article from his pocket. "Ginny, a week ago, would you have thought this was possible?"

She stared down at the wrinkled paper in her lap and didn't feel the least bit like laughing anymore. "No."

"Me either. But now...well, I'm having to rethink a lot of things."

"But Max...okay. Let's just say for a minute your crazy theory is true. Why wouldn't I remember any of this stuff from 1984, like Mom does? How come she remembers it and I don't?"

Max frowned. "Don't you ever read any science fiction?"

"Yeah, sometimes."

Max made a "tsking" sound. "Then you should understand how time travel works. This has already happened in your mom's life, but it hasn't happened to you yet." Ginny stared at him blankly, so he went on, "Look, think of 1984 as a place—a place that you're going to visit, but you haven't yet. Your mom is from that place, so she's able to tell you all about it."

Ginny sat for a moment, twisting her hair and trying to absorb this.

As he got to his feet, Max sighed. "Your mother's been through a lot. She's been scared, and she's been told she's insane so many times. She's probably made herself sick by now. Maybe you should leave her alone for a while."

"But she needs to know."

Max nodded slowly. "That's true."

"And I need her to know." Ginny jumped to her feet and grabbed the basketball, throwing it wildly in the general direction of the hoop. It missed, of course, and banged into the garage door. She cursed.

"Ginny, please—"

She whirled on him. "I need my mother, Max. Do you understand that? I might as well have been some kind of demon sent to destroy her life, because that's exactly what I've done." The feeling of hot tears on her face surprised her. "Blast it! All I seem to do lately is cry."

"That's not true. You throw a lot of temper tantrums, too."

She jerked her hands away from her eyes and glared at him. He took a step back and held up his hands. "Don't hurt me," he said. But the sides of his mouth were twitching.

She found herself smiling, too. "What would I do without you, Max?"

"You got me."

"Yeah, I do." She stepped toward him, and this time he held his ground. She pulled him into a hug. "Thank you."

For a moment he didn't seem to know what to do. Then she felt his arms go around her, holding her in an embrace that was warm and safe and wonderful.

She pulled away from him as a truck swung into the driveway. Oh, great. Alec.

She watched in wonder as he somehow managed to swagger just getting out of his vehicle.

He folded his arms and studied her and Max. "Well, don't y'all look sweet?"

"What are you doing here, Alec?"

He frowned, as though puzzled. "Just coming to see my girl, obviously."

She scoffed. "Have you forgotten the other night?"

"No," he said, "but I'm prepared to forgive you."

Ginny felt her mouth drop open.

"Look, Matthews," Max said, "she doesn't want anything else to do with you."

Alec guffawed. "What, she prefers you now?" He glared at Ginny, while still talking to Max. "Well, maybe that makes sense, you know? You're a freak and so is she. I should have known…"

Alec ranted on, and Max answered him again, but Ginny quit listening. She turned, climbed the porch steps, and went inside.

Her phone rang a few minutes later, as she lay limply across her bed. She started not to answer, but then saw it was Max and decided she better make sure he was alive. "Hello?"

"You okay?"

"Stop asking me that, like I'm going to disappear into some kind of space-time void at any minute."

"All right, all right."

"So you two didn't kill each other?"

"Nah. Matthews lost steam when you seemed so completely disinterested. Hey—thanks for all your support, by the way."

"Sorry. I just don't have much support to give right now."

"Yeah, well…anyway, since we got interrupted, I didn't get to tell you the main thing I came for."

"Oh, really." She was aware the words came out flat, disinterested. But that's still how she felt.

"I didn't find that picture we were talking about, but I did look at some more microfilm. I found a longer story that identified your mother and a guy named Hunter Isaacs as the kids who found Jordan."

"Yeah, he was Mom's fiancé." She sat up, feeling a little pique of interest in spite of herself.

"Not just that, but I looked him up and—get this. He still lives here in town. I don't have his home address, but his office is right off the square. He's a lawyer."

Ginny's brain still felt sluggish. She wouldn't have been able to say what she thought about Max's news, but on some deeper level, she knew. Her hands started shaking so hard she dropped the phone. Jerking it back up, she started babbling before she could even get the receiver near her mouth. "What do you think I should do? Go see him? I mean…do you think I could?"

"I think we can," Max said, emphasizing "we."

"Thank you, Max. When?"

"How about after school tomorrow?"

"School." Ginny sighed. "How am I going to sit through school with all this going on?"

"At least it's the last day before summer. You can put up with one day."

"Maybe. I thought it was bad trying to concentrate when my folks were bickering all the time, but it's quiet as a tomb around here now and I think it's worse."

"Yeah, it's pretty quiet over here, too," Max said, "but I haven't accomplished much this evening."

"Kelsey's not home studying?"

Max snorted. "You must be joking. I never have a clue where she is, but she's seldom here. Dad and The Woman are out tonight, too. She made him take her out to dinner."

"Oh, she forced him, huh?" Ginny said the words automatically, but her mind was running on another track…down the stairs from Max's bedroom, into the study that was Anna Shaw's office.

Ginny sat up straight at the thought of the house, totally empty except for Max…and Anna's records.

"Max!"

"Yeah?"

He sounded startled, and she knew she had broken into him talking about something, but she didn't have a clue what.

"I just thought of something," she said. "Does your stepmother keep her office door locked?"

"She's not my stepmother."

"Okay, whatever. Does she or not?"

"I don't know, actually. It's always closed, and it's not like I've tried to get in."

"So go try it and tell me. Or—oh, never mind." Ginny jumped to her feet. "I'm coming right over."

CHAPTER TWENTY-ONE

Max put his hand on the doorknob at Ms. Shaw's office, and after the slightest hesitation, gave it a turn. "It's unlocked," he said. He sounded quite glum about it.

Ginny felt like shouting with joy. She reached past him and pushed open the door. "Look, you can just go back upstairs if you want to. If I get caught, you can tell them I said I was going to the kitchen to get a drink and you had no idea what I was up to."

"No. We can do it faster if we both look. Anna's pretty disorganized. There's no telling where your mom's records will be."

"I don't want you to get in any trouble."

"I think I've been in trouble since the moment I first laid eyes on you."

That was either an insult or the sweetest thing anyone had ever said to her, but Ginny didn't have time to figure it out now.

"Max—"

"If we're gonna do it, let's do it," he said, easing through the doorway and into the dark study.

He didn't turn a light on, but instead handed Ginny one of two flashlights he had grabbed. Max seemed surprised that the file cabinets were actually neatly labeled, so it was pretty easy to tell which one should have Mom's file. Unfortunately, the drawer was locked.

"Oh, great," Ginny said. "What now?"

Max gazed around the room. "We need to find the key. Try to think like Anna." He gave an exaggerated shudder. "Oh, the horror."

Ignoring him, Ginny opened and shut the desk drawers that weren't secured. Paper clips, pens, breath mints. She did find a couple of little keys, but they didn't fit the file cabinet. They just wasted her time.

"Let me try those," Max said.

She tossed the keys to him, and watched vacantly as he bent down to a credenza behind the desk. Would Ms. Shaw hide the keys? Ginny wondered as her gaze went around the room to the books on the shelves, the ornamental porcelain boxes on tables. No, that didn't make sense. This was an office, not a pirate ship.

"Hey!" Max called suddenly, pulling out a heap of papers.

Ginny drew in a sharp breath. "You found them?"

"No, I mean…not your mom's stuff. But wow."

"What?"

"It's stuff about Anna, her last job at the hospital and all." Max started to shake his head as he thumbed through the stack. "You know all that rubbish she says about leaving that lucrative job at the hospital and setting up her own practice so she could help people more personally and blah, blah, blah…well, according to this she had no choice."

"What do you mean?"

"Looks like she was fired, or…oh, man." He looked up at Ginny, eyes wide. Even though she had been growing impatient that he was side-tracking their search, she felt herself getting curious.

"What now?"

"According to this, she was fired because her credentials didn't check out." Max's eyes grew distant as he mused. "I wonder what credentials she really does have. I mean, was it just that she lied about something to get that high-powered job at the hospital, or should she not even be counseling at all?"

Ginny waved her hand, dismissing the whole subject. "I can't think about that right now. We're running out of time. The keys obviously aren't in here. Could she have left them somewhere else in the house or do you think she took them with her?"

Max took a deep breath. "I can't go in there."

"Where?"

"Their bedroom." He did the shudder thing again.

"Oh for Pete's sake. Point me in the right direction."

Max led her to the stairs and pointed toward a doorway just in sight at the top. As she ran up the steps, she called back over her shoulder, "If they come home while I'm in there just tell them I'm crazy. Everyone will believe it."

Fortunately, she found a key ring on one of the night stands almost immediately. Grabbing them up, she saw a couple of petite keys that could possibly fit a filing cabinet and made a beeline back to Ms. Shaw's study. Somehow she'd rather be caught there than in the woman's bedroom.

She came so close to success, so close she could literally touch it. The first of the little keys opened the file cabinet, and she thumbed through the files at lightning speed, with Max holding a flashlight over the drawer so she could read the names.

"Hey, there's a file that says Andrew Callahan," he said.

It took her a moment to recognize their principal's name. She spared him a quick look, then kept thumbing. "So?"

"Oh, no reason. Just sayin'."

She smiled, hearing the slightly wistful note in his voice. "You know you wouldn't have looked."

"Hmmm…glad you were here to keep me honest."

Ginny gasped as she saw the word "Crosby." "I think I found it!" she called to Max. Simultaneously, she ripped the folder from the drawer and the flashlight from Max's hand and was just about to open the file when the room suddenly flooded with light.

Her heart jumped so hard it was obviously trying to flee her body. Coward. Of course, she would have fled, too, if she had the chance. Anything rather than facing those four cold, angry eyes right now—two belonging to Ms. Shaw, and two to Max's father.

☙

Anna pushed the drawer shut with a firm click after replacing the file, then turned to look down at her and Max where they sat huddled on the couch. Her face was cool and composed. No slamming, no yelling. So why was Ginny so nervous? Mr. Ferguson was studying Max sadly, like some highly disappointing experiment result in the bottom of a petrie dish.

"Why would you do such a thing, Max?" Mr. Ferguson asked him. "You know those files are a sacred trust. People confide their most intimate fears and dreams to Anna, and they expect that information to be safe."

"I wasn't snooping through the files. We…I mean, I—"

"Not you. Me," Ginny said.

"Anyway, we just wanted to see where Ginny's mother is. We weren't going to read anything else."

Anna laughed sharply. "And I suppose you managed to find her file without seeing anyone else's name in there?"

Max opened his mouth, then closed it. Ginny knew he was thinking of the principal's file.

The woman smiled in triumph. "I thought so." She crossed her arms and learned down toward Max. "Some people don't even want it to be known that they come here. They have a right to their privacy."

"And a girl has a right to know where her sick mother is." Max's face was blazing red as he faced off with Ms. Shaw. Ginny figured he would fight with the woman over almost anything, but she still felt touched by his sticking up for her.

Amazingly, Ms. Shaw nodded thoughtfully. "You may have a point, Max." She sat down across from them. "Nobody's been trying to punish Rose or Ginny, you understand that, don't you?"

He shrugged, while Ginny bit her tongue.

"In Rose's frame of mind, it just wouldn't have been good for her to see Ginny again. And it probably would have meant another trauma for Ginny." She fell silent, biting her lip and apparently thinking.

Max prompted, "Has something changed?"

"Rose is calmer. She's definitely made some improvement."

Ginny exchanged a look with Max. Had those people finally managed to convince Mom that she was delusional? The thought made Ginny queasy, but she didn't express the thought, not when Ms. Shaw seemed to be bending in their direction. Instead she said, "You think it might be all right now? For us to see each other, I mean."

"Well, I'll have to talk to Dr. Carswell, but we'll see."

Ginny nodded. Considering the trouble they were in and their total failure at finding Mom's location, it was the best she could hope for. "Thanks, Ms. Shaw," she said, getting to her feet and preparing to make a break for it along with Max.

Mr. Ferguson, however, was standing by the doorway. His arm

shot out like a railway crossing barrier, signaling that they better stop if they didn't want to get run over. Glaring at Max, he said, "There's still this little matter of your breaking and entering."

"Oh."

"Uh-huh." He turned his arm so his palm was up. "Gimme."

Max shook his head as though bewildered, his face looking totally innocent. "Give you what?"

"Car keys," the man said. "Hand 'em over."

Max sighed, but dug in his pocket and fished out the keys to the Civic. "Man, I only just got it. I've barely gotten to drive it."

"Yeah, well, think about that before you pull a stunt like this again."

Max gazed mournfully at his father, who retreated toward the kitchen as he jingled the Civic's keys in his hand.

Ginny turned to watch Ms. Shaw return Mom's file to the drawer and lock it. Then, she noticed, Ms. Shaw straightened up and looked toward the credenza where Max had found the papers about why she lost her last job. The woman's eyes grew thoughtful as she tapped her lower lip with her finger.

Quickly, before Ms. Shaw could speculate too much, Ginny said to her, "Can I ask you something?"

She raised her eyebrows, as though expecting the worst. But she said, "Sure. Fire away."

"This Jordan person that Mom is so obsessed with—did you know her?"

She lifted her shoulders and let them fall. "Vaguely. I met her a few times."

"And you don't think she looks like me?"

She pursed her lips. "Max, do you remember my cousin Sylvia?"

"Uh…sort of," he said.

"You've met her three times. Once at that wedding. Once we went to see her when she had a layover at the airport. So tell me exactly what she looks like."

"Well…she had brown hair."

"What color are her eyes? How tall was she?"

"I don't know. That was a long time ago, and anyway, I only met her a few times."

"Exactly. Except for the way she came into our lives, this Jordan person wasn't that big a deal—and it was twenty-five years ago. She was only around for a few weeks. She was quiet and boring as far as I can recall. The most striking thing about her was that black hair."

"Like mine," Ginny said.

Sighing, Anna looked at her. "Yes. I sincerely wish you hadn't done that to your hair."

"Yeah, me too." She crossed her arms across her chest. "It would have been nice if someone had told me more, so I would have known."

Ms. Shaw laughed. "I don't suppose it ever occurred to any of us that it was something you might do. 'Don't dye your hair jet black, Ginny. It will make you look more like that strange girl.' But honestly, other than the hair, I couldn't tell you whether you're like her. Jordan just wasn't that big a part of our lives."

"She must have been important to my mom."

"Or she's become important over time—a fixation. The idea of her means something to Rose. That doesn't mean Jordan herself did."

Ginny felt herself being pulled along by the logic of her argument, until she reminded herself of that picture—apparently of herself in a 1984 newspaper, with a detailed description right down to her tattoo.

Max mumbled his thanks and started to pull Ginny toward the doorway, but he paused before leaving as another thought apparently struck him. "So whatever happened to this Jordan, anyway?"

Anna thought for a minute, then shook her head. "I don't know. One day she just wasn't around anymore."

CHAPTER TWENTY-TWO

Since Max—who had been driving Ginny to school—was carless, she really needed to ask Daddy for a ride. But when he started in on her at breakfast again about getting counseling, she had no desire whatsoever to ride with him. She let him leave for work without mentioning her transportation problem. She'd walk if she had to.

As it turned out, walking wasn't necessary. A car honked for her at eight, same as usual. Pulling the kitchen curtain aside, she saw Max's father's BMW in the driveway. Its window slid down and Max waved cheerfully from the passenger seat.

Grabbing her backpack, she hurried out to the car and then slid down in the back seat, hoping Mr. Ferguson couldn't see her in the rear view. Although why she should be embarrassed she didn't really know. They were the ones conspiring to hold her mother hostage. All of them but Max. He was still looking at her, a little anxiously, maybe wondering if she was mad at him. She smiled and mouthed the words, "Thanks anyway."

They rode in silence for a moment. Ginny searched desperately for something safe to talk about. Then, instead of saying something safe, she blurted out, "Mr. Ferguson, you're a scientist. Will you please tell your son that time travel isn't possible!"

Mr. Ferguson turned to look at Max, who shrugged and tried to look casual. "We have some very deep discussions."

Mr. Ferguson guffawed. "Sounds like you were having a Star Trek discussion to me." He flashed Ginny a smile in the rear view. "I'd love to be able to convince him that a lot of this fantasy stuff isn't real, but I haven't been successful yet."

"Yes, but time travel," Ginny persisted. "I mean…that's totally ridiculous, right?"

"Well…depends on what you mean by the phrase. We don't usually say 'time travel,' for instance, because that implies movement. We generally use terms like 'closed timelike curves,' and we speculate about whether spacetime might be warped, or contain world lines that can be looped back upon themselves, or—"

"But is it possible?" Ginny tried not to scream.

"Well…" Mr. Ferguson blew out his breath. "Depends on who you ask. That's rather like asking whether God is real."

Max glared at him, while Ginny felt her spirits starting to sink.

"You're probably familiar already with Einstein's concepts of general and special relativity, in which a person hypothetically traveling away from the Earth at the speed of light, then turning around and coming back to Earth at slightly less than light speed would have experienced far less of what we call time than the people who stayed on Earth. He could therefore, theoretically, travel into the Earth's future."

"What about traveling into the past?"

"That's trickier, because of the causality problem—in other words, having a result appear before the causal agent that produces it." For the next few minutes, Mr. Ferguson rattled on about entropy and the arrow of time and used about a million words that she couldn't have even repeated, until he said one that she seized upon.

"Wormholes! I've heard of those."

Max huffed. "Of course you have. They're a very convenient device in loads of science fiction. Want to travel across the galaxy in a nanosecond? Pop into a wormhole. Go back in time? Suddenly there's a wormhole."

Mr. Ferguson nodded. "True, but the theory is far more complex. You would first have to construct a traversable wormhole—and even if such a thing were possible, many hypothesize that any matter actually entering a wormhole would be instantly destroyed."

"So it's not possible," Ginny stated, feeling a sliver of relief.

"God created space and time," Max declared. "He exists outside of it, and he isn't limited to our pitiful little three or four dimensions. If he wanted to intervene—"

A groan from Max's dad cut him off. "You pull that trump card every time. It isn't fair and it isn't science."

"Oh, really? How about your physics colleagues, who discover they were wrong about the universe being infinite and always existing? They discover it actually has a definite beginning in the Big Bang, like the Bible said all along—so what do they do? Say, oh well, there must be more than one universe, because we're not giving up on infinity and non-creation. Or let's see, maybe it's an infinite bounce and it will happen over and over again! You refuse to give up faith in your ideas even when evidence goes against you."

"Now, Max, you know I find much of the multiverse theory to be—"

"You're passing our turn-off!" Ginny called out, never more relieved to see the drab brick school building.

Mr. Ferguson hit the brakes hard, then swerved into the driveway so fast that Ginny wondered if he had just slowed their aging by a second or two.

As he stopped the car in front of the entrance, he chuckled. "Well, Ginny, I think we tried to solve all the mysteries of religion and creation and physics in one short car ride. Not an attainable goal, but an enjoyable one. We'll have to do this again soon."

"Sure, Mr. Ferguson," Ginny said, thinking to herself that she was going to start walking to school.

As Mr. Ferguson drove away, Ginny glared at Max. "Was that little discussion supposed to make me feel better?"

"Knowledge is power."

"Yeah, I feel so much more powerful now." Suddenly, from out of nowhere, Ginny felt as though someone were choking her. She gasped for breath and grabbed for Max's arm as her ears started to ring and a black film seemed to come down over the landscape. *Oh no, oh no, no, no.* What if this were it? What if she were about to disappear into some sort of parallel universe or void or—

She came back to her senses and found Max holding onto her arms and looking urgently into her eyes. "Ginny, calm down. Take a deep breath. Breathe."

She tried, but she was still gasping, struggling to suck it in.

Finally she managed to say, "What is it? What happened?"

"I think you're just having a panic attack." He looked around and maneuvered her over to a bench. "Sit down for a minute."

She looked around, mainly to see if anyone was staring. But no one was around at all. "Did the bell ring?"

"Yeah, but don't worry about it. You want me to take you to the clinic?"

"No, I'm okay."

"Really?"

"No. Max, what am I going to do?" She made herself slow down and breathe as she felt the hysteria starting to rise again. "I can't even find my mother. What if I really do disappear? How would anyone ever find me? Who would come looking for me?" She searched his eyes, hoping for hope. "What happened to Jordan? What's going to happen to me?"

Max squeezed her hand. "We're gonna find out."

"How?"

He stood up. "We're going to see Hunter Isaacs."

She got to her feet alongside him, holding onto the back of the bench for support. "This afternoon?"

"Right now."

"But we'll miss school."

"We can't wait. You may not have time."

That struck her as bizarrely funny, and she started to laugh. Max frowned for a moment, then his brain caught up with hers and he smiled. "Come on." He nodded in a westerly direction, toward the town square.

They walked beyond the square and located the address. It marked a complex of one-story brick office buildings, neatly landscaped with knee-high shrubbery and all alike in every way. They wandered aimlessly through the maze of CPAs and orthodontists until the numbering system made sense and they could zero in on 22-A. They stood for a moment staring at the wall in front of them, marked by a plain white door with a window to the left. Two bronze plates on the door read, "Mitchell & Isaacs, Attorneys at Law," and "No Solicitors."

Max reached for the handle, then paused and looked back when he realized Ginny wasn't following. "What's wrong?"

"I'm not sure we should just barge in there."

"Why not? We're not solicitors."

He pushed the door open and went in without looking back. After another moment of hesitation, she followed him in, although she hung back when he approached the reception desk. Hiding behind him didn't work, though. The receptionist's eyes took in Max, frowned a little, then zeroed in on Ginny and stayed there, staring. At first she wondered why, until she thought about her Goth black hair and black clothes, which probably contrasted nicely with the shocked-white face she'd been wearing for the last couple of days. Probably a little too Addams Family for this place.

"May I help you?" the receptionist asked, in a tone that said, "You better explain what you want pretty darn quickly."

"We'd like to see Mr. Isaacs."

Ginny was impressed with Max for sounding so cool and confident.

The woman wasn't. "Do you have an appointment?"

"No, but—"

"Actually, Mr. Isaacs isn't here right now."

"We'll wait for him."

The woman made a huffing noise. "It might be quite a while. I'm not sure exactly what time he'll be back."

"It's okay. We'll wait."

She tried one last time. "There's still the little matter of you not having an appointment. Mr. Isaacs is a very busy man."

Max glanced back at Ginny. "He'll want to see us. I'm sure of it."

The couch and chairs in the waiting area were uncomfortably close to the reception desk, but the woman pointedly went back to her typing and refused to look at them. Anyway, at least they'd know when Hunter Isaacs came in. There didn't appear to be any other way to get into the offices than to walk through here and past the sentry's desk.

They sat in silence and fidgeted for a half hour or so. Every now and then they caught the receptionist sneaking a glance at them. Max would smile broadly at her and she would quickly look back at her screen. Ginny picked up a couple of magazines and flipped through them, trying at least to look busy, but they were all about finance and investing. Glancing at one, Max snorted. "I never have been able to picture having so much money that you would consider it recreation to read about what to do with it."

Ginny twisted around on the couch, propped her arm on the back and stared out at the parking lot. "I can't believe I'm doing this."

"Yeah, well, if this whole thing wasn't so unbelievable, we wouldn't have to be doing this."

A moment of silence.

"Ginny?"

"Yeah?"

"I'd come look for you."

She looked at him, puzzled. His cheeks were flaming red as he grabbed one of the magazines and stared down at it, suddenly finding it fascinating after all. And then it hit her—the memory of what she had said back in the school parking lot—and she felt her eyes filling with tears. She nodded slowly. "I bet you'd find me, too."

He didn't look up, but she saw the sides of his mouth twitch in a smile. Not knowing what to say next, Ginny turned back to the window and watched vacantly as a car rolled across the pavement to the parking spaces just outside. A silver car. The door opened, and the driver got out, stood up.

She jumped up off the couch and started toward the door, wanting to run. Realizing that the only door led out to the parking lot and the car, she stopped short.

"What is it? Ginny?"

She whirled back around toward Max, trying to catch her breath. The receptionist had stopped her typing and was pretty wide-eyed herself. Max stood up and started toward Ginny. "Are you sick?"

She couldn't speak for a second, then nodded. "Yes. I'm sick." She turned toward the woman at the desk. "Where's your bathroom? Quick!"

The lady pointed to the hallway behind her. "First door on the right."

❧

Ginny closed the lid on the toilet and sat on top of it, knees drawn to her chest, for what seemed a long time. When someone tapped lightly on the door, she had to clear her throat a couple of times before she could get out words. "Who is it?"

Max's voice responded, sounding hushed and urgent. "Open the door, okay?"

She pulled it open a crack, and he pushed inside with her. She caught a glimpse of the receptionist's shocked face just before the door closed.

Max didn't waste any time. "I saw the silver Lexus outside. I take it that's the guy who was following you."

She nodded.

He took a deep breath. "It's Hunter Isaacs."

"Yeah, I kinda figured. It makes sense—now."

Max fidgeted for a moment, then said, "What do you want to do? He's agreed to see us."

"You're kidding. How'd you manage that?"

"Showed him that newspaper clipping and told him the girl in the picture was here to see him."

"You didn't."

"I did."

"And he understood what you were talking about?"

"He pretended not to...but then he didn't seem all that confused or surprised. So what do you want to do?"

Her brain felt numb. "I don't know. What do you think, Max?"

"It's up to you, okay? On the one hand, he's been acting like a creep, following you around. Maybe we should go to the police first—or our parents. But then again..."

"Then again?"

"Snitching on this guy won't get us any information. And he obviously knows something."

Ginny felt the mental wheels finally starting to turn. She felt her blood pumping through her chest, pounding in her fingers. "You're right, Max." She pulled the door open, then tried to smile. "Information. It's what we came for, isn't it?"

Ginny's pulse accelerated when she walked into Hunter Isaacs' office and she had to look at the scary man from the mall again, face to face. Her reaction was nothing compared to his, though. His mouth fell open, and he dropped the pen he was holding as she walked in. He completely ignored Max to stare at her. As they settled themselves in two leather chairs in front of his desk, he blinked as though pulling himself together. He looked from one to the other of them, questioning, then finally demanded, "Well? One of you want to tell me what this is about?"

"Why don't you tell me?" Ginny was almost happy to feel herself getting angry. Anger felt better than fear any day. "Tell me why you've been following me, ever since you ran into me in the mall that day."

"That was you?" He cocked his head and studied her. "You look different now. The hair." He laughed harshly. "You're really going for the look, aren't you?" Now he leaned forward, clutching the edge of the desk with his hands. "Who are you? Is she your mother?"

Ginny nodded. "Yes. Rose Crosby—Rose Remington—is my mother."

"Rose?" He frowned, looking befuddled. "Rose is your mother?"

"Isn't that what you meant?"

He didn't answer. He looked over at Max. "Let me see that piece of paper."

Max pulled it from his pocket and handed it over without unfolding it. Isaacs fumbled with it as he smoothed it out. He stared down at the picture in silence until Ginny wanted to scream.

Finally he looked up. He spoke, but he simply repeated, "Rose Remington is your mother?"

Ginny slapped her hand on her knee in frustration. "Yes, I think we've established that. Now why don't you tell me what's going on?"

"Why do you think I know?"

Ginny shot up from the chair. She wasn't sure what she intended to do, but too much energy was pumping through her. Why wasn't he helping them? As Max had put it, she didn't have time to waste. She took a step toward the desk, and her face must have looked fierce because this tall, strong man jerked back in his chair away from her. She felt Max's fingers close around her hand, and she stopped. He tugged lightly on her arm, and she sat back down.

Thankfully, Max spoke for her. "We think you know something because you're the one who was doing the following. Why is that?"

He swiveled in the big leather chair so he could look out the window. "I was just shocked that day in the mall, that's all." He nodded toward Ginny. "She looked so familiar."

Max tapped the picture on the desk. "Like her?"

"Yes. Sort of. Her hair was the wrong color, but I always knew Jordan's hair was dyed, anyway. Otherwise, everything was so similar.

The face, the build. The way she walked, and her eyes—oh, man, those eyes. That sort of breathy voice. Even the way she was twirling her hair around her finger." He turned his chair back around to face Ginny. "I apologize if I scared you. I really didn't mean to, and I wouldn't have done it if I thought you would notice. I just wanted one more look—or maybe to see who your family was. Simple curiosity, nothing more. You looked so much like Jordan, I figured you must be related to her. I wondered if you were her daughter, but then, I knew that couldn't be."

Ginny frowned. "How did you know that?"

"What? Oh…" The question seemed to catch him off guard. "I don't mean it was impossible…I just didn't think Jordan had been in this part of the world for a long, long time."

"Why not? Where did she go?"

He shrugged. "I have no idea. As far away from Rose Remington as she could get, I imagine." He leaned forward again, his mouth twisted in a smile. "I know what you're about to say. 'Why?'"

Ginny closed her mouth. She had been about to say just that.

He shook his head. "You sound very much like my two-year-old. 'Why, why, why?'" Isaacs turned the photocopy so the picture was right side up as he looked at it. "Has your mother ever told you about this night?"

Ginny nodded. "A little."

"Well, Carla Remington was not exactly a generous woman, but for some reason she agreed to let the girl stay with them. For a little while, everything was fine. The girl—we called her Jordan. I mean, we had to call her something—would get a little down and moody. Who wouldn't, if they'd been injured and couldn't remember how it happened? Couldn't remember anything about their lives? But for the most part, Jordan tried to make the best of things. I thought she was actually good for Rose."

"In what way?" Ginny asked.

Hunter hesitated. "I don't know how your mother is now, but back then, she…was very fragile. Emotionally, I mean." He looked at Ginny as though waiting for confirmation, but she refused to give any. She met his gaze and waited. "When things got stressful, she would get a little paranoid. Sometimes she saw things, or heard voices."

"Did you know all that when you got engaged to her?" Ginny

said.

"Yes, but I thought she was finally well. The more she pulled away from that mother of hers, the stronger she got. I thought when we were married and she was free, everything would be okay."

"But you changed your mind?"

"I did…after Jordan came." He sighed. "At first, the three of us did a lot of stuff together. We had a lot of fun. But then, Rose started to slide into one of her jealous moods. She became more and more unreasonable. Eventually she was…" He paused again, searching Ginny's face as though trying to read her. He shrugged. "She was violent. Toward me, but mainly toward Jordan."

"Violent? How?"

He considered for a moment, then shook his head. "Look, there's no point in going into all that. The thing is, your mom drove Jordan away. As far as I know, the girl was physically okay, but she hadn't recovered her memory. And for all we knew, someone had hurt her on purpose, that night we found her. The doctor said it appeared she had been hit with a blunt instrument. She certainly didn't need to go off on her own, with no family or friends to take care of her, no money."

"Sounds like you cared about her a lot," Max said.

He turned his focus to Max. "I didn't want anything to happen to her. She was a sweet kid." He looked out the window. "I didn't want anything to happen to her."

Ginny remembered what Mom had told her and asked, "Did Jordan actually say she was leaving because of my mom?"

He shifted his eyes away from her. "She didn't have to tell me. I knew."

"Where did she go?"

"I don't know where she went. She just went."

Max leaned forward. "Did she talk to you first? Or to somebody? I mean, if somebody had tried to hurt her that night you found her, then maybe that person showed up again and—"

He stood up, cutting off Max's speech. "I've told you what I know, okay? That's it." He nodded curtly to them in turn. "Good day to you both."

Once outside, Max said, "So. Are we going back to school?"

Ginny shook her head. "I just don't think I can. Anyway, it's

May 28, very last day of the term, so what's the point?"

Max stopped so suddenly she almost ran into him. "May 28."

"Yeah? So?"

Once again, Max pulled out the article. He stared down at it, his eyes huge. "Ginny, the date of this article is May 29, 1984."

"Again…so?"

"So that means your mom and Isaacs found Jordan the night before, on the twenty-eighth."

"So you want us to buy Mom a cake or something to commemorate?" Ginny started walking again, not waiting to see if Max followed but sure that he would. The heat was getting to her, even if it was only May, and she did not intend to stand around with him with the sun blaring down on her head while he talked nonsense about dates. And then it hit her. "Oh!" This time, she was the one to come to a sudden halt. "You mean that it might be related somehow, assuming your crazy time travel thing is right. That if I appear in 1984 on May 28, then maybe I leave here…"

"Today," Max finished for her, his voice barely a whisper.

She took a few steps forward, then stopped and came back. She was pacing in circles, but she couldn't stand still. "So what should I…what should I do? I can't stand the thought of sitting in a classroom, but maybe I shouldn't go anywhere near the house or the pond. Where can I possibly—"

"Ginny, calm down."

Max's touch on her hand brought her to a stop. He gazed at her intently. "Come on. Let's go to my house."

She nodded, and they started off again. Within minutes, she was soaked with unlady-like sweat. "Man, it's hot," she said, pulling her sticky hair up off her neck.

"Yeah, well, sorry about the walk. I did something stupid to impress a girl and lost my car in the process."

"What a geek."

"You said it." After a beat, Max said, "You know why I got the car in the first place, right?"

She managed to smile at him. "To attract girls?"

Max laughed. "Yeah, there's nothing like an aging Civic for sex appeal." His eyes grew serious. "I wanted to be able to drive you, to look after you, after hearing about the creep in the silver Lexus."

Ginny tried to say something, but her throat was suddenly tight with emotion.

Max chuckled. "So what do I do today? Take you to see the creep with the silver Lexus."

As they entered Max's kitchen, he stopped on a dime and spat out one of his forbidden words. Ms. Shaw was there. Apparently she wasn't delighted to see him, either.

"What are you two doing here?" she asked.

Max recovered quickly, so quickly Ginny had to wonder if he slipped things past Anna pretty often. Then again, he had made a complete foul-up of sneaking info from her mother's file. Now, though, he relaxed and spoke calmly. "We're on lunch break. They're having tuna casserole in the cafeteria."

"Oh. You have time to walk all the way here and back?"

"I thought so when we started."

Ms. Shaw crossed her arms and stared him down. "Max, is this some kind of ploy to get your car back?"

He grinned. "Is it working?"

"No. And don't expect me to write you any sort of excuse if you're late." Turning on her heel, the woman stalked from the room.

Ginny raised her eyebrows at Max. "I thought you church-goin' types didn't lie."

"What lie? They are having tuna casserole in the cafeteria today, so—hey!"

"What?"

"Your mom's name is on this." Max was pulling a file folder out from under a newspaper. He picked it up and flipped it open, then looked at Ginny, an amazed expression on his face. "This is the same folder that was in the file cabinet in her study."

Ginny gasped. "Let me see." Practically jerking it from Max's hand, she saw he was right. She quickly started flipping through the pages, her hands shaking so that several pages fell out. "The name of her hospital's got to be in here. It just has to."

Max's voice came from down low, as he bent to pick up the fallen pages. "Seems a little odd, doesn't it?"

"What?"

"She had everything locked up like Fort Knox when we were trying to break in. Now the file is just lying here in plain sight? It's too easy."

"I think I'm entitled to a little bit of easy," Ginny grumped, accepting the dropped papers from him and sticking them in at random. "Besides, no offense, but based on that stuff we found about your stepmom and her last job, she's obviously not the most professional person in the world."

"Yeah…"

Max still sounded worried, but Ginny didn't care. She made herself flip quickly past the notes on Mom's therapy sessions, focusing on finding that one important piece of information. And suddenly, there it was. Dated the day after the big blow-up about Ginny's hair, there was a note from Anna. "Admitted to River View, Newnan," Ginny read.

Max nodded. "I know where that is. Next county over, about a half hour from here."

"Will you take me?"

Max's face clouded. "Ginny, you know Dad took my car away for a month."

Ginny choked off a scream. Didn't Max realize how important this was? But looking at the struggle in his face, she knew he did realize. He was obviously in the grip of a moral dilemma because of her. She tried to throw him a lifeline. "He didn't say you couldn't drive at all, just that you couldn't drive your own car, right?"

"Umm…well…I don't know that it came up, but it was probably implied that—"

"Good. Then we'll walk to my house and get Mom's car."

"What!" Max started to laugh weakly. "Oh, great. So instead of getting in trouble with my dad about my grounding, I'll get arrested for car theft."

Ginny threw up her hands. "Fine." She headed for the door. "I'll do it myself."

"You can't drive."

"I'll figure it out."

"Oh, for Pete's sake."

She felt his hand on her shoulder and stopped, allowing him to turn her toward him.

"I'll drive you," he said.

"Thanks, Max." She bit her lip to stop it quivering. "I'm really sorry, but I don't have anybody else."

"It's okay. Come on."

As they went out the door, he moaned.

"What now?"

"It just occurred to me we're ditching school for the rest of the day, too."

"Just as well hanged for a dragon as for an egg," Ginny said.

Max grinned at her, his eyes full of admiration. "How can I resist a girl that quotes Harry Potter at me?"

"Mrs. Figg, actually."

"I know, I know."

After a moment of walking, Max said thoughtfully, "Ginny…assuming the worst, or the weirdest, does happen, and you really do end up, well, back there…"

"Yes?" she snapped.

"We should figure out some way for you to leave us a message. Maybe we could decide on a place in your house for you to leave a note or something, somewhere it wouldn't be found over the years, letting us know you're there and you're…okay."

Ginny stopped.

"What?" he asked her.

"Max, I just thought of something. Maybe I…" she tried to figure out how to say it. The words didn't make sense, but she said them anyway. "Maybe I already did."

She ran into the house, to the junk drawer where she had thrown the yellow, moldy scrap of paper all those weeks ago. Then she shoved it at Max, choking out the words, "I found this down in the basement, up in the ceiling of all places."

Max looked down at the paper for a long moment, without speaking. Finally he looked up. "Obviously part of it is missing."

"I know. I couldn't make anything out of it."

"It could say a lot of things, but…one of those things would be, June or July something, 1984, Max, Mom, I'm…something."

"I'm J-O," Ginny murmured.

"JORDAN?" Max practically squeaked. He cleared his throat and tried to speak normally again. "And then that could be your signature in cursive. Ginny."

"Yeah," Ginny said. That light-headed feeling washed over her again as she stared at the letters, realizing for the first time how much the looping "n-y" did, indeed, look like her signature. A signature that her hand had not made…at least, not yet.

CHAPTER TWENTY-THREE

When Mom appeared in the hospital's common room, Ginny was glad for the bandanna tied around her head. As they were getting into Mom's Escort to drive over here, Max had said, "Hey! Put something over that scary hair before you see your mother."

Apparently the strategy worked. Mom appeared nervous, hugging her arms tight across her chest as she looked at Ginny. But the expression in her eyes was soft and hopeful, and she smiled tentatively as she looked at her. What would Ginny do without Max?

"You remember Max, don't you?" she awkwardly asked her mother.

"Yes, of course. It's good to see you, Max."

"I brought him along for moral support."

Mom looked down at the floor. "I'm sorry you need moral support, Ginny."

"No, I didn't mean it like that—"

"It's okay, honey. I've put you through a terrible time, I know that." She looked up and met Ginny's eyes. "I know I was deluded. You're my daughter, no one else. I'm so ashamed—"

"No, Mom, don't say that." She took a deep breath. "You were right all along."

"What?"

Ginny felt Max touch her arm. "Careful." For a minute, she

wondered why he was warning her. He knew the truth. He leaned in toward her and murmured, so low she could barely hear him, "Careful how you tell her."

She looked at her mother and knew he was right. Mom hugged herself even tighter, and her smile had faded. Her voice had a ragged edge as she asked again, "What do you mean, I was right?"

Ginny looked around and spotted a sofa in a quiet corner. She motioned her head toward it. "Let's go sit down, okay?"

Mom nodded.

Max cleared his throat. "I'll just wait for you in the lobby."

"No!" Ginny felt panic tighten her throat. "Come with us." She looked at her mother. "You don't mind, do you, Mom?"

Mom frowned in confusion, but she answered, "Of course not." She flashed a shaky smile in Max's direction.

He shrugged. "Sorry."

They trooped over to the sofa, a bland beige affair that was actually pretty comfy. The whole area was more homey and comfortable than she would have thought, with little clusters of people at card tables or reading in squashy armchairs.

Ginny licked her lips. Her throat felt so dry she wondered if she would croak like a frog when she tried to get out the words. Somehow she managed. "You shouldn't be here, Mom." Almost shyly, she reached for her mother's hand. "I believe you."

Mom let out a breath. "Oh, honey. That's sweet of you, really, but—"

"It has nothing to do with being sweet. I believe you because you were right. I know that now."

Mom tilted her head and studied her. "Now, Ginny…how could you possibly know that?"

Ginny looked at Max, who shrugged, then reached into his pocket and pulled out the paper. By now it was pretty crumpled. Ginny smoothed it out as best she could and tried to pass it across to her mother. "Because I've seen it for myself." Mom made no move to take the paper. "It's a picture, and a news story about—"

"I know what it is." Mom jerked her head and looked away. "I've seen it before. I don't want to see it again."

"But Mom—"

"What are you trying to do to me?" She lurched to her feet and glared down at Ginny, who shrank back against the couch. "Do you know how hard it's been, how hard I've worked trying to get rid of these crazy ideas? I've finally calmed down, I'm able to look at you without seeing *her*, and now you want to start all that up again?"

From the corner of her eye, Ginny saw a woman in scrubs approaching. No wonder. Mom's voice had grown pretty loud.

Ginny, on the other hand, could do little more than whisper. "Mom, I'm trying to help."

"Help me! I half think you've known what you were doing all along. That you're doing this on purpose."

It was so close to what that lawyer had said that for a second, Ginny doubted herself. Was there any way she could have been doing this on purpose? Adopting the girl's mannerisms, dyeing her hair? But there was no way she could have known any of this, was there?

The nurse arrived and placed her hand on Mom's arm. "Mrs. Crosby."

Mom jerked away from her, then stopped and held up her hands. "I'm sorry, Katherine."

The nurse—Katherine?—smiled but put her hand firmly back on Mom's arm. "That's okay, Mrs. Crosby." She turned toward Ginny with a big fake smile plastered on her face. "I think you need to be going now. You can come again later."

"No, I can't. I might not have a later." Ginny felt Max's hand on her arm, trying to restrain her the way the nurse was restraining Mom. She shook him off and took a step toward her mother, shoving the photocopied picture toward her. "This is me, don't you understand? It's already happened to you, but it hasn't happened to me yet."

She heard Max murmuring in her ear, the way he'd done a few minutes ago. "Careful, Ginny, or they're gonna give you a room here, too."

"I don't care."

Mom had turned and was walking away from her, back toward the hallway. People were starting to look at them. Patients and visitors stared, and a couple of other staffers in scrubs moved in Ginny's direction. She didn't care. She called toward her mother's retreating form, "Mom! Mom, please!" She hated herself for it, but she started to cry, the kind of jagged, messy crying that probably could land you in a place like this. She needed to stop, but all she could do was sob and call after her, "Please don't leave me. I don't know what to do. Mom, please!"

Mom stopped. She twisted out of the nurse's arm and turned around. Ginny wasn't even sure whether she ran forward, or Mom ran back toward her. Either way, she found herself crying against her mother's shoulder, feeling her mother stroke the back of her hair. The bandanna came undone so that all that ugly black hair streamed out, but still Rose stroked and whispered, "It's okay, honey. Everything's going to be all right. We'll get past this, you'll see."

Somehow, in the midst of that crying jag, Ginny started to giggle. The wildest thought came to her. Mom was in the psychiatric hospital and was acting perfectly reasonable and sane, while Ginny totally lost it. Mom had been put in here because no one believed her supposed delusions—and now Ginny was trying to convince her to believe. And apparently, failing miserably.

She pulled away and looked at her mother, trying to read the expression in her eyes. Thankfully, she saw love, and concern, but she also saw fear and bewilderment. How could this be going so wrong?

Katherine and a guy in scrubs pulled at them, pulling them apart. "I think you and your mother both need a little time to rest and calm down, okay? You can come back again—but you need to bring your father with you next time."

Ginny blinked, and Mom was gone.

CHAPTER TWENTY-FOUR

Max took her home, but not right away. They drove around and talked, and got a Coke and sat in Mom's Escort and talked for a while, until Ginny calmed down enough to go home. She twitched the curtain at the front door aside and watched him walk away in the direction of his own house. And then she heard something—creaking floorboards down in the basement.

It couldn't be Daddy. Too early for him, and anyway, his truck wasn't outside. She jerked up the phone and hit the speed dial for Max's cell. She cut him off before he could complete the word "Hello."

"Somebody's in here. In the basement."

"I'll be right there."

She threw the phone down and headed for the front door. She tried to tell herself she was crazy, an idiot to panic over creaking noises in this house. It creaked all the time. But she didn't care. She shook all over and every nerve ending told her to run. She moved as quickly as possible without causing the floorboards under the old carpet to groan, herself. Whatever was in the basement, she didn't want to alert it to her presence.

She didn't make it to the door before the noise changed. The subtle creaking changed to the distinct clomp, clomp, clomp of feet coming up the stairs. At the same time, she saw a shadowy figure moving across the porch toward the front door. Max!

Forget about making noise. She broke into a run, covering the remaining distance to the doorway in two flying leaps, and grabbed the doorknob.

"Ginny!"

"Ginny!"

She twisted her neck back and forth, trying to look everywhere at once as someone called her name in front of her, behind her. She flung open the door, and there was Max. She whirled around and found herself facing...

"Mom!"

As she stared in disbelief at the thin, pale figure of her mother, she wanted to run again. Out the door and away. Toward her mother, to throw her arms around her and beg to be held. She didn't do either. She stood rooted in place. "Mom, what are you doing here?"

Rose twisted her hands in a nervous motion, but her voice was calm. "It sounded like you needed me, so this is where I should be."

Now Ginny could move. She ran and threw her arms around her mother, relieved that first the first time in ages she could feel strength radiating from this tiny woman's body into hers. Strength, not fear.

Ginny drew away and looked at her. "But how did you get them to let you go?"

Rose laughed. "I wasn't kidnapped, honey. I checked myself into that hospital, so when I decided to leave, they couldn't stop me." She grimaced. "No matter what they thought about it."

"Wow, just like a celebrity." Max closed the front door after making this pronouncement. Ginny and Mom both turned to look at him. "Except of course they're usually in for doing drugs. Uh…" He coughed. "Sorry, I didn't mean…"

Wonder of wonders, Mom smiled at him. "Max, honey, are you here all the time now?"

He blushed and coughed again. "Well, I mean…"

Ginny moved to stand beside him. She put her hand lightly on his arm and faced her mother. "Max is always here. And thank God he is."

Soon they were seated together again, just as they had been at the hospital, with Ginny and Mom side by side on the couch and Max in an armchair close to Ginny. Just the same, yet everything was different. The house was quiet, no nervous chatter from patients or family members. No one watched them. But beyond that, Mom seemed more relaxed, more her old self—the old self from months ago. Mom even took Ginny's hand and held it loosely, comfortably in her own. Ginny felt her tangled nerves relaxing.

Mom took a deep breath. "Okay. So tell me what you were trying to say back at the hospital."

They told her, Ginny and Max, sometimes separately and sometimes talking all at once. Max jumped into the story when she started to stumble, and Ginny reigned him in when he got ahead of himself. She watched her mother's eyes as they talked, first widening, then narrowing practically to slits. What did that mean? Impatience? Anger? Disbelief? Mom's fingers tightened around hers, then went limp and turned almost completely loose.

Finally, Ginny and Max wound down. They sat in silence and waited for Mom to speak.

She held out her hand. "Let me see that newspaper picture."

Max glanced at Ginny. She nodded. He pulled out the crumpled paper.

Ginny held her breath as Mom took it from him, smoothed out the wrinkles, held it under the light to study it more carefully. She prepared herself for another fit of nerves, wondering what she would do if Mom freaked out now, with no nurses around to help them. The paper shook slightly as Mom held it under the lamp, but otherwise, she showed no emotion. She cleared her throat and said, "Yes, it looks like Ginny. There's no denying that." She laid the clipping on the side table and looked at them. "I have another blurry old photo that I showed to your father. He very wisely pointed out that a resemblance in an old photo didn't mean all that much."

Had Ginny heard right? Wisely? Her father was wise to make Mom believe a lie?

Mom went on. "You can't tell that much from a picture. You can read anything into them." She shook her head. "Ginny, I feel terrible. I'm afraid you've talked yourself into a delusion in some sort of misguided effort to support me."

"What!"

"It's true, isn't it? You didn't believe any of this until I went in the hospital." She laid her hand on top of Ginny's. "I can imagine how upsetting all that was for you. Maybe so disturbing you'd rather believe it's true than believe I…" Mom's voice faltered. "That I was sick."

Ginny pulled her hand away. "Is that what they taught you in the hospital?"

"It makes sense, doesn't it? Lots of sicknesses are contagious, Ginny. I'd hate to think that I've made you live in such an unhealthy atmosphere that I've contaminated you, somehow transferred my delusions onto you."

"You sound brainwashed."

"I went into that hospital to get well, Ginny. To be able to see my daughter again instead of a hallucination."

Ginny looked straight into Mom's eyes. "So you don't see Jordan at all anymore? She's completely gone?"

Mom blinked. She tried to hold Ginny's gaze, but she looked away. "Getting completely well takes time. You resemble Jordan, there's no denying it. But I know what's true now."

Angry, frustrated words bubbled up into Ginny's mouth. She fought to push them back down. She turned to Max and said through gritted teeth, "Say something!"

He started. He licked his lips and leaned forward in the chair. "Well, ah…why don't you show her the tattoo?"

"Tattoo?" Mom asked. Ginny noted she went a bit paler at the word.

Ginny nodded. "That's right." She pulled down the collar of her shirt, exposing the dove and olive branch. She felt a perverse pleasure as Mom's eyes grew wide. "Is this a hallucination, too?"

Mom sounded a little breathless as she asked, "When did you get that tattoo, Ginny?"

Ginny got to her feet and stood looking down at her mother. "What are you trying to say?" She grabbed the clipping and shook it at Mom. "That I ran out and got this tattoo after I read the article?"

"Well, I've never seen it before."

"There's a lot you haven't seen the past few months."

Ginny felt Max standing next to her, touching her gently on the arm. "Mrs. Crosby, I can vouch for the fact that Ginny already had that tattoo when we found this article about Jordan." He put his hands up. "Not that I'd seen it before then. I mean, she showed me when we found the picture. And I wasn't with her when she got it or anything. I don't know anything about that, I just—what?"

Mom had started to smile as Max bumbled through his speech, and Ginny felt herself starting to giggle. She collapsed onto the couch next to her mother, and the two of them laughed in earnest at Max's indignant expression. Finally, Max smiled, too.

As the giggles petered out, Ginny felt hollow, as though the laughter had blasted all the emotion out of her. She felt drained and tired. Where could this conversation possibly go now?

As she had said earlier, thank God for Max. He snapped his fingers. "I just thought of something else. Ginny. Show her the note."

Ginny ran to her room and fetched it from her desk drawer. Five minutes later, Mom sat staring at the note in silence. There didn't seem anything else for them to say. They told her how Ginny found it. They told her what they thought. "That note is from me, Mom," Ginny said quietly. "I know there are letters missing, but I'm sure I know what it says. 'June'—or maybe July—'1984. Max, Mom, I'm here. I'm JORDAN. Ginny.' Look at that 'y' at the end, the way it loops and curls. It's like my signature. I don't know any other way to interpret it. I was there—back there with you in 1984."

Mom shook her head slowly back and forth. "No, Ginny, that can't be true. It just can't."

Ginny slapped the couch in frustration. "What's it going to take to make you believe this?"

"You don't understand, Ginny. I can't believe this."

"Why not?"

"Because this girl—" Mom tapped her finger on the photocopied picture. "This girl died in 1984."

Part V

Rose, 2009

CHAPTER TWENTY-FIVE

Rose was sitting alone in the living room, the lights turned off to allay the pounding in her head, when she heard Ben's soft voice from the doorway. "Why are you sitting in the dark, baby? You okay?"

A flood of elation washed over her just as the room flooded with light. For a brief moment, she thought he was actually addressing her with concern and affection in his voice. Then she saw the surprise on his face.

"I thought it was Ginny in here," he snapped. "What are you doing here?"

She forced herself to meet his harsh gaze. "Last time I checked, this was still my home. And my daughter needed me."

Ben snorted. "Oh, now she's your daughter again?"

"She always has been. Always."

Ben looked around the room. "Where is Ginny?"

"She's in the bathroom. She was upset so I told her to go take a hot bath. I thought it would help her relax."

"Yeah, I imagine she was upset. Having you show back up all of a sudden." Ben turned his head toward the hallway. The sound of the water running into the tub could clearly be heard, so maybe he believed her.

"You don't understand, Ben. That's why I came home, because Ginny was upset."

"What do you mean?"

"She visited me in the hospital today."

"She did? How'd she find you?"

"I don't know. But she wasn't doing very well." Rose stood up and started to pace. "She needs me here, Ben. She needs her mother."

"Okay. And what made you decide that now, after all these months of me trying to tell you how much she needs you?"

Rose turned to face him. She opened her mouth to speak, then closed it again. She shrugged. "Maybe I'm getting better, Ben. Maybe I just see things a lot more clearly now."

"I wish I could believe that, Rose."

"A few weeks ago, I promised you that I would never hurt Ginny. That I would do whatever was needed to avoid that. And I made good on that promise, didn't I? You didn't have to force me into that hospital. I went of my own free will."

Ben nodded. "That's true. But are you saying you're all of a sudden cured? That you don't believe all that stuff about Ginny turning into someone else?"

She hesitated, biting her lip. Finally she said, "I don't believe there are any ghosts in this house, or that Ginny is possessed. No." As for what she thought about all that stuff Ginny and Max had told her, she had no idea. But she wasn't about to share any of that with Ben. He was studying her intently as it was, as though trying to gauge her state of mind and decide whether to call someone to come haul her back to the hospital.

Finally, he said flatly, "So you believe Ginny is Ginny."

She smiled. Well, even if Ginny and Max's bizarre theory was true, she could still answer that one. "Ginny is Ginny. Yes. Absolutely."

Ben fell into one of the armchairs and rubbed his face with his hands. "I don't know what to say."

She sat down on the couch and faced him, until he took his hands away from his forehead and looked her in the eye. Then she said, "I know I've let you down the past few months. I fell apart under all the pressure. I wasn't honest with you about my job. But you know, you disappointed me, too."

"When?"

She let out her breath in frustration. "When you sold my land without my permission, maybe?"

"Oh, please, not again." He waved a hand, dismissing her argument. "You were in no shape to make rational decisions. So I had to."

She stood up, moving so that she stood right in front of his chair. She liked the feeling it gave her, towering over him and for once having him look up at her. "Let me tell you the point, Ben. I know I've been weak. I've been confused. But that was no reason for you to start treating me like an idiot—like someone without a brain in her head. I wasn't incompetent. Not a few weeks ago, and not now."

"I know that—"

"No, I don't think you do. No one's known that about me for a long time." She sat down on the coffee table across from him. "People have been treating me like this all my life. Weak. Incompetent. That's Rose. Maybe I deserved that, because I let them treat me that way." When she spoke again, she spoke softly, so that he leaned forward to hear her. "What I've never understood is why— if someone gets sick, or weak, why no one seems to love them anymore."

His face close to hers, he whispered in response, "That's ridiculous, Rose."

"You stopped loving me."

"No, I didn't."

"When I let you down. When I didn't behave the way a wife and mother were supposed to—"

"I hated it. I didn't know what to do. But I never stopped loving you."

He picked up her hand, squeezed it gently. They hadn't been this close, hadn't touched one another in so long. She gazed into his eyes, looking for affection, looking for hope.

And then she jerked her hand back with a gasp.

"What's the matter?" he asked, frowning.

"The water's still running."

"What?" He pushed his hair back off his forehead and sat back in the chair, looking a little disoriented.

Rose jumped to her feet. "Ginny. The bath water's been running all this time. Something's wrong."

She heard him padding across the shag carpeting behind her as she headed toward Ginny's bathroom. Her heart lurched as she saw a trickle of water coming from underneath the closed bathroom door.

Ben pushed past her and threw open the door, and she saw

water rushing over the side of the tub. After twisting the faucets to stop the flow, he stood looking around the empty room. "So where is she?"

Rose could barely speak. "She's gone."

She could feel herself falling—mentally, emotionally. She shook her head, trying to keep calm and focused, but she felt herself losing it. Was she seeing things—or rather, not seeing things? She remembered Ginny coming in here, turning on the water. She couldn't have vanished into thin air, could she? Had something happened that she couldn't remember? She pressed her palms against her cheeks and shook her head back and forth. "This can't be happening. No, no, no."

"Stop it, Rose!" Ben's voice hit her like a slap in the face. "You said you were going to be strong for her. That she needs you. So let's see you do it."

She forced herself to take a deep breath, and after a moment, the spinning room seemed to settle down. "I'm sorry, I—I just. I'm all right now."

He started out of the bathroom, and she followed close behind. Their feet made a squishing sound on the soaked carpet.

"Nothing terrible has happened," Ben said. "She's just not in the bathroom. You know how teenagers are. She probably got a phone call and is outside yakking on the cell and not giving a thought to the bath water." By now he had reached the door that led from Ginny's room to the back yard. He twisted the knob and jerked, but it didn't give.

As the implication of that hit Rose, her hand went to her throat. "It's locked?"

He nodded. The door had a dead bolt that could be turned from this side of the door. From the outside you had to have a key to lock or unlock it. He turned the bolt and opened the door. "This is weird. If she went outside in a hurry, she wouldn't have brought her key and locked the door. Would she?" He turned to Rose.

She was shaking like a leaf, but managed to keep her voice calm. "So maybe she's still inside," she said. "I'll check my bedroom."

"Okay. And I'll check the front yard. Maybe she went out through the front hall."

A few minutes later she stood back in the foyer, her hands on her hips as she turned in a slow circle, looking around the house and thinking hard. A quick search of the house had produced no sign of Ginny. She heard footsteps coming up the porch steps and hurried to the doorway, just in time to see Ben coming in alone. She let out her breath in disappointment. "No sign of her, huh?"

He shook his head. "I even looked into the pecan grove, as far as I could see."

Rose crossed her arms tight across her chest. "I can't really say I'm surprised. I'm pretty sure she didn't go outside."

"How do you know?"

"Wasn't the front door locked, too?"

"Yes. All the doors were locked."

She held up a set of keys. "She couldn't have locked them without these. Not from the outside." She tucked the keys into her pocket. "They were in her purse. It's in her bedroom, too. A girl doesn't leave without her purse."

"So what are we saying? She's not in the house but she couldn't have left the house?"

"I don't know."

Ben started for the basement steps. "I'm gonna look down here."

"I just did."

"So I'm looking again."

For lack of any better ideas, Rose wandered back to the bathroom. And this time, she saw it.

"Ben!" she started to scream. "Ben! Get up here!"

He came bounding through the doorway, his gaze darting around the room. "What is it? Did you find—oh. Oh, no."

He was looking where she was pointing, at the sink.

How they had missed it the first time she couldn't imagine. Maybe because you sort of had to stand over the sink and look down, and they had only been looking for Ginny. But there, plain as day, were bright red fingerprints on the edge of the sink, a perfect impression of four bloody fingers gripping on for dear life.

CHAPTER TWENTY-SIX

Rose rubbed her eyes, hoping her vision would clear and that horrible red stain would no longer be there. She rubbed at her forehead, wishing her head would clear. Blood! Why would there be blood? Even if that story that Ginny and Max had told her was true and Ginny had somehow slipped away into another time, why would there be blood?

Ben's voice made her jump. "Okay, that's it." He started out of the bathroom. "I'm calling the police."

"The police!"

He paused and looked at her. "Do you have a better idea?"

She shook her head. "No, I—whatever you think is best."

She stood watching him as he dialed 911, hugging herself tightly as she heard him say the impossible words. "My daughter seems to be missing. And we found blood in the bathroom."

The doorbell rang. Ben stopped in mid-sentence and looked at her. She ran toward the door, hoping it would be Ginny, whether that made any sense or not. She flung the door back, and there, of course, was Anna. Who else?

As usual, Anna took charge. "Rose. Max got home a while ago and he told me you'd left the hospital." Her gaze swept down Rose's body and back up again. Rose automatically put her hand up to straighten her hair and wipe her eyes, picturing in her mind how wild and disheveled she must look. Probably had black mascara streaks down her face. Then she made herself drop her hand back down to her side. What did she care about any of that now?

"Rose, is everything all right? Is something wrong?"

"Yes, as a matter of fact, Anna, this is not a good time. Could you come back later—"

"What's going on, Rose? Is Ginny all right?"

Rose frowned. "Why would you ask about Ginny?" A movement out in the yard distracted her. A car was pulling into the drive. "Excuse me." She pushed past Anna and saw that it was the police—already. They hadn't sounded the siren, thank God.

Anna followed Rose and the police right on back into the house, as though she belonged there. But at least she stayed quiet, for the most part, while Rose and Ben told their stories. Rose kept her voice as even as she possibly could as she told about the events of the day—well, most of them. She left out all mention of the Ginny/Jordan issue, and she certainly didn't mention Ginny's time travel theory. As it was, she could see the wheels turning in the policemen's heads as she admitted that she had been in a psychiatric facility until this afternoon, and that she had left without being officially released. And then one of them turned to Ben and said, "Did you see your daughter after you got home?"

"No. I heard the water running. Rose said she was drawing a bath."

"But you didn't actually see her."

Ben glanced at Rose. "No."

Ah, yes. The wheels were clicking into place.

The other one consulted his notepad and said, "And you say the doors were all locked, and that if they had been locked from the outside, that would require a key, correct?"

"That's right."

"And you have your daughter's keys, as well as your own?"

She and Ben both produced their house keys.

"And does anyone else have a key to your house?"

"No," Rose said.

Ben didn't say anything right away. She looked at him, and he glanced away, but he answered. "No," he said.

In the chaos of the next hour or so, they made phone calls and tramped up and down the basement steps and brought in reinforcements, and she and Ben conducted them about the house and property and answered questions and talked and talked and talked.

Somehow, she found herself alone with Anna at one point. She tried to correct that situation by scooting into another room, but Anna grabbed her arm. "Rose, you can tell me."

"Tell you what?"

"What happened to Ginny."

"What makes you think I know?"

Anna snorted. "Maybe because you're the only other one who was here? And because I know how you felt about her."

Rose jerked her arm away. "First of all, I love her. Second, that's present tense. I still love her, because she's alive."

"Oh, well—of course she is. But I mean." Anna laughed, and Rose thought the sound was jagged and nervous. Briefly, she wondered why. "Ginny couldn't just disappear into thin air, could she?"

Rose heard voices and footsteps. Some of the cops were coming back, so Rose spoke quickly. "I need to tell you something, Anna. You're fired."

"What?"

"You heard me. I don't need your services as a therapist anymore. Dr. Carswell is doing a fine job. And I don't know of any other reason for you to be here, do you?"

Anna stood up straighter, so that she was looking down at Rose when she answered. "Well, I thought we were friends. Old friends."

Rose shook her head. "I don't think we were ever really friends." Ben walked past the doorway, and she saw Anna's gaze flicker toward him. Rose smiled grimly. "And I don't think I'm the one you're interested in now."

"I don't know what you're insinuating—"

"Oh, of course you do." She moved toward the doorway, motioning for Anna to come along. "Like I said, I don't think we'll be needing your services anymore."

For a few minutes after seeing Anna out, Rose felt strong and proud of herself. Then she glanced out the window and saw Anna huddled in conversation with Ben.

So had she really accomplished anything at all?

CHAPTER TWENTY-SEVEN

In no time, the house was like Grand Central Station, with police and volunteers and friends coming in and out, and the SUVs of the media pulling in and out of their roadside parking places. The noise had become a background hum as Rose sat and waited and listened more to the voice inside her own head, accusing her, speculating, wondering. But then a couple of the voices outside grew so loud that she couldn't ignore them and, crossing to the narrow window by the front door, she lifted the curtain and looked out.

It was Max and that other boy…what was his name? Alec Something. The one who had made Ginny so upset on her birthday. The two stood facing off like cats yowling before the brawl. She stood still, listening, and had no trouble hearing every word they were shouting at each other.

"What are you doing here, Matthews?"

"I would think that's pretty obvious. I'm worried about my girlfriend."

Rose snorted, remembering how Ginny had felt about this boy of late.

"I seem to recall she dumped you," Max said.

The taller boy—"Matthews"—smiled grimly. "No, she didn't. But I guess you can say anything you like, when she's not around to contradict you."

Max laughed. "Yeah, apparently you can."

He tried to step around the guy and go up the steps, but Matthews stepped in front of him. "Look, you little freak, I think you know a lot more about this than you're telling."

"What do you mean by that?"

"You're a freak and everybody knows it. And you've been bothering Ginny for weeks, following her around. You probably had plenty of opportunity to steal her key. Maybe you even convinced her to give you one, who knows? But if anybody knows what happened to her, my bet's on you."

"Yeah, well, good luck with that."

Again, Max tried for the steps. This time the tall boy grabbed his arm and jerked him, and Rose decided that was enough. Pulling the door open, Rose looked at the tall boy and said, "Pushing people around seems to be a habit with you, doesn't it?"

He dropped Max's arm and looked at her with a deep frown. "Excuse me?"

Ignoring him, she turned to Max and said, "Come on in."

Once Max was inside, Rose slammed the front door and turned the dead bolt. Apparently the Matthews boy didn't care much for her rudeness. After a second, she heard him yell, "Yeah, that's right. Let the creep in. Ginny told me about you. You're all a bunch of freaks. No wonder Ginny's missing."

Leaning against the doorway, Rose pressed her hand against her chest. Her heart felt as though it were about to beat its way through. She felt Max touch her lightly on the arm.

"Don't worry about him. No one's gonna listen to him. He's like one of those creepy stalker types from a movie."

She jerked up her head to stare at him. "I never thought...you don't suppose...I wonder if he could be the one that hurt Ginny."

Max looked puzzled, which in turn confused her.

"Hurt Ginny?" he said.

She pushed stray hair out of her face. She couldn't imagine what she must look like. "You do know Ginny is missing, right? Isn't that why you're here?"

"Yes, of course, but..." His voice drifted off, and he stood biting his lower lip and considering her, as though trying to figure out how to say something.

And then she realized. "Oh, Max...you're not thinking...I mean, please. Just don't even start with that again."

His voice was low, but his eyes flashed with determination. "But Mrs. Crosby, this is exactly what we talked about. Ginny vanishing into...you know. And it even happened on the very day we were talking about."

She heard the phone ring in the kitchen, heard Ben say, "Hello?"

Waving Max off, she started that way, as always practically dizzy with intoxicating measures of both hope and fear at the possibility of news. But Ben appeared in the kitchen doorway, punching off the portable phone and shaking his head. "Just a reporter." Handing the phone off to her, he wandered off toward his bedroom.

She rounded on Max. "Look, I don't know what happened to Ginny. But I know I can't start talking about time travel theories. They'll lock me up for sure this time, with no choice of getting back out. And I need to be free to try to help Ginny."

"Okay, great. I want to help Ginny, too. How do we do that?"

She waved her hand and looked very unsure. "We do what we're doing. We look for her."

"But what good will that do, if—"

"Max, stop it!" She sighed and looked at him, her eyes almost pleading. "I don't know what happened to Ginny. I agree it's pretty bizarre, that she's just seemed to vanish into thin air." She put up her hand to quiet him. "But that's real blood we found in there, Max."

She heard him gasp. So Anna hadn't told everything.

"You found blood?"

She nodded. "Something very real happened to her. We have to proceed on that assumption."

For a moment he was silent, and she thought she had won. But then he whispered, "Jordan had a head injury."

"Stop it, Max!" Practically choking, she gasped out the words. "You're killing me."

She saw his eyes reddening, and he was biting his lip again. "It's killing me, too, Mrs. Crosby. It's just that…I promised Ginny that if this happened, that if she disappeared, I would find her. And I would do anything, absolutely anything, to keep that promise. Only I don't have a clue how."

Rose felt herself melting. She reached out and took the boy's hand. "No, if your theory is correct, I don't see any way we could go after her, anyhow. So maybe it's better to do it my way. Not rule out any possibilities. Think of anything you can that might help us find Ginny if some perfectly ordinary evil has gotten after her." He looked off into the distance, and she was pleased to see that he did seem to be thinking it over. "What about Alec Matthews?" she prompted.

"Do you know any more about him? Do you think it's possible that Ginny might have given him a key?"

"No, I don't," he said, sounding very sure. After a moment of silence, he said, "Actually, there was another weird guy that followed Ginny around and scared her."

"You're kidding. Ginny never mentioned anything like that to me."

"Well, at first she was afraid she was being paranoid. And then we found out who it was and, well…we thought it was okay, that his excuse made sense, but now…"

"Max," she said sharply. "Just tell me. Who was it?"

"Your old fiancé. Hunter Isaacs."

Rose had to lean against the door to keep from falling down in a heap.

CHAPTER TWENTY-EIGHT

The lawyer's receptionist looked up at Ben and smiled as he closed the door behind him. Glancing at Ben, Rose could see why. He had made an effort to look like a prospective client, and in the process had somehow managed to look handsome and confident in spite of the dark circles under his eyes. His smile was still brilliant, even though she knew him well enough to recognize how fake it was, as was the hearty tone of his voice.

"Hello," he said. "We don't have an appointment. Something's come up sort of suddenly, and I—well, I've heard Mr. Isaacs might be the one to help us. Do you think he might have a minute?"

"Um…let's see." She squinted at something on the computer screen, presumably the lawyer's calendar. "He might have a few minutes, but Judge Matson is coming by." She stood up. "Tell you what. Let me just pop back here and check."

"Thanks."

As she walked down the hall, Ben pulled out a roll of Tums and munched on a couple of the powdery tablets. He grimaced and held out the roll to Rose, offering her one. She started to take one, but as she heard footsteps returning down the hallway, it fell to the floor from her stiff fingers. She didn't bother to pick it up.

What were they doing here, she wondered. After Max had told them the incredible story of Hunter's following Ginny around a couple of times, and his and Ginny's confrontation with the man, she and Ben had dutifully passed on the information to the police. The lead investigator then reported back to them that they had spoken with Mr. Isaacs and determined he had nothing to do with Ginny's disappearance.

But Ben had not accepted that. In fact, as the hours went by with no leads, he had paced and raged more and more, and Hunter's name came up a lot. "He's a big wig in this town," Ben growled. "He fed them some line and probably called his buddy the police chief and it was over. But he's the only person we know of who's threatened our little girl, isn't he?"

Rose hadn't said much as Ben railed like that. Part of her was relieved—and also a little bewildered—that he wasn't accusing her. Another part rolled the idea around in her head, the idea that Hunter could have turned into the kind of person who could stalk and then harm her daughter. True, he had betrayed her with Jordan, but then…he had also protected Rose in the ugly aftermath, when he could have told things that would have put her away.

No, she didn't, couldn't believe this of Hunter. More than likely, he had just been startled and fascinated by Ginny's resemblance to Jordan just as she had. But she didn't want to say any of that to Ben, so she had just remained silent.

Until today, when he came out of his bedroom dressed in his only blazer and tie and declared that he was going to pay a little visit to Mr. Isaacs. She couldn't let him go alone. He had murder in his eyes. So she had steeled herself and insisted that she come, too, not allowing herself the temptation of thinking it over. But now that she was here, she couldn't imagine it. Not just facing Hunter, but seeing him with Ben, maybe hearing secrets spilling from her former fiancé that she had never planned to share, even with her husband.

Especially with her husband.

The receptionist reappeared and motioned for them to follow her. "He can give you ten minutes, all right?"

"Sounds great," Ben said, in that same fake voice.

He started down the hallway after the receptionist, but she found that her legs had gone as stiff and cold as her fingers. She couldn't move. Hunter Isaacs was at the end of that corridor. Hunter! She couldn't possibly face him, she couldn't—

"Rose, you coming?"

The sharp sound of Ben's voice snapped her into movement, like a riding crop against a horse's side. Her legs jerked and moved her toward him, toward the end of the hallway, even though her mind still screamed in protest.

As they reached the threshold of his office, she peeked around Ben and saw the attorney rising to his feet, buttoning his coat, as though preparing for a new client. He reached across the desk and held his hand out to Ben. "I'm Hunter Isaacs. How can I help—"

He broke off, spotting Rose as Ben moved to shake his hand and left her exposed, alone.

For a moment they both stood silent. Then she heard Ben's wry voice. "I believe you two know each other."

Hunter's face flooded with color, and she saw his eyes narrow with an expression of displeasure that was so familiar that it nearly knocked the breath from her.

"When are you people going to let it go?" he demanded, his voice low and almost hissing.

"What do you mean?" Ben had dropped all pretense. He stood tense, fists clenched as though preparing for the fight that Rose had feared. "You mean let it go that you were stalking my daughter—who has now disappeared."

Hunter's gaze flickered toward his receptionist, who was still standing in the doorway, wide-eyed. "Mr. Isaacs, I'm sorry, I—"

"No problem," he said. "I can handle this."

Shutting the door on her, he rounded on Rose and Ben. "Your kids have been here. The police have been here. I'm sick of this whole thing."

"I believe you started it by following my daughter and scaring her half to death."

"Yes, I admitted that I wanted to get a better look at her. She looked so familiar."

An odd expression crossed Ben's face. "You mean she reminded you of Rose?"

Hunter shook his head. "I'm not going into all of this again. You know the story by now, I'm sure." He leveled his gaze at Rose. "It's really remarkable, isn't it? How much she's like Jordan?"

A week or two ago, Rose would have given anything to hear someone confirm her story. To see the flicker of…what? Insecurity? Wonder? Something new was in Ben's eyes as he looked at her, as he digested what Hunter was saying. Was he starting to believe her, even a little? But what did it matter now, except to make Rose even more frightened that something terrifying and unnatural was happening to her daughter?

All she could manage in response to Hunter's question was a jerky nod of her head.

His voice and his expression softened. "I take it your daughter is still missing?"

This time she managed a choked whisper. "Yes."

"I'm sorry, Rose. I truly am. But I can't help you. I wanted to get a closer look at her because of the resemblance. That's all." He turned to Ben. "I'm sure the police told you that the day your daughter went missing—"

"Ginny," Rose murmured. "Her name is Ginny."

"I was here in this office with my secretary right outside until a colleague picked me up and we drove to Atlanta."

She saw Ben's shoulders slump. "Yeah. They told us you were at a conference."

"And made a speech in front of about two hundred people."

"Yeah."

For a long moment, no one moved or spoke. None of them seemed to know how to continue or how to end the scene, either.

Then Hunter leaned against his desk and stroked his chin, eyeing them warily. "Look, I hate to ask this, but was your daughter at all…disturbed?"

Ben drew himself up to his full, impressive height. "What the devil do you mean by that?"

Hunter put up his hands. "I just mean…well, when she was in here with that boy, she had dyed her hair to look like Jordan and was dressed sort of like her. I mean, she looked even more like Jordan than the first time I saw her, and I just wondered if she…"

"If she's like the rest of the Remington family?" Rose said quietly. "Disturbed like her good ole mom?"

"No, Rose, not like that." He studied her for a long moment, until she squirmed. "Are you sure you want to keep talking about this?"

She met his gaze. "I'm sure. Say whatever you like. I've got to…" She licked her lips, feeling her mouth go dry. "I don't know what to do for Ginny, so I've got to go over anything that might help."

He nodded slowly. "Look…why don't you folks sit down, all right?" He returned to his seat behind the desk while Rose and Ben fell into chairs. Then he leaned toward them. "As I told your daughter and the boy with her, I was momentarily shocked when I saw your daughter in the mall. Because yes, she does look remarkably like Jordan. I wondered if the girl might be Jordan's daughter, that's all. And that intrigued me quite a bit. I wanted to know."

"Know what?" Ben asked.

Hunter looked at her again, and she lifted her chin. "He wanted to know for sure whether Jordan is dead," she said.

Ben shook his head. "I still don't get it."

"You've never told him about all this?" Hunter asked her.

"No. But…it's time. Tell him."

"You sure that's what you want? I mean…why don't you tell it?"

She shook her head, unable to speak at all.

"Okay." Hunter turned his attention to Ben. "You do at least know about the girl…Jordan?"

Ben laughed drily. "Oh, yeah."

Leaning back, Hunter pressed his fingers together into a sort of tent shape. "Rose at first was really close to this girl. Her mother, too." He shook his head. "In fact, that was the weirdest thing of all, how Carla Remington took to the girl. But then Rose got it in her head that something was going on between Jordan and me. And you know Rose. Once she gets an idea in her head, she hangs onto it."

Ben glanced over at her—but neither confirmed nor denied. "Go on."

"They started fussing and fighting like cats. One night, Anna told me they had gone down to the pond together. I thought that was pretty strange, because Rose had a thing about that pond."

"Still does."

She started to feel a little prickle of irritation worming its way into the fear. Yes, she'd asked him to tell the story, but she hadn't asked him to proceed as though she wasn't in the room. And it wasn't quite right, was it? The story? Did Anna really tell him that she and Jordan had gone down that path together?

Hunter's story was rolling on. "Rose hated that pond. Didn't want to go near it. So when I heard she'd gone with Jordan down there, it made me nervous."

"Nervous? Why? I mean, sure it's strange, but…surely you didn't think Rose would harm the girl, did you?"

"Actually I was afraid Jordan was up to something. What did we really know about her, after all? So I decided I better go down there and see what was going on. It was dark by then, so I got a flashlight—I mean, that was weird, too, that they would go down there at night. The trail had gotten all weedy and overgrown because it wasn't used, and Rose was nervous about snakes.

"Anyway, I went down the trail to the pond, and at first I didn't see her. But I heard someone crying. I found Rose sitting on the ground near the pond with her knees drawn up to her chest, shaking and bawling. I sat down next to her and asked what was going on. So then she started to tell me some bizarre story."

Rose leaned forward, covering her face with her hands.

"First, Rose was convinced I'd had a rendezvous to meet Jordan down at the pond. So she had followed the girl down there to confront us."

"And did you?" Ben asked him. "Have a date to meet Jordan, I mean?"

"Of course not. Like I said, who knows what that girl was up to?"

"Stop it!" The words ripped from her in a shout, so loud that both men jumped and looked at her.

Hunter pursed his lips and glared at her with familiar disapproval. "You asked me to tell the story."

"I thought you would tell the truth."

Hunter threw up his hands. "You gotta be kidding me. After all these years, you're still going to say—"

"That you were there with her," Rose said. She was shaking all over, but with anger, not fear. "I saw you with her, saw you holding her and kissing her—"

"No, you did not."

"Okay, okay, both of you stop it," Ben said. He wiped a shaky hand across his mouth. "I don't really care about any of this unless it has something to do with Ginny."

Hunter frowned. "And I never said it did. You two are the ones who pushed your way into my office."

As if on cue, the phone on his desk buzzed. As he picked it up, he said, "That's my secretary. I'm sure Judge Matson is here." Into the phone, he said, "Yes, yes. We'll be finished in just a minute." Dropping the phone back in the cradle, he stood up. "Well, if you don't want to hear any more from me, I'm sure Rose will tell you her version of the story."

"I want to hear it from you. What happened when you got to the pond?" Ben held his hand up, silencing Rose's protests. "Whenever it was you got there."

"Rose was hysterical. According to her, she had just killed Jordan."

"What!"

"That's right."

Ben turned slowly to face her. "I suppose he's lying about that, too?"

"No," she whispered. "That part is true."

"You killed her!"

"I think...I didn't mean to. It was an accident."

"What happened?"

She took a deep breath. "I...I had seen Jordan with Hunter, and then he pulled away from her and left, so I confronted her, or...I guess I sort of jumped on her. I...we got into an argument, and then a scuffle, right by the pond and I sort of shoved her and she lost her balance. Jordan fell into the water and then...she never came up."

Ben turned to Hunter. "Is that right?"

"That's what she told me, yeah. So I took the flashlight and I looked. I looked everywhere. I even dove into the water and looked."

"And?"

"And nothing. No Jordan."

"Did you call the police?"

"No."

"Why not?"

"Would you have?"

"Of course."

"Really?" Hunter folded his arms. "I wonder. Here were the possibilities. Rose was being hysterical and crazy. Calling the police would just get her into trouble. Or...Rose had just accidentally killed this girl. If that was the case, what good could the police have done?"

"They could have done something."

"Like what? Notify Jordan's family? They hadn't managed to figure out where she came from. Punish her killer? That was my fiancée—the woman you're married to now—and I frankly felt I owed her more than I owed some girl who showed up out of nowhere." Hunter pointed at Ben. "You would have done the same thing and you know it." He shrugged. "Besides, I always figured that

Jordan just got her memory back and went home."

"Really?" Rose whispered, for some reason feeling a little stirring of hope. "Even after what I told you? Even after there was never any sign of her again?"

"Especially when we never heard from her again." He looked from Rose to Ben. "You understand, don't you?"

Ben's forehead creased in thought. "Because the body didn't come to the surface?"

"Exactly. If Rose's story was true, the body would have floated. Someone would have found it. No one ever did. Still, a part of me wondered what exactly did happen, it was all so weird. So when I saw your daughter in the mall...well, I guess I wanted to know. After all this time, I was hoping to finally know for sure that she was alive, and that I did the right thing."

They walked to Ben's car in silence. But as they pulled on the highway, he said, "So. Why did you two break up?"

"Excuse me? Did you not just hear that story?"

"So you broke off the engagement because you thought he cheated on you?'

"No. He dumped me right after."

Ben looked surprised. "I don't get that. You'd think he must have loved you quite a bit, if he was willing to risk helping you cover up a death."

"Unless he was lying about being there with her."

"Even so...it's one thing to cheat on a girlfriend. Another to be involved in a girl's death, or even in covering it up."

Rose sighed. "Hunter was all about covering things up. He had big plans—law school, politics, with an eventual stop at the Governor's Mansion." *Although he didn't seem to make it very far.* She almost smiled in satisfaction as the thought popped into her head, but the moment faded quickly as she remembered why they had come. *Ginny.* She tried to pull her weary, drifting mind back onto track. "Anyway, after that night, Hunter couldn't risk being connected with someone like me. He knew there were two possibilities. Either I was crazy, or I had just killed a girl."

She watched Ben thinking that one over as he started the car. She could almost hear the wheels going round: *Yeah, I know how he feels. Those are the same possibilities I'm facing now...*

And sure enough, he was sitting lost in thought, his fists clenched on the steering wheel as he stared through the windshield. "Oh, lordy, Rose, I just realized..."

"What?" she choked out.

He turned to stare at her, looking deeply troubled. "I didn't want to mention this to you because I didn't want to upset you, but...well, I have a feeling you may be about to get your answer about whether that Jordan girl drowned or not."

"What do you mean?"

"The police told me last night that they had to check out the pond to see if maybe...well, you know. If Ginny had an accident or something." He took a deep breath and closed his eyes. "They have divers in the pond this morning."

CHAPTER TWENTY-NINE

L ittle knots of men stood around the edges of the pond and conferred, supervised, gossiped, speculated—who knew what all those men were doing. As Rose and Ben stepped off the path and into the clearing, a couple of them broke off talking and stared.

She had known they would check the pond, of course. And honestly, she wanted them to, for Ginny's sake, just in case—although the thought of what else they might find filled her with dread. She shook her head to clear away the nightmarish images of herself being dragged away to prison. No. She couldn't think of any of that. Ginny had to be found, whatever it took. They had to check the pond, just in case. They were running out of options. Judging by the way the detectives spoke to her, the way they looked at her, their first choice would probably have been to arrest Rose and interrogate her until she revealed the location of the body. That's what they believed, she was sure of it—that there was a body, and Rose was responsible for it. They were just itching for a bit of evidence.

And they were probably right about her guilt, after all. They just had their dates wrong. She shuddered at the thought.

Ben came to a halt near one of the detectives, his hands jammed down in his pockets and his shoulders hunched as though he were cold, even though the morning sun was already scorching. "Have they found anything?"

Captain Rollins shook his head and frowned. "No, but you

shouldn't be down here."

"Why not?"

"Well." He looked down at his shoe. "Just in case."

One of the other plain clothes policemen walked up. "I don't think we're going to be finding anything. Not today, anyway."

"Why do you say that?" Rose asked.

He nodded toward a woman walking toward them. A woman who looked decidedly odd out here in the Georgia woods dressed in a wetsuit. "Madeline and her bunch have been in the water for a couple of hours, but they can't tell much. It's too dark."

"Dark, muddy, tangled with roots. You name it." The woman ran her hand through her wet curls, then stuck her hand out as though for Rose to shake it. Then she realized what she was doing and drew it back. "Sorry."

"Oh, no problem."

"I'm Madeline Johnson."

"Thank you so much for being here, Ms. Johnson. But…it sounds as though you aren't able to tell much."

She shook her head, sending a little spray of water droplets. "Visibility's about two inches."

Rose glanced out at the pond. The water had been stirred so that it was even muddier than usual. She could imagine how hard it must be to see through that. She tried to keep her voice from sounding as frustrated as she felt. "Surely there's something you can do. I mean, obviously I don't want you to find Ginny's body—but I do want to know that she's *not* there. You're not just quitting, are you?" She looked from the diver, to the cop, to Ben. "Are we?"

"Of course not." Ben turned to Madeline. "How could a little puddle like that defeat a pro like you?"

Against her will, Rose felt her lips tilting into a smile. For once, she was happy to let Ben flirt. Maybe it would help.

It didn't seem to work on Madeline, though. "Puddle! It may not look that big to you, but it's forty to eighty feet deep in places."

Rose felt the familiar flutter in her stomach as she looked at the pond this time. Eighty feet of darkness, filled with long grasping fingers of root and weed. Ginny could be in there.

Captain Rollins cleared his throat, and he sounded hoarse when he spoke. "Look, folks, this isn't where you need to be."

Rose tried to control the edge in her voice. "This is where you're looking for my daughter. Where else do you think I should be?"

"Back at your house, manning the phones."

"A volunteer is doing that. Someone perfectly capable of taking messages as well as me."

Rollins put up his hands.

"You do look exhausted," Ben said, his voice surprisingly gentle. "Look, they're quitting anyway. Let's get you back to the house."

The searchers did, in fact, start climbing out of the muddy crater right about then. Ben was in the very act of turning Rose away from the dwindling activity when they heard a shout from one of the last divers.

Rose broke free of Ben's arm and whirled back around. The searchers who had just quit were running back, converging at the end of the pond farthest from her and Ben. The two down in the water shouted back up at them, and one started to climb back down. As she and Ben ran to join the group, Captain Rollins immediately moved to intercept them.

"I'm sorry, folks, but you're definitely going to have to leave now."

"You've obviously found something," Ben said.

Rollins sighed and wiped sweat off his forehead. "Yes sir, we have found something. But it's not your daughter."

Rose tried to force out the words. "What did you find?"

"Mrs. Crosby, as I said, it's nothing to do with your daughter. But this may be a crime scene now, so you have got to leave."

"Tell us what you found and we'll go," Ben said, sounding choked.

Rollins started to shake his head.

Rose whispered. "You found remains, didn't you? Human remains."

After a long silence, the detective sighed. "Yes ma'am, we did."

Ben threw up his hands. "Then how can you say it's nothing to do with us? How do you know it's not Ginny?"

"Because we found skeletal remains, Mr. Crosby."

"What?"

"Bones. These remains have been here far longer than your daughter's been missing."

Ben appeared dazed. "How long?"

"I couldn't begin to tell you that. Just let us do our jobs right now, and maybe we can tell you soon, okay?"

As he strode away, Rose murmured to Ben, "I can."

"What?"

"I can tell you how long they've been there." She looked up at him, feeling tears rush to her eyes. "Since 1984."

Part VI

The Pond

CHAPTER THIRTY
1984

Her knee made sharp contact with the ground as she pitched forward. Pain shot through her as the skin of her kneecap peeled back. Her bare hands hit the dirt next as she fell to all fours. The jolt of the fall was like the shock of falling out of bed, jarring her awake. She pulled herself up to a sitting position, rubbing her knee, and looked around. She tried to remember what she had been doing before the fall—even in the seconds preceding it. Was she sleep-walking?

She looked around but couldn't see much. A thin beam of moonlight trickled through pine tree limbs. The buzzing and chirping of night things sounded familiar and alien all at once—too loud, too intimate.

This was strange. Her mind registered that as a cool fact, then stopped. It pursued the idea no further.

A breeze fluttered across her skin, and she shivered. *Strange.* The night was warm, but her bare skin felt damp and vulnerable. *Bare skin.* She held out her arms and looked down at her body. Her skin glowed white in the moonlight. She wore a damp camisole and a silky skirt that was tangling around her legs. Nothing else.

Strange. The word formed again in her brain, and she tried to hang onto it, tried to latch onto it to see where it would take her. But it slipped away from her.

She hugged her arms to her chest as another breeze touched her, then drew her attention to a small body of water as it gently rippled the surface. The moonlight sparkled on the surface, rhythmically as the water sloshed. It drew her in. She could feel herself glazing over, growing sleepy, watching the tiny flashes of light, listening to the gentle splashes.

Then the light grew around her, brighter and brighter, drowning her in light. She put up one hand to ward it off. She touched her throbbing head with the other hand. More wetness. Sticky wet. She whimpered, feeling stabbed by the bright light. Headlights, she realized. A car.

Two figures, silhouetted in the light, approached her. Slowly, she brought her hand up in front of her face and whispered, "That light. It hurts my head."

CHAPTER THIRTY-ONE
Rose, 2009

"Could we hold off on telling the police, do you think?"

Ben didn't seem to hear her. Or maybe he just didn't want to talk. He continued to sit across from her in the New Room, his face buried in his hands. She cleared her throat and tried to raise her voice above a whisper, although she didn't want to speak loudly enough to be heard by the volunteers in the kitchen. "Do you think we can hold off on telling the police?" she said again.

This time his head popped up, and he looked almost surprised. "About what?"

It was her turn to be surprised. Dropping her voice to a whisper, she said, "About what I did, back in 1984, to...her?"

Ben made a noise of frustration. "I'm sorry, but I don't care about that right now. All I care about is Ginny."

And what if they're one and the same? She couldn't seem to stop the thought from running through her head, even though she knew she needed to squash it. She certainly couldn't share that thought with Ben.

"I know I need to confess about what I did." She drew in her breath, steeling herself. "And I will, but right now, I just can't be locked up somewhere because of what happened with Jordan. I need to be free. If I can do anything to help Ginny—"

"Yeah, yeah, of course." He waved his hand, carelessly dismissing her fears, her future. "Let's just worry about Ginny right now, okay?"

As she tried to nod, loud voices sounded in the kitchen. As Ben

237

shot to his feet, Max came bursting through the door, looking wild-eyed and pale.

"Is it true?" Max turned from her to Ben, then back again. "They found a body in the lake?"

"Calm down," Ben said. "It wasn't Ginny."

"How do you know?"

"The police said the remains are skeletal. They're from…" His eyes flickered toward Rose for only the barest moment. "Well, they've been there for years."

"Since 1984," Max said, sounding grim.

"What? How did you…I mean, why would you say that?" Ben asked.

Max turned to Rose. "You haven't told him?"

"Told me what?"

Rose struggled to speak. "Max, don't. Please. Not now. We're so upset—"

"We should be upset!" Max turned pleading eyes to Rose. "What are we going to do? I told her I'd come look for her if this happened."

"Rose, what is this?" Ben asked her.

"Have you shown him the note?" Max continued earnestly. "That'll convince him, like it did you."

Rose clapped her hands over her ears. "Stop it!"

"What note?" Ben's voice sounded deadly. "If there is something about my daughter's disappearance that I don't know, someone better tell me right now."

Rose sighed heavily. "Max doesn't know anything, Ben. He—and Ginny along with him—just had this bizarre theory."

"Bizarre?" Max practically spat the word as he dug down in his pocket. "That's not what you said when Ginny and I talked to you about it earlier." He pulled out the yellowing scrap of paper. "When we showed you this."

Rose rubbed her aching forehead. "I don't know what to think, frankly."

"Show me," Ben said quietly.

"Okay." Max breathed in deeply. "But first I need to give you some background." He glanced at Rose. "Since apparently she's not going to."

Max settled himself in an armchair, then started telling the same story that he and Ginny had told Rose earlier, before she disappeared. The moment Max mentioned the idea that Ginny might have bodily gone back to 1984, Ben fell back in his chair and groaned. "No, no, no, please! Please tell me I'm not sitting here listening to such nonsense when my daughter is missing!"

"I know it sounds crazy—"

"You got that right."

"But there's evidence." First, he pulled out the article from the paper and passed it across to Ben. As the man scanned it, Max filled him in about Ginny's tattoo. "That's what made it completely real for us—for me and Ginny," he said. "And after, when we were discussing the possibility…that Ginny was going to make some sort of jump through time and visit 1984, I said that if she did, we should decide somewhere that she would leave a note so we would know. And she sort of gasped and said that reminded her of something. She had found a piece of a note up in the basement ceiling weeks ago. So she went and got it." He looked down at the paper. "At the time she couldn't figure out what it said, because part of it is torn away, but now it seems pretty clear. 'Max, Mom, I'm here. I'm JORDAN.' And then it's signed. 'Ginny.'"

Silence fell.

Ben appeared dazed. "I'm sorry to say this, son, but how do I know you didn't write that this morning?" He held up his hands as Max protested. "Or even that Ginny wrote it recently, as a part of this game you were playing."

"It isn't a game," Max said angrily. "Look, my dad will tell you that a lot of physicists believe time travel is possible." He tapped the scrap of paper. "He also looked at this paper and said that it and the ink are old."

"So what! It's scattered letters. No whole words. You could read anything into this thing." He turned to Rose. "Please tell me you don't believe this."

"Oh, Ben…" She had never felt so tired, so defeated, in her life, but she forced herself to look him in the eye. "Here's what I believe. I'm going to be locked up soon, either for what I did to that girl in 1984, or because I'm crazy. So I might as well tell you straight. I think my daughter vanished into thin air—vanished from a locked-up house. I think she is right now back in 1984, walking around as that girl Jordan…" Rose's eyes filled with tears. "And waiting for me to kill her there."

CHAPTER THIRTY-TWO
1984

She followed them around and tried to help as they prepared for the girl Rose's eighteenth birthday party. That's what she did every day. Drift around behind them, as purposeless as a leaf blown on the wind, and just about as empty of thought.

No, that wasn't entirely true, she realized, as she accepted a stack of plates from Mrs. Remington to take out to the picnic table. She was empty of memory, but not thought. Her brain churned away at high speed all the time, trying to make connections, trying to remember. The forgetfulness was horrifying, as though her brain was constantly trying to get at an itch it couldn't scratch.

She supposed that was understandable. What made her wonder was the sense of urgency, as though something horrible would happen if she didn't remember and remember soon.

As people arrived and started to chatter and laugh and grow louder, she pulled inside herself and grew more quiet. She felt too tall and gangly and obvious, wishing she were as petite as Rose, as able to slip into a crowd and disappear. And Rose did keep disappearing, blast her! That was another odd thing, the way she kept feeling as though she needed to cling to Rose, and not because she wanted Rose to protect her. For some odd reason, she felt that tiny, timid Rose needed looking after, and that she was the one to do it. As though she were in a fit state to protect anyone!

"Who are you looking for?" came a smooth voice from behind her.

She didn't have to turn to recognize the voice. "Your fiancée," she said, annoyed. But not just at Hunter. She was annoyed at herself for the way her pulse picked up speed whenever she heard him speak.

He nodded slowly, studying her. "She's over there. Starting to open her presents."

"Oh."

She turned toward him, looked deep into his eyes, and he didn't look away. Vaguely, she heard squeals of delight as Rose opened a present. "Do you love her?" she asked.

"I'm engaged to her, aren't I?"

"That's not really an answer."

He shrugged. "Sometimes you can't have exactly what you want. So you have to get as close as you can." His eyes burned into her. "The trouble is, when you do that, how do you know when you're as close as you can get? What if something comes along that's even closer?"

A chill crept through her. "Doesn't sound like a very good deal for Rose. Why don't you just go after exactly who you want?"

"Not possible. She's dead."

"Oh."

"You have her eyes." He lifted his hand and appeared to be about to touch her face, when a squeal from Rose caused him to jerk it back.

"Look, Hunter!" she called out. "Look what your mother gave us!"

"Us?" he said. "It's your birthday. I'm not supposed to get presents."

Jordan—that's what they were calling her now—felt a thrill at how smoothly he turned on the charm for Rose, after what he had been saying. After he was about to stroke her face!

Poor Rose was blushing, completely unaware. "It's for our apartment." She held up an amazing quilt, made of hundreds of jewel-toned prints put together in such a way that the colors bled from one to another.

"For your bed," said his mother.

"Oh, I see," Hunter answered, flashing his white teeth.

For a moment, they were quiet, watching Rose open a couple more packages. She felt so terrible for Rose, so happily tearing into her packages, planning her life with this guy. Should she tell her what her boyfriend had just said? Should she destroy Rose's happiness that way?

"Let's see," Rose was saying. "Only two left."

"Open mine," Anna said, pushing a small package toward her.

As Rose reached toward the couple of boxes left, Jordan felt warm breath against her neck. Hunter was leaning in close to her as he whispered, "I'm not as bad as you think I am."

"What?" She thought she saw Rose pause with the little box in her hand and look at them. She started to pull away from him, but his voice was still low and she had to lean in to hear. "The love of my life is dead. So it's not as though I'm going to be cheating on Rose with her."

"No. You're just going to be on the lookout for anyone that comes closer than Rose."

"That's not true. I've never been on the lookout." For the first time, she saw pain in his eyes. "You just showed up out of nowhere."

"Me!"

Rose was opening the little box, while Anna watched with an expectant smile on her face. But Rose kept glancing Jordan's way. At her and Hunter.

"I'm going to move up closer to the action." As she stood up, planning to move as far away from Hunter as possible, she simultaneously felt him grab her hand and felt something brush against her leg. She jerked her hand away from Hunter and reached down to her leg, feeling the soft fur of a cat.

"Hey there," she said to the gray tom, who was looking up at her as though they were old friends. "I haven't seen you around here before."

"That's Star," said Hunter. "Rose's cat. He disappears for days at a time but always shows back up."

"Star." She studied the cat, an odd feeling washing over her. "Star..."

"Yeah. Really clever, huh?" Hunter reached down and stroked the cat's forehead, which had a star-shaped white blaze.

And suddenly, everything flooded in on her, a dizzying wave of knowledge and memory, so many scenes and pictures and thoughts that she was almost knocked over by the force of them. Mom and Daddy, and this same yard...only different. Noisier. More traffic noises. Fewer trees and flowers. Arguments and hurt feelings and the path back to the pond. Max! And Alec, reaching up into her ceiling tiles and pulling out a squirming gray kitten with a white star on its forehead. A star exactly like the one on this grown cat, twining and twisting around her ankles.

She dropped back down into the chair.

"What's the matter?" she heard Hunter say.

She jerked her head around at the sound of his voice, staring at him, feeling her mouth drop open. She was staring at the living embodiment of the drawing from her wall, the soulful-looking boy who had occupied so many of her dreams. Hunter Isaacs. Her mother's ex-fiancé.

Her mother…

It was a dream, it had to be a dream. It felt like one. There sat her mother, only different, like an old picture of her mother come to life. But real and solid, only feet away from her, a teen-ager with a radiant face, pulling a small box out of wrapping paper while a lot of other people beamed at her.

Other people…

Max's step-mom! It had to be her, although her hair was a sleek, natural-looking blonde instead of the bleached-straw stuff she had today.

Today…

But this is today.

She jerked her head around at the thought, looking at the people. Seeing the other boy from the picture on her bedroom wall. Hunter's brother, Jake. She stared back at the house, looking the same as when she lived there. The same, only different…the trim a different color. But then Daddy had painted it. Or Daddy would paint it. Sometime in the future.

Oh, dear God, it was real. Max had been right. She had landed back here in her mother's past, in her mother's girlhood, just as they had talked about. But no. No, that was idiotic. Her head felt fuzzy and dreamy. She was dreaming, that was it. She needed to sit quietly, to breathe the fresh air until she could think clearly again. Or until she woke up.

"Are you okay?"

She jumped at the sound of Hunter's voice next to her. She stared at him wildly. He was still there. Her mother's fiancé, the same guy she had met as a pudgy forty-something lawyer. Only now he looked rugged and fit and his face was smooth and tan.

He repeated the question. "Are you okay?"

Was she okay! She started to laugh, wondering if she should ask his opinion about that. Let's see. As far as she could tell, she was attending her own mother's eighteenth birthday party. So was she okay?

Wait a minute. Her mother's eighteenth birthday party. Something dramatic had happened at it, hadn't it? What had Mom told her, during that long talk when she told her all about Jordan, and why she had come to dislike her—*me!*—so much. Mom had thought that Jordan and Hunter snuck away from the party together, but something else…something before that.

Ginny watched as Teen Mom absently opened a box and reached in. A box from Anna. Suddenly it hit her. Jumping up, she threw herself toward her mother, knocking Mrs. Isaacs and Anna aside, reaching across the table and snatching the box away, throwing it down.

Chaos ensued, during which Ginny saw the story that Mom had told her playing out in greater detail, with dialogue added. It was like reading a synopsis of a movie and then going to see it. Just as Mom had told her, she (Jordan!) pointed out that the gift from Anna was almond soap, and they all realized that Mom was deathly allergic, and Ms. Shaw apologized, and everyone was horrified and thanked her. Mom obviously had a good memory. Except for one thing. Either Mom hadn't noticed or hadn't remembered how Anna, after delivering heartfelt apologies and swearing she was about to faint from the horror of it all, snuck a poisonous glance at Ginny, as though she were angry that the girl had shamed her and thrown her present to the ground, in spite of her good reason for it. Strange.

Eventually the party, though more subdued, got back into swing. But Ginny couldn't join in. She felt stunned. She retreated to the perimeter and tried to think.

Could this be the reason she had come—or been sent—to the past? So she could save her mother's life? Surely there would have been a simpler way. But…

Her head began to ache as she tried to think it through. This was so totally bizarre. She wouldn't have even known there was almond soap in that box if her mother hadn't told her the story about Jordan saving her from it. Her mother only had the story to tell her because it had already happened in 1984. So where did the knowledge about the almond soap come from? It was like a circle going round and round, 1984 to 2009 and back again.

Okay, breathe, she told herself. Think. There would be time later to try to figure out all this philosophical stuff. What should she do now? What was she supposed to do?

But nothing practical would come. The only thought that did come was the memory of her mother telling her that she had killed the girl Jordan back in 1984. And Mom had been so upset that, like an idiot, Ginny hadn't allowed her to go on with the story. Hadn't allowed her to give the details about what had happened between them so that maybe she could avoid it now.

She shook her head, hard, trying to clear it. She couldn't think about that right now, either. She tried to focus on some action, any tangible thing she could do to try and help herself. And then she remembered the note in the basement ceiling.

Quietly getting to her feet, she headed to the house and crept down the stairs, feeling the need to be quiet even though everyone else was still outside. She felt different now than when she had gone out of the house a couple of hours ago. Now she not only felt like an intruder, but like the only solid thing in the place. She felt as though she were walking on steps made of memory and sunbeams, that she would crash through them and fall into oblivion if she stepped too hard or made too much noise.

Once in the basement, she pulled one of the dining room chairs across the floor and stood under the spot of the ceiling that, to the best of her recollection, was the place she had put the note.

The note…

Idiot! Climbing down from the chair, she found a pen in her pocket and looked around until she found a box with an old composition notebook and tore a page from it. She paused before writing, trying to remember exactly how the scrap of note that she had found had looked. Shouldn't she make it match? That seemed like an important point, somehow. What if she wrote it differently? Could she screw up the space-time continuum? Could she do some little something wrong that would change things forever, so that she could never get home?

Then again, judging by what had just happened at the party, it didn't seem she had to put forth any effort at all, that things would come out the way they were supposed to—the way they already had—regardless of whether she put any thought into it. She shivered at that thought, once again hearing Mom's hysterical voice saying, "That girl died in 1984."

A wave of dizziness came over her at that thought. She climbed back up on the chair and pushed open the tiny window, hurriedly taking gulps of fresh air. But then a noise from upstairs made her jump. She might not have much time. Clutching the pen and trying to write in spite of her trembling hand, she dashed out a few hurried words. "Max Mom I'm here. I'm JORDAN!"

Okay, she definitely heard footsteps now. She shoved up the ceiling tile and tucked the folded paper to one side, over the next tile. As she did, her fingers met something solid, something leathery.

At first she jerked away, picturing all sorts of unpleasant, moldering things that might be hidden away in that dark place. The note was in its place and she needed to get out of here. But for some reason, she couldn't tear herself away. The cold, clammy object seemed to be holding her in place, drawing her, so that she stood on tiptoe on the chair and reached up a second time.

She tried to peer inside, but even as tall as she was, she was too short and the space was too dark for her to see anything. She stretched her hand up and felt inside, fighting the urge to draw her fingers back as her mind happily provided her pictures of rats, spiders, rotting skeletons, all sorts of pleasant images. But she pushed forward and again felt the leathery object. She tried to grasp it but her fingers just slid along it, not getting a good hold. She moved upward, trying to find a strap or a corner or something to grasp, and instead encountered what felt like a bunch of papers sticking out. She grabbed those and pulled.

She found herself looking down at a packet of what appeared to be loose-leaf binder paper, and at least the top ones were covered in handwritten blue ink. She started to smooth out the packet when she heard a foot on the top step and crammed the whole packet down into her pocket. She had just managed to climb down from the chair when Mom appeared.

How young and beautiful Mom looked—more radiant and golden than Ginny's earliest memories. Feeling a rush of love and fear, Ginny had to fight the urge to run over to the girl and throw her arms around her. But Teen Mom was glaring at her, not recognizing her, with her eyes filled with suspicion.

"What are you doing down here?" Mom demanded.

"I just...I thought I heard something." Ginny couldn't seem to meet Rose's eyes. "Guess I was wrong." She darted toward the stairs before Rose could ask any more questions.

Ginny didn't find an opportunity to take a look at what she had pulled from the ceiling right away. Mrs. Remington—Grandma!—spied her coming out of the house and called her over to eat. Mom followed in a few minutes and sat across the picnic table from her, giving her sour looks from time to time. Hunter reappeared even later than the two of them, mumbling something about taking a walk to clear his head. Star the cat stayed close by Ginny's feet and occasionally looked up at her with hopeful eyes and mewed. Jake joked that the cat thought he had found a sucker as Ginny slipped him bites of steak, but the cat actually ignored the meat offerings after the first bite or two, and Ginny found herself peering back into his golden eyes, wondering if he, too, had somehow skipped through whatever wormhole had brought her here, had disappeared from Grandma's crumbling 2009 ranch house as a kitten and managed to grow up here before Ginny appeared. Is that why he was staring at her? Did he remember escaping from the cardboard box in her bedroom and scrambling up the quilt on her bed, snuggling up to her and purring?

"You're not eating much," Grandma observed. "Are you all right?"

"She's fine," Mom said, popping a chip into her mouth and crunching down on it.

Ginny stared at her. What was the matter with Teen Mom? She was cutting into her steak with such energy that it was scary, as though she was picturing herself laying into something other than steak. Of course, Mom had told her something about this party, something that had upset her beyond the near-poisoning and had caused her not to feel grateful to Jordan as she should. Ginny tried to remember the rest of the story, but her head felt as though it were packed with cotton, like her mouth after dental work stuffed with gauze and suffocating. She just couldn't remember everything clearly.

She ached to crawl away from them all and take a look at the papers she had pulled out of the ceiling. Maybe there were some answers there. Maybe Mom and Max knew she was here and had left some kind of communication there, the way she had left the note…no. That was stupid. They couldn't stick something in a ceiling tile in 2009 and expect someone in 1984 to find it. That would only work the other way round. She could leave things here for them to find, but there was no way they could communicate with her. A sense of panic and claustrophobia threatened to finish filling her head up with fuzz, so that she couldn't think or remember at all. She grabbed at her paper cup full of tea and gulped at it.

"You look terrible," Grandma declared. "Is your head hurting again?"

"A little," Ginny said. She started to climb out of the picnic table bench. "I think I'm going to go lie down."

"That sounds like an excellent idea," Grandma said.

"Yes, it does," Mom said. The quiet, unfriendly sound of her voice made Ginny feel sad and even more alone.

Once in her room, Ginny settled cross-legged on the bed and pulled the papers from her pocket, feeling a thrill of excitement and hope. If she were in a novel or a movie, this would be the part where she found the clues that would make everything start to fall into place. She scanned through the papers quickly before she started to read each word, trying to get an overview of what she had found, but that proved more difficult than she had expected.

She made a stack of what appeared to be letters—or at least, they sounded as though one person was addressing another. But they weren't really in the form of letters. No "Dear Whoever," and no "Love Whoever" at the end. But they had a date at the top, all of which appeared to be during a four-month time period in 1980. And they said things like, "I know you're afraid we went too far. But is there really any such thing? Or is that a term that the old and frightened have made up to keep us in our place? To keep us from finding the fields of bliss that you and I both seek…"

Fields of bliss? Eeewww.

Ginny could only figure that these letters were written by a guy to a girl. The letter-writer might be more intellectual—and more creative—than Alec Matthews, but he was no doubt after the same thing. Were the letters written to Mom? By Hunter? But that didn't make sense, did it? In 1980, Mom would have been fourteen. She appeared timid and uncertain enough even now, at eighteen. Ginny didn't picture her in that kind of relationship when she was basically a kid.

She pushed that pile aside and started sorting the remaining scraps of paper, which were in a totally different handwriting and mostly in a dark black ink. There were all kinds of papers—parts of torn envelopes, lined paper like from a school composition book, even a couple of napkins. Whoever had written this stuff, she seemed to grab her pen and write whenever the urge struck and on whatever was at hand. Some of it was weird poetry, mostly about angels and visions of fire and stuff that Ginny couldn't begin to understand. Other writings were more like diary entries, but those weren't much more helpful, except in helping Ginny finally identify the writer as her Aunt Livvy. With that realization, Ginny cursed and threw the whole stack down on the floor.

What possible good could this stuff do her? Even in 1984, Aunt Livvy was dead. Whatever she had gotten into, it was over and done with. And besides, Ginny had never met her and knew very little about her. So she hadn't just made some bizarre leap through time to do something for her Aunt Livvy, had she? Surely this had to do with helping Mom, with changing something or protecting her from something, or…

Or maybe it didn't have any reason at all.

That thought knocked all the energy from her. She collapsed backward against the pillows and stared at the ceiling.

What made her think this weirdness had some purpose? It wasn't like in the movies, where some mysterious stranger comes up and tells you that you've got a lesson to learn or a mission to accomplish and that something bizarre is going to happen to you until that's done. There was Clarence in *It's a Wonderful Life*, and that black dude in *Family Man*, and, oh, lots of other examples she had thought of. But Ginny had heard no voices, received no instructions. She had just…what?

She squinted her eyes as though trying to see through the ceiling and thought. What exactly had happened? She remembered talking in the living room with Mom and Max. And Mom got all upset and then Ginny, herself, had started to get a little hysterical. So Mom stroked her and told her to go take a hot bath, and Max said he better go home. And then…what? She had been standing out by the pond, half naked and wet, and Mom and Hunter's car had pulled up. Just like in

Mom's story.

The pond…

Ginny nearly jumped out of her skin at a sudden scratching sound at the window. She laughed with relief when she saw Star crammed onto the narrow window ledge outside, pawing at the screen and begging to come in. The screen was securely attached, so Ginny opened the door to the porch and called to him. He reached her in about three bounds and touched Ginny's nose with his when she picked him up. She studied his face as she carried him back to her room. The star marking was exactly like the one on the abandoned kitten she had found in 2009, even the way the top of the star marking leaned to the left. Could it be possible that this was the same kitten?

She snorted. Of course it was possible. Whether she was in a deluded dream or a real universe with real time travel, anything was possible in this world.

"Where did you come from?" she asked him as she set him down on the bed. She scratched his ears and tried to remember what Mom had told her about finding the kitten that reminded her of the one Ginny found in the basement. "Let's see…according to Mom, she and Aunt Livvy, plus Hunter and Jake, found you floating on a log in the middle of the pond."

The pond again. Mom was terrified of that pond, and Grandma Carla was, too. Was there something outlandish about the pond? Maybe this was all a big physics problem, like a wormhole or some magnetic weirdness about the pond. She and the kitten had both been found there. So maybe they'd both had some kind of mind-bending science accident, which was interesting and terrifying and all that, but not really meaningful. No *Wonderful Life* stuff for Ginny. No purpose to this business at all.

But…it didn't really feel like that. Even during those days of blank un-remembering, she had felt it. The urgency, a kind of nudging and tugging at her spirit. The voice that wasn't a voice really but that got its message across anyway. *Do something.*

But about what?

She sighed, picking up the papers from the floor and stacking them on the bed. But Star dove into them in a sudden burst of playfulness and scattered them again, so Ginny just left them where they were.

She tried desperately to think of something else to do. Maybe she needed to talk to Mom, to think of a way to feel her out and see if there was something going on in her life that Ginny needed to help with. Then she remembered how Mom had looked at her and spoken to her at lunch. Lovely. Still, it would have to be done. Maybe Ginny could apologize first for, well, whatever it was Mom thought she had done.

Ginny crossed to the window and looked toward the picnic table under the trees. The party appeared to have broken up. Grandma and Mrs. Isaacs were gathering up scraps and putting paper plates into trash bags. Mom and Hunter were nowhere to be seen.

And Ginny wanted to do something now. She suddenly thought about pulling those papers out of the ceiling earlier, about feeling something else up there. Something solid and leathery. Of course, it was probably another dead end, but still. She needed to do something, and now was the time, before Grandma settled into the New Room for her night of TV and made it impossible for Ginny to get down into the basement.

With Star creeping along behind her, Ginny quickly headed back to the basement stairs.

CHAPTER THIRTY-THREE
Rose, 2009

Like every night of late, Rose lay awake staring at the dark ceiling, every muscle in her body tensed to the point of pain. Her head throbbed with lack of sleep, but she couldn't stop thinking about...everything. Not for the first time, she wished things were better with Ben, that he was here next to her, holding her, sharing all this with her.

Still, things with Ben could be a lot worse. He was at least in the same house with her. And—wonder of wonders—he didn't seem to think Rose was guilty of hurting Ginny. After seeing how the cops eyed her, the things they were saying about her on TV, she had asked him directly.

He had looked down at his feet, then up at the sky, anywhere but at her. Then, finally, he had said, "I won't lie. I've thought about it a lot, but...you're different now, Rose. Or you were different a few weeks ago, I guess is more like it. Anyway, if you had hurt Ginny, you would have done it in one of your mad frenzies. I would have come home and found you crying and hysterical."

"Like Hunter after I hurt Jordan," she said quietly.

"Yeah, well...whatever. Anyway, you wouldn't have hidden her body. You *couldn't* have. As far as I can tell, you only had a few minutes between the time Max left and the time I came home. How could you have moved Ginny all by yourself and in that amount of time, when she outweighed you by about twenty pounds? And where would you have put her that the police and the volunteer searchers couldn't have found her by now?"

As Rose remembered this conversation, she thought about the way the police had gone through the house, pulling it apart, analyzing every scrap of paper and peering into every corner, every cupboard, everywhere that a body could possibly have been hidden away. Had they raised the ceiling tiles in the basement? Surely they had. That's where Ginny had found the note that Max now insisted was from Ginny back in the past. In all seriousness, Max had told them that he and Ginny decided that was the place she should tuck away messages to them if she did actually end up in the past.

So…if Max's crazy theory was correct, and Ginny was back there right now, was it possible she had left other messages for them that hadn't been found yet?

She didn't see how that was possible. Surely either Ginny would have found any other notes months ago, or the police would have dragged them out during their search and demanded to know the meaning of them. She smiled. Even more likely, Max had already looked and hadn't found anything from Ginny.

Still, she had to do something.

Throwing off the covers, she pulled her jeans on and headed for the basement.

CHAPTER THIRTY-FOUR
Ginny, 1984

A s Ginny eased into the New Room, she saw Grandma Carla coming in from the kitchen. No way to sneak down to the basement without being seen now.

"Feeling better?" Even with a nice question like that, the woman's voice was harsh as sandpaper.

"Uh...yes, thanks."

"Good. Then come help me pick up a few things at the store. I thought we'd have leftovers but not with that plague of locusts. And of course Rose isn't giving a thought to what we'll eat tomorrow. I let her run off with that Hunter because goodness knows she needs him to take care of her. She'll never take care of herself."

"You're going out? I think I'll just stay here and rest—"

"Nonsense. A nice drive might help clear your head. You're never going to remember anything just sitting around here."

You'd be very surprised, Ginny thought. Sighing deeply, she gave up and followed Grandma Carla.

As she buckled herself into the passenger seat of Grandma's Buick—the same one that huddled under a dirty plastic cover in the back yard in real time—Ginny felt nervous. Grandma had always scared her. Even that summer when Ginny visited her and the woman was trying to be nice in her own drill-sergeant way. Even as she lay supposedly helpless in the nursing home bed, fixing her wild and troubled eyes on Ginny and trying to talk. And especially now, at the height of her power and sheer meanness.

"Why did you let me stay with you?" The question popped out

before Ginny could stop it.

"Why shouldn't I? It was the decent thing to do, wasn't it?"

"It just doesn't seem like something you would do."

She laughed sharply. "How would you know what's typical for me? You don't know anything about me."

This time Ginny said the words. "You'd be surprised what I know."

Grandma Carla turned to look at her, then faced the road again. "I suppose Rose has been telling tales about me. How mean I am. How unfair I am." She snorted. "I'm surprised you weren't afraid to get in the car with me. I might just dump you in the woods somewhere, like a stray dog."

A shiver ran through Ginny. Actually, a very similar thought had occurred to her. She told herself not to be an idiot, that this was Grandma after all, not an axe murderer. And the picture ran through her head again, of Grandma in the nursing home, trying to reach out to Ginny. The fear fled, leaving in its wake a feeling of deep sadness.

"I've seen what will happen to you," she whispered. "I've seen what you'll become."

Grandma whipped around to face Ginny, pulling the steering wheel with her and causing the car to swerve. "You've *seen* what *will* happen?" As she directed the car back to the middle of the lane, she started to laugh again, but Ginny thought her face looked whiter. "Oh, that's rich." Taking one hand off the wheel, she shook her finger in Ginny's face. "You listen to me, young lady. That nonsense won't work on me. You're no ghost or angel or anything particularly special. Just a silly girl that got herself into trouble. You asked me why I let you stay with us. Well, it was mainly because of Rose. If she didn't have a chance to get to know you, to see how perfectly ordinary you are, she would have been imagining all kinds of things about you. I wanted to show her the truth."

"What truth?"

"That there's nothing extraordinary out there. That no matter how terrible—or how wonderful—things may look in this life, it's all just plain old plain old underneath." Again that razor sharp laugh. "Oddly enough, even the Bible says that, doesn't it? Ashes to ashes and dust to dust." She let out a peculiarly wistful sigh. "Ashes and dust. That's all this whole world comes down to."

Now Ginny laughed. "Wow. No wonder you're always in a bad

mood."

Grandma flashed a scathing look at her before turning back to the road.

Ginny felt her laughter fading. "Trouble is, it's not true."

"Oh, really? Then prove it."

Ginny thought hard, trying to think of something she could tell Grandma to convince her that she wasn't just a girl who'd gotten a knock on the head, that something extraordinary really was going on. For a second, she was distracted wondering why she wanted to convince Grandma of that, but she quickly shrugged the doubt aside. That nudging in her spirit was back, and it seemed absolutely vital that Grandma believe her. She could barely breathe with the enormity of it, could hardly think for the mental picture of Grandma the way she would be, old and speechless and reaching out to Ginny…

Calling her Jordan. Begging her for help.

Suddenly it hit her. When Ginny had visited Grandma that summer, a church sermon about the Good Samaritan had reminded the woman of something that happened with Ginny's grandfather, a story she said she hadn't told anyone else.

Ginny said tentatively, "On the day that Mo—uh, Rose was born—your husband was driving you to the hospital. And you passed by a car that had run off the road and into a tree. Your husband started to pull over to help, to see if anyone was hurt, which made you angry because you were in labor, after all. You told him to forget it, because you were in a hurry. And he looked at you and said very quietly, 'I'm sure those other folks who passed by the injured man in the Good Samaritan story thought they had important things to do, too.' And then he mentioned how far apart your contractions were, and how it would only take a minute to help—which it did, but still—it hurt your feelings so bad that you thought about it for years, that you brought it up to him over and over, but now, sometimes, you think about what a good man he was—"

"Get out of the car." The woman's face was livid as she veered onto the shoulder of the road and shut down the car's engine.

Ginny looked around. There was a gas station across the road, but nothing else. What in the world was Grandma talking about?

The woman shoved Ginny's shoulder. "You heard me. Get out."

Ginny felt drained and weak, as though her shaky legs would never support her. But obediently, she climbed out. With the door still open, she peered back inside. "What are you doing? Are you getting out?"

"No, I'm not. Like I said before, I think a little change of scenery and some air will do you good."

"Are you...are you throwing me out? Out of your house too, I mean?" Ginny felt dazed, felt horrified that she might have somehow screwed up everything. Mom's stories hadn't included anything about Jordan fighting with Grandma or being evicted from their house. Had she somehow managed to mess up the future? Or was she supposed to go back and change things, and this was actually a measure of success?

"What happens from here is entirely up to you," Grandma said. "I personally have a feeling this whole memory loss business is a sham, anyway. So maybe it's time for you to go home. Here, take this."

Ginny looked down at what the woman had just shoved into her hand. A dime. Utterly perplexed, she asked, "What's this for?"

"The pay phone." She jerked her head in the direction of the nearby gas station, and Ginny saw an old-fashioned phone booth out near the road. "Maybe it's time for you to call some of your own people to come get you. If you really don't have anywhere to go, I'm not throwing you out. Like I said, I'm not afraid of you. But I won't have you filling Rose's head with nonsense. You can think about that on the walk back, if that's what you decide."

"The walk back?" Ginny tried to remember just how far they had driven. Everything looked so different in 1984, without all the subdivisions and stores she was used to along the roads—probably not built yet. But she thought they had driven at least three or four miles.

"It won't kill you." Grandma barked out a laugh. "Whenever I got hurt or sick, my daddy used to say, 'Walk it off, girl.' Always worked, too. So I'll see you later...or I won't. Whatever you decide."

With that, the woman reached across the seat, grabbed the door and pulled it shut, leaving Ginny standing outside.

CHAPTER THIRTY-FIVE
Rose, 2009

Rose dragged one of the old dining chairs across the basement floor, hardly feeling its weight as it scraped against the concrete. She breathed in slowly and tried to calm herself before climbing onto the rickety surface. Breaking her leg wouldn't make her feel any better.

After taking a moment to steady herself, she reached up as high as she could and pushed up the tile with her fingertips. For the thousandth time in her life, she cursed her height, or lack thereof. Ginny was so much taller. If she did put something up here, she probably pushed it further back than Rose could reach.

Boxes were stacked all along the wall next to her. The pile next to the chair wasn't much higher than the seat she was standing on, but she put one foot on it and pushed herself upward, anyway, trying not to think how precarious her position was. Straining with all her might and coming as close as she could to balancing on the very edges of her toes, she pushed her hand into the dark space and felt around.

Immediately, she had to fight the urge not to jerk it back and jump—or fall—down. Her fingers rolled across damp and slimy goop, and fragments of—something. But not paper. She definitely didn't feel any paper. She was about to give up the job when, forcing herself to make one last sweep to the left and right, her hand touched something fairly large. She shuddered at the feel of it. It had a damp feel to it, as well, and was soft and squishy. All sorts of nasty thoughts started to go through her mind, but then she felt a handle, and realized she was probably feeling a leather purse or tote bag or something. So she resolutely grabbed onto the strap and pulled, and after a struggle that almost left her a heap on the floor, she found herself holding a brown leather hobo-type handbag.

Climbing down from the chair with her musty-smelling prize, something stirred at the back of her mind. The purse didn't so much look familiar as feel familiar, as though the sight of it was bypassing her conscious memory and stirring her blood to pulse faster through her veins.

It didn't take her long to realize why. When she pulled the bag open and peered inside, a flood of memories came boiling out of it. The silver hairbrush. The denim wallet. It was all so achingly, painfully familiar. It was Livvy's purse.

But why! Why in the world would Livvy's purse still be in this house, let alone hidden away in the ceiling?

The weekend that Livvy died, she had driven down to Florida by herself to take a look at Florida State, the college she wanted to attend. Before she arrived, she had been in a fiery car accident. Supposedly, everything was a total loss—the car she had rented, her possessions, her body. That's why Mamma had returned with nothing but Livvy's ashes.

So...why was her purse still here?

Suddenly, Rose was filled with an overwhelming urge to go talk to her mamma, if such a thing was even possible. Mamma had talked very little in the past weeks, but she knew Rose and was aware of her surroundings. You could just tell it in her eyes.

As Rose jumped to her feet and started toward her bedroom to dress, it occurred to her that, interesting as this discovery was, it had nothing to do with Ginny or her current problem. Then again, she had no idea where to start trying to help Ginny, or even decide exactly what was going on. And she'd been neglecting her mother of late, anyway.

No, going to see Mamma certainly wouldn't hurt.

CHAPTER THIRTY-SIX
Ginny, 1984

Ginny figured the pay phone wasn't going to do her much good. Even an iPhone wouldn't be able to place a call twenty or thirty years into the future. So she started walking, back toward Grandma's house.

She had been walking maybe twenty minutes or so and already felt sticky and sweaty when a car slowed down next to her. She didn't have time to worry about who was in the car before Anna's head popped out the driver's side window. "Hey!" she called cheerily. "What are you doing?"

"Long story."

"So hop in and tell me. Unless, of course, you're trying to get exercise or something."

"Not this much exercise. Thanks." As she ran around to the passenger side, another memory came flooding back, of Anna driving her home the day of the basketball fight. Was Anna always prowling around to see what she could get into? But that was mean. Ginny should be grateful the woman always seemed to be around.

Anna's mouth fell open as Ginny told her what had happened with Grandma, leaving out her prophecies about the future, of course.

"I knew the old bat was crazy, but throwing a recuperating accident victim out by the road is just cruel," Anna said.

The words made Ginny squirm. Maybe she shouldn't have told Anna. She wasn't here to turn people against Grandma. On the other hand, Anna Shaw was Mom's friend in the future, right? Plus a counselor.

That thought made Ginny curious. "Anna, you're in college already, right?"

"Yep. Jake and Hunter and I are juniors."

"What's your major?"

"Psychology. Why do you ask?"

"Oh, I just thought I'd heard that somewhere."

Anna chuckled. "Probably from Jake. He likes to say I study psychology so I'll be better able to manipulate people."

Ginny forced herself to laugh. "Yeah, funny…umm, I was wondering if your studies have given you any insight into Mrs. Remington…or Rose either, for that matter."

Anna shot her a curious look. "Has Rose done something strange?"

"Well, no, just…" Ginny's voice trailed off. Again, she didn't want to hurt her family's reputation. But she needed help. She felt her mind sliding away from the Anna in the car as she tried to remember what she knew about the other Anna…Ms. Shaw. Hadn't she and Max found out something odd about Ms. Shaw and her counseling? Sometimes memories were bright and clear, like the one of Anna picking her up. But most of the time, the future felt almost as foggy in Ginny's head as it must to everyone else here in the eighties. Like she could see a dim silhouette of 2009 in her mind, but the details were blacked out. Could that mean it was in flux, that it might be changing while she was back here fiddling around with things?

She gave her head a determined shake, trying to dislodge the distractions. She needed to focus on where she was right now.

"She…Rose, I mean…just seems very insecure to me. And I guess I can see why, with her mother criticizing and harping on her all the time. Have they always been that way?"

"If anything, Carla was worse."

"Worse!"

"Yep. Rose's father committed suicide, you know."

"Yeah, I know."

"Half the people in town think she drove him to it."

"Really? How?"

Anna looked thoughtful. "You know, when I get around to doing my psychology thesis, I think I'm going to do a study about why in the world opposite personality types are so attracted to each other when they're courting—and then want to mold their mate into an exact clone of themselves after marriage."

"Is that what happened with Mrs. Remington?"

"With a vengeance. You know her. Practical to the extreme. From what Rose tells me, their father was a dreamer and a poet, and he swept Miss Carla off her feet with all his romantic ways. Then when they were married, she expected him to magically change into an ambitious business man, a practical head of the household. When he didn't, she made his life miserable. I've heard stories of how she belittled him in public, how she kept him under her thumb—well, it would make your flesh crawl. Everybody around here liked him and felt sorry for him, I think.

"You'd think Carla Remington would have learned something from that experience, but apparently not. Unfortunately, both her daughters took after their daddy and had their heads in the clouds, and she's been determined to stamp it out. I can't tell you how many times I've heard her say to Livvy or Rose, 'You don't want to end up like your father, do you?'"

"Mo—um, Rose—doesn't seem to be doing too well to me. I guess losing her father and her sister like that was pretty devastating."

"It absolutely was. Especially losing Livvy. I think their father's death made Livvy go sort of weird, and then when Livvy died, Rose fell apart."

"How?"

"She had some kind of breakdown right after they found out Livvy was dead. She was hallucinating and really out of it. She spent a couple of weeks in a hospital. Even after she got out, she seemed…different. Scared of everything. Especially water."

Ginny perked up. "Water? She hasn't always been afraid of water?"

"No, not at all. In fact, when the four of us—Jake and me, and Hunter and Livvy—wanted to hang out at the pond and not have kids bothering us, we had to chase her away all the time."

Ginny briefly pictured the drawings on the wall back home, how the artist always appeared to be spying on her subjects as they lounged by the pond.

"But then, after Livvy was gone, suddenly Rose was afraid to go down to the pond."

Ginny struggled to think through the fog, to remember if Mom had ever told her why she was so afraid of the water. Or whether she had talked much about Aunt Livvy and her death. Talking as much to herself as to Anna, she mused, "Could she be connecting Livvy and the pond in her mind, somehow? Because Livvy hung out down there and didn't want her to come? Or when she was spying on y'all and doing her drawings—"

"Her what?"

"—could she have seen something happen? Maybe something bad happened to Livvy sometime, and after Livvy was dead, she didn't want to think about it?"

Anna shook her head. "I don't remember anything bad ever happening at the pond. It was really nice back then. Makes me sick that we stopped going." After a long, thoughtful pause, Anna added, "Of course, Livvy did get pretty strange that last year or so. Different."

"How?"

"She got obsessed with angels, for one thing. I guess that was natural to be interested in spiritual stuff for a while after her dad died, but it got old. She couldn't think of anything else. Then her whole personality started changing. Instead of talking incessantly about all this weird stuff, she got quiet and withdrawn."

"Maybe she realized you weren't interested in what she wanted to talk about."

"It wasn't so much that she was boring us. More like…scaring us."

"Scaring you!"

"Yeah. Mostly we were worried about her, because she was so obsessed. She went from telling us about books she'd read, about people who thought they were saved by angels, to telling us there were ways to try to contact them and communicate with them. I know Hunter was totally freaked out by it all."

"So he didn't go along with any of it…you know, just to keep her happy?"

"Hunter? Oh, please! Surely you realize how important it is to him for everything to be all traditional and normal. I guess that's why she got so quiet, come to think of it. Because she really did love Hunter."

Ginny thought of the scraps of letters she'd found in the basement ceiling. She spoke slowly, the idea forming in her mind as she talked. "Do you think maybe Livvy met someone else? Someone who shared her passion?"

Anna lurched around to face her, eyes wide. "Why would you say that?"

Something kept Ginny from mentioning the letters. "No reason. Just thinking out loud."

Anna appeared to relax. "I don't think Livvy had anyone else. I certainly never met anyone else around here whose head was sufficiently up in the clouds to put up with her, and I don't think her mind was on man-hunting. She loved Hunter in her way, but she wasn't desperate for him the way Rose is now."

"Pretty weird, isn't it…that he's ending up with Livvy's sister?"

Anna snorted. "It's as close to dear departed Livvy as he can get, isn't it?" She shot Ginny a sly look. "Or at least she was, until you came along."

"What!"

"You look more like Livvy—especially your eyes." Anna sighed. "It'll be wonderful when Rose is married to Hunter and out of her mother's clutches. Maybe she can start to recuperate when she can actually make a life of her own."

Ginny rubbed at her aching forehead, slightly mollified. "Yeah, well…what if that doesn't happen?" Even worse, Ginny thought wryly, what if it did? Her very existence depended on Mom being dumped by Hunter Isaacs and ending up with Ben Crosby.

"Oh, it'll happen. Unless you're intending to steal him away. You're not, are you?"

"Of course not."

"Then I'm sure Rose will be a dull old married woman before you know it." She whipped the car into the Remingtons' driveway so fast that Ginny slid against the door. "Here we are. Do you want me to wait and see if the old dragon lets you back in?"

"No, that's okay."

"Suit yourself." Anna shrugged and drove away as soon as Ginny's feet hit the ground.

As Ginny turned slowly toward the house, she wondered just how Grandma was going to react to her homecoming. Would she be surprised that "Jordan" had come back? Had she seriously thought that Jordan was faking amnesia (well, okay, she kind of was) and could just call someone to come get her? Or maybe by now Grandma was feeling bad about what she had done and would be ready to apologize.

It wasn't going to take Ginny long to find out. As she trudged toward the front door, she could see Grandma staring out the kitchen window at her.

CHAPTER THIRTY-SEVEN
Rose, 2009

Mamma was out in the common area when Rose arrived. She'd been strapped into her special reclining chair and wheeled in front of the TV, but she was staring up at the ceiling and didn't even turn her head when Rose walked up.

"Mamma?" She touched the woman on her left arm but wondered if she could feel the contact. That was the arm that had been partially paralyzed by the stroke.

Either she did feel or hear Rose, because she rotated her head in Rose's direction. Her face lit up with recognition, and a delight that brought a lump to Rose's throat.

Swallowing hard, Rose said, "I'm so sorry I haven't been to see you in a while. I've been having a lot of trouble."

Mamma didn't move, but her smile faded.

"I need to talk to you. Can I...can I take you back to your room?"

The woman made a small movement of her head which Rose took as permission to move her. In the few minutes it took to wheel her mother back to her bedroom, she realized she didn't know how to go about talking with her mother. When she had visited before, Mamma had seemed anxious to communicate with her and had strained to form words, but her voice was so low and so slurred that Rose couldn't understand a thing. By the end of their visits, Rose's facial muscles would ache with the strain of smiling and she would nod as though she understood and make little sounds of understanding. Meanwhile, Mamma would get more and more agitated at obviously not being understood, so that Rose invariably cut the visits short with a promise to come again soon and an order for Mamma to relax and rest up. The only time Mamma had spoken with any distinction had been when she reached out to Ginny and said the word "Jordan," loud and clear.

Rose was thinking about that as she settled Mamma in her room and took a chair facing hers. "You knew, didn't you?" she whispered. "How much Ginny is like Jordan?"

Again that little movement of Mamma's head.

Rose started to go further, to ask her, "Is she Jordan?" But she stopped. At least in the old days, a question like that would have made Mamma livid. You were not supposed to consider unreasonable, unearthly foolishness. Mamma seemed to have changed, but still, Rose needed to tread carefully.

"Mamma," she said slowly, "this is really important. I can't go into why right now, but...I need to ask you some things about Livvy."

No movement from Mamma, but her eyes were sharp and bright. And she was listening. They had told Rose after the stroke that Mamma's hearing was sharp as ever.

"I need to know..." She breathed deeply. "I need to know if Livvy really did die in a car wreck in Florida."

No movement. No sound. Mamma just stared at her. Had she understood?

"You see, I found her purse in the house...your house. Her wallet and her driver's license and everything, and it just made me wonder. I know you know the truth. You're the one who drove to Florida to collect her ashes. So...is it true? Was there a car crash...did everything burn?"

After a long moment, Mamma shook her head.

"No?" Rose gasped. She felt as though Mamma had punched her, even though she had half expected this answer.

Rose forced herself to go on. "Did she really die?"

A nod for yes.

Her heart pounded in her throat, making her own speech difficult. "Did someone...did someone kill her?"

A long pause, and then...a nod.

"Who? Who killed her?"

At this, Mamma became agitated, moving in the chair and appearing to try to sit up straight. She was trying to speak, like she used to right after the stroke, but as always, Rose couldn't get a thing out of the low, urgent mumbling.

Rose put her hands on her mother's shoulders and gently pushed her back. "Mamma, calm down. I'm here. I'll ask differently, okay? We'll figure it out."

Mamma collapsed against the back of the chair and closed her eyes, breathing hard.

"I'm going to get a nurse, okay? I want to make sure you're all right."

Rose ran from the room and toward the nurse's station, her mind racing almost as fast as her pulse.

Did she really want to pursue this line of questioning? After all, what could it have to do with Ginny at this point, and finding Ginny was all that was important right now. All this stuff about Livvy was just a distraction, wasn't it?

But what if…

If Livvy hadn't died in Florida, had never even left home, then something had happened to her here. That brought up some terrible possibilities, including one that Rose didn't want to contemplate. She had never spoken her fears out loud to anyone, had never been completely open even with the doctors when she was hospitalized as a teenager. But there was a hole in her memory, like a blank spot on a tape recording where the offensive part had been edited out. And the blank spot was right around the time that Livvy died.

Rose had always assumed that was because she was so traumatized by Livvy's death, but what if…what if she had actually done something to Livvy? It could have been an accident, like what happened with Jordan. As close as she and Livvy were, they did fight sometimes. Sometimes things got nasty.

Rose came to a stop in the middle of the hallway. Maybe she was on the wrong track altogether. Maybe someone had hurt Livvy, but maybe it wasn't Rose. Maybe it was Mamma.

Rose started violently as someone stepped in front of her and said, "Rose? Is that you?"

Stepping back, she practically fell over an old man in a wheelchair. The younger man who had spoken to her laughed and grabbed her arm.

As she righted herself, she found herself staring straight at the chest of a deputy sheriff's uniform. She yanked her arm, fearing for one second that she was being arrested. Then she found herself looking into a pair of familiar eyes, eyes that brought a flood of memories washing over her. One of the memories was recent—herself and Ginny looking at those drawings on her bedroom wall. Ginny laughing and reporting the nicknames she had given the two boys in the drawings: Soulful and Trouble.

And now here Trouble was standing right in front of Rose, shaking his head and saying, "Same old Rose. Head in the clouds, as usual."

His hair was shorter and there were new laugh lines around his eyes. But she would have recognized Jake Isaacs anywhere.

CHAPTER THIRTY-EIGHT
Ginny, 1984

I n the time it had taken Ginny to walk and ride home, Grandma had apparently skipped the grocery store and started drinking. At least, she smelled like she was drinking, and when she spoke, her words weren't as crisp as usual.

"So..." she said, standing with her arms crossed and her eyes looking fearful—something Ginny hadn't seen in her before. "You came back."

"I have nowhere else to go."

Grandma made a sharp move of her head, as though trying to shake it on a sore neck. "No. I don't believe that."

Ginny remained silent, staying near the doorway in case things turned ugly. Right now, Grandma bore a lot of resemblance to Mom when she had been having one of her "Jordan" fits.

"Who are you?" Taking a couple of strides toward her, the woman almost pinned Ginny against the doorway. She was breathing in Ginny's face as she continued—and oh yeah, she was definitely drinking. "Did Livvy send you?"

"Did Livvy...what? You mean your daughter? How could she send me? Isn't she dead?"

A sharp laugh. "What does that matter to you? Aren't you supposed to be an angel or something? Were you sent to punish me or torment me?"

At those words, Ginny felt an odd sense of exhaustion, not to mention déjà vu. It was like having Mom in her face all over again, accusing her of being Jordan and thinking she had been sent to punish or torment for something that happened in the past. Now this bizarre, supernatural thing had propelled Ginny into that past, and what was happening? Another mystery, apparently from further back. More accusations. She wondered vaguely if she was going to find herself propelled even further back in time to deal with this, and then Livvy would send her spiraling back to try to save her suicide-father, and so on and so on until she found herself in the Garden of Eden trying to keep Eve from eating the apple.

She felt hysterical laughter bubbling up in her throat, but the feeling died when Grandma backed away from her and said, "You know what happened to Livvy. She knows...she knows I'm sorry, doesn't she?"

The words spilled out before Ginny had time to think about them. "If you're really sorry, you can be forgiven. I promise you. But I need to help Rose."

"Rose?" Grandma appeared startled, but after a moment's thought, she nodded slowly. "I know. Rose was damaged, too, wasn't she? I didn't mean that to happen."

"I know you didn't. It's too late to help Livvy now, but we can still help Rose. And that will help you." Up until now, the words had been flowing out of Ginny as though from an outside source—or rather, from some independent spirit inside her, guiding her. Now she made the mistake of stopping to think, and to grow curious. "Mrs. Remington, why don't you tell me...what exactly happened to Livvy?"

Now Grandma's eyes sharpened, narrowed with suspicion. "What do you mean? You don't know?"

"Well, I...I thought it would do you good to tell me."

Grandma's expression was returning to its normal alert state. Obviously she hadn't drunk enough to get Ginny all the way through this conversation. She rubbed her forehead as though trying to finish waking herself. "I apologize for...well, I had a little wine and apparently...I've been rambling. I hope you didn't take my little jokes too seriously. I believe I'm going to go lie down now. The party and...the scare with Rose...I'm worn out. Good night."

CHAPTER THIRTY-NINE
Rose, 2009

Mamma drifted off to sleep as Jake and Rose sat by her bed—Rose in an uncomfortable, unpadded chair, and Jake in Mamma's wheelchair. Except for the fact that he had apparently become an officer of the law, she felt lucky to have run into him. He had known which nurse to call to come check on Mamma when Rose explained how agitated she had become, and had stayed by her side as the nurse checked Mamma and pronounced her to be all right, just a little more excited than usual.

Mamma had recognized Jake when he came in, even after all these years. She had reached her good arm out to him and tried to smile.

Suddenly a thought came to Rose. "Have you visited Mamma since she's been here?"

"I have. Several times, actually."

Rose nodded. "I thought you must have. I just remembered that Anna said your father is in here, too." She felt a pang of guilt as she admitted knowing this, remembering that Mr. Isaacs had almost become her father-in-law once upon a time. She should have visited him at least once.

"So...how you holding up?" Jake said. His voice was totally devoid of the cockiness she remembered. "With your daughter missing, I mean."

"You don't know? Surely if the TV doesn't give you enough of the gory details, your cop buddies fill you in." She was sorry for the words even before they finished ripping out of her. She drew a steadying breath and started to apologize.

"It's okay," Jake said, putting up a hand to stop her. "I can't imagine how you even manage to function with all this going on." He looked down at his shoes, rocking the wheelchair back and forth with his feet.

She cleared her throat. "I just can't believe you're a..." She gestured toward his badge. "You know. I would have been less surprised to find out you were in jail."

He laughed. "I know, I know." Then his eyes grew serious. "Let's just say some things happened that made me see the error of my ways."

"Oh, uh...good. I guess."

Rose reflected how the years had changed things. Hunter had been the knockout, the dreamy hunk that all the girls wanted. Now he looked sour and pudgy next to Jake, whose job obviously kept him in better physical shape, and whose eyes were bright and kind.

As she looked into those eyes, the words popped out of her mouth. "I have got to figure out how to talk to Mamma."

"It's rough, I know. Dad wasn't able to talk at all when he first had his stroke, but he's gotten a lot better. Do you have a good speech therapist?"

She felt like moaning with frustration. "I don't know...I mean...I put her in here because they were supposed to help her with rehabilitation, and I do come to see her, but as for the details..."

"I know. I understand."

"No, you don't! I must look horrible to you. I've lost my daughter and I'm not taking care of my mother—"

"No, no, I didn't say anything like that. Look, I know that—" He broke off to glance at Mamma, as though confirming she was asleep. Lowering his voice, he continued. "I know how difficult she was when you were growing up. I know you've been estranged for years. I think it's wonderful that you're here at all, and thinking about how to help her get better, when you've got such a horrible situation with your daughter on your mind."

What would Jake think of her if he knew she was only concerned about Mamma's speech because of what she needed to get out of her? She breathed in deeply, trying to clear her head. She could drown herself in guilt later. Right now she had to press on. "So Mr. Isaacs can talk now?"

"Fairly well."

"How long did it take him to reach that point?"

"Oh, well, he's improved an inch at a time, I guess, and he's still improving. The first few months—"

"Months!" She gasped in horror. "I don't have months. I need to ask Mamma some things now. Some things about…Ginny."

"Your daughter?"

"That's right."

Jake leaned back in his seat and seemed to be pondering the problem. After a long moment, he asked, "Do you know what kind of stroke damage she has? Whether her problem is just with speaking, or with language in general?"

"I'm sorry, I don't understand."

"Strokes cause a lot of different kinds of damage, depending on what part of the brain is affected. Sometimes it's pretty widespread. People don't understand language and can't use it at all after the stroke. But other times, they know the words, but just have trouble moving their mouths and talking. My dad, for example, could write notes to us and type on a keyboard before he could speak. We have a specially adapted laptop for him now."

"So it's possible that Mamma—oh!" She felt herself starting to smile as she realized where Jake was going with this.

Jake put his hands up, cautioning. "There's no guarantee it would work. She might have problems with language in general, not just with speech—"

"But she might not." Rose started scrambling in her handbag. "I think I have a notepad and a pen in here somewhere."

In spite of his pessimistic warning, Jake jumped to his feet and hurried toward the door. "I'll get Dad's laptop, too. When she wakes up, we'll try it all."

In his haste to get out the doorway, Jake collided with someone coming in. As he gushed apologies and stepped away from the newcomer, Rose gasped. "Anna!"

Jake fell silent, his eyes growing wide with surprise as he echoed Rose. "Anna!"

The woman's mouth twisted. "Yes, it's me. Glad we have that settled." She looked from Jake to Rose, then back again. "What are you doing here?"

"What am *I* doing here?" Rose said. "This is my mother's room.

What are you doing here, that's what I'd like to know."

"I'm the staff psychologist here, you may recall."

As their voices rose, Mamma shifted in the bed and opened her eyes. She glanced at Rose before settling her gaze on Anna, and then she started to moan.

Anna gestured toward the old woman. "I think it's good I stopped by. You're obviously upsetting her." Her eyes narrowed. "Let me ask you again. What are you two doing?"

Jake laughed, but the sound was rough. "Lordy, Anna, you make it sound like we were beating her up or something. We were just talking about getting my dad's laptop to see if she could type a little, maybe write a few notes, something to communicate with Rose."

Mamma moaned louder and struggled in the bed, as though trying to sit up.

"No. Absolutely not."

"What!" Rose couldn't believe what she was hearing. "How dare you!"

"It's my job, making sure the patients are calm and healthy emotionally. I think Carla's got enough to deal with without your bringing your, um…problems in here."

Rose tightened her fingers around her purse strap, clenched her teeth together until her jaws ached.

Anna had opened the door and was gesturing them into the hallway. "I need to do my job here and take care of your mother. The two of you need to leave."

Rose hesitated for a moment. Never in her life—not even in her frenzies of fear when she thought Ginny was Jordan—had she felt such a strong desire to lash out, to hurt someone. But she absolutely could not lose control, or she'd end up locked away and completely useless to Ginny. Forcing herself to relax, she nodded. "All right, Anna. I'm going. For now."

She turned to Jake, who was looking back and forth between the two women with a puzzled expression on his face. "Thanks for your help. I'm definitely going to try your idea." She met Anna's eyes, for once feeling steady and strong. "Because I will, somehow, communicate with Mamma."

ଓ

Rose was still shaking with rage when she pulled into her driveway. Being pelted with shouts from reporters and curiosity-seekers as she dashed from her car to the house didn't help, so when she found Max sitting at the kitchen table, she nearly took his head off.

"What do you want now?" she snapped.

He blinked, looking startled, but stood up straight and faced her. "Something occurred to me."

Rolling her eyes, Rose threw her purse on the table. "I can't listen to any more of this. Not now."

"Please, it's important."

"No, I mean it, not now." She started toward the doorway, needing the sanctuary of her bedroom, but Max jumped in front of her.

Waving that cursed newspaper clipping at her, he pleaded, "Look at it. Look at the date."

Figuring it was the quickest way to get rid of him, she snatched the paper away from him and glanced down at it. "May 29. So?"

"So that means y'all found Jordan on May 28, the same day that Ginny disappeared in this year!"

Rose shifted her weight from one foot to another, trying not to think about the pounding in her head. "Again, so?"

"So maybe the dates always match up. Today is June 28, 2009. Maybe Ginny right now is living June 28, 1984."

With a deep sigh, Rose tried to push past Max and continue toward her room. Again, he jumped in front of her. "Please, Mrs. Crosby. Just tell me one thing and then I'll leave you alone."

"All right, fine." She folded her arms. "What?"

"You said Jordan died in 1984—but you said she fell in the water, right? And she didn't surface? What was the date it happened—the date in 1984?"

She felt herself faltering, going weak at the knees. Reaching out for the door jamb for support, she said, "Wh-what? Why do you ask that?"

"Don't you see? If she disappeared from here on the same day, maybe she's coming back on the same day."

Again she pushed past him, shaking her head and rejecting the idea. "No, Max. No."

"But if we know the date, maybe—"

"Stop it!" She whirled to face him, making him jump. "Let it go, Max!"

"But why? Why don't you want—"

"Don't you understand! They found a skeleton in that pond." She jabbed her finger in his face, punctuating each word. "You better hope you're not right about this time travel business, because if you are, Ginny's remains are on a table at the Medical Examiner's Office right now."

As she turned away from him one more time, Rose saw that Max was now the one holding onto the door jamb for support.

CHAPTER FORTY
Ginny, 1984

Ginny sat up in the New Room and waited for Teen Mom to get home from her date with Hunter. When she came through from the kitchen, she didn't notice Ginny at first. She was looking down at the floor and her shoulders slumped, giving Ginny the impression of a glum girl who'd had a very bad day—which of course she had. Their picnic at the lake had turned out just the way Mom had related it to her in 2009, with Ginny and Mom both ending up half-drowned and Mom humiliated. Even as Ginny had realized she was living out Mom's story, she hadn't been able to figure out whether to try to change it or just lean back and go with it.

"Rose?"

Mom gasped, then saw Ginny and relaxed. "Oh, I didn't notice you."

"Sorry. Have a good time with Hunter?"

"Yes. Of course."

Yeah, sure. That's why you look like you've been sucking on sour lemons. "That's good. I just wanted to make sure you were okay. You know, after what happened at the lake."

"I'm fine," Mom said coldly.

Ginny leaned back into the armchair and tried to appear casual. Pointing at the coffee table, she said, "I made some popcorn. Want some?"

Mom shook her head. "No, thanks. I've been eating all day."

"Sit down with me, at least. I couldn't sleep and I've got a Stephen King movie on. He's been around forever, I guess."

"What?"

"Oh, nothing. Want a Coke?"

Mom sat down, but perched on the edge of the couch, as though she was only planning to stay a minute, to be polite. "I don't think watching Stephen King and drinking caffeine will help you sleep."

"Oddly enough, it usually does."

"Usually? Are you remembering things?"

"Oh, I...I just meant since I've been here. I've sat in here by myself a lot when I couldn't sleep."

"Oh." In spite of what she had said, Mom reached out and took a handful of popcorn.

After a moment of conversationless munching and pretending to watch Jack Nicholson break down a door with an axe, Ginny said, "Rose? What happened that made you afraid of water?"

"What? Oh...I don't know."

"I figured you must have nearly drowned at some point."

Rose shrugged. "If I did, I don't remember it. Things just changed. One day I liked it and the next day, it terrified me. My doctor said..." Her voice trailed off, and she looked at Ginny as though just realizing she was there. The coldness returned to her voice, and she stood up. Almost echoing her mother, she said, "It's been a long day. I'm worn out and I'm going to lie down."

Almost crying with frustration, Ginny watched her young mother-to-be's back retreating into the hallway. She sank back into the couch and watched Jack finish demolishing the door, knowing exactly how he must feel.

A few days later, Ginny was alone in the house when she heard a car pull up and a horn blowing insistently. Going outside, she saw Anna rolling down the car's window.

"Hey," Ginny said.

"Hey." Anna glanced toward the house, as though confirming they were alone. "I've been thinking about our conversation...you know, about Rose suddenly becoming afraid of water."

"Yes?"

"I've tried to feel her out about it from time to time, and honestly...I think she may have the same problem you do."

"Which would be...what?"

"Amnesia, of course. Except hers is more selective, just one event. Like maybe she's repressed something." Anna stopped and laughed. "I'm a psychology major, remember?"

"So...how do you get somebody to remember? If it's something they've repressed on purpose?"

Anna sighed. "There are lots of arguments about all that. Freud believed memories were permanent, but others believe that some memories can be lost forever."

Ginny waved that away. "Let's say Freud is right, and the memory is still there. Do your experts have any ways of getting old memories back?"

Anna grimaced. "Hypnosis, which I don't know how to do. Electrodes to the brain, which, again..."

"We can't do." Ginny thought for a moment, pulling a strand of her hair forward and twisting it around her finger.

Anna said, "My textbooks also say something about using cues to help people call up memories."

"Cues..." Ginny suddenly thought how her own memories had come gushing back when she saw Star walking through the yard. The house, the people, none of that had done it...but the yard *plus* the cat had.

As though reading her mind, Anna was saying, "The cue could be as simple as putting her in a similar situation."

"What do you mean?"

Anna leaned out the window, her face close to Ginny's. "Maybe we need to get Rose back to the pond."

Ginny started to nod, but then thought of something. "Wait a minute. She's been to the pond recently, remember? The night they found me. It didn't help her memory or her fears."

"Yes, but you said it—that was the night they found you. There was nothing familiar about the pond that night, to take her mentally back to some other time. That night was way too exciting and bizarre. We need to get her down there when things are more ordinary."

"You might just be right," Ginny said. "But it doesn't matter, because she won't go back there. She already tried to stay away, and after what happened when Hunter dragged her back there and they found me, she'll never set foot near that pond again."

"There might be a way," Anna mused. "I can think of one thing more powerful in Rose Remington than fear."

"What's that?"

"Jealousy." Anna's eyes were intense. "If I told her I'd overheard that you and Hunter were going to have a little rendezvous down at the pond—"

"No. No way." Ginny shook her head so hard a pain shot through it. "She would hate me forever, and be more damaged than any fear of water has made her."

Anna laughed and slapped playfully at her arm. "Only for a very little while, silly girl. Once she gets down to the pond, she finds out there was no meeting—no one there but her good friends Jordan and Anna."

"You would be there, too?"

"I'd come down with her, and we could explain together that we just wanted to help her heal."

Ginny stood silent, rubbing her aching head. Memories of 2009 were still fuzzy about the edges, but something made her uncomfortable about this whole idea. Something horrible had happened between Rose and Jordan in 1984. With a shiver, Ginny remembered once again that, according to Mom, Jordan ended up dead.

"Well?" Anna prodded. "What do you think?"

She thought she was terrified, scared to death that she was walking into something she didn't quite understand, something dark and inevitable like Fate. But what else could she do? Time had convulsed and spit her out here for a reason, and that reason was not to sit and grow old waiting for 2009 to roll around a second time. She had to find out the truth, had to help her mom.

She nodded slowly. "All right, Anna. We can try."

.

CHAPTER FORTY-ONE
Rose, 2009

Rose kept an eye out for Anna as she maneuvered through the halls of the nursing home. She had no intention of backing down from Anna today, but avoiding a scene would be even better, so she felt relieved when she didn't see the woman.

Or she did feel relieved, until she pushed open the door to Mamma's room and saw Anna, her back to the door, bending down over the bed and pulling Mamma's pillow out from under her head and lowering it down to the sleeping woman's face—

"Anna!" Rose crossed the room in long strides and snatched the pillow from Anna. "What the devil do you think you're doing!"

Anna folded her arms and met Rose's angry gaze. "I was trying to make your mother more comfortable."

Rose drew a deep breath and steeled herself. "I don't think you were helping, Anna. I think—"

"So, Rose," Anna broke in smoothly. "How did you do it?"

"Wha-what?" Confusion threw her off the track. "How did I do what?"

"You know." Anna crossed over to her, searched her eyes. "How did you manage to hide her in the little bit of time you had?"

"Just what are you accusing me of?"

Anna's eyes narrowed. "I know you only had a few minutes between the time Max left your house that day and the time Ben got home. How did you manage to get her out of that bathroom and cover your tracks in that amount of time?"

Trying to remain calm, she said, "I didn't do anything to Ginny."

Anna ignored this. "Did you stash her in the house somewhere? I mean, you must have, but where? And how, without leaving any sign at all?" She shook her head. "I must say, Rose, I didn't think you had it in you."

If she hadn't known better, she would have sworn the gleam in Anna's eyes came from admiration. Before she could answer, Rose heard the door swing open behind her, and saw Anna's gaze shift in that direction. Before Rose could turn, Anna grabbed the pillow Rose was still holding and yanked it, practically pulling Rose over as she screamed, "Give me that, Rose! Oh, Jake, thank heavens. Help me stop her!"

Rose let go of the pillow so suddenly that Anna staggered backwards. Turning, she saw Jake standing in the doorway, looking confused. Anna stood near Mamma's bed, clutching the pillow to her chest and taking deep heaving breaths as though she'd been wrestling an alligator. "Thank goodness you came when you did!" Anna gasped to Jake. "I walked in and she—she was trying to smother her mother with this pillow!" She shook the pillow for effect.

Rose felt a bubble of hysterical laughter welling up in her at the absurdity of it all, but the urge died quickly as she saw that Mamma had woken up and looked frightened, and that Jake was giving Rose a look of deep suspicion.

"Jake, it was her!" Rose pointed a shaky finger toward Anna. "She was bending over Mamma with the pillow when I came in, about to put it over her face."

"What?" He turned a questioning look on Anna.

Anna frowned, a perfect mask of concern on her face, and she spoke softly this time. "Rose is delusional again, Jake. I've been her therapist for a while now, and…well, you remember how she is."

The words hit her like icy water, melting her confidence and resolve. As Jake turned on her with an intense, questioning look, Rose felt herself shrinking. She wanted to slink out of the room and be alone and…no. She couldn't fall apart. Not now.

She squared her shoulders. "You don't want me to communicate with my mother, do you, Anna? When I walked in, you were bending over her with her pillow. You were about to…do something."

Anna threw up her hands. "Do you see, Jake? Delusional." Her voice grew rough. "I didn't want to do this, Rose. I was hoping you were getting better, but now people are getting hurt." She turned to

Jake. "I want you to arrest her."

"What!" Rose gasped.

Jake blanched. "Arrest her? You mean…what for?"

"What for! I just told you I saw her trying to kill her mother. And as for Ginny…I'm not sure what she did with her, or whether the girl is still alive, but I'm sure she's responsible."

Jake put up his hand, silencing Rose's protests. "You have any proof, Anna?"

Again the dramatic sigh. "I was her counselor, so I know quite a bit. I've tried to keep it all confidential, but when lives are at stake, that's when the confidentiality has to end."

"And what exactly do you know?" Jake said.

Rose felt her face burning as Anna started to spill her most private confessions to Jake—all her fears as she'd watched Ginny grow more and more like Jordan, her insane dread that Ginny somehow *was* Jordan. She finished up by saying, "Rose fell apart when they found that skeleton in the pond. She actually thinks that's Ginny, even though it's been there for years and years. I hear her latest delusion has something to do with time travel."

Rose gasped. Where was Anna getting all this information? From Max? Or even worse, from Ben? "No," she said firmly, "I do not think that body is Ginny."

"You know who that body really is, don't you, Jake?" Anna continued.

He frowned, looking wary. "Who?"

"Jordan—the girl we knew in 1984. Rose confessed that to me, too—how she killed that girl back in 1984."

Rose shook her head. "No." She didn't remember telling Anna anything about that last day with Jordan.

Jake was squirming, licking his lips, almost as though Anna was accusing him of something. He didn't say anything.

Anna plowed ahead. "She told me she was jealous of Hunter and Jordan. That she followed them down to the pond and got in a fight with the girl and, well, drowned her."

Rose gasped. She had *not* told Anna that.

Jake's body had gone rigid with tension, and he stared at Anna. "Well," he said slowly, "don't you imagine that's just another one of Rose's wild stories?"

"I might have…until they found that skeleton."

"Yeah...how 'bout that?" Jake studied his fingernails. "Does her daughter really look that much like her...like Jordan?"

Anna looked annoyed. "I don't know. Who remembers that girl? Do you?"

Jake shrugged. "Just curious, you know. It's kind of a crazy story."

"Her family has always been full of wild stories. I could do an entire textbook on the Remingtons. Remember Livvy and her angels?"

"None of this has anything to do with Ginny's disappearance!" Rose had heard enough. "And none of it means I hurt my daughter."

From the bed, there came a moaning noise, and they all turned to look at Carla. Her mouth was hanging open and a trail of drool ran down her cheek as she struggled to make a word. "J-J-J."

Rose ran to her side and, holding her hand, wiped her face and tried to soothe her. In as calm a voice as possible, she said to the other two, "I'm going to ask both of you to please get out and leave me to tend to my mother."

Jake said, "You know what, Anna? Rose is right. Telling unbelievable stories doesn't necessarily equal murder, or even violence. Anyway, you should tell it to the GBI detectives. I'm not involved in this case."

Anna's eyes blazed. "Look, *Deputy*, I heard this woman confess to killing Jordan and to planning to kill her daughter, who is missing. Then I walked in on her about to kill her mother. If you allow her to roam around free and something happens, there will be consequences, do you understand me?"

Before Rose's fascinated eyes, Jake seemed to be growing younger, less sure of himself—morphing into the old Jake who lived squarely under Anna's thumb. Rose said quickly, "Jake, she's the one you should arrest. She's the one that was about to hurt Mamma."

Jake put up his hands. "All right, here's what we're going to do. All three of us are going down to the station, and you can talk to the detectives who make a lot more money than I do and are paid to straighten this kind of mess out." As they both started to protest, he raised his voice. "And that is FINAL!"

CHAPTER FORTY-TWO
Ginny, 1984

Ginny sat on the porch steps, fidgeting and watching the sun sink lower over the pecan trees and procrastinating. She should get on down to the pond so she didn't have to negotiate that trail in the dark. Even with a flashlight, that would be harder, and Anna had told her she would bring Rose down to the pond just after dark. So she should go on down there and get in place.

But something held her back, some heavy feeling of dread that made it hard to draw breath into her lungs, let alone stand and walk toward that dark place.

Steeling herself, she grabbed the wood post and pulled herself to her feet. It's your mother, she told herself. It'll be all right. Still...

As she stepped into the shadows of the trail, she remembered times when Mom had been so freaked-out, almost unrecognizable with paranoia and obsession. That's the Rose Remington she might be facing tonight.

But really, was Mom even the one she was worried about? As that thought occurred to her, she stopped. No, it wasn't Mom, it was Anna she was afraid of—but why?

She could feel the shadows growing around her as she wasted precious time, so she forced her heavy legs to move again. She felt a trickle of sweat run down her thighs, and she slapped at a mosquito buzzing next to her ear. It was like walking into the Okefenokee back here. But at least the trail was cleaner than in 2009, which was fortunate because of course she'd forgotten that flashlight.

She didn't like Anna, that was for certain. Anna had been trying to seduce her dad back in 2009, had maybe even succeeded. But in 1984, the girl seemed genuinely concerned about Mom, so maybe Ginny was just being crazy. She snorted. She had just used the phrase "back in 2009" to herself, and believed it. Of course she was crazy.

As she squished her way down the trail—there had been a gully washer last night and this morning—she couldn't stop thinking about Anna. Conversations with the young Anna, observations of middle-aged Anna, all of it kept flashing through her head. The only time she had ever talked to Old Anna alone had been that time the woman picked her up when she was walking back from the mall. What had they talked about? She frowned and concentrated, trying to ignore the soft rustlings starting in the dark underbrush to her left.

That day had been so wild, with the fight at the gym and Creepy Guy at the mall. That conversation with Anna had seemed so insignificant by comparison, except for…the tattoo! Again Ginny stopped short, this time touching her shirt at the place that it hid her tattoo of a dove and an olive branch. The tattoo that had so disturbed her mother in 2009. The tattoo she had gotten mostly because of the story middle-aged Anna had told her in the car.

But Anna hadn't mentioned anything about the girl Jordan having that tattoo. Ginny rubbed her temples furiously, wishing she could clear away all the cobwebs and finally, finally understand. Had Anna been up to something, trying to manipulate her? Of course, she hadn't been Mom's counselor yet, hadn't heard the story of her obsession, so maybe she simply hadn't mentioned Jordan's tattoo in the car that day because she hadn't thought it was relevant. Maybe didn't even remember.

Ginny sighed, listening to the last stirrings and sleepy chirpings of the birds settling into their nests. The light was gone. She would have to feel her way along and get on down to the pond, whether she wanted to or not. As confused as she was, she knew the key to clearing away the cobwebs was at the pond tonight. She braced her shoulders and took a step forward, toward the dark water that lay sleeping under a still, moonless sky.

CHAPTER FORTY-THREE
Rose, 2009

Rose fumed in the back of Jake's patrol car. She could not believe he had put her in the car with him for the ride "downtown" and let Anna drive herself. Well, at least she could see Anna's SUV in front of them, so she knew Anna wasn't hovering over Mamma with a pillow again. Otherwise, things looked pretty bad. She didn't want to think about life a couple of hours from now, after the media—and Ben—found out about her trip down to the station. Worst of all, she'd be trapped, unable to do anything to look for Ginny or try to help her. She could kick herself for ever confiding anything to Anna, for letting herself fall apart and act like a fear-crazed maniac a few weeks ago, so that everyone thought she was capable of murdering her daughter now.

"You okay back there?"

She jumped as Jake's voice cut into her meditation.

"Just peachy," she said, smoothing her hair and trying to pull herself together.

"Look, I…I'm sorry I made you ride with me, but I wanted a few minutes alone with you. There were a couple of things I wanted to talk to you about. Your daughter…was she really so similar to that Jordan girl?"

"First of all," Rose snapped, "don't talk about my daughter in the past tense."

"Sorry."

"And second, I don't want to talk about this anymore. It has nothing to do—"

"It's important, Rose. Were they, I mean are they, oh for Pete's sake, I'm just trying to figure out if they're the same size, because I remember that girl Jordan being tall."

Rose heaved a deep sigh. "Yes, Ginny is tall, the same height Jordan was. Why are you so interested in this?"

"If that's true, I can tell you for sure that skeleton they found doesn't belong to either one of them."

"What!" Rose sat up straight. "How do you know?"

"When they found it, I was interested. I, um…had my reasons. And I can tell you that whoever that was, she was a lot shorter than Jordan or your daughter." He jerked his head toward Rose's reflection in the rear view mirror. "More like your size."

Rose fell back against the seat again, amazed. "My size?" she said weakly, as her head spun with the possibilities. Jake was right. Both Ginny and Jordan—whether they were the same or separate—were considerably taller and larger than her. So if that skeleton wasn't either one of them, then who…

"When I heard about the skeleton, my first thought, of course," Jake was continuing, "was that they'd found Jordan's remains."

"Really?" She stared at him in the rear view. "Did you think Jordan was dead? I mean…Hunter swears he didn't…I mean…"

"I was there that night."

"What!" She gulped, trying to force herself not to blurt out something she might regret. "I don't understand. What night?"

Jake laughed roughly. "Oh, of course you understand. That night you thought Hunter and Jordan were going to have a big rendezvous down at the pond, and you went stomping down there in a jealous rage and ended up…well, Anna told me you got in a fight with her. And Jordan was gone the next day. I was always afraid something really bad had happened." His eyes met hers in the mirror. "So naturally, when they found that skeleton, I wondered."

"That's ridiculous." Her voice sounded raspy; the words felt like dry husks choking her. "Anyway, how did you know about that meeting? Oh. I guess Anna told you, huh?"

"Anna didn't just tell me. She gave me a role in the play." Again he glanced up. "I was Hunter."

"I'm sorry." She shook her head. "You were…Hunter?"

"You never figured it out, even after all this time?" When she didn't answer, he prodded her. "Didn't Hunter deny meeting Jordan down at the pond?"

"Of course he did. But I saw him—I saw him holding her, kissing her—and then slinking away through the trees, like a coward."

"It was me. You saw me."

"No—no, I didn't. I saw Hunter's dark green shirt I gave him, and he had short hair, not shaggy like yours."

"Yeah, Anna fixed me up pretty good, didn't she? I was a dead ringer for my dear bro, at least from behind."

"Anna—but why would she do that?"

His eyes stayed on the road, but she saw his shoulders lift in a shrug. "Because she's Anna. Manipulation is her favorite hobby, although…her second favorite thing was always exacting revenge on girls who stole her men."

Rose was beginning to wonder if this was ever going to make any sense. "So why did she want revenge on me? I certainly didn't steal you from her. Neither did Jordan, to my knowledge."

"Not me. Hunter." He heaved a deep sigh. "It was always Hunter she wanted."

Rose closed her eyes for a moment, trying to process this. Had she ever noticed, ever seen anything to indicate that Anna was pining away for Hunter? It was hard to imagine Anna pining for anything or anyone, actually. She always seemed so self-contained, so self-confident, so…self-absorbed. Without opening her eyes, Rose mused, "I don't get it. You and Anna always seemed so close, so perfect for each other."

Hunter laughed, a sort of dry-popcorn sound that reminded her of her own hoarse, reluctant throat. "Nobody understood Anna and me—except Anna and me. We were a good fit, all right, but not because we were crazy about each other like everybody thought."

"Why, then?"

"First, because we were both so crazy about someone else. For her it was Hunter, and for me, well…Livvy."

Rose drew in a sharp breath, shocked.

"That's what really bonded us to begin with. Even though I thought I was covering up my feelings really well—'

"You were, trust me."

"Not to Anna. She saw right through me, and pretty soon I was pouring my heart out to her about my great unrequited love for

Livvy. And then she confessed to me about Hunter. And at first we were just sort of leaning on each other, crying on each other's shoulder. But then…" Jake's speech petered out, and he went silent.

"Then what?" She leaned as far forward as she could.

"Then Anna started getting ideas. And me, like an idiot—I went along. We, uh—Lord, I hate to tell you this."

"What did you do?" she choked out.

"Anna came up with this idea to break up Hunter and Livvy. But, well…it didn't work out very well."

A heavy feeling of dread came over her. "What did you do?"

"Anna said…she said that if Hunter really understood Livvy, he wouldn't be so attracted to her. As for me, I loved Livvy's weird ideas. That was all part of her charm. But Anna said Livvy covered up most of her really crazy ideas around Hunter, and that we needed to, well…encourage her flakiness. Bring it out into the open, so Hunter could see."

"And how did you do that?"

"At first it was just Anna. She pretended to be really interested in all the strange stuff that Livvy was into…the angels and spirits and ghosts, and I don't know what all. She started telling Livvy wild stories about things she had seen—but begging her to keep it to herself, of course. Then eventually, she suggested things like séances, and she got a book about contacting angels and suggested they learn to call on angels for help and advice. And uh…that's where I came in."

Rose waited.

"If there was a séance, I was the spirit. If they were following some kind of instructions for summoning an angel, I made sure they got a response." He fell silent for a long moment. "I thought it was all in good fun at the time. Shoot, I even thought it was good for Livvy—you know, so she wasn't always so disappointed."

Rose sat without speaking, remembering the last year of Livvy's life, remembering how she grew more and more silent and withdrawn, yet seemed to vibrate with a quiet energy, glowed as though lit by some inward fire of the soul. Scenes Rose hadn't remembered for years came flooding back…

…The night Livvy came home early from a date with Hunter, and knelt on the floor next to Rose's bed and whispered that she and Hunter had argued because Hunter said she needed to pull herself together and not be so "crazy." Livvy hadn't seemed as upset as Rose would have expected. In a trembling voice, Livvy had breathed into the night that she wouldn't miss Hunter so much if he left her, that there were bigger things than romance, things more powerful, more eternal. It had been Rose who cried herself to sleep after that talk.

…The constant rows between Livvy and Mamma, as Livvy frequently cut classes and disappeared, failed exams or skipped them altogether. Those fights usually ended with Livvy screaming that she didn't care about school, that she might just leave early anyway and go somewhere that people understood her, understood the universe.

…The last night Rose ever saw her sister…waking up and hearing Livvy's bedroom door onto the porch opening…looking out and seeing Livvy crossing the porch, going down the steps, her skin glowing white in the strong light from the moon.

Rose cried out, the memory cutting through her like a knife.

Jake hit the brakes in reflex. "Hey! What's wrong?"

The memory was so clear, so sharp, and yet she hadn't thought of it in, how long? Maybe not since Livvy died. Five minutes ago she would have sworn that she didn't remember when she last saw Livvy, that she only knew some happy memories of childhood when she still had Daddy and Livvy, and then very bleak memories of when they were gone, with no clear transition between the two.

"Rose? What's wrong?" Jake repeated.

She ignored him, squeezing her eyes shut and concentrating on that long-ago night. In her mind, she watched Livvy gliding toward the woods. And then, floating just at the edge of the woods, reaching out for Livvy, there was something white and shimmery, something that had frozen Rose's blood in her veins. Livvy marching out to meet her angel. Livvy, never seen again…

"Was it you?" she choked out, strangled.

"Huh?"

"The last night I saw Livvy, I saw her walking away from the house, and I could have sworn there was something in the woods, something, like…"

She couldn't manage to finish the sentence, but it didn't matter. Jake barked out a laugh. "Yeah, it was me. Livvy's angel. Pretty impressive, huh?"

Rose struggled to remember Livvy coming back that night, but no…she had never seen her sister again, had she? She had fallen asleep at the window, waiting. But supposedly Livvy had left the next day for her fatal trip to Florida, hadn't she?

"Did something happen that night, Jake?" she asked him.

"Yeah, it kind of blew up in our faces that night," Jake said. He laughed again. "For the first time, she caught up with her 'angel,' found out it was me in a cheesy costume with Anna shining a flashlight on me for effect." Any trace of derision, of sarcastic humor, left Jake's voice. "She was devastated."

Rose moaned, picturing her poor, trusting sister having her faith jerked away from her—faith in her angels, faith in her friends.

"So what did she do?"

Jake shrugged. "What you'd expect. She cried, she called us some pretty ugly names. It was…horrible. I knew she could never care about me after that, and besides, it was just…well, I felt really awful about it."

Now it was Rose who laughed, completely without humor. "And yet, you jumped right back in with Anna and helped her play tricks on Jordan and me."

"I know," Jake said. "And I can't explain it except to say that I was incredibly stupid when I was younger. Plus, there's something about Anna. She knows how to manipulate people, how to charm them into doing what she wants. And I don't know…after Livvy was gone, maybe I did start to fall for her a little."

"So why did Anna want to torment poor Jordan? Was she still after Hunter?"

"Oh, yeah, and…she really hates you, Rose. You do realize that, don't you? She hated you back then, and she still hates you now."

"But why? What did I ever do to…oh. Her campaign against Livvy backfired, didn't it?" Rose said slowly, thinking. "Hunter never dumped her, and when Livvy died, he still didn't go for Anna. He went for…me."

"Yeah, Anna was furious." He jerked a hand through his hair, causing it to stand on end. "It was pretty scary."

"And I never knew a thing. She was always so friendly, so smooth around me."

"Not behind your back, believe me. And then when that Jordan girl came along and Hunter started flirting a little with her, that was just about more than Anna could take—being that far down on his list! So, she came up with a plan to get at both of you at once!"

"And you went along with it."

"I did," Jake said, with a note of disgust in his voice. "We were pretty inseparable by then. And I wanted her to calm down and move on. But I tell you, Rose, that night when we pulled that trick on you and Jordan—that was it for me."

"Oh, really? Why is that?"

"Because that night, our stupid pranks really caused damage—not just mental anguish, like I know we caused you and Livvy. But that Mrr." In the mirror, Rose saw his Adam's apple working, as though he was swallowing hard. "Maybe even got killed. I swore, never again. I'd have nothing else to do with Anna—and no more foolishness. Yep, that was the night I decided to get my act together, became a new man. July 2, 1984."

The significance of the date hit them both at the same time, but Jake spoke first. "Hey, July 2! Same as today." He raised one hand as though holding a champagne glass and toasting himself. "Here's to twenty-five years as an honest man."

Same as today!

Rose's last conversation with Max came back to her, as he begged for the date that Jordan was last seen in 1984. Because, according to him, Ginny might be coming home that night. But that was absurd, right? And especially in light of Jake's revelations. Had there ever been anything supernatural in her life, anything to give her faith? Or were there simply charlatans and fakers, ill-meaning people disguising themselves as angels of light?

But then again...

She thought of that scrap of paper, yellow with age but with pieces of words that appeared to be in Ginny's handwriting, words that could be a part of a cry: "Max, Mom, I'm here. I'm JORDAN."

Only scraps of words. Maybe that's not what they said. But could she risk it?

If Max was right, Ginny would end up going into that pond in 1984 on this very evening. And that meant...what? That she would resurface in the pond tonight, in 2009? Assuming Rose allowed herself to believe that some power had caused her daughter to travel in time, did that mean that power couldn't move Ginny in space, as well? Would the girl have to come and go through the same portal? But wait, Ginny had disappeared from the bathroom in the house a few weeks ago, but they had found Jordan down at the pond in 1984.

Rose started to shake her head, remembering something else—Mamma raging at her, the night they found Jordan, about having to clean up the water in the bathroom, down the hallway, all the way to the door. She remembered thinking how ridiculous it was to be arguing over something so trivial when they were at the hospital with a strange, injured girl. Plus, Rose had burned with the unfairness of being shamed in front of people when she knew she hadn't dripped any water on Mamma's precious floors. So had Ginny appeared in 1984 in the bathroom, and dazed and injured, wandered around in the dark until she ended up at the pond?

No, no, it was all so outrageous, it just couldn't be true. But...could she take a chance? She lifted her head and noted with horror that the sun was sinking. Night would be falling soon. And Ginny—her sweet Ginny who had never learned to swim because her idiot mother was so terrified of water—might find herself floundering in that dark, deep pool of water, all alone. Just like that kitten they had found in the pond so very long ago.

"Jake," she said abruptly, before she had completely thought out what she would say to him.

"Yeah?"

"You've got to take me to the pond. Now."

"You gotta be kidding me."

"No, I'm not." She edged forward in her seat. "I absolutely have to go there now. It's imperative."

"Oh, really? And why is that?"

Her mind raced, trying desperately to think of some reason that would motivate Jake to do something so preposterous. Telling him that her time-traveling daughter might be about to reappear in the pond and therefore might drown probably wouldn't do it. Before she could stop herself, she spit out the one thing she could think of. "Because. I have to show you where I hid Ginny's body."

CHAPTER FORTY-FOUR
Ginny, 1984

Ginny stopped short. She had reached the edge of the clearing and could see the pond, but that wasn't all she saw. Hunter was standing at the edge, his hands shoved into his pockets and his head down, staring at the water.

What was Hunter doing here! Anna had sworn this was all a ruse to get Mom down to the water, that Hunter wouldn't actually be involved. Maybe it was just a coincidence. He did come down here from time to time. But Ginny didn't like it. Mom was due here any minute. True, Anna was supposed to be with her, but still. She turned to leave.

"Jordan!"

Before she could slip back into the woods, Hunter had seen her. Only it wasn't Hunter. It was Jake, dressed in Hunter's favorite shirt, his hair shorter than usual.

"Why do you look like this?" she asked, as he walked toward her.

"Like what?" He grinned, looking as mischievous as ever. Mischievous, not dangerous, and yet, she instinctively took a step back as he reached her.

"Like Hunter," she said.

His gaze went past her, over her shoulder, and she heard leaves rustling behind her as someone approached. To her amazement, he suddenly grabbed her and pulled her close, turning her as he started to kiss her, so that she was facing the trail through the woods and his back was to it. So she had a clear view, in the last dying light, of her young mother standing a few feet away, her eyes wide with horror and her hand clamped over her mouth.

Mom turned and started to run away, back to the trail, but Ginny wrenched herself out of Jake's grasp. "Mom—uh, Rose! No, please, wait!"

She took off after Mom, and with her longer legs caught up and grabbed her by the shoulder before she could leave the clearing. "No, listen! You don't understand."

To her shock, Mom whirled and shoved her, so hard that she fell with a painful thud on her bottom. Her mother, who normally seemed so tiny, towered over her like a giant, her hair flying wildly about as she bent low over Ginny and shoved a finger into her face. "Don't tell me I don't understand. I'm not blind, and I'm not an idiot!"

"No, no, of course not." Ginny wiggled back from her. "But it wasn't Hunter. It was Jake, playing one of his tricks. Jake, tell her!" She twisted her head to look back in his direction, but he was gone.

There was no one in the clearing but the two of them—Ginny, and this stranger mother, with murder burning in her eyes.

CHAPTER FORTY-FIVE
Rose, 2009

As they pulled onto the logging trail to go back to the pond, Jake decided to call for reinforcements. The radio responded with dead air. "What the…"

"Don't you remember?" She watched without much interest as he continued to punch the button. "Radios and things don't work back here."

"Oh." He pursed his lips, looking uncertain. "I really should call this in."

She huffed. "Yeah, because I'm so dangerous."

"You're confessing to killing your daughter, aren't you?"

Just hearing the horrible words made her shudder, but she forced herself to shrug. "The situation was entirely different."

The car was slowing. "Maybe you just need to make your confession to one of the detectives and bring them back here."

"No! It has to be you. It has to be now."

"Why me?"

She licked her lips. "I know you. I'm not showing anyone but you where I…where I put her."

"I don't believe any of this, you know," Jake said. "No way I believe Rose Remington murdered her daughter."

She laughed harshly. "You're the only one."

Jake sighed. "Oh, all right." He rolled to a stop with the edge of the pond in sight. "Come on."

After a few minutes of her aimlessly leading him around the pond, it was Jake who was annoyed. "What's going on, Rose?" he snapped. "What are we really doing here?"

"I told you." She jutted her chin out in defiance. "I killed Ginny and she's back here. It's just..." She looked around, glad for once to see the deepening shadows, because if Ginny appeared back here, it would be after dark. She had to stall. "I don't remember exactly where. It's getting dark, and anyway, I was obviously in a state at the time."

The birdsong died down, as the birds retired for the night. A cricket whined, and the outline of leaves and branches melted into an indistinguishable mass. But the pond remained dead quiet. And then there was a ripple, a slosh, fifteen yards or so away.

She was straining to see the source when Jake jerked her arm. "Come on, let's go."

"No." She tried to yank away from him, wincing as he tightened his grip. "We can't leave."

"I don't know what you're up to, but it's over. Let's go."

She twisted and pulled back toward the pond, listening and straining her eyes. The pond was quiet again as Jake dragged her back toward the car. She groaned in frustration as he opened the back door and motioned for her to get inside.

Then a woman's voice called, "Hey! Stop!"

Anna had walked from the trail and was approaching them.

"What are you doing here?" Jake asked.

"I was keeping an eye on you in my rear view mirror and I saw you turn down the pond road. Naturally I was curious as to why." She nodded toward the trail. "I parked further up so as not to...disturb you."

As Jake explained the situation, Anna's eyes moved coolly over Rose's face. "But then she didn't show you anything?" she asked him.

"Of course not. She's stalling. But time's up. We're leaving."

"Hold on a minute," Anna said. "She may be telling the truth."

Rose felt Jake release a little pressure on her arm, and she stood up straight next to the car.

"What do you mean?" he asked.

Anna ignored him and turned to Rose. "Where did you put her? Ginny's body?"

"We've been through this already," Jake said. "No doubt you saw us wandering around back here and—"

"Okay, I was stalling then," Rose gushed, trying to think. "But I, uh…she's actually in the pond. I put her in the pond."

Anna huffed. "No, you didn't. They've already searched that pond, remember? And the remains they found weren't Ginny's."

The last flicker of sunlight disappeared. Rose stood in the gloom, fidgeting in frustration, listening to the water slosh in the darkness and picturing her darling Ginny slipping into that black water.

And suddenly, the scene in her mind shifted. Once again an old memory came rushing back, only this time just a flash…Livvy's white face, then her hands, slipping beneath the water, disappearing from sight forever.

"Livvy!" She gasped, looking at Anna. "That was Livvy's body they found."

"So you finally remember," Anna said. She sighed. "That's unfortunate. Your amnesia was always so convenient. Still, it's not as though you're going to tell anyone, is it?"

"Wait a minute," Jake said. "Livvy?" He looked from one to the other. "But…Livvy died in a car accident."

"No." Rose shook her head, thinking hard. "No."

She stared at the dark water, and suddenly it was as though the scene tilted, grew less clear. She was staring at the same moonlit pond, but from a different vantage point. She was looking down on the rocky ledge where she never liked to go, not even when she was young and used to swim. It was the point the boys used to dive from, into the deepest part of the flooded quarry, and now she was looking down on it, from a few feet above, looking at Mamma and Anna…with Livvy lying pale and still at their feet. And they were dragging something to her…the anchor from Daddy's old boat…tying it around Livvy's ankles, tight. The two women pushed and tugged, as though dealing with dead weight. And then, the person Rose loved more than anything, at least at that time, disappeared over the side. A splash below, a flash of Livvy's white robe billowing around her, and then she was gone.

A cry tore out of Rose, shattering her memory. She looked at them wildly—at Anna with her knowing smile, and Jake with his wide, shocked eyes. "Mamma! Mamma and Anna put Livvy in that horrible black water."

CHAPTER FORTY-SIX
Ginny, 1984

S omehow, Ginny managed to throw off the tiny fury of arms and legs attacking her and scramble to her feet. Mom was between her and the trail back to the house, so she turned and ran blindly back in the opposite direction.

As she ran, she thought she saw movement in the trees. Someone on the trail leading back to the Isaacs' house.

"Jake!" she cried. "Jake, come back!"

She ran along the shoreline, toward the trail and Jake's vanishing form. Then a hand grabbed her arm, stopped her so suddenly that she slid back on the gravel. Trying to throw off Mom's hand and regain her balance at the same time, she flailed her arms and rocked on her feet. Mom lost her grip and fell to her bottom with a gasp, but the stones continued to roll under Ginny's soles, and she felt herself sliding downhill, down toward the water. She threw her arms out wildly and scrambled with her feet, trying to get her balance, trying to catch hold of something, anything that would stop her momentum toward the edge.

She saw Mom trying to get to her feet and reach out at the same time, the anger gone from her face, replaced by white-faced horror.

Ginny reached out for Mom's hand, but she couldn't close the space in time. She hit the ground, feeling the dirt cake under fingernails as she tried to clutch the ground. And then she was over the side, falling, feeling the shock of the cold water as it closed around her, as it pushed itself into her nose and mouth and ears.

CHAPTER FORTY-SEVEN
Rose, 2009

"Anna…Rose?" Jake looked from one to the other, dawning horror in his face. "What in the world are you two talking about? Miz Remington…and Anna…you killed Livvy?"

"No," Anna scoffed. "Of course not."

"Then what—"

"Rose's crazy sister killed herself." Anna turned toward Jake. "Or I guess you could say that you and I killed her…well, mostly you." She chuckled.

"What the devil do you mean by that! I never hurt Livvy."

"Of course you did. You helped me deceive her, helped me fill her up with the notion that this world is full of magical, wonderful things…and then you completely destroyed her faith that night."

"That night…" His Adam's apple worked up and down. "That night she found out it was me playing the trick on her, pretending to be her angel…that's the night she killed herself?"

"That very night." Anna's voice was almost cheerful, but then she turned serious. "And then I cleaned up the mess all by myself—or rather, with a little help from Mrs. Remington." She stepped closer to Jake, punched her finger in his face. "I knew you all too well—knew that if they started looking into why poor, sweet Livvy killed herself, you'd fall apart. Even if there was nothing we could actually go to prison for, we wouldn't come out looking too well in the community."

"And Hunter would have hated you," Rose murmured.

"Exactly. So with my usual quick thinking, I thought of one person who had just as much as me to lose, if another member of her family turned out to be crazy—crazy to the point of suicide." She folded her arms in triumph. "Carla Remington." She continued, addressing Jake. "After you skulked away that night, leaving poor little Livvy so devastated, I stayed around to watch the show. She sat next to the pond bawling and shaking…well, I have to tell you, it felt sort of good."

"Good!" Jake buried his face in his hands.

Anna's voice went cold. "When I play a game, I don't go all weepy and sad for the other team when I finally win. Especially not when the game is so, so big." Now she looked at Rose. "Anyway, I was starting to get bored—Livvy had stopped her weeping and carrying on and was just sitting on the bank near the rope swing, staring out at the pond. Then suddenly, just when I was about to leave, she jumped up and tied the rope around her neck. For a minute, she still just stood there, staring out at the water, but I wasn't bored anymore, because I knew what she was about to do. I was transfixed, wondering…would she really have the guts to do it…to jump out over the pond with that rope around her neck?"

Rose heard a low moaning sound and thought at first it was coming out of her own mouth, out of her heart, but then she realized it was Jake.

"You just stood there, knowing what she was about to do, and…and let her?"

Anna studied him. "I used to think you and I were a great team, even if I never was really attracted to you. Now I can't imagine why I ever spent so much time with a weakling like you." She shrugged. "But really, it wasn't that long that she stood there. Probably thirty seconds at the most. And then she made up her mind, and ran for the edge, and just…jumped."

Rose felt bile boiling up in her throat and fought the urge to vomit. "And again, you did nothing, while she was hanging there…dying."

"Don't worry, I can ease your mind there, at least. It killed her right away, I think."

"The remains they found…the neck was broken," Jake said flatly, sounding as though he were in shock.

"So…I thought the obstacle standing between Hunter and me

was finally gone." Her cold gaze turned on Rose. "Obviously I was wrong, but for a few deluded moments I was happy. At the same time, as I said, I really didn't want a big hullabaloo about what happened to poor Livvy. If nothing else, it would turn her into a martyr that Hunter could moon over for years. I briefly thought about cutting her down and putting her in the water, myself, but then she would just be missing. Again, that would lead to an investigation, and to trouble. And again, Hunter could pine and worry for ages. So then I thought of dear Mrs. Remington." The corners of her mouth twitched. "I have this one great ability. I can spot where a person is weak—what they're secretly longing for."

"Just like the snake in the Garden," Jake muttered.

"I knew what Carla Remington wanted. Respectability. Admiration. Normalcy. She had tried to whip her weird family into shape to get that, and it had backfired. She knew what people were whispering about her, that she had driven her poor husband to suicide. Now they wouldn't just be whispering. It would be unbearable—'that Remington family, they're all nuts. That Carla Remington drove another one to suicide.'" Anna smiled. "So I mussed myself up, and went and pounded on Mrs. Remington's door."

Rose heard it, clear as a bell, even though she hadn't remembered it for years. The pounding on the door, and Anna's hysterical voice telling a sleepy and irritable Mamma that Livvy was dead, was hanging from the rope swing over the deep water of the pond. The words had struck Rose so immediately, so deeply that her mind started to fog over even then, so that she found it hard to concentrate on anything that followed. She remembered some talk of calling the police, and—as Anna had just now reminded her—some talk from Anna about poor Mrs. Remington, what people were going to think. Anna had sworn she was angry at Livvy for being so selfish, hurting her family like this. What would people think of poor little Rose now—would they be waiting for her to do something similar? If Livvy was going to take her life, why didn't she drown herself, hide herself under the water where she couldn't hurt her family so badly?

Mamma had snapped at Anna that none of that mattered now...but it did.

Mamma asked Anna to go down to the pond with her and try to get Livvy down—because maybe Anna was wrong about her being dead. Hanging was a devilish thing. Sometimes it wasn't as quick and humane as people thought. Maybe Livvy, even now, was suffocating.

Rose hadn't waited to hear any more. She had slipped away, out the door and down the trail to the pond.

And now she saw it again, in her memory. The horrible sight that had greeted her, horrible even by the dim light of a quarter moon, so terrible that her mind wouldn't let her go near it again for twenty-five years. But Livvy wasn't suspended over the deep water, as Anna had said. The rope hung from a tree on the land, and to dive into the pond you had to jump on it and swing out over the water. So if Livvy could get up into the tree and get the rope loose, she could lower Livvy to the ground and maybe, maybe, as Mamma had hoped, save her.

Rose was up the tree and out on the branch in a flash—then crying in frustration as she realized she had nothing to cut the rope with, and that there was no way she could loose those ancient knots with bare fingers, especially with the weight hanging from it and pulling it taut. She was about to start screaming with horror and frustration when she saw lights bobbing through the darkness, coming toward her...two people with flashlights...Anna and Mamma.

Two practical women, who did what had to be done...so of course, they had brought a knife. As Rose shrank back further into the darkness, jammed up against the solid trunk of the tree, Anna started to saw through the rope, and it seemed to go on and on, the sawing noise, the violent shaking of the limb...on and on, until finally they lowered Livvy to the ground.

Anna stood still, arms crossed, as Mamma dropped to her knees beside the still form of Rose's sister, calling her name, shaking her as though she were asleep, laying her head against Livvy's chest and listening. But it didn't matter. As Anna had said, Livvy was clearly gone.

Finally, Anna bent down over Mamma, put her hand on Mamma's shoulder. "You've got to hide her," Anna said. "You can't let anyone know."

"What?" Mamma said sharply. "What are you talking about!"

There was a lot of talking, a lot of arguing back and forth. Rose couldn't remember any of it clearly, except for one line. Clear as a bell, Anna's voice had rung out. "Mrs. Remington, you've got to do this for Rose. If we don't cover this up, do you think any decent boy will ever have her? Do you think any normal family would ever accept one of the crazy Remingtons, if word of this gets out?"

That's when Rose's mind truly started shutting down, because that's when Mamma went insane. As Rose hid motionless in the tree, she watched as Anna and her mother retrieved the anchor from Daddy's old jon boat and secured it to Livvy's body. The two women had to work together, dragging the heavy, limp form that had been her sister to the edge of the rock where the boys always jumped. A push, a splash...a flash of white as her robe bubbled up around her, like Ophelia...and then she slid beneath the black.

Mamma had jerked around with a horrific cry at that moment, and her flashlight beam had arced wildly, lighting up Rose in the tree for the barest moment, so that Anna and Mamma could see her clearly if they looked up...

Anna's voice jerked Rose back to the present. She was telling Jake the same thing that Rose was remembering—only without the gut-wrenching horror.

She turned to Rose. "I was there for you and your mother. I offered solace to Mrs. Remington. Helped her figure out that cover story." She laughed. "Even helped her pick out the urn for the, ummm...'ashes.'" She studied Rose with satisfaction. "Your mother told me you weren't handling things well, and she didn't want you upset, and that we would never mention any of this again. Which was fine with me, of course. I certainly didn't want to set fire to the loose cannon."

"I blocked it out or something," Rose said dreamily. "I woke up next day feeling like I'd had nightmares but...I believed Mamma's story just like everybody else. Until now."

Jake licked his lips. His face was ashen. "I didn't know, Rose. I never knew."

"And now you do," Anna said, her voice hard. She looked from Rose to Jake. "So what do you intend to do about it?"

Rose felt stunned, unable to think—and judging from Jake's silence, he felt the same. "I, ah...I don't know—"

"Then let me try to help you two along in your thinking." Turning to Jake, she said, "Deputy Sheriff or no, you will keep your mouth shut about all this, do you understand me? You took part in everything with me back then. If you start opening up doors I've been so careful to nail shut, I promise you, you will suffer more than me."

She whirled around to face Rose. "And you—you will stop trying to get your batty old mother to talk."

"Why should I?" Rose crossed her arms. "I didn't do anything to Livvy. I hid in a tree and saw what you did, that's all."

Anna laughed harshly. "Who is going to believe your story over mine, Rose? I'm a respected member of the community, a therapist. You're one of the crazy Remingtons, whose daughter is currently missing and presumed dead." Anna took a step closer to Rose, and lowered her voice. "How did you do it, Rose? Seriously, where is Ginny's body?"

"Why do you want to know so badly? Why do you keep asking me that?" Rose was simply stalling—at first. As long as they stood by the car talking, they were where she needed to be. "What does Ginny's disappearance have to do with you? It's almost as if you were—" She stopped, stared at Anna, thinking hard. Once again, realization came flooding in, only this time, there were no memories. Just ideas. Deductions. Truth.

"You were there," Rose said. "Weren't you, Anna?" As Anna smiled broadly, Rose tried to push away the next thought, but it wouldn't budge. "You had a key to my house, didn't you?"

Anna shrugged. "I didn't steal it or anything." Her eyes positively danced with glee. "You know where I got it, don't you, Rose?"

"From Ben, I imagine," Rose said flatly. "I thought I heard something in the house, that day I came back from the hospital. I looked around a little, but then Ginny and Max showed up, and we were all upset. We started talking, and I forgot about the noise. You were somewhere nearby when the kids were telling me everything they had found out. About Jordan—and about their time travel theory."

Anna said nothing, just smiled, listening.

"And then Ginny got all upset, and I sent her in to take a bath, and then—what did you do, Anna? There was blood on the sink. Did you hurt Ginny? You did, didn't you?"

Anna's mouth twisted up in a sneer. "Whatever do you mean? I thought she, uh...time traveled."

"Okay, that's it," Jake said, jerking open the police car door.

"We're going back to the original plan. Down to the station, both of you, to get this sorted out."

For the first time, Anna appeared surprised, uncertain. "You must be joking. Didn't you hear what I said? I'll drag you down with me, I promise you—"

"You can try," Jake said. "I hate for people to know what a jerk I was as a kid, I don't deny it. But I made myself a promise a long time ago that I would never be that person again. I've just discovered you had a key to Rose's house and were probably there when her daughter disappeared. I know what you're like, Anna. It's time for everyone else to know, too. Let's go."

Jake grabbed Anna's arm, tried to propel her into the car—and then a lot of things happened all at once. Rose heard another splash in the pond, and she whirled and tried to run toward it. She felt Jake jerking her backward, and Anna must have been struggling with him, too. She felt Jake lurch, felt herself stumbling, and suddenly there was a shot—so close and loud that her ears rang.

Jake fell. For a brief moment, he lay on the ground struggling to breathe, a look of intense surprise in his eyes. Then his eyelids flickered and closed.

"Jake!" Rose screamed. She dropped to her knees next to him, trying to assess the damage. His shirt was wet with blood, but she felt his stomach moving up and down. He was still breathing. His gun holster was empty. Looking up, she found Anna standing over them, still pointing the gun.

"He made me do it," Anna said casually. "You saw that, I'm sure."

Rose gulped, unable to speak.

"Well, anyway…now that we're alone, we can talk a little more freely. You asked if I hurt Ginny. Well, yes…of course I did. I was hiding in the bathroom closet when she came in for her bath. As I came out, she saw me in the mirror, and when she turned toward me, I hit her in the head with an old rusty towel rod I'd found lying on the closet floor." She shook her head. "Don't you ever throw anything away?" Anna took a deep breath and closed her eyes. "Ah well, we all make mistakes. You should be a better housekeeper. I shouldn't have taken the towel rod away with me. I was going to finish your brat off with it, wipe my prints off and leave it there. See if that would finally—*finally*—get you what you deserved.

"I had to get drastic, because no matter what I did, it didn't seem to stick. They called me that day and told me you had left the hospital, so I headed to your house to see—I mean, I couldn't believe you could be slipping back into your old life, scot-free—and so soon! But there you were, fresh out of the loony bin, back in Ben's house, even back in good with your dear, sweet daughter." She made a noise of frustration. "Months ago, I tried slipping some of Henry's oral diabetes medicine to Ben when he and I were having a drink together. Not enough to kill him, you understand. Just enough to make him sick, because I knew he would suspect you, Rose. But even that didn't work."

"No, it worked," Rose said. "You poisoned his mind against me pretty effectively."

She grimaced. "He was attracted to me, wanted to spend lots of time with me. But when he did, he mostly wanted to talk about *you*." She practically spat the last word, glaring at Rose as she did.

Rose struggled to breathe. But the pond was still. The splash must have been from a fish. Trying to keep an eye on the water, she gasped, "Please, just tell me. What happened to Ginny? Is she alive?"

Anna put the gunless hand on her hip. "Now, how would I know? That's what I want you to tell me!"

"Wh—what?" And then Rose understood. "She vanished, didn't she? Ginny just vanished into thin air, while you were in there with her."

Anna waved the gun about in her excitement. "I knew it! I knew it was you—knew you could explain it."

Rose felt hysterical laughter bubbling out of her. "You know already, Anna. She time traveled."

"Oh, puh-leeze! I hit her in the head. She was dazed, crawling around on the floor, and I was about to put her out of her misery. But then I heard a man's voice in the living room. I went to the door and listened, just for a second, just long enough to know it was Ben. Then I turned around and—she was gone." Anna took a menacing step toward Rose. "I looked all over that room, looked to see if the closet connected to another one. There was no window. But you grew up in that house. I figure you found her later, finished her off. Because we all know...you Remingtons are crazy."

Another splashing sound came from the pond—only this time louder, and it was followed by a strangled-sounding cry. The moonlight illuminated a shape in the deep end of the pond, struggling and flailing, then disappearing under the surface.

Anna stared, her mouth open and the gun dangling slackly in her hand.

Without thinking, Rose shoved the other woman as hard as she could, and as Anna stumbled away from her and then—judging by the thud—fell, Rose ran for it. She ran toward the water just as hard, just as single-mindedly as she had run away from it all those years, running in at the shallow end and then, as soon as the level reached her thighs, starting to swim toward her drowning daughter with strong, sure strokes. Because it had to be Ginny out there. Even though Rose could barely see more than a dark head bobbing up and then disappearing, she knew it was Ginny—and that she wouldn't last long without help.

Rose was closing the distance between them when she heard a sharp cracking sound, and felt a sting in her shoulder. But it didn't slow her down. At least not at first.

Two more strokes, three more.

Her left arm started to burn and to feel heavy. She kicked harder. "Ginny!"

Rose briefly saw Ginny's face as it sank down into the darkness. She wasn't struggling anymore. Rose drew all her strength to cover the last few yards before Ginny disappeared for the last time, but she suddenly felt dizzy and weak. What was wrong? And then it hit her…Anna had shot her!

She tried to ignore the pain and the light feeling in her head, lifting her head out of the water for a deep breath before stretching out again toward the spot where Ginny was sinking. In fact, by the time she reached the spot, she had to tread water and feel about, because the ripples on the surface were the only sign of her daughter. But she found Ginny's cold, limp hand and, with her one good arm, groped for Ginny's head and got it above the water.

As she clumsily tried to keep her own head above water while maneuvering her unconscious daughter into position for towing, she wondered why Anna hadn't shot again, and where she was. As her eyes scanned the shoreline, she heard another crack, and a yell. In the dim light, she thought she saw more than one form thrashing about on the shore. Had Jake regained consciousness and started to put up a fight? Had someone else appeared on the scene to help her?

What if she finally managed to drag Ginny to shore only to find Anna standing there waiting, gun in hand and ready to finish them both off?

The buzzing sound started to fill her ears again, and the dark shapes grew even dimmer. She forced herself to concentrate. *Keep your head up. And Ginny's. Kick. Stroke. Eyes on the shoreline. It's getting closer. If you don't make it to shore it won't matter whether Anna is there or not.*

Had the moon gone behind a cloud? Suddenly even the dim light faded. She couldn't see how far she was from the shore, or what was going on with the struggling bodies. The yells faded, drowned by the roaring sound from inside her own head. She gasped for breath, but apparently had allowed her head to sink because she drew in water and started to choke. Her heart thudded in panic as she felt herself sinking, then realized her feet were touching the bottom. She must be right at the shore, if she could just push herself up, pull Ginny's head back above the surface...

Her arms refused to obey this time. She was slipping away, away from the surface, away from consciousness. Away from Ginny.

CHAPTER FORTY-EIGHT
Ginny, 2009

When Ginny first hit the water, it was a nasty, cold, physical force assaulting her inside and out. She fought against it, trying to shut her lungs against it, pushing it away with her arms and struggling for the surface. And then…everything changed.

She opened her eyes. No water rushed in to sting. Everything was still dark, but now she floated and breathed, as light as though she were air herself. At first there was no sound, but then she started to hear murmuring voices. How long this went on, she couldn't have told. Time seemed to have no meaning, and it could have been a few minutes or a few years. She floated long enough to learn to tune in on one voice at a time, like tuning in to a particular radio station, and it would come into sharp focus. A lot of it made no sense. Strange voices seemed to be pouring their hearts out, confessing terrible pains and wrongdoings, begging for favors. And then one voice stood out—it was Grandma's voice. She was whispering but strong, not like the grandma in the nursing home but like the vital woman Ginny had stayed with that summer, years ago.

"Please…" Grandma was saying. "I've done such terrible, terrible things. My daughter…she's all I have left, and she's ruined. Please…"

Ginny had a sense that the voice would have gone on for a long, long time, confessing and pleading. But the station started to fade. Her head filled with a roar like static, and then suddenly she was fighting again, sinking into cold water, her lungs and eyes burning.

She popped above the surface for a second, and thrust her arms out to her sides to try to keep herself up, but down she went again.

The second time she pulled her head above the water, she could have sworn she saw Mom's face. Not young Rose, but Mom, like she should be, swimming purposefully toward her. Ginny reached toward her but the water rushed over her again and she flailed in panic, trying so hard not to gasp for breath and take in water.

The roaring in her head grew deafening, and then everything went dark.

Before she opened her eyes again, she became aware—aware of someone speaking to her, someone squeezing her hand. She fought to open her eyes.

Max's face hovered over hers.

"You're here," Ginny managed to croak.

"Of course I'm here." His shaky voice didn't match up to his cocky talk. "I told you I'd find you, didn't I?"

She was shivering with cold, but a sudden warmth flooded through her, and she felt herself starting to smile. "Yeah, you did." She grabbed at his arm, trying to pull herself up, then froze. Anna—middle-aged Anna—sat a few feet away, leaning against a tree with her hands behind her and glaring. Two shapes lay on the ground, unmoving. One appeared to be a man and the other was...

"Mom!" Ginny scrambled up, trying to ignore the dizziness in her head. "Mom, what's wrong!"

She felt Max grabbing her, pulling her back down. "Take it easy. You almost drowned."

She threw off his arm and crawled the few feet to her mother's side. Mom was unconscious, and a bright red stain spread across her blouse. "Mom? What happened!"

Max jerked his head toward Anna. "She shot your mom, and that cop. She shot at us, too, but your dad and I managed to take her down."

"You and my...dad?" Ginny looked around blankly, but didn't see him.

"He ran back to the house to get help. Shouldn't take long with all the media hanging around. After the gunfire, some of them will probably be here any minute."

"Daddy...but how, I mean..." Her gaze fell on the other limp form on the ground, who was covered by a lacy white sweater. "And who is that?"

"We can talk about that later. But he's going to be okay too, I think." Max took her hand. "The important thing is, you're home, and everything's going to be fine. Even your mom."

Without letting go of Max, Ginny took her mother's limp fingers in her other hand. Now she noticed that Mom was covered with two shirts: Dad's ratty old plaid that Mom wanted him to throw away, and a cotton button-down she had often seen Max wearing over his t-shirts.

"I'm not great at emergencies," Max said, "but I knew they needed to be kept warm as possible. Anna sacrificed her sweater for the cop—not willingly, of course. And I also kept pressure on your mom's wound at first, but it stopped bleeding. That's a good sign, don't you think?"

"I hope so," she said, squeezing both hands she was holding—and feeling her heart leap with joy when Mom briefly squeezed back.

Max had said it. She was home, sitting on solid ground, hanging onto the people she loved. She looked into his wide puppy eyes. "I feel like I haven't seen you for years."

He laughed. "About twenty-five of them?"

"At least." She gripped his hand even tighter. "You don't think I'll just…slip away again, do you?"

He shook his head. "No. Everything's come out the way it was supposed to. You're home."

CHAPTER FORTY-NINE
Ginny, 2009

At first, Ginny felt no sense of déjà vu. Maybe that was because she was keeping her eyes down, trying not to see the casket at the front of the church as she slid into the pew. Maybe it was because, when she finally did look up, there were too many other emotions crowding out that feeling of having been here before. Even though she'd never met Aunt Livvy, she felt a deep sorrow for the girl that had suffered so much in life, then waited for all those years to have her family acknowledge what happened and say good-bye.

It was taking a lot of courage for Grandma to do the right thing now. Her confession—communicated through Mom—of what she and Anna had done when Aunt Livvy committed suicide all those years ago was so deliciously gruesome that the story was everywhere, on TV news and crime shows, the Internet, newspapers. People spread every little tidbit like wildfire jumping from one Facebook or Twitter account to the next. Even after all these days, the family had to fight their way through a crowd of reporters and curiosity-seekers into the church.

Max, sitting on her left side, squeezed her hand and smiled at her. She smiled back, and now that her head was up, she couldn't stop herself from looking at the casket. Daddy and Mom had wheeled Grandma up next to it, then retreated to the side to give her some privacy. The coffin was closed, of course, but Grandma had wanted some time to whisper to Livvy, anyway—to ask forgiveness, maybe, or say good-bye. Maybe to pray, who knew? The woman's speech was still garbled, but she was making progress now. Ginny felt certain that, even though Grandma was whispering and slurring her words, she was being understood. Welcomed. Forgiven.

At least all the police trouble was over with. Years ago, Grandma would have been in serious trouble for covering up Livvy's death the way she did, and for putting her body in the pond. But no one had the stomach to send her to jail now.

And Ginny had been able to get the police off their backs as far as her disappearance—telling them how Anna had appeared in the bathroom as she was undressing for her bath and hit her over the head. The police were easy. School was hard.

If she had drawn stares and whispers and been considered a scary freak just for moving into the old Remington house and wearing semi-Goth clothes, the unwelcome attention was off the charts now. But she had mainly dreaded facing Alec and Kelsey, and at least that hadn't been so terrible. Actually, she really hadn't faced Kelsey. Her father had picked her up the day after Anna was arrested and moved her back to his house in Gwinnett County. And Alec had a new girlfriend—Heather Tanner, of course, Kelsey's best friend that Ginny had replaced on the basketball team—and had moved on and forgotten Ginny in the way that shallow people do. In fact, when their eyes met in the hall, she wasn't entirely certain whether he was doing a great job of freezing her out, or really didn't remember her all that much.

It wasn't so easy getting the reporters and the gossips and curiosity seekers to lose interest, because she couldn't give a good explanation for where she had been all those days she was missing. She just told them she didn't really know what had happened after she blacked out in the bathroom, and truer words were never spoken. What exactly had happened, after all? She couldn't explain it.

People a lot smarter than her were at a loss. A few days ago, several of them had sat together and tried to hash it all out, make some sense of everything. Daddy and Mom and herself, Max, Grandma, and even Max's dad. That poor man had still looked shell-shocked, and no wonder—finding out the truth about Anna, fending off the press after she was arrested, and then struggling to make sense of what Max and Ginny were telling him about what happened.

"Stop trying to explain it with science, Dad," Max had told him.

"You'll make your head explode, and anyway, this is beyond science." His eyes had glowed as he continued, "This is about the eternal—beyond time. And a power beyond the natural world."

"No." Mr. Ferguson had shook his head, disarranging his messy hair even further. "The fact that electronics fail around that pond shows there's something natural about this whole thing."

Ginny hated to burst his bubble, but she had to say it. "I don't think it's just the pond. I jumped in time—"

Max's father and Daddy both winced.

"Or disappeared, or however you want to phrase it, from the bathroom, not from the pond. And it happened before, when I was little, in Grandma's church. So it's not as though the pond is magic."

Daddy was giving her a strange look. "So it's something...something extraordinary about Ginny?" he said uncertainly. "Some special ability or—"

"No," Ginny said sharply. They all stared at her, waiting for her to explain, but she couldn't put it into words, all the thoughts rushing through her head. The knowledge that Anna had been planning to kill her, only she had been swept away from danger in a miraculous way. That feeling of some Spirit nudging her, guiding her throughout her time in 1984. The knowledge that that Spirit was now inside her, hers forever. She had talked to Max about it, and she now knew what he meant about being filled up, only she wasn't ready to talk about it, about that Power she was just getting to know.

The silence stretched out.

Then Grandma spoke—low and slurred and indistinct, but a miracle nevertheless, that she was slowly starting to speak again at all. "I prayed...for my family...my girls...and she was sent."

Ginny felt tears coming to her eyes, and felt a surge of affection as she saw Max nodding his head.

But this time it was her own daddy who objected. "But that doesn't make sense, either. If this crazy, supernatural thing happened as an answer to an old woman's prayers—prayers for all these past tragedies to be fixed or changed—then why wasn't Ginny sent back further? Why didn't she prevent Livvy from killing herself?"

"It wasn't about Livvy," Max said. "It was about Ginny and her mom and her grandmom. Anyway, if you start saying, why didn't she go back further and fix things, where would it end? Why didn't she go back before Livvy and stop their father from killing himself? Or back before that, to fix whatever happened with his parents? It would never end."

"Yeah, but really, nothing was changed." Ben frowned. "So maybe Henry is right and it was some freak of nature. Because otherwise, what was the point?"

Mom sat down between Ginny and Grandma, and taking both their hands, linked them all together. "Everything has changed," she said.

"I don't think I was sent to change events," Ginny said slowly. "It wasn't about changing so much as…discovering…interpreting." She looked from one puzzled face to another. "Do you know what I mean?"

Only Mom and Max nodded, but her heart warmed, anyway, basking in the glow of family and calm and—finally!—understanding.

Strengthened by this memory, she lifted her head and looked squarely at the front of the church, at Grandma and the casket.

And that's when the déjà vu hit.

She had seen all this before—this sanctuary, the polished wood casket with the blanket of wildflowers, Grandma in the wheelchair. Only she had seen it from a slightly different angle—further back, lower down, peering around the end of one of the pews.

Ginny whirled and searched for her—the little girl who had crept out from under the pew and peered around, terrified at the sudden emptiness of the church, at the coffin and the flowers and the sad music. And then she saw her, a flash of a white face peeping out at her, like a scared kitten hiding in the bushes. Huge, dark eyes with sweaty wisps of hair sweeping across them.

Feeling the breath being squeezed from her, Ginny took a step toward the girl. She wanted to talk to her, embrace her, tell her everything would be fine. For a moment she had a desperate urge even to catch her and hang on, to travel back with her like a Harry Potter character in a side-along apparition. Because she knew the girl would disappear and soon, back to that impossible land of Ginny's childhood. Even now, her form appeared to be blurring around the edges, growing more transparent. Ginny took a step toward the little girl.

A hand pulled her back.

Mom was peering into her face, her forehead creased with concern. "Ginny? Are you all right? You look so pale."

Ginny looked back, out into the church again, just in time to see it. The girl seemed to dissolve, growing transparent before fading completely from view.

The child was gone.

Mom was rubbing her arm. "Ginny? Honey?"

Ginny felt a lump forming in her throat. She wondered if she would ever see the little girl again, would ever again transcend the boundaries of space and time. Or for as long as she lived on this earth, would she just be plain old Ginny, stuck inside the walls of time like everyone else?

But as she felt Mom's hand on her arm, saw Daddy and Max both gazing at her from the pews—one with fatherly concern and one with big adoring puppy eyes—she felt laughter bubbling up inside her.

All was well.

ᘓ

ACKNOWLEDGEMENTS

This being my second published novel, this is also my second time to write acknowledgements, and I'm even more terrified to start naming names. The first time, I was slightly nervous I would forget to mention someone important. Actually, I did worse than that. I forgot to include a thank-you to the lovely and gracious Ane Mulligan for suggesting the title of my book, *Summer's Winter*. But I told her I did include her in the acknowledgements. It's a good thing she *is* lovely and gracious, or I would have been in serious trouble. So anyway, a bit late, but thank you, Ane—for the title, and for not making me feel too humiliated!

I seriously hope I won't make a blunder this time, but I have a bad feeling. If there's one thing I've learned in the past year, it's that working full-time, taking care of family, and being an author all at the same time can make you very absent-minded. But here goes…

Thanks to hubby Dave Grant for always believing in me and for putting up with all the time I spend on this writing obsession—and for also being a great friend. And I especially want to thank my beautiful sister, Frankie Israel. I think she sold more books for me than anyone last year and was my chief cheerleader. I wish I could afford to hire her as my full-time publicist! Thank you so much for being such an amazing sister and friend. And thanks to Kristi Israel for understanding, for listening and praying, and for spreading the word! And to my mother, Ewell Johns, I'm so grateful for showing me the meaning of strength and perseverance.

Thanks to all the people who put in serious amounts of time to help make *Jordan's Shadow* the best that it could be. I had a fabulous team of Beta readers who gave me great input about the story and characters: Frankie Israel, Amy Winfrey, Ann Williams, Judy Ellis,

Susan Jordan, Brittany Jordan, Leslie Sowell, Megan Rosenberger, Rebecca Jones, and SarahAnn Dozier.

It's so great to have friends with helpful super powers! Laura Wilson used her graphic design skills to produce *Jordan's* amazing cover, and Sandra Mayo once again provided professional proofreading. Carlos Avila made an awesome book trailer for *Summer's Winter.* Thanks, guys!

Thanks to all the people who helped spread the word on the release of my first book, headed up launch parties, and supplied constant encouragement. First, my work colleagues Felicia Haywood, Ann Williams, Judy Ellis, Pat Borck, Chris Nylund, April Warren, and Ashley Evans. And so many people in the Covenant Class at First Presbyterian Church—Pat Kinser, Fran Drummond and Carolese Gullatt in particular. And Susie and Brittany and Amy—I mentioned them as Beta readers, but they did so much more. And all my friends at the John 3:16 Marketing Network, who never failed to provide answers to my questions and a shoulder to cry on if needed.

Thanks to my writer friends who gave me endorsements and told their readers about me, especially Elizabeth Musser, Nancy Grace and John Granger.

And last but not least, I thank God for providing the opportunity to fulfill my writing dream—the opportunity as well as the resources like time and money and energy. I'm lacking in all those, and I work myself into a tizzy realizing I am not enough. Then I remember how Jesus took a few loaves and fishes and multiplied them to accomplish His purpose—to feed thousands—and I know He can multiply me. I constantly remind myself I serve a loaves and fishes God.

ABOUT THE AUTHOR

Robin Johns Grant lives in Georgia with her husband Dave and formerly feral felines Mini Pearl and Luna. She now has her best day job ever as a college librarian, which keeps her young by allowing her to hang out with students. Over the years, she did a lot of crazy fan stuff and was overly-involved with books and movies like Harry Potter and *Star Wars*, which helped her dream up Jeanine and Jamie's story for *Summer's Winter*. Robin was named 2014 Author of the Year by the Georgia Association of College Stores, and *Summer's Winter* won a bronze medal in the Romance-Suspense category of the International Readers' Favorite Book Awards.

If you liked *Jordan's Shadow*, be sure to read
Summer's Winter!

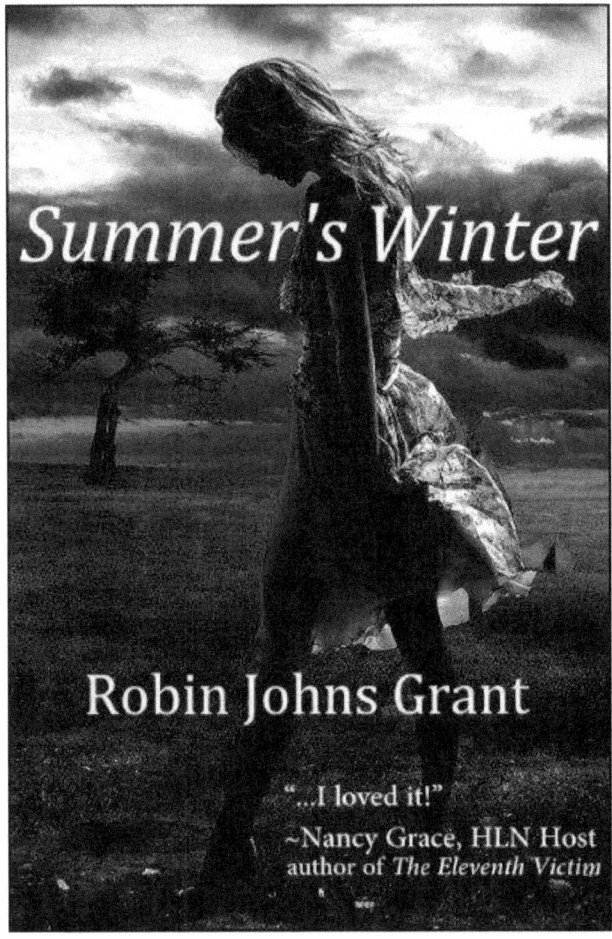

When a Georgia college student finally connects with film
star Jamie Newkirk, the object of her obsession, will it be a
dream come true? Or will she be pulled into his nightmare of
secrets, control, and death?

www.ingramcontent.com/pod-product-compliance
Lightning Source LLC
Chambersburg PA
CBHW061128200626
46817CB00016B/376